THE ONCE
AND FUTURE ME

THE ONCE
AND FUTURE ME

A NOVEL

MELISSA PACE

HENRY HOLT AND COMPANY
NEW YORK

Henry Holt and Company
Publishers since 1866
120 Broadway
New York, New York 10271
www.henryholt.com

Henry Holt® and Ⓗ® are registered trademarks of Macmillan Publishing Group, LLC.

Distributed in Canada by Raincoast Book Distribution Limited

Library of Congress Cataloging-in-Publication Data

Names: Pace, Melissa Duggan, author.
Title: The once and future me : a novel / Melissa Pace.
Description: First edition. | New York : Henry Holt and Company, 2025.
Identifiers: LCCN 2024050245 | ISBN 9781250358677 (hardcover) |
    ISBN 9781250358660 (ebook)
Subjects: LCGFT: Psychological fiction. | Novels.
Classification: LCC PS3616.A32555 O53 2025 | DDC 813/.6—dc23/
    eng/20241028
LC record available at https://lccn.loc.gov/2024050245

Our books may be purchased in bulk for promotional, educational, or business use. Please contact your local bookseller or the Macmillan Corporate and Premium Sales Department at (800) 221-7945, extension 5442, or by e-mail at MacmillanSpecialMarkets@macmillan.com.

First Edition 2025

Designed by Meryl Sussman Levavi

Printed in the United States of America

10 9 8 7 6 5 4 3 2 1

This is a work of fiction. All of the characters, organizations, and events portrayed in this novel either are products of the author's imagination or are used fictitiously.

Published by arrangement with Henry Holt and Company.

To Chris, who never doubted.

And to my parents, Andy and Betty Duggan, who let me build worlds instead of napping.

the thing I came for:
the wreck and not the story of the wreck
the thing itself and not the myth

—Adrienne Rich, "Diving into the Wreck" (1973)

This book contains elements of historical fiction and thus some events and timelines have been altered to better suit the narrative.

THE ONCE

AND FUTURE ME

PROLOGUE

DEATH IS LOUDER *than I thought it would be.*

I could have predicted the blinding white light. Some close to the end would speak of a radiant beam that beckoned. And they were right—it is beautiful, shot through with bits of brilliant color that fly by me like heavenly confetti.

But the roar. No one mentioned the roar.

Its vibrations course through me, voltaic and swift, carving what feel like vast networks of roads and tunnels deep into my being. And there's a taste. Metallic. Just a tinge that hints at conduction. Maybe that's it, maybe together the thundering light and I complete some sort of vast, eternal circuit, and that's all there is. No heaven, no hell, just the white roar, everlasting and indifferent.

All my sins, if not forgiven, at least forgotten.

Oblivion. I can live with that.

So we proceed, the white roar and I, hurtling through the cosmos till I lose all sense of time, space, and myself. It's perfect, and it lasts and lasts—until it doesn't.

Without warning, the white roar pulls away, leaving me alone in the dark, trying to remember how to breathe.

Trying to remember anything at all.

CHAPTER 1

M Y FIRST BREATHS come guttural and convulsive, like those of a drowning victim finally breaking the surface. But what surface? Where am I?

The air feels steamy, ripe with the sour tang of damp woolens, diesel, and Naugahyde. I'm definitely in a vehicle. Can feel a rumbling, a sickening sense of motion—and a jagged, ringing pain between my ears, like someone's wedged a piece of flint deep inside my brain. I want so badly to escape it, to slide back down into the dark and its painless sleep.

But then I hear her. The voice in my head. She's vigilant and pushy. Issuing her orders like some surly fairy godmother:

Eyes open, this is not the time for sleep.

You've got things to do. Important things.

Such as? But like me, the *voice* appears to have no answers. Just that vague things-to-do edict she won't stop repeating.

So I open my eyes—

But all I see is a roiling blur of color and shadow, bobbing and weaving across my field of vision. I try to will just a piece of this dizzying sideshow into focus, the swirling mass of red, blue, and green inches from my face, concentrate till at last the image comes clear:

My plaid dress peeking out from under my winter coat.

My sluggish eyes drift slowly across it till they come to my red purse, the one with the shiny gold clasp shaped like a clamshell.

My hand is clutching it so tightly my knuckles are bloodless white. I try to relax my hand's death grip but find I have no power over my fingers. My head's no different. It's slumped against a window, and with each bump in the road, my temple beats painfully against the rattling glass, and I am powerless to stop it.

Why the hell can't I move?

What's happened to me?

Urr-creeeeeek! The sound of grinding gears reverberates painfully inside my tender ears, interrupting my alarm. And its distinctive tortured shriek tells me something: I'm on a school bus.

And not alone. There are voices, female voices, coming from the front of the bus. I nudge my eyes that way and see a half dozen students. They're dressed like me: I can see the bottoms of their dresses showing beneath their long winter coats. While I watch, one of them, a squirrelly brunette, pops up out of her seat. There's a manila tag hanging from a string around her neck like she's a rug being shipped to some far-off destination. "My family never said we'd be going on a trip," she complains in a chirpy voice while she absently twists a lock of her long brown hair around a finger.

"Siddown before I come back there and make you," the driver yells. Harsh, even for a school bus driver—and as the girl sinks back into her seat, I drag my eyes to the fogged-up window for a hint of where the man is taking us.

That's when I see the bars.

Bars on the windows. Not a school bus.

I put a pin in my alarm. Use the adrenaline now barreling through my frozen body to focus. Outside it's sleeting, and we're driving parallel to a tall wrought iron fence whose pointed uprights stretch into the gray distance like an army of black spears. The bus's gears groan into downshift and it slows, turning into a driveway and stopping in front of an imposing gate flanked by tall brick columns.

A man in a slicker emerges from a small building just inside the gate, and as he goes to unlock it, my eyes drift back to the brick column, squint to make out the words on its bronze plaque through the steamy glass: HANOVER STATE PSYCHIATRIC HOSPITAL.

These women are mentals?

Then why am I on this bus with them? I'm not a patient. I'm . . . I'm . . .

And I wait for an answer, but nothing comes.

Why the hell can't I remember who I am?

I need to get off this bus—!

"The Lord always provides a way," says someone behind me. I can just make her out two rows back and across the aisle: a woman with auburn hair divided into two braids who's staring at me with a look of crazed enthusiasm. Grade school hairstyle aside, she's old, close to twenty-five—just about at her quarter hour.

As the bus rumbles back to life and begins ascending the long, curved driveway, the woman darts across the aisle and slides, saddle shoes first, into the seat beside me. "I told them all God would save me from this place, bring me back to the trains. Someone has to watch over them, signal the Lord when it's time," she says, then examines a hank of my hair. "And just look at the perfect lamb He's sent to do it."

Lamb?

She reaches out with both hands, touches my ears, then pulls them back to examine the scarlet slick now on her fingertips.

My blood.

"'For the life of a creature is in the blood,'" she says to the heavens, "'and I have given it to you to make atonement for yourselves on the altar.'"

Leviticus 17:11. Crazy lady knows her scripture. And apparently so do I.

The woman continues her talk of God, trains, and plans, and I'm trying hard to follow her fervent whispers, but there's a problem:

little black spots are beginning to spread across my eyes, the ringing in my ears is growing, and my shoulders are getting so heavy . . .

I said not the time for sleep! the *voice* scolds.

And I fight like hell to stay conscious, but no amount of flight or fight's going to stop the gathering darkness, and as the woman in braids pulls the red purse from my steadfast fingers, I slip down into the velvety black.

CHAPTER 2

WHEN I COME to, I find I'm sitting upright on the bus seat, knees together, hands neatly folded in my lap. The woman in braids has arranged me like a doll. And taken my purse.

"Up and at 'em."

Coming down the bus aisle toward me is a sallow, doughy-faced nurse. Under her navy coat, she wears a crisp white uniform—dress, stockings, shoes, and a hat that resembles an elaborately folded dinner napkin. Her name tag reads VIRGINIA WALLACE, R.N.

But it's her wrinkles that have my attention. Most are small, almost invisible—but there. "You're thirty-five at least, way beyond your quarter hour. How the hell can that be?"

Nurse Wallace doesn't answer. Too busy staring at my bloody ears. "What the devil have you gone and done to yourself?" she asks.

My eyes flick from one end of the bus to the other. It's empty now, the patients all lined up outside in the sleet, where a nurse with a clipboard is hastily reading their tags and checking them off her list. But the woman who stole my purse isn't among them, isn't anywhere that I can see, and my pulse begins to quicken.

"Where did she go, that woman in braids?" I ask.

"Afraid I don't know who you're talking about," the nurse says as she frees something caught behind my shoulder: a patient ID tag hanging from a string around my neck—just like the others.

Was it always there?

It can't have been. Right?

You bet your ass that's right.

I struggle for recall while Nurse Wallace reads the tag: "'Dorothy Frasier.' Well, it looks like you've reached the end of your yellow brick road, Dorothy. Time to line up with the other patients—"

"Dorothy? No. That's not mine. I'm not a patient . . . That nutcase bitch with the braids, she must be Dorothy . . . Must've put this on me when she stole my purse—"

"Okay, time to go," the marly nurse says, and her meaty hand grabs my arm.

This woman is not your friend. Do what needs to be done.

And as the nurse starts to hoist me up, my body finally sparks to life, and I twist out of her grasp. She comes right back at me, seizing my wrist and wrenching it up behind me till my knuckles are kissing the base of my neck.

But rather than feeling shock or panic at the pain, I find instead a strange certainty that I am in control. That part of me is letting her do this, gauging her skills, testing her capabilities.

Nurse Wallace shoves me forward, and before I can consider my options, weigh my next move, I discover the choice has been made for me—

By me.

Suddenly I'm stepping backward, closing the gap between us, then throwing my head back till it slams into her forehead with a *crunnnnkkkk.*

I ignore this newest, sharpest pain and seize Nurse Wallace. My movements are so smooth. Sure. In one fluid action, I pin her arm back and muscle her into a nearby row, shoving her face hard against the window. Then I grab hold of her hair bun, ready in the next moment to smash her temple into the seatback's metal bar.

But that's the next moment.

In this present moment, she's looking at me with frightened bunny rabbit eyes, and I freeze.

What the hell am I doing?

Only what's necessary to contain the threat.

What did the *voice* just say?

A wave of nausea now rolls up my spine and time seems to stretch as the sick hangs there, about to break. I drop the nurse and she falls into the seat, where she watches me, waiting for my next move. That makes two of us—till calls for help from the nurse outside pierce my daze: "Gus, come quick! One of the transfers is attacking Miss Wallace!"

Time to go.

I charge through the bus's open doors into the frozen rain—and find in front of me a mammoth building, so vast it spans my entire field of vision. Hanover State Psychiatric Hospital. It's a Gothic beast of brick and stone, all peaked roofs and turrets. A looming clock tower rises from its center, flanked on both sides by sprawling, three-story wings that turn a corner every fifty yards or so, corrugating outward into the frosty distance.

Someone's breathing hard. Closing in on me is a bearlike attendant in all-white—Gus, no doubt. Gus's steamy breath gathers in clouds on either side of his wet face like a locomotive. He slows a few feet short of me and holds out his hand. "Come, let's get you out of this nasty rain, dear," he drawls extra slow, like he's afraid I might get confused. "It's nice and warm inside . . ."

A myriad of violent options to deal with him come to mind, but I don't want a replay of what just happened on the bus. Gus is large, but I sense a softness in him like a three-minute egg. So, I stand my ground and wait till he reaches for me, his balance dependent on success in the grab. When he lunges, I duck out of reach, and the guy tumbles hard onto the wet asphalt.

I run but get only a few yards before someone else grabs me.

"Gotcha." It's another attendant, greasier and smaller than Gus. Cocky though. "Why all the hurry to leave us, sweetheart?" he says with a grin, revealing a crooked outcropping of teeth. "You look like someone Lester'd like to see stick around." Somewhere along the way, this creep has banked a whole lot of confidence, and Lester's damn sure how this is all gonna play out.

But apparently, I am also sure.

Before I know it, I'm leaning in on him hard, ramming my loafer as far up Lester's crotch as it'll travel. As he doubles over in pain, I help his head into my rising knee, and he staggers a step or two before toppling to the ground. Again, it's all instinct, like I have no choice in the actions my body is gleefully taking.

That's it. You know he had it coming. Now look for your exit.

But which way?

A hundred yards to the left, under the awning at the top of the hospital's grand main entrance steps, is a uniformed policeman in what looks like a cowboy hat handing some woman over to a nurse.

So, I sprint in the other direction, across the hospital's sprawling lawn dotted with trees that retain just a few scarlet leaves, heading for the distant end of the building's right wing. My penny loafers slip and slide on the icy grass as I tear across Hanover's grounds. My dress is equally unfit for fleeing—too tight on top but too loose on the bottom, its skirt plumped up like a half-filled balloon by starched petticoats that scratch at my thighs with each stride.

A brief rifling through the two patch pockets on the front of my dress and those of my coat reveals nothing of use, just a crumpled-up ball of yellow paper and a couple sticks of gum.

"Best run like the wind, sweetness!" someone calls to me. I look up and see in one of Hanover's windows the pale, spectral face of a woman pressed up against its bars. "Before they gets dibs on you!"

I sense she speaks from experience and pick up my speed.

Soon I'm rounding Hanover's far corner and can see for the first time, down its long back slope, past outbuildings, hedges, and driveway, what I was hoping for: a chain-link fence. It's at least ten feet high and topped with barbed wire—but unlike the wrought iron in front, chain-link can be climbed rain or shine. I may not recall my name, but some part of me knows this fact with absolute certainty.

I charge down the frozen hill for it but don't get far before I hear a man's shouts coming from a couple hundred feet back, "Miss! You need to stop!"

Fuck. I force my legs to pump faster, trying to outrun my latest pursuer. Soon, I'm passing through what must be Hanover's cemetery. It's filled with dozens of rusting t-shaped grave markers, each stamped with just a number. At the edge of this dismal field is the thicket of shrubs I saw from the top of the hill. I run along beside it till I spy a narrow break in the bushes. Through it I can just make out Hanover's driveway and the chain-link fence beyond.

On the other side of that fence is a town I can hide in.

I'm about to cut through the gap when there's another shout: "Please, miss, hold it right there." My pursuer is extremely polite. And close. Too close.

Get the hell out of there! the *voice* scolds.

But I want a look at him. Not sure why I do. Curiosity? The quiet note of decency in his voice? Whatever the reason, it's a stupid move, but I do it anyway, glance over my shoulder—and see it's the policeman in the cowboy hat I saw turning the woman over to a nurse.

He's less than twenty feet away and closing—

I bolt through the break in the hedges, branches full of thorns clawing at me as I stumble past, till finally I burst out onto the driveway—

And see it too late: an old car speeding down the hill toward me.

Amazing the things your mind can ponder in a split second, even as your body freezes up and betrays you. Mine, for instance, is able to gauge that the car whose license plate says 1954 VIRGINIA is traveling at a speed that will likely be fatal for me. Also, that its driver, now slamming on his brakes (too late), is wearing a hat. Fedora? I wonder idly, in that last moment before impact—

But suddenly my hand's yanked back and I'm sailing through the air like a Chihuahua on a preschooler's leash. We barrel-roll across the wet asphalt, me and the cowboy policeman who's plucked me from death, and when we come to a stop, I'm looking up at a star-shaped badge that reads DEPUTY SHERIFF, CULPEPER COUNTY, OFFICER THOMAS R. WORTHY.

The deputy looks down at me. "Are you okay? Your ears, they're bleed—"

But he's interrupted by the driver of the car. "Tell 'em to get a tighter leash on these lunatics before someone gets hurt," the guy shouts before driving off.

"He's wrong. I'm not a mental!" I say. "This is all a mistake. She switched places with me on the transport bus."

"Who?"

"A patient. Dorothy Frasier. Complete mental, obsessed with blood and atonement . . . and trains. She must've put her ID tag on me after she stole my purse," I tell him. "They think I'm her, but I'm not!"

Officer Worthy's blue eyes survey mine a long moment, trying to appraise my sanity.

"Then who *are* you?" he asks. Such a simple question. For which I have no answer. I can feel the existential panic in me rising again, and I look away from the deputy to shake it off. But this only quickens his interest. "Do you not know your name?" he asks.

Stop answering this guy's questions and get the hell out of there!

"You've got to let me go," I tell him, trying to squirm free.

"I'm afraid I can't do that, miss."

You know what you need to do.

I quietly reach for a nearby stone. Won't hit him hard, just enough to stun so I can make it over the fence. It's no more than fifteen feet away. But Officer Worthy must sense my plan. As my hand grabs the rock, his comes down on mine, pinning it to the asphalt inches from my face. On his fingers I see a wedding band and a second ring whose elaborate engraving says VIRGINIA TECH, CLASS OF 1950.

Something about those words addles me a moment, long enough for him to flip me onto my stomach. Bits of wet gravel dig into my cheek as it meets the ground. Then I feel something cold enclose my wrist, followed by a series of clicks as he locks the handcuffs on.

"The year, what year is it?" I ask as he helps me to my feet.

He looks at me a quizzically. "It's 1954."

1954. I guess that's right . . . It's just something about it feels *off*. Then again, my brain's taken a big hit sometime in the last hour. Everything's feeling a little off. I need out of these cuffs. Time to beg.

It's not pretty. The words tumble out in a shameless heap meant to draw sympathy and/or woo. "Please, you've got to believe me, I don't belong in that place. You could still let me go," I plead as he picks up his sheriff's deputy hat that fell off during our tussle.

"Sorry, miss," he says, putting his cowboy hat back on, "I just can't do that. It's for your own good—"

"So, you're just going to hand me over to them, no questions asked, Lone Ranger?"

He cocks his head, surprised by my cowboy crack. "If a mistake's been made, I'm sure the doctors at the hospital will straighten things out—"

"Go to hell," I say. Wooing is officially over.

A moment later, Lester, the attendant, emerges from the nearby bushes, still pale from our last interaction. "Thanks for the assistance, Deputy, we're having a little trouble with Dorothy—"

"Don't call me that," I snap back.

"One of today's transfers from County," he says to Officer Worthy.

"He's wrong. I told you, I'm not a patient!"

"She's a bit unsettled by the new surroundings," Lester says as he takes me from Officer Worthy. Then the asshole whispers in my aching ear, "But I knew when you thought it over, you'd decide to stay. Make some new friends."

"Someone at Hanover should double-check her identification," Officer Worthy says to him. "She said a woman on the bus—"

Lester laughs. "You're not falling for her story, are you, Deputy?

They all got one, 'bout who they *really* are. Why they don't belong at Hanover. They believe it, too. Can't help themselves. But don't you worry, we got things well in hand up on the hill. Haven't misplaced a patient yet," he says, winking, and he's starting to pull me away when I hear that distinctive *urr-creeeeeek!* — the transport bus, heading back down the driveway to the front gate.

It takes a couple of tries, but I wrench myself free of Lester just in time to glimpse the bus as it rumbles past — and there, in the vehicle's steamy, rain-spattered rear window, I swear I see the ghostly contours of the woman in braids.

I point to the departing bus, about to ask Officer Worthy if he saw her too, when his eyes flick to Lester. "Hey, what are you doing?" he shouts at the attendant.

I turn in time to catch the word TIMEX on Lester's watch just before it contacts my face. Can feel my whole body fly in the direction of his backhand as everything dissolves in a blur.

CHAPTER 3

M Y HEAD'S THROBBING from its latest blow, my vision still bordering on double, as Lester escorts me down some shadowy steps a
short distance from Hanover's front entrance, into a grim subterra-
nean room marked RECEPTION. The door to the outside slams shut
behind us with disturbing finality.

I need to keep my head till I can figure out my next plan.

Lights suspended from the ceiling cast ghostly circular patterns on
its gray-and-white checkerboard floor. Behind a large desk is a nurse
filling out paperwork, who doesn't look up as I beg her to listen to
my story.

Lester pulls me under one of the lights, removes the handcuffs
and coat. I fight to keep myself in check as he performs a search of
me that is more about his lingering pat down than finding actual
contraband. The reception nurse is more thorough, stops Lester as
he's leading me away to search the pockets on the front of my dress
that he's neglected. Pulls out the pack of gum. "For your safety no
outside food is allowed inside the hospital," she says, then confiscates
the pennies from my loafers as well. For safety.

Lester leads me away, and the hospital's odor, a suffocating mix of
disinfectants, cleansers, and bodily fluids, grows stronger the deeper
into the building he takes me. When he pulls out his retractable key
ring and unlocks a door labeled WOMEN'S WING, I note the lock's a
Titan mortise—rock solid, small to no chance of picking it. Like the

climbability of chain-link, it's another vaguely criminal fact I am certain of.

I also note that I might know how to pick a lock.

We pass a door marked EAST-WEST CORRIDOR, and I see through its window a hallway stretching into the dim basement distance like a subway tunnel.

Soon we come to an elevator. A Black custodian is mopping the checkerboard floor nearby in a steady circular rhythm. Lester inserts a key, then pushes the elevator's up button.

While we wait, I try to press my temples to relieve the pressure, careful to avoid the tender, swollen spot where Lester's hand landed. "Here, miss." I look up and see the custodian's holding out a clean, white handkerchief and gesturing to my bloody ears.

"Thanks," I say, take the offering—

And immediately feel myself tearing up at his kind gesture.

What the hell is wrong with me?

I manage to stifle my weird emotional response and have just begun cleaning off my ears when Lester snatches the bloody hand-kerchief away and hands it back to the custodian.

"Joe, is it?" he asks the man.

"Yes, sir," the custodian answers.

"Well, Joe, you being new here, I'm gonna give you a big ol' bene-fit of the doubt and assume no one's told you it's a rule we don't share personal items with the patients."

Joe silently endures Lester's lecture, tucks the bloodied square back in his pocket, and returns to mopping while we step into the elevator.

A dim fluorescent light flickers from its ceiling as it slowly rises to 1. When it bounces to a stop, we head down a wide, bright hall-way to an office marked DR. EUSTACE SHERMAN.

Good, a doctor. Someone who'll see how ridiculous this whole mix-up is—and with the rum to get me released.

In the doctor's waiting room Lester leads me toward a desk where a young woman in pearls sits behind a nameplate that reads MISS

JANE CAMPBELL She's typing on a manual typewriter the size of a small boulder, and the keys' *thwack, thwack* staccato is reverberating painfully through my tender head.

Above her hangs a clock, next to a wall calendar featuring a boy in a Pilgrim hat. Days one through twelve are neatly checked off. It's November twelfth. Not a big surprise, judging by the almost-bare trees I saw on the grounds.

Miss Campbell glances at me, then addresses Lester. "You can bring Dorothy back. He's expecting her."

Dorothy—each time they call me that ludicrous name, I want to smack someone. But that's not how I get the hell out of this place. So, I drop my urge into a little mental drawer and slam it shut. The move feels effortless, well practiced. It's possible I have hundreds of mental drawers, an entire tansu chest of them in my head, storing all my most unhelpful thoughts.

Lester takes me down a short hall to an office where a man in a white coat sits behind an enormous wooden desk polished to a high shine. He's poring over a file.

"Doctor," I say to him, "there's been a huge misunderstanding—"

He raises his finger but doesn't look up. Lester seats me in one of two chairs facing the desk and stands nearby.

While we wait, I scan the room, filing away details. Exits other than the obvious? Just two windows with fixed bars over them. Potential weapons? I like the coatrack in the corner.

Dr. Sherman's a collector. Above him hang several framed butterflies pinned under glass. And his bookshelves are filled with objects that look plundered from a natural history museum: an elephant tusk, African masks, and a group of small primitive female figures with ample breasts. Close by is a nautilus shell, split down the middle and mounted on a spike, its secret Fibonacci chambers laid bare for all to see.

Among an infinite set of possibilities is one where my escape depends on the clever use of nautilus shell and busty clay figure, so no object is beneath note. I'm guessing my compulsive cataloguing of weapons is a habit born of both intense need and copious repetition—and I wonder just what kind of messed-up life situation would provide those two things.

It's a habit that's kept you alive, hasn't it?

The *voice*—always there with the cold-blooded commentary when she senses a threat or thinks I'm taking one too lightly. My own mental watchdog. Has she always been with me? And why?

When Dr. Sherman finally glances up from his file at me, he looks utterly fascinated. Which makes two of us: the doctor has even more wrinkles than Nurse Wallace. "You and the nurse on the bus, you're both so . . . old. How is that even possible?"

The doctor smiles, then says in a thick Scottish accent, "Why don't you and I have ourselves a little chat." He comes over to my chair, and his cologne—a heady mix of leather, cedar, and soap—envelopes me. "I'm Dr. Sherman," he says, offering his hand.

"Careful, Doctor," Lester cautions.

"Oh, I think we'll be fine, Lester," the doctor says. After I shake his hand, he takes the seat next to me and eyes my scrapes and bruises. "I apologize if the staff was a bit . . . overzealous. You *were* quite impressive out there. Saw you myself from the window. So, I hear you're having a bit of trouble remembering who you are—yet quite sure you don't belong here?"

You bet your ass we don't belong here.

"I told them there's been a mistake," I say. "I'm not Dorothy Frasier. There was a woman in braids on the bus who was clearly unhinged. She must be—"

"The real Dorothy," he says, grabbing the file off his desk, "who you believe stole your handbag."

"This Dorothy person might still be on the bus," I tell him. "If we act fast, get word to the driver, he can grabble 'n' snag her."

"'Grabble and snag,' is that what you said?" the doctor asks.

"Yeah. Why?"

He doesn't answer, just jots a note in the file. "And you believe Dorothy switched places with you on the patient transport bus?"

Memories of my bewildering experience on the bus have already begun to take on a faded, unfocused quality, like an old photo. It's unnerving—and something I keep to myself. "I told them she must've put her ID tag on me. Feggin' bitch. If we can just get back my purse—"

"You think it'll contain a driver's license telling us who you really are?" he asks.

"Maybe . . . or some other clue to go on."

"I see." Dr. Sherman quietly examines the tag, and I start to think I've gotten through to him, that maybe the deputy was right, the doctor *will* straighten all of this out. But then he turns to Lester. "I've said it for years, these war surplus tags County insists on using for transfers are a problem. Their mobility leads to just this kind of upset."

"You don't understand! This tag isn't—"

"I know it's confusing," Dr. Sherman says softly to me, "but not to worry, you'll be getting more secure identification soon, an ID band that isn't going anywhere."

"You aren't hearing me. I'm not who you think I am," I say with all the calm I can muster.

"Dear, eight women stepped onto the transport bus at Culpeper County Hospital. And eight women, including yourself, stepped off it here. How do you explain that?"

"The real Dorothy hid in the back with my purse. I'm sure I saw her!"

But am I, really?

Nothing's clear at this point, and I can feel the pain and pressure in my head begin to build as Sherman continues. "Let's suppose that were true and this woman hid to elude capture. It still doesn't explain why *you* were on that bus, now does it?"

"There's a reason. Something important I had to do . . . I just can't remember what it is. I must've hit my head in the bus, driver took a turn too sharply, and I got concussion. Then *he* clocked me," and I nod to Lester. "None of this feels right . . . makes sense . . ."

"I understand," the doctor says. "Along with the physical examination Dr. Sackler will perform up in the infirmary, we'll be running some psychological assessment tests to better determine the nature of your amnesia—"

"The *nature* of my amnesia? I just told you my head was injured—"

Dr. Sherman pats the air in front of him like he's trying to soothe it. Or me. "Sometimes, when a patient experiences events or learns things their mind finds too overwhelming to cope with, it'll block those memories, deny them to protect itself. But, dear, it's vital for your recovery that you begin to face reality, no matter how painful it might be—starting with the fact there was no woman in braids on that bus."

"You're wrong, she—"

"'Dorothy Frasier,'" he says, starting to read from the file. "'From Littleford, Virginia. Twenty-three years old. Currently under a court-ordered commitment of not less than twelve months. Transferred today from Culpeper County Hospital to Hanover State for evaluation and treatment. Onset two years ago of steadily worsening psychotic episodes marked by blackouts, delusions of grandeur, paranoiac, multifocal hallucinations.'" He looks up. "Have you been hearing voices, Dorothy?"

None of your fucking business.

So, I guess that's a yes to voices—but don't we all hear a voice from time to time, nudging us to do more, be better? Mine's just a bit harsher than most—definitely not something I'll be discussing with this guy.

"I may be having . . . a little trouble remembering who I am, how I got on that bus," I say, "but I know I'm not crazy—and I sure as hell am not Dorothy Frasier."

But Sherman keeps reading. "'As the disease has progressed, it's been marked by an increasing lack of concern for appearance, hygiene, as well as an escalation in lewd and antisocial behavior, aggression, and'—"

"We're wasting time!" I say, and try to stand, but Lester stops me.

"'. . . violence toward self,'" Sherman continues, "'culminating in a recent suicide attempt.'"

Suicide? I try directing my thoughts away from that word to something more useful, like acquiring the coatrack to use as a cudgel, but my mind keeps circling back.

Because suicide feels . . . possible.

The doctor watches for my response, but I give none, coolly tug the cuffs of my cardigan up, cross my arms, and look at him with my best stone-cold poker face—

Only Dr. Sherman seems far more interested in my crossed arms than my poker face. "County's records are lacking as usual, but it's pretty clear the method." What is he talking about? "May I see your hands?"

Not much choice with Lester still spoiling for a fight behind me. I hold both out, but Dr. Sherman takes just my right, gently turns it palm up—

And there on my wrist is a two-inch scar. What the hell?

It's recently healed, dark pink and slightly raised, flanked by dots from suture holes. I stare at the seam in disbelief as the throbbing in my head intensifies.

Why did I do it?

Sherman stands up. "I think that's enough for today. Give yourself some time to settle in, dear. Things will start to make more sense. Speaking of time," he says, looking at his watch, "I'm late for the staff meeting again. I swear they'll be docking my pay soon, eh, Lester?" And they share a chuckle before Dr. Sherman turns back to me. "Come."

In the waiting room he hands Miss Campbell the file along with a note he's written. "See that Miss Wallace gets the change in orders."

"Yes, Doctor," she says.

* * *

I walk in stunned silence between Dr. Sherman and Lester down the long, broad hallway, brain churning with possible suicide motives.

So, you've had some dark days. Doesn't make you Dorothy.

Why you did it won't get you out of here. So table it.

Soon we come to another metal gate marked NORTH WING, WOMEN'S WARDS. A nurse on the other side buzzes us through, and we continue on, passing female patients wandering the hall or sitting on the benches lining it. Most seem intimidated by Dr. Sherman and avoid eye contact.

"I'd like you to meet someone," Sherman says to me, and leads me to a patient cowering nearby. She's maybe thirty—hard to tell with all the worry perched on her face. "This is Lillian. Lillian, meet Dorothy."

The woman looks at me, or rather through me, for the briefest of moments before seizing my arm and pulling me close. "Careful where you step!" she whispers. "The Soviets, they've been laying their electromines everywhere to prevent our forces from retaking the land. See them, there, there, and there?" she says, pointing about the hallway. "Those spies of theirs are communicating on their wristwatch phones, making plans all through the seven kingdoms—"

"Lillian, you can go ahead and let go of Dorothy," Sherman says to her. When she doesn't respond, he gently peels the woman's hand off my arm. She doesn't seem to notice. "That's a good girl," the doctor says to the woman, like she's his loyal dog, before continuing down the hall. Lester nudges me to follow.

"At the onset of one of her schizophrenic episodes," Dr. Sherman says, "Lillian is actually quite aware of what's happening to her. Can even describe the upset she feels as the visual and auditory distortions set in. These worlds she imagines are outlandishly complex and elaborate, full of scheming players and intrigue, high stakes and drama, and they quickly begin to take hold of her. And as you just saw, once she's in the full thrall of an episode, the visions are so real to her, she can no longer distinguish them from reality."

We reach an open door marked CONFERENCE ROOM, and two

doctors in ties, white coats, and brown lace-up shoes nod to Sherman as they walk past us into the room.

"It's patients like you and Lillian who truly need Hanover. Not just its protection and care, but its state-of-the-art treatments, should they be necessary."

"But I'm not a schizophrenic!" I say, grabbing his jacket. He quickly removes my hand, flustered at my touch. Looks to see if anyone's watching before turning back to me. "Medical progress is never a smooth road, but if you'll open up, tell me what you're seeing and hearing, I promise to help you get beyond the denial, manage the symptoms so you can begin to separate substance from fantasy."

"Why aren't you listening to me? I'm not Dorothy Frasier. I don't belong here!"

He smiles. "Dorothy, beyond the twelve months, your commitment to Hanover is at *my* discretion. I determine when you can be safely released. So, cooperation, *that's* the key to going home."

Home.

Haven't the slightest idea where—or what—that is. Just know I won't be waiting for this patronizing asshole to give it to me. Time to find another way out of Hanover. "I want to speak to someone else—"

But he disappears into the room with the other doctors, and Lester pulls me away, down the long hall. "Come, darlin'. It's bath time."

CHAPTER 4

A LARGE GERMANIC NURSE with steel wool hair and forearms like bratwurst answers a door marked LAVATORY. "She's late," she complains to Lester, then turns to me. "Come."

"See you around, darlin'," Lester whispers, and hands me off.

The lavatory is immense and institutional, long on tiled walls, short on privacy. We pass by doorless toilet stalls, then a row of sinks — and I spot another patient out of the corner of my eye. She's twitchy and disheveled, cagey eyes darting around six ways from Sunday, cuts and bruises on her cheeks. When I turn toward her, she turns —

And I realize I'm looking at myself in a metal mirror bolted to the wall. I'm in my early twenties, with long brownish-red hair that's half fallen out of a barrette. Big hazel eyes, full lips, a few freckles scattered across my cheekbones. Me. Whoever the hell that is.

"Over here," Germanic says, and I join her in a changing area outfitted with benches covered with piles of newly admitted patients' clothes. The squirrelly brunette with the chirpy voice from the bus is at the end of a line of now-naked women snaking through a steamy doorway into what I'm guessing is the shower room beyond.

"Everything off. Leave it all on the bench," Germanic barks, then disappears into the shower room.

As I kick off my shoes, my eyes roam the room, scoping for possible escape options. A band of windows runs above the benches. Could they be stacked? Nope, bolted to the floor.

I shed the ID tag, socks, and sweater, then unzip the dress. When it's off, I discover, hanging from my neck, a silver medal flanked by a half dozen small wooden beads. Engraved on its front are the words GEORGETOWN COUNTRY DAY LATIN AWARD. And on its back, *Memento Audere Semper.* Roughly translated: "Remember to always dare."

So I know Latin. Not the most useful of clues, but it's something.

I tug my meringue-like petticoat to the floor and step out of the frothy heap, then turn away from the women to slip off my bra and underwear. The move feels a bit rote, like I'm going through the motions of modesty. Am I demure?

Doubtful.

I am cold though. The room's frigid, and goose bumps are spreading over my body as I pile my clothes, hair barrette, and manila ID tag on the bench. I'm about to join the brunette at the end of the line when I spy that thin, pink incision on my wrist.

Just how much have I forgotten?

And what other clues about me lie in plain sight? I start the premortem at my feet: dirty toenails but otherwise unremarkable. Traveling up my right leg, I find nothing. But the left's a different story. A long scar snakes up the thigh, bent halfway like a broken branch. Nearby it are two small, round deformations. I find a third on my upper arm. Unlike my wrist, these scars are old. Puncture wounds? Burns?

What kind of a person amasses this kind of damage? I run my finger over one, and a scene flashes through my mind:

The round scar's now a freshly healed wound, still deep pink—and a man's fingers pass over it before coming to rest on my shoulder. He's standing right behind me, his tan, muscular leg alongside mine, its blond hairs lit by a sun low in the sky.

Soon I feel his kisses, light and stealthy on my shoulder. When his lips skip over the strap of my swimsuit and begin working their way toward my neck, I pull his hand to my lips, kiss the quarter-moon scar on the center of his palm.

That's when I first hear it.

Laughter. A boy's weightless, joyful laughter nearby. And it's in this moment, amid the man's kisses and the boy's mirth, that I'm filled with so much love it feels like my heart will burst.

Then the man's kisses reach the nape of my neck, and I feel something new, a need, unruly and raw, building inside me.

He gently tugs my earlobe, and I turn to face him —

But as quick as it appeared in my mind's eye, the scene cuts out, and no amount of racking my brain will bring more.

That intense feeling of love I just experienced in its recollection makes me know with absolute certainty that the man, his kisses, and quarter-moon scar, the boy's laughter — it all happened.

My first real memory of life before waking on that bus. But who — and where — is that man? Is he searching for me?

Does he even know I'm lost?

A couple of my fellow passengers return from the showers, shivering, wet, and clutching their small white towels. They look like they've been through the ringer.

The squirrely brunette has now reached the doorway, and when I fall in line behind her, she turns. "Hi, I'm Betsy," she says, in her high-pitched voice, idly spooling her hair around a finger. I nod, having no name to offer in return.

Just ahead of Betsy is a woman I don't remember from the bus. She's fortyish, with gray-flecked hair and suspicious eyes that circle the room, looking for threats. A kindred spirit.

"Did you know there's a transmitter in my head?" Betsy asks me, pointing to her temple. "It's true. My brother put it there . . . to keep an eye on me." Betsy's crazy talk draws the attention of the gray-haired woman ahead of her, and her vigilant eyes briefly land on the two of us before moving on.

Soon the line advances and we enter the shower room. Along one wall are a half dozen stalls. Standing across from the nearest one is a tall, cage-like structure studded with nozzles controlled by a nurse inside it. She sprays the patient currently cowering in front of her with a sulfurous yellow fluid that quickly inundates her.

Germanic's in charge of wrangling patients into the line of fire. "Next," she barks at the twitchy gray-haired woman ahead of us, but she refuses to advance. "We don't have all day. Step to the wall for the insecticidal." She pronounces it *inzectizidal*. Yeah.

When Germanic starts to drag the woman toward it, I step out of line. "Is that really necessary?" I ask, and the two turn around. "She's clearly clean enough for *this* place."

But Germanic's not listening—she's spotted my Latin medal. "Give me the necklace."

My hand instinctively wraps around this lone tangible connection I have to my real self. But short of escalation, there's little choice, and I take it off, drop it into Germanic's chapped hand. The nurse slips it in her pocket then pulls the twitchy gray-haired woman to the wall.

As Betsy and I watch the woman being sprayed, she chirps, "Her name's Mary Droesch. I'd be careful of her. Overheard the nurses say Mary attacked her boss 'cause she was in love with him and couldn't understand why he didn't love her back. Put the guy in the hospital. Her sister and some doctors decided she was insane, and a judge sent her here. A local sheriff's deputy brought her in just an hour ago."

The same one who chased me down, Officer Worthy. The Lone Ranger. So Mary Droesch was the woman he was delivering to the nurse.

When I'm done with the delousing, I take a scratchy towel and head back to the changing room. My pile of belongings on the bench is smaller now—the petticoat's gone. It must've been deemed too buoyant for Hanover. I pull my damp hair into the barrette, then begin to put my clothes and ID tag back on.

Soon Betsy and the others finish dressing and exit, leaving just Mary Droesch and me. She turns around, sharp eyes fixed on mine. "You shouldn't have done that. Defend me."

"Yeah," I say to the ungrateful lunatic, "from what I hear, you're more than capable of fighting your own battles."

Mary smiles. It's a thin smile, like a grim Cheshire cat's. "My crime of passion. Good story, isn't it? Full of unrequited love, vengeance, violence. It certainly served its purpose."

"Purpose?" I ask.

"No one's going to listen to a jealous madwoman," she says, pulling on a pilly old blue cardigan someone knit long ago. "They needed a crime that wouldn't attract attention, get the wrong people asking the right questions. Something small . . . domestic. So they could lock me away in here."

Wow. Even more of a loon than Betsy. But I must admit I'm intrigued. "Who's this 'they' you're talking about?" I ask as I pull on my own sweater.

But before she can answer, Germanic enters. "You two, time's up. Come," she says, clapping, and we follow her out into the hallway and join the last few women still in line at a half-open Dutch door labeled INTAKE. A pretty nurse with big doe eyes is manning its window. She briefly looks up, surveying those of us still in line, before returning to whatever it is she's doing.

I repeat my question to Mary. "So, who's 'they'?"

Mary Droesch's eyes flick around, checking for any fellow loons listening in, before answering. "The ones who don't want you to know the truth," she whispers.

Okaaaay, should never have pressed the unhinged woman to elaborate. That's my fault.

I nod politely and the two of us wait in silence till it's Mary Droesch's turn. She steps up to intake's half door, and the doe-eyed nurse gently asks, "Mary, can you give me your wrist?" The paranoid woman reluctantly holds out her arm and Doe-Eyes secures an ID band on it, then directs her to stand with the others gathered by Gus, the large attendant I dodged by the bus earlier.

When I advance to the window, the nurse smiles timidly at me.

Her name tag says EVELYN GIBBS, R.N. "Dorothy Frasier," Nurse Gibbs says, reading the manila ID tag. "I've got something for you," she says, and holds out her hand. In it is the Latin medal. "Just keep it tucked under your dress, out of sight."

The kind gesture in the middle of this callous place catches me off guard, and just like when the janitor gave me his handkerchief, my eyes are inconveniently filling with tears. I try but fail to stop them, and in moments one is sliding down my cheek.

Crying'll get you killed.

I ignore the *voice*'s creepy warning. Turn away from the nurse to wipe my eyes and put the necklace back on. When I'm done, Nurse Gibbs says softly, "Can you give me your right hand, honey?" I hold it out, and she slips a plastic-coated band around my wrist and locks it on by tightening its metal cleat with a small tool. It reads: PATIENT W8209. DOROTHY FRASIER. SUICIDE RISK. EVAL. My new and improved ID, just as Sherman promised.

"You came on a good day at least," Gibbs says brightly. "Tonight's Thanksgiving here at Hanover."

"But today's the twelfth."

"It does sound odd, doesn't it? Hanover celebrates it early, so staff can be here with you . . . and also be with their families for the actual holiday." Gibbs leans in close. "I saw you from the front steps earlier." So Gibbs was the nurse the deputy was handing Mary Droesch over to. "The way you fought, it was amazing," she gushes. "Where'd you ever learn to do that?"

I have no answer for her.

"Gosh, right, your memory," she says. "Sorry, sometimes I can be a real dunce—"

"Still here, Miss Gibbs?" It's Nurse Wallace approaching, clipboard in hand. She doesn't look happy, though that might be on account of her eye, now swollen partially shut. I quietly slip into the crowd of Mary, Betsy, and the others gathered by Gus.

"Let's get you on your way, shall we?" Wallace says to Gibbs, as she consults her clipboard. "Mary Droesch and Betsy Apel, you're to go with Miss Gibbs to the Unit."

The Unit. Sounds ominous. Mary must share my sentiment 'cause her eyes are darting double-time as she joins Betsy and Miss Gibbs. The three soon disappear around the corner.

"Stein, Alemi, Flores, Young, and Frasier—you all come with me," Gus says to us in his slow drawl.

"Not Frasier," Wallace says, sounding a little ticked. "Dr. Sherman's made a change in her orders. She'll be joining Kasten and Delucia in A-Ward for evaluation."

"Yes, ma'am," Gus says, and leads his charges away.

"Come, ladies," Wallace says to the three of us remaining, and we follow her down the long hall.

* * *

We're passing a door marked SECLUSION when we hear almost animalistic cries coming from its other side, followed by a *THUMP*.

What the hell?

Wallace peers through the door's porthole window, then quickly unlocks it, and we follow her down a short corridor lined with a half dozen padded cells, each with a small window in its door. Halfway down it a wild-eyed, shrieking patient in a straitjacket is kicking an attendant she's somehow managed to knock to the ground.

Wallace plants us near the end of the hall, in front of a vacant cell. "Don't move," she says to us, then goes to help the downed attendant. While we wait, I check out the lock on the open cell door behind us and see it's a Wilcox double cylinder, keyed entry on both sides. The Wilcox is a shitty pin-and-tumbler lock, easily picked. Interesting.

As we wait for them to wrangle the patient, something bright red in the window of the cell door at the end of the hall catches my eye. I slip away from the others, peer through the glass window, and find not a cell but a tree. Bright crimson, its leaves lit by the sun finally breaking through the clouds.

But enough about the tree. The point is, I'm not standing in front of a cell door but an outside exit—one that bypasses all hallways, security gates, and creepy staff. Examining its lock, I can't believe my further luck: also a crappy Wilcox double cylinder.

This is going to be easier than I thought. I close my eyes and picture the Wilcox's pins and tumblers—and what it'll take to overcome them. I'll need something that can act as a tension wrench. The metal clasp of my barrette should work. And the pick? A piece of metal thin enough to get in there but with enough flex to push the pins—

"Dorothy!" I look up, see Wallace standing by the other two patients, arms crossed. When I rejoin them, she says, "I fear you've somehow gotten the wrong impression of me, so let's start over, shall we? I'm Miss Wallace, matron of this section and all the wards within it."

I get it, lady, you are all-powerful.

"As matron," Wallace continues, "I can determine just how agreeable your life at Hanover will be. Whether you get privileges, whether you get a toothbrush, whether you get toothpaste *for* that toothbrush. If you act out like you've done today or again disrespect my or any member of my staff's authority, you'll be in a restraint and locked in one of these cells so fast it'll make your head spin. So remember, I'm watching you."

I'm assuming with the good eye . . .

Maybe I deserve the nurse's venom. Whoever I am, I'm kind of a bitch.

CHAPTER 5

I LOOK THROUGH THE reinforced glass observation window into A-Ward's dayroom. It's surprisingly pleasant, lit by large windows and filled with white wicker chairs and tables. Two dozen women mill about or sit.

A wall clock by the nurses' station says three o'clock.

Wallace opens the dayroom door and I hear the white-noise murmur of the room's inhabitants. "You three will be in A-Ward while the doctors determine the best placement for you. I suggest joining those ladies," and she points to a nearby table where women are weaving strips of fabric onto square frames. "They're making pot holders to be sold at the local market. Making yourself useful with a homemaking task helps keep the mind out of trouble and prepares you for the day you might return home."

The other two head for the crafts table to join their fellow sweatshop workers, but I hang back, eyeballing the nurses' station window for possible lock picks—till I see Wallace's good eye on me. So I go to a nearby stack of magazines.

It's a grab bag of choices: on the top of the pile is *Life* magazine, whose cover features a picture of two men pointing to a towering, twisting structure that looks like it's made of marbles and toothpicks. The headline reads: "Uncovering the Mystery of DNA's Double Helix Structure: James Watson & Francis Crick."

I flip to the next, *Amazing Stories*, whose cover is a colorful illustration of dinosaurs menacing a man holding up a small device with a spiral antenna. I flip to the next magazine, *Woman's Day*, and thumb through its well-worn pages past ads for catsup, detergent, and scary white lingerie, till I come to one in which a woman holds a large thermometer. Below her are the words "Ferber, the meat thermometer that tells you the temp HE likes it."

Who is *HE*? And why does she care?

When Wallace turns away, I put the magazine down—and notice a cluster of patients nearby now whispering as they watch me. Like Nurse Gibbs, they seem to have caught a glimpse of my attempted escape. More gossip for the Hanover grapevine.

I head for a nearby bookshelf, and among the battered novels I find *For Whom the Bell Tolls* and *The Sun Also Rises* by Hemingway. Though my memory is currently Swiss cheese, I'm quite certain I like the lean writing of this man so keen to prove he's a man. I'm snagging both books when I hear happy music coming from a black-and-white TV housed in a metal cage across the room.

I walk over and see an elegant woman in pearls with pert, pointy breasts and a tiny waist on the old TV's small, blurry screen. She's smiling as she cranks open a large metal tin, peeling off its top to reveal something that looks an awful lot like a lung, though the can insists it's a ham.

Now she's got the ham-lung in a pan and anoints it with circles of pineapple before popping it into an oven. A clock's hands spin rapidly around, and as the music crescendos, the woman joyfully carries the finished ham-lung into her dining room, where husband, daughter, and son wait. As the woman places the maybe-organ before them, she turns to us. "Harvey's precooked hams. You owe your family the very best," she says, then winks at me.

There's something intoxicating about this woman's certainty of her place in her safe, canned ham-lung world—and I find myself caught up in a sort of happiness by proxy.

But my reverie's interrupted by whisper-shouts.

"Hey, hey there!"

Lillian, the woman who grabbed me earlier, is waving me over with a fanned-out deck of cards. Lillian's all smiles now, no sign of her recent Soviet electric land mine fears. More important, the table she sits at is next to a window whose grate I'd like to check out, so I join her.

"Hello there. My name's Lillian," she says as I sit down at the table. She seems to have no memory of our recent encounter. "Care to join me in a round of hearts?" Lillian proposes as she starts dealing cards. But then she pauses. "I heard you don't recall a thing about yourself. Suppose you don't even like hearts?" A distinct possibility. But Lillian must decide it's worth the risk because she returns to dealing.

"Shouldn't you be working on a pot holder for Miss Wallace?" I ask her.

"Dr. Sherman said not to worry about going home yet or pot holders. Says there's other ways to be of use in A-Ward. Besides, card games are on the list," Lillian says, and points to a sign on the wall that reads: "Miss Wallace's suggested activities: reading, checkers, cards, mah-jongg, and approved crafts."

Below it is a second sign: "Ladies, show courtesy for those taking care of you. Never curse. Use your better words and don't forget your *may I*'s, *pleases*, *thank yous* and *yes ma'ams*. — Miss Wallace."

"Quite the respect junkie, Miss Wallace," I say.

"She was a big shot army nurse in Korea. A major," Lillian says. "I think she misses all the rules."

I reach down to quietly pull on the steel window grille next to me. Solidly bolted to the wall. No play. Not promising.

"Plotting your escape so soon?"

I look up, expecting some eagle-eyed nurse has spotted me casing the place, but it's a patient. She's in her early twenties, blond and perky in a fluffy pink angora sweater. "Georgina Douglas," she says, extending her hand to me. "I saw you earlier, fighting your way through Nurse Wallace and her henchmen. Dorothy, is it?"

"Not my name," I say, ignoring the hand, and she pulls it back, miffed.

"Then what *is* your name?" she asks.

"Not your problem," I say.

Lillian taps her arm. "Georgie, she's got amnesia."

Georgie looks at me. "So, Not-Dorothy's feeling a bit confused about where she's landed? I'll give you the nutshell version. This is A-Ward, filled with the basically sane and the only *slightly* insane: your nervous breakdowns, alkies, depressives, manics, degenerates — ladies who want too much or the wrong kind of sex—"

"Is there a wrong kind?" I ask.

Georgie ignores my wisecrack. "We even have some schizophrenics. But mild schizos — not the going-on-about-the-devil-at-all-hours kind. Or the swearing, combative kind," she says, eyes on me. "Agreeable ones like Lil here."

Lillian smiles, happy where she's landed in Georgie's sanity peck order. "Thanks, Georgie," she says, then turns to me. "We ladies of A-Ward are the luckiest patients at Hanover."

"Luckiest?" I ask, eyeing the women doing semicompulsory crafts.

"We've got privileges the others don't," Lillian says. "Movie night, badminton, ballroom dancing—"

"Sure, that's all very nice," Georgie says, "but our biggest privilege — we only get talk therapy, none of Hanover's 'state-of-the-art' treatments."

"So, why are *you* here in A-Ward, among the lucky?" I ask her.

"No big mystery. I'm a convalescent. Checked in temporarily for nervous exhaustion. Daddy thought I could use some rest to rebuild my strength."

"Georgie's father's a real big cheese of something or other. Rich and powerful," Lillian adds.

"We chose Hanover because it's discreet," Georgie says, pulling a pill off her pink sweater. "Not like those gossip mill clinics closer to D.C. Plus Daddy happens to know Dr. Sherman, so it was the natural choice."

Georgie's eyes are blinking double-time and her smile's trying a bit too hard.

She's lying, but the what and why of the lie aren't clear.

"Come January I'll be back home," Georgie says, "rested and refreshed. And do you know why? I follow the rules. Don't give the staff any trouble."

"Yeah. You don't wanna make the doctors or nurses mad, make 'em think you're difficult," Lillian says, slowly shaking her head. "Or you'll end up down-alphabet."

"Down-alphabet?" I ask.

"Hanover talk," Georgie explains. "What ward you end up on after the observation period depends on how hard the doctors and nurses think it'll be to manage you."

"Meaning?" I ask.

Georgie grabs the cards out of Lillian's hand, gathers up the rest, then lays one in the center of the table. Taps it. "At Hanover's center is the administration building—visitors' room, doctors' offices, book-keeping, infirmary, the tower. To its left is the men's wing, to its right, the women's, both three stories, jiggering out section by section," she says as she lays cards on either side of the first in a stepped pattern that forms a jagged V.

"I'm familiar," I say.

She smiles. "Right, you've already toured the grounds," she says, winking, then taps the two cards flanking the center one. "The first section of each wing holds A-, B-, and C-Wards. All have fairly light security 'cause we give staff the least trouble. Don't have too many 'oppositional tendencies' is how the doctors put it."

"We're missing the fewest marbles," Lillian adds.

"But the further down-alphabet you're sent," Georgie says, "the more care and security you're going to get. And treatments—I've heard hydrotherapy, insulin, electroshock. Lil knows firsthand."

Lillian nods solemnly. "And they don't just use the treatments to treat."

"What do you mean?" I ask.

"If a patient acts up too much, they shock 'em," Lillian says. "Calms us down real fast." Lillian's "electro-mines" she imagined in the hallway earlier—are her ECT experiences filtering down into her delusions?

"Plus the shocks wipe out a patient's recent memories," Georgie says. "So they forget ever even being upset."

"Like shaking an Etch A Sketch," Lillian says, shivering at the thought. "We tried our best not to be shook."

Jesus.

Georgie taps a card. "G-Ward, that's where security tightens and the real chronics start: schizos, psychotics, assorted gorks and catatonics who've lost their connection to reality, too difficult—or dangerous— for their families to take care of. Those patients rarely leave Hanover."

"Some get buried right on the grounds," Lillian says.

All those numbered graves I saw. Chronics.

Georgie taps the farthest card. "At the end are the violent and disturbed wards. They hardly leave their rooms." Like that patient shouting her warning to me through the bars as I ran past earlier. "Right now, they're evaluating you," Georgie says, eyes leveled on me, "deciding just how much trouble you'll be. So, I'd be good, Miss Not-Dorothy. Go along to get along, or you'll find yourself down-alphabet."

"Or worse," says Lillian as we watch Georgie sashay away.

"Worse?" I ask but she doesn't answer, her attention now drawn to something in the room. Something I can't see. Fear now floods her face, and she grips the table tight.

"What is it, Lillian?"

"It's coming back," she says, shaking her head, then looks at me. "I don't want this . . ."

"What?"

"My ghost world—all those electro-mines planted out in that cornfield. It's gonna trap me inside it . . . like a room with no doors or windows to escape." She looks away from me. "That sound, that awful blue sound when someone steps on one . . ."

I put my hand on her shoulder. "Then stay here with me, Lillian," I say, but she doesn't seem to hear. Instead she slides down off the chair onto the checkerboard floor and slowly rocks back and forth.

CHAPTER 6

Hours later a recovered Lillian and I wait in line in the kitchen's serving area, the walls of which have been decorated with giant cutouts of Pilgrims and Indians. Up ahead a woman in a hairnet behind the counter doles out food.

Fake Thanksgiving at Hanover.

It's probably not the best celebration of the holiday feast I've enjoyed in my life, but someone's about to hand me a plate of hot food—and one can hardly argue with that situation.

The kitchen worker loads up our trays—a slice of turkey roll bathed in yellowish gravy, a "holiday medley" of peas, carrots, and corn, and a slice of pumpkin pie.

While we wait for the patient ahead of us to decide what silverware to take, I take in her crude, choppy crew cut. Someone's shorn off her hair like you would a sheep's, with little care as to the outcome.

Lillian whispers, "Lobotomy. Dr. Sherman performs them on really sick patients, the difficult ones that nothing else works for. Helps them become more normal. I heard he takes something that looks like an ice pick and hammers it through there," she says, pointing to the inner corner of my eye, "till he reaches the brain. Then he sort of swings it back and forth to cut whatever it is that's causing the problem. They say it's all terribly scientific." We watch the woman still hesitating over cutlery. "The doctor just needs a little more practice. She's gonna be a while."

Jesus. Get me out of this place.

Lillian reaches around the woman and grabs our silverware.

The dining hall is huge, with a soaring ceiling supported by giant wood beams. And loud: the deafening din of a couple hundred highly vocal women almost drowns out the ringing still in my ears. I follow Lillian down its center aisle, passing by rows and rows of tables topped with today's preholiday art project: construction paper turkeys.

As we sit down at a table near the far end, Lillian warns, "You need to be a bit careful tonight. Normally this dining hall's just for A- to C-Ward patients. But since it's Thanksgiving, patients from some down-alphabet wards are here for the holiday celebration. And some of them can be *scrappy*."

A woman at the end of the table gazes out through the hole she's eaten out of the slice of turkey plastered to her face. Gravy drips slowly down it as she speaks to no one in particular: ". . . so I said to John, you and the kids can make your own goddamn dinner . . ."

"She's harmless. It's those two you need to watch out for. Norma and Carol over there," Lillian says, nodding to a couple of Paul Bunyan–size women laughing hysterically a few tables away. "F-Ward psychopaths."

The number of staff overseeing the dining hall is small: Gus, Lester, and Germanic Nurse. Joe, the custodian who lent me his handkerchief earlier, is mopping up medley spillage—peas, corn, and carrots in a blast radius around a table near the center of the room.

Soon Wallace and Gibbs, the doe-eyed nurse from intake, appear, leading a handful of patients down the center aisle. Thin creatures with drawn faces and large, dull eyes, dressed in faded gray gowns that hang limply from their sharp collarbones. They trail with slow, teetering gaits behind the nurses. I see drool glistening on the chin of one.

Nurse Wallace pauses the group near our table, waiting for Georgie, who's blocking the aisle, to move. While the debutante searches for a table to grace with her presence, I spot a loose hairpin jutting from Wallace's tightly coiled bun, trying to escape its gravitational force— a potential lock pick.

Wallace grows impatient with Georgie and points to our table. "Sit there, Georgina."

"Yes, ma'am," Georgie says with a smile. She plunks down across from me, the smile for Wallace gone, and watches me eat. "Lord, you'd think you hadn't eaten for days the way you're tearing through that pressed turkey."

"Is that going to be a problem for you?" I ask.

"Depends. Will you close your mouth when you chew?"

"Please don't fight, ladies," Lillian urges fretfully. "The nurses'll hear."

But Wallace and Gibbs are moving on with their charges. As the last one, a middle-aged woman in pointy cat's-eye glasses, shuffles past Norma, the psychopath leans into the aisle and taunts, "Hey, gork, Gene Kelly teach you those dance steps?"

Norma's sidekick, Carol, laughs so hard she chokes, sending veggie shrapnel into her friend's face—causing Norma to shift her bullying from Glasses to Carol.

Wallace and Gibbs hear none of it; they're busy seating their docile charges at a nearby table that's already been set with spoons in bowls containing what looks like our holiday dinner—if you ran it through a chipper-shredder. Festive. Having settled the last of their patients, the nurses walk away.

I watch Glasses slowly bring a spoonful of turkey mush to her mouth, hand curled tight around her utensil to ensure its safe journey. "Who are those women?" I ask.

"Patients from Dr. Sherman's Unit downstairs," Lillian says. The Unit—where Betsy and Mary were sent. "On holidays, the doctor allows anyone who can make the trip to come up here for the special dinner."

Wonder why Betsy and Mary wouldn't have qualified. They're definitely in better shape than these women. Glasses's spoon is almost at her lips when the food spills out of it. The woman stares at the empty utensil, at a loss.

"Not exactly *Quiz Bowl* contestants," Georgie adds, having deemed our conversation worthy of her attention.

"What exactly *is* the Unit?" I ask them.

Lillian shrugs. "Not really sure."

"I know. My father told me," says Georgie. "It's an experimental facility. Dr. Sherman's conducting government-funded research down there on how a damaged mind can be rehabilitated. Even made well again. He's been developing various new treatment regimens on severely ill patients brought in specifically for them. Daddy says it's all very hush-hush, part of the cold war effort. Apparently, even the patients' families aren't told exactly what's being done."

The zombies chew slowly, dull eyes down. "What do you think is being done to them?" I ask Georgie.

"Hard to say," she answers. "They don't let us anywhere near the Unit patients."

"They're afraid we'll hurt them," Lillian says.

"Probably for the best," Georgie says. "Look at them, like baby deer."

"Oh no, that's trouble," Lillian says as she watches Norma heading down the aisle toward the Unit table, dragging her spoon across tabletops as she goes. Wallace and the rest of the staff are preoccupied with some shouting match at the other end of the room. Norma reaches the Unit's table and starts scooping pureed pie from the helpless women's bowls into her own mouth.

But when she tries swiping Glasses's bowl, the woman bats her away with her own spoon.

"Someone's still got some fight in her," says Georgie.

Seeing Glasses about to get her ass whooped sparks something in me, and just like in the shower line with Mary Droesch, I feel this urge bordering on compulsion to involve myself. Idiotic, I know, and I try changing the subject in my head to anything else — the weather, Officer Worthy's clear blue eyes, the suspect mole on Lillian's upper lip. But now the *voice* puts the urge into words:

Trust your gut. Go to her.

And I have to admit, she's awfully persuasive.

As I rise, Georgie puts her hand on my arm. "Let that be."

"Go along to get along?" I ask.

"Exactly. Do not stick your neck out for anyone here."

But I ignore her, head for the Unit table, and just as Norma takes a swing at Glasses, I slide between them and block it.

Norma comes after me now, shouting, "Find your own damn pie, Wonder Woman!" But I silence her dessert tirade with a hook kick, raising my knee and extending it outward, then snapping it back till my heel impacts Norma's jaw with a satisfying thump.

Norma recovers surprisingly quickly and again turns to Glasses, about to grab her by the throat, when I seize her arm, wrap my leg around hers, and pull her to the ground. I'm preparing to flip her when I find myself pausing and checking the crowd, which now includes Sherman, standing in the doorway, observing.

There's something I'm waiting for but I'm not quite sure what it is—till I see it: Wallace and her loose hairpin heading straight for me, straitjacket in hand. Gibbs, along with Gus, Lester, and a couple other attendants, follow.

I surrender to Hanover's arithmetic. Don't resist as Lester and Gus pull me off Norma, and Wallace opens the restraint meant for me. It's an old one; stenciled on the shoulder are the words HANOVER LUNATIC HOSPITAL. A return address should I go lost.

As Lester pins my left arm down, he says to Gus, "I swear these women'd eat each other alive if we let 'em. Wouldn't you, darlin'?" he asks, winking at me.

Gus ignores Lester's fantasy date musings and concentrates on pinning my legs, allowing Wallace to begin her work. And even though this apparently *was* my plan, as the nurse deftly thrusts my arm into the stiff canvas of the restraint, a sort of primitive panic starts to fill me. But when she leans over me for the second arm—and I see that loose hairpin so tantalizingly close, I remember what I'm after. I lift my head, try to snag it with my teeth but fail.

Damn. I try again, fail again. She's now got both arms completely in the long sleeves. Time's up. But then there's a scream. Norma's bitten an attendant. Wallace turns her head toward the noise — bringing her hairpin a shade closer. I try one last time and, hallelujah, my teeth connect with metal.

As I slip the hairpin quickly into my mouth, I sense eyes on me and look up to find Georgie watching. But she says nothing.

When they stand me up and cross my arms, I notice two things: one, that I've quietly filled my lungs to capacity. And two, that I'm flexing every muscle in my upper body to its maximum, holding this pumped-up stance as they work.

This new awareness of my intention to be big prompts questions. Did I help Glasses like I tried to help Mary Droesch — and in the process find I could obtain this piece of metal? Or did some cunning part of me see the opportunity, weigh the risks, then engineer this little drama to score it? The person who'd do that is a calculating bitch.

Am I her? Am I a calculating bitch?

Just practical. You saved Glasses and gained the tool that'll get you out of here.

Don't overthink it.

The *voice* is right. I'm a couple picked locks away from escape; I'll worry about my shady motivations when I'm free.

I smell Sherman's approaching cologne. "You see what I mean?" Wallace says to him. "Dorothy should be moved to a more appropriate ward —"

Sherman cuts her off. "Seclusion till they've calmed down."

"Yes, Doctor," a chagrinned Wallace says. After she's finished securing the last buckle, a trussed-up Norma and I are led down the main corridor. Even though Norma's from F-Ward, the staff must prefer not to drag riled-up patients all the way back to their own wards. Both of us are taken to A-Ward's nearby seclusion hall — home of the crappy locks.

Gus takes Norma to her cell while Lester unlocks mine and flicks on the light. The small, low-ceilinged cell is built for claustrophobia. Its padded floor and walls must've started out white, but years of women writhing over their surfaces have given them a patina of psycho-beige.

Lester waits till I've kicked off my shoes, then pulls me into the cell and draws me close. Odors of cigarettes and menthol compete for supremacy in his mouth as he strokes my cheek.

I so want to bite.

Easy. Keep it together.

"Lester, you coming or what?" shouts Gus from down the hall.

"Killjoy," Lester mutters, then yells, "Yeah, be right there."

He shoves me to the floor and exits. When the door locks with a *thwock*, I put my interlude with Lester into one of my mental drawers, relax my flexed muscles—and find I've now got some slack in the jacket.

Time to leverage it. Hairpin clutched in my teeth, I manage to stand up, exhale, and hug myself till I'm as small as possible, then twist around till I'm able to slide my hand up to my shoulder. And I'm about to maneuver the crook of my elbow over my head and shed this garment, when I feel something—

The slightest vibration in my toes. It's subtle, barely a whisper. So I stop a moment to better define it—and see the most beautiful rainbow halo form around the lightbulb above me. Soon the whisper in my feet grows to a buzz, like tiny ghost bees are trapped inside them. In seconds the buzz has worked its way up my legs and spine, to my head, where it begins to percolate, growing in sound and discomfort till it's like a thousand jackhammers are drilling into me.

It's a familiar roar. And a familiar pain.

This has all happened before.

Suddenly, there's a blinding light, and I shut my eyes against the white roar. Let the hairpin drop. Let the cell fill with my screams.

CHAPTER 7

'M UPRIGHT. I know that. Head down, eyes shut, sucking great rafts of air into my greedy lungs while I let the pain and dizziness recede. Can feel the straitjacket still restraining me. Its snug embrace is oddly comforting. I keep my head down, slowly open my eyes, but the cell floor is just a shadowy blur of shapes. I stare, conjuring focus till I can barely make them out: black snakes, dozens of them surrounding me, their serpentine bodies slithering over my feet.

What the hell is going on?

I try not to make any sudden movements, slowly raise my pounding head—and see, looming high above, dark creatures with glowing blue eyes that blink as they watch me. When I look away from them, ghostly trails of blue stretch across my eyes . . .

How did I get here?

And where *is* here?

Soon, sounds of feet *clattering* down metal steps. And a girl's faraway voice: "We're coming, Bix!"

Bix? Sherman said they'd be performing some tests on me. This must be one of them, some sort of psychological evaluation . . . Or maybe some sick behavioral experiment they're running. Part of the doctors' research. They must've drugged me, then put me in this room of snakes to observe my reactions. Maybe the girl is their research assistant, coming to tell me the testing is over and let me out of here . . .

This isn't some experiment or test. This is real.

Bullshit.

Now another voice, this one male and closer. "Christ, that's a straitjacket on her! I said something like this would happen if we sent *her* back. She's a leader in the Child's Army, for God's sake. Frightens the hell out of people *here*—can you imagine her effect on people *there*? And we expected Bix with her proclivity for violence to land in 1954 and just . . . blend?"

"Bix's *proclivities* are why we sent her, Gideon," the girl says. "It's not exactly safe there—"

"Or *here* anymore, thanks to her—now that we've got the Tabula Rasa's goon squad breathing down our necks. It's only a matter of time—"

"We just barely got her back. Can you give it a rest, Gideon?" the girl says.

I squint, trying to make out the approaching lab assistants through my hazy eyes as they emerge from the shadows. The girl's East Asian, in her twenties, with a brow furrowed deep enough to plant cabbage. The guy's Black, also in his twenties, though his glasses sit low on his nose like a cranky old man's.

Trailing behind them are a half dozen more figures, and panic starts to spread through me as they approach. I try to back away but trip and land among the snakes, bound up, helpless—

Only now I see they aren't snakes. They're electrical cables, dozens crisscrossing the floor. And the towering shadows with the blue eyes—some sort of black equipment stacked high, their blue running lights blinking on and off.

"Back off, give us some space!" the guy shouts at the others behind them, and they retreat into the shadows.

"You gave us a real scare there, Bix," the girl says as she kneels down beside me among the cables. "Something went wrong with the machine in your initial jump. A glitch."

"It sent your fragging levels through the roof," the guy says, "messed with some of the settings, which might have skewed your landing coordinates."

"Worst of all it cut your tether," the girl says. "So we couldn't bring you back remotely."

Coordinates? Tethers? Fragging? The jargon's got to be part of the experiment. Doctors want to see how I react to all the BS being flung at me.

"Thank God you managed to trigger your link inside that restraint," the girl says, "got yourself back here. We want to hear all about the jump: everything you saw, what you were able to learn. But first let's get you out of that thing."

She reaches for one of my restraint ties, and I feel a rising alarm as her hands come closer. "Get the fuck away!" I roar, and the two assistants back up. "Where are they?"

"Who?" the girl asks.

"The doctors running this fucked-up experiment, observing me." I search the shadows for a sign of them. "Are they out there, hidden in the dark?" I ask.

The two stare at me in weird, stunned silence for a moment before the guy says to the girl under his breath, "Holy shit, she has zero idea who she—or we—are. That fragging did a helluva lot more than mess with her tether."

The girl nods slowly, then whispers back: "Major memory loss. Shit. Looks like some distortion in her perception of reality as well. Without an exam, it's hard to tell the full extent of the neural damage—"

"Me waking on that patient transport bus—was that all part of this experiment? Did you drug me then too?" I ask.

"Bix came to on a patient bus?" the guy says. "Those landing coordinates were definitely fucked-up."

That chopped-off name again. "Bix?" I ask.

"That's you," the girl says to me. "It's short for Beatrix Parrish. I'm Kyung. And this is Gideon."

The Gideon guy has pulled a small object shaped like a pack of gum from his pocket and is now pointing it at me. What the hell is that? "What could the doctors possibly be testing with this psychological experiment?" I ask them.

"It's okay, Bix," the Kyung one says. "Gideon made some adjustments to the machine after we realized something had gone wrong with your first jump. He's just scanning your disc to see if they helped." There's a *beep* sound, and Gideon looks at his pack-of-gum object. "Well?" she asks him.

"Modifications worked . . . mostly," he says. "But she's still fragging some with each jump. I'll tweak it some more, get the neural damage down to acceptable levels before we send anyone else," he says, then disappears into the blue-eyed shadows.

Kyung turns to me. "Can you tell me what happened back there?"

"Back where? I want to speak to whoever's running this—"

But I'm interrupted by a door BANGING open somewhere. Moments later a guy is bounding toward me, wavy hair flopping with each step. "Bix!"

"Ethan, wait!" Kyung yells, and he stops just short of me. "That anomaly during her initial jump—it was a lot more serious than we thought. There's been some brain trauma. She doesn't know us. *Any* of us."

Sadness and anger seem to be fighting for dominion over the guy's face as he kneels down close to me. "I'm Ethan," he says, trying to smile as he eyes my cuts and bruises. And even though I know all of this is some elaborate setup of Sherman's, something about this guy's struggling grin gets to me. Soon big, stupid tears are escaping my eyes and falling to the floor.

Ethan looks shocked by my display.

"Emotional lability," Kyung says. "Means there's been damage to her frontal lobe, causing her to experience confusion over what she's feeling and how to manage it." Ethan glares at her. "It's possible all of this could resolve with time—"

"You never should've sent her before we fully understood the machine," he says.

"The clock's ticking for all of us, Ethan," she says. "Someone needed to go."

"So you signed Bix up for your deadly mission."

"She volunteered!"

The bees are back.

Can feel the buzzing in my feet starting to rise up the long bones of my legs.

Ethan knows nothing of the bees rising. "You should've refused, Kyung. Bix was in no state to decide—"

"She's an adult, fully capable of making her own choices."

Now the bees have reached the base of my skull and the roar begins to build.

"You knew she'd do whatever she could to stop the Guest," Ethan says. "And you took advantage."

The Guest. The words fill me with stomach-twisting dread—and questions.

The pain's now reaching a crescendo between my ears, and I just want to curl up in a ball and shut all of this out. But I can't—because part of me needs an answer: "Tell me who the Guest is, Ethan!" I shout, just before I'm swept away by the white roar, back into the dark.

CHAPTER 8

FEEL LIKE I'M both inside my body and watching it from some great distance . . .

"And Ethan, is he still here in the seclusion cell with us?" I hear Dr. Sherman ask.

Don't tell this asshole one more goddamn thing!

The *voice*'s harangue rouses me from my gauzy stupor. I look around—

And find I am indeed back in my cell, Dr. Sherman crouched next to me on its padded floor.

That room with the blue-eyed shadows gone. Those squabbling lab assistants gone.

How is that possible? It was all just here! But my panicky thoughts are interrupted by Sherman, who's acting like nothing has changed. "Maybe I could speak to Ethan," he says, "help you sort things out. About Bix, your mission . . ."

Ethan. The mission. What the hell have I been telling this guy?

No doubt too much. Time to end this session.

So I force an easy smile onto my face and say with great coyness, "Mission? I'll show you mine if you show me yours, Doctor. Just gonna need you to untie the restraint, let me slip into something more *comfortable*." My fake come-on has the desired effect on the easily flustered Sherman: his face turns beet red, and he jumps to his feet to put some distance between himself and my sexual advances—cutting short his inquisition. I can see little beads of sweat cropping up along his thinning hairline.

"We'll talk more about this tomorrow, Dorothy," he says, and goes out to speak to Lester in the hallway.

I see something peeking out from under my shoulder—the hairpin. I just manage to get it back in my mouth and slide the restraint sleeve I worked up to my shoulder back into its place before the attendant hauls me to my feet.

* * *

I'm lying, ravenous with hunger, in one of two dozen beds in A-Ward's dormitory two. Everyone else is asleep, except Lillian, quietly talking to herself as she creeps, free range, across the floor in the dark. Not me. Though they removed the straitjacket, I'm still restrained, bound to the bed, arms and legs separated, each ankle and wrist cuffed and lashed tight. Full-on Gullivered, there's nothing for me to do but listen to my grumbling stomach, run my tongue over the hairpin, and contemplate what just happened.

Or rather didn't happen.

'Cause I've figured it out. Those people, their mysterious machine, the white roar, of course it wasn't some doctor's test—it was a dream. A fuzzy, fucked-up dream fueled by my concussions. Just the random misfirings of neurons in my punch-drunk brain as my subconscious was trying to make sense of this strange day.

What you experienced was real. It happened.

Nope. A dream, nothing more.

The future isn't something you can just ignore. You heard Ethan and Kyung—you're there to carry out a mission.

"Wild cherry Life Saver?" Georgie asks, plopping down on the edge of my bed with a pack of candy. "You look like you could use one," she says, peeling back the wrapper.

"How did you get those? We're not supposed to have—"

"This, my dear, is what going along to get along—and the proper bribe — can get you." She pulls a candy from the roll, and I start sali-vating like Pavlov's dog. I've definitely tasted wild cherry Life Savers before.

Georgie holds it in front of my mouth. "I imagine things are a bit crowded in there. Why don't you give me the hairpin?" I hesitate. "If I was going to turn you in, I'd have done it by now."

True. I push the piece of metal out, and Georgie gingerly takes it and places the candy on my tongue.

Such mouthwatering joy! While I take in the amazingness of the little red candy, Georgie lifts my blanket and reaches for the hem of my dress. "I could see it on your face as they marched you and Norma off. You engineered that fight in the dining hall. All to get them to put you in seclusion armed with this," she says, holding up the hairpin. She levels her eyes at me. "I've a feeling you're quite capable of finding your way out of a restraint, using this to pick a lock. Which means you were minutes from possible escape."

She is not wrong.

Georgie slides the hairpin into my dress hem, then stares at me. "So, why scream and bring everyone running? What happened to you in that seclusion cell?"

I briefly fantasize about telling Georgie of the dream. What it would be like to unburden myself like that, to lessen my fucked-up nightmare's frightening power in the sharing of it. But I let the temp-tation pass.

"Come on, faster," Lillian urges some invisible sidekick as she creeps past us on the floor. "We've gotta reach the lighthouse before they search the coast!"

"Lord," Georgie says to me, "Lillian really needs to ditch that imaginary friend she's dragging along. Clearly they're slowing her down." And now I can't help thinking about my own imaginary dream friends. Georgie notices. "Something's got you spooked. What is it?"

Not one word.

This isn't a slumber party where we braid each other's hair and spill our secrets. Bad enough Dr. Sherman knows about the mission. Kyung said it's dangerous here. Trust no one. Depend on no one.

Then again, the *voice* is demented enough to believe my nightmare was real, so not the best judge of this situation. Over her protests ringing through my brain, I tell Georgie about waking on the bus, the real Dorothy stealing my purse, the mystery man I remember kissing me, my wild nightmare, Ethan, Kyung—and damn, it feels good to let it all out.

"I know it was just a crazy dream brought on by a couple of blows to the head," I say, "but there was something about it that felt so . . . real."

Georgie now has that slightly constipated look of someone trying to spare you pain.

"Say it," I tell her.

"I just think before you make your escape from Hanover, go running off into the night, you might want to take a step back, look at your state of affairs objectively."

"My state of affairs?"

"Dreaming about being on some vital—but screwed-up—mission, for these people who call you Bex—"

"Bix."

"Pardon me, Bix. But what if it wasn't a dream? What if it was a hallucination your waking mind cooked up—and it's not the first? You said things seemed 'off' on the bus. Surreal. Maybe the 'real Dorothy' stealing your purse was also a hallucination—"

"No. That was real."

"Do you have any proof?"

"You think I'm Dorothy Frasier."

"If you can't prove you're not, then shouldn't you at least entertain the possibility? Face the truth of who you are and why you were on that bus no matter what that is?"

Bitch.

But understandable. All Georgie knows is I'm a woman who woke on a bus with no memory, wearing a schizophrenic patient's ID tag and insisting that same patient switched identities with her before stealing her purse and disappearing into thin air. And tonight this woman, on the verge of escape, couldn't keep herself from alerting her jailers with bloodcurdling screams. That woman sounds pretty certifiable to me.

So I shouldn't be angry at Georgie for offering up her *helpful* advice. And I definitely shouldn't act on the impulse to hurt her back—

But I do.

"And who are *you*, really, Georgie? Are you really just here for 'exhaustion'? Is that all your daddy is worried about?" Georgie shoots me a look that's equal parts hate and hurt, then heads back to her bed.

So I lie awake, watching Lillian circling the room and trying to wedge Georgie's worrisome words into one of my mental drawers.

CHAPTER 9

N OW HOLD STILL, sugar. We just want to make sure one of those cuts doesn't get infected," says a kindly horse-faced nurse, Miss O'Brien. She's holding the largest needle I've (probably) ever seen. I'm dressed in a cloth gown, sitting on a chilly metal examining table in the third-floor infirmary's procedure room. Its walls are tiled in green, giving it a vaguely morgue-y feel.

While she gives me the tetanus shot, I scan the room for possible weapons. But anything of use has been safely secured in its drawers and cabinets.

As the nurse puts a Band-Aid on me, a short doctor in a white coat enters. He wears a headband with a little round mirror attached to its front like a cartoon doctor.

"Dorothy, I'm Dr. Sackler. My, aren't you pretty," he says, looking me over. Guess that's a gold star on the looks portion of the medical exam. "Dr. Sherman's spoken to me about your case. So I hear you've been having a little trouble remembering things, aren't sure if you bumped your head?"

"No, I'm completely sure. It happened on the transport bus. Then that creepy attendant, Lester, knocked me out, so that's two concussions in under an hour—"

"I see someone's been busy playing doctor," he says, chuckling and patting my leg. "But before you make your diagnosis, how about I take a look?" I nod to the cartoon doctor, and he says, "Tell me if anything I touch hurts," as he begins probing my scalp with his hands. "Have you felt any symptoms from these *concussions* of yours?"

"Yes. A throbbing pain in my ears. And they were ringing. Still ringing," I tell him.

"Well, that's not good, is it?" Dr. Sackler says absently, then turns to his nurse. "No obvious signs of swelling or injury to the head, other than the facial contusions and bruises." While Nurse O'Brien jots a note in the chart, the doctor points to a picture on the wall of a Dalmatian in a fireman's hat. "Now, I need you to look at the funny dog for me while I examine your eyes for signs of concussion."

I stare at his hilarious dog while the doctor shines a light in my eyes. "Dr. Sherman told me about last night," he says, looking extra hard at me as he moves the light to my other eye. "Sounds like you got a little carried away in all the excitement." Sherman's shared the story of my little come-on to him last night with Dr. Sackler. Looks like nurses and patients aren't the only sources of gossip at Hanover. I don't respond to the doctor's fishing expedition, and he returns to the eye exam. "There's a slight difference in pupil size," he says to the nurse. "Nothing significant."

"It must be from whatever happened to me on that bus," I say, but he just smiles politely. "If you don't believe me, run tests. Do a . . . a . . ." And I rack my brain for the name of the test I mean.

But Dr. Sackler's moved on—to the small, round, divot-like scars on my arm. He flips down his mirror thing, reflecting the light from the lamp and throwing them into high relief. "Possible puncture . . . or burn marks." He and Nurse O'Brien exchange looks.

"Those aren't important—" I start to say, but the doctor interrupts. He's spotted something else.

"Hmm. Dried blood in the ear. Hold still, Dorothy," he says, and I listen to his slow, steady breath as he peers for a long moment into my right ear with his little light, then repeats the exam on the left. "No sign of infection—yet both eardrums have recently been perforated.

Violently. That would explain the auditory distortions and the blood." The doctor exchanges another look with his nurse, then puts his hand on my knee. "Did you put something into your ears, Dorothy?"

"No! I would never hurt myself," I say, moving my knee out from under his hand. "It's what I've been trying to tell you, I was injured on the bus!"

"Okay, that's fine, Dorothy," he says, and gives me a smile and a nod. Smile-nods, I've noticed, are used by Hanover staff to avoid all manner of tears and trouble. They make the patient feel good about what she's just said—or done—when maybe she shouldn't be so proud. A participation trophy handed out by the face.

Nurse O'Brien pulls two metal levers from the end of the table and unfolds them. Each has an oblong ring on its end.

"Dear, I'm gonna need you to slide your fanny down here and lie back, so we can have a look," the doctor says.

"Why?"

"Just a brief exam. Dr. Sherman wants you to have a full workup, make sure everything's in working order before deciding on the best therapy for you."

"What kind of therapy?"

"I'm sure he'll have that discussion with you when the time comes," he says, taking a seat on a rolling stool.

Nurse O'Brien puts a tray holding a beak-shaped metal instrument on a nearby rolling table, then flicks on a bright standing lamp. "Nothing to be afraid of, sugar. You've most likely had an internal exam before. Come, scooch on down."

Do I have a choice?

When my butt's hanging just off the end of the table, she lifts my feet up and onto the cool metal rings, then drapes a sheet over my knees, blocking my view. "Good girl," I hear Dr. Sackler say through the sheet. "Now take a deep breath and try to relax while I insert the speculum."

I hear the pieces of the thing clanking together. Feel the cold metal slide in, then the pinching pressure stretching my insides apart. As he ratchets the metal blades farther and farther open, there's a sense of air reaching places it's not meant to. When the metal has brought me several degrees beyond comfortable, I hear a click and feel the vibrations of a nut being spun and tightened to lock it like a tire being changed.

The sensation of hardware acting upon flesh at my core is unnerving—but familiar. The horse-faced nurse was right; I've definitely had an internal before. Dr. Sackler brings the lamp closer, and I feel its radiating warmth as it lights me up brighter than a prison yard during a jailbreak. He peers around for a long minute, very quiet, then unlatches the speculum and withdraws it.

"Okay, all done," he says, popping back into view. Then he turns to Nurse O'Brien and says a little sourly, "Let Sherman know he can have his sign-off."

"What does that mean?" I ask.

"It means everything's looking just fine, Dorothy," he says, smiling. "You're in tip-top shape." Then he turns back to Nurse O'Brien, now lowering my legs. "Is there a directive on file for her?"

"Not that I know of," the nurse says.

"Let's find out. Definitely something that should be taken into consideration."

"A *directive*?" I ask.

"Just some housekeeping," he says, "one of several forms that needs updating to ensure you're getting the proper care. Nothing you need to worry about, Dorothy." He stands, then pulls off his thick brown rubber gloves and picks up the file. "We don't want your records to be incomplete, now, do we? You can go ahead and get dressed," he says, and exits.

CHAPTER 10

AVE YOU HEARD of something called a directive?" I ask Lillian as we watch Lester set up a card table nearby in the dayroom.

"Directive? Nope. What is it?"

"Don't know. Something the infirmary doctor mentioned."

Lillian shrugs. "What'd you do to Georgie?" she asks, watching her eyeballing us from the other side of the dayroom. "She sure looks . . . wound up."

I shrug. Georgie's distance today is just fine. I don't need any more of her well-meaning opinions distracting me from my plans. Tonight, I will once again get myself sent off to seclusion—and this time nothing will stop me from escaping Hanover.

"Find yourself a partner, ladies," Lester shouts, opening up a suitcase on the card table. Inside is a record player. Time for one of A-Ward's perks: ballroom dancing.

While the women of A-Ward pair off, Lillian with another schizophrenic, Georgie with a Nordic alcoholic named Maren, I try to slip out into the hall, but Lester spots me. "Frasier, get on back here and find yourself a special someone."

By the time I rejoin the group, Maren's dumped Georgie for a pigeon-toed manic, leaving just me and the disgruntled cheerleader without partners.

"Looks like you two ladies'll be coupling up today," Lester says, and puts a single on the turntable.

When the crackly music begins to pour from the speaker, Georgie reluctantly takes my hand, and we settle into a silent slow dance. But unfortunately the frosty quiet doesn't last. On our tenth trip around the room, Georgie says, "Sorry about last night. Sometimes I can be a bit . . . bossy. That thing I said about you being Dorothy . . ."

Nope. Don't want to revisit her logical but incorrect assumptions about what I confided in a moment of weakness. But apparently this is what we are doing.

It's not like I didn't warn you.

Georgie continues, "I shouldn't have tried to tell you what to do, Bix."

"You're calling me Bix now?"

She shrugs. "Beats calling you Not-Dorothy." I'm tempted to correct her: I'm neither Bix nor Dorothy. But I don't, hoping we can return to polite silence. "Is there something you'd like to say to me?" Georgie asks, angling for an apology. But that part of my brain feels creaky. Rusted over. Pretty sure saying "I'm sorry" is a rarity for me, whoever I am.

I shake my head no and direct my attention to the strange single we're now dancing to: Bing Crosby singing "Till the End of the World." It's an emotional goulash of a tune, the lyrics all about watching the death of our world during some sort of nuclear Armageddon picnic with your sweetheart—yet the piece is inexplicably upbeat, full of happy horns, tinkly piano, and Bing's honey-coated voice extolling the virtues of just sitting back and letting the end times roll.

But Georgie perseveres. "Since you told me a secret last night, it's only fair I share one too. You were right, Bix, my father didn't send me here for exhaustion."

"Oh?"

"I should've been more careful," she continues, "waited till we couldn't possibly be discovered. But I was too impatient . . . I guess Taylor was my crazy-maker."

"What do you mean 'crazy-maker'?" I ask.

"That person, thing, or idea you'll risk all for. Everyone at

Hanover's got one. Lillian's would be maintaining her privileges. Maren's an alkie, so hers is probably a bottle of ninety proof Norwegian aquavit. I'm guessing yours is freedom—"

"You were explaining why you're here," I say. "Who's Taylor?"

"Right. Taylor was my doubles partner for tennis. One day, my father found us making out on the pool house couch after practice."

"So?"

"I'm not talking about *mixed* doubles. Taylor is—"

"A girl. I get it. So you like girls. It's not like that's a crime. Or a mental condition," I say, laughing.

But Georgie's not amused. "That's exactly what lesbianism is. Classified as an illness of pathologically deviant sexual behavior. Perversion. Doctors, their books—the whole *normal* world—says so."

"That's ridiculous," I say. "Sex is just sex, Georgie, however you slice it. A way to get your yah-yahs out, have some fun, blow off steam. You're overthinking it."

"Overthinking it?" Georgie stares at me, quiet a moment, head making little nods like she's working out a new algebraic theorem in her head. "Now I understand. Your coarse language, you thinking there's nothing wrong with my past sexual behavior—Dr. Sherman calls that an antisocial belief system. Says that inability to tell good from bad is a symptom of disease."

Georgie's turning into a regular Freud. "You actually believe you're sick?" I ask.

"Of course! The illness has sent me off track, made me act in ways nature never intended. Unacceptable ways. I'm here to get back on track."

"Sounds more like you're here to avoid the truth about yourself. Going along to get along," I say louder than I mean to.

"If anyone's running from herself, it's you, *Bix*," Georgie hisses back.

I drop her hand, and the two of us stand motionless among the dancing women. Our dustup has gotten the attention of Wallace and another nurse, who are now watching us from the nurses' station. Georgie's desperate to end the scrutiny. "Come on," she says, gesturing for me to rejoin her.

I'm shaking my head when the *voice* intercedes.

Debating morality in this nuthouse accomplishes nothing.

You can get on your soapbox when you're out of Hanover. Till then, leave the mentals to their opinions and move on.

Though the *voice* is currently concussed enough to believe in missions and machines and nerds with lost tethers, when it comes to tactics and keeping my ass out of trouble, her hard-boiled advice remains solid. So I do what she says and retake Georgie's hand.

As we again begin weaving our way through the women, I try to keep things neutral. "So, you agreed to come here for treatment?"

She nods. "Daddy just wants what's best for me. And discretion. We both do." This is so many degrees of troubling and twisted. But I don't interrupt. "And no one'll be the wiser," Georgie continues. "My father's told everyone I'm on a grand tour of the Orient with a distant cousin. Even had me write out postcards. They're being posted from places like Kathmandu, Singapore, all over."

A plan to keep up appearances that's global in scale. Creepy but impressive. "So, how's the treatment going?" I ask.

"Good, I'm making progress," she says, nodding vigorously. "Eventually, it'll be easier to be normal, feel the way I'm supposed to feel. What matters is that come January, when I leave Hanover, it'll be manageable."

"You're trying to make who you fall in love with 'manageable'? I don't think it works quite the way you think it does—"

"Frasier!" Wallace calls from the nurses' station, once again halting our dance. "Come get your pass. You've got an appointment with Dr. Sherman."

Shit. When I get to the window, the nurse rips a filled-out pass from her pad and hands it to me. "Show this to the nurse at the gate."

I'm about to leave the dayroom when Georgie stops me. "Don't make things harder on yourself than they have to be, Bix. Show Dr. Sherman you can be cooperative. That you deserve to stay in A-Ward."

"And how do you suggest I do that?"

"Play ball. Make him feel *instrumental*. Dr. Sherman loves to feel instrumental," she says.

"I don't follow."

"Let him witness a breakthrough. Confess something, something personal. Doesn't have to be big or even true. Just some shameful tidbit he thinks he got you to dredge up. So he feels he's—"

"Won?"

She nods. "He's a man. They all crave a win. So give it to him."

* * *

A nurse at the gate checks my ID against my slip, then buzzes me through, and I walk down the hall to Sherman's office.

His assistant, Miss Campbell, doesn't hear me enter, absorbed with jotting a note down on her pink pad. I clear my throat, and she jumps a little. "You're early. Take a seat," she says, then uses a small key hidden in the top drawer of her desk to unlock the mammoth file cabinet behind her and retrieve a file.

Soon Sherman and a patient emerge from the inner office, and he glances over at me before taking the pink phone message slip Miss Campbell is offering him. "That sheriff's deputy, the one who helped with her," she says, nodding at me. "He's still asking to speak with you." Lone Ranger wants a word. Too little, too late. Sherman swaps files with Miss Campbell and waves for me to follow him.

As Sherman takes the seat next to me, I consider Georgie's advice, try to invent some embarrassing personal story I can tearfully confide that'll keep the doctor satisfied till I can escape this place. But I don't get a chance. "I'm interested in what happened last night in the seclusion cell," he says. "Your screams, what you thought was happening to you . . . and your rather *assertive* behavior with me afterward. Help me understand—"

"It was just a dream. I really don't remember any of it," I say.

"Oh, I see. A dream," he says. The way Sherman says "dream" tells me he agrees with Georgie—it was more than a dream. "Yes, dreams can be hard to recall. So why don't I tell you what you told me, and let's see if that sparks something." He reads from Dorothy's file: "You wanted someone named Ethan to tell you who 'the guest' is. You said that stopping this guest was the reason he and others sent you on a mission. Any of this sounding familiar?"

God, I really did babble. I shrug noncommittedly. Georgie would not be pleased.

He smiles. "Dear, you were transferred to Hanover so we can help you get better. But I'm going to need your assistance to do that. Starting with this," he says, patting a box on his desk. "Inside it are tests designed to pinpoint your memory deficits."

"I'll pass."

Sherman looks at me, fingertips together, in here-is-the-church-there-is-the-steeple formation. "May I be frank?" he asks.

"Not sure how I'd stop you."

"Dorothy, until you stop fighting the process, are willing to do what it takes to learn the truth about yourself," he says, "you won't find peace."

I want the words the doctor's just uttered to be like all his other words: pure quackery, misdirected, easily dismissed.

But they are not.

If I'm not Dorothy, not Bix, then who *am* I? What *is* the truth about myself? Without that answer, Sherman's right, I'll never feel whole.

But the one person who knows who I really am and why I was on that bus is the mystery man from my true north memory. The one with the crescent-shaped scar on his hand and the kisses. The one I felt such overflowing love for. But the only chance of finding him is to get back my purse from the real Dorothy. And she's definitely not going to be hiding out at home. I'll need some way of tracking her down.

Sherman continues, "You were sent here because I can help you find that peace. But first I need to know what we're dealing with." He opens Dorothy Frasier's file, and I spy the words "Washington, D.C." and "Incident Report" on a stack of pale yellow sheets.

"What are those?" I ask.

"Police reports. It seems you have a couple of places you're repeatedly drawn to during your episodes. Your 'haunts,' as it were. Been picked up from them many times."

Dorothy's haunts—places she'd go to repeatedly . . .

Places you could track her to. Get your bag back.

"I'd like to see those reports," I say, but Sherman closes the file. "They might help me remember."

"Now, let's not get ahead of ourselves. I'll decide when it's appropriate for you to read them."

Dr. Decider of what's appropriate for all others. This quack. I consider making my own decision and snatching the file out of his power-hungry little hands but stop myself. "How about we make a deal," I say. "I answer your test questions, and you let me see those reports?"

* * *

My brain's tapped out. It's been close to an hour of taking Dr. Sherman's tests, ID'ing all the photos I was able to from his box, answering as many tedious questions as I could.

My answers each occupy a spot in my memory, but they're unconnected to each other, this time or this place, just free-floating islands of facts amid a sea of blank. Will I ever get back my life?

"And no personal memories have returned to you?" he asks.

Sherman's question catches me off guard, and the image of my mystery man with the soft kisses briefly ricochets through my mind, making me hesitate. "N . . . No."

"Did you recall something?"

"It's nothing."

"What did you remember?"

I can hear Georgie telling me to toss my recollection to Sherman like some doggie treat. Make him a winner. Easiest thing in the world. But it's my one certain memory, my true north, and I don't feel like making it public. "It's personal."

"If you won't share your thoughts, how can we —"

"I took your tests, answered every question I could. Now it's time. Show me the police reports. That was our deal!"

"The *deal* here at Hanover is to always cooperate." He closes the memory box, picks up the file, and stands. "If you won't be forthcoming with me, I cannot be with you."

"You made a promise."

"I made a decision. But in light of your refusal to fully comply and how worked up you're getting, I've *reconsidered* my decision. You're clearly not ready to view these records."

Asshole.

CHAPTER II

Tonight we privileged A-Warders are enjoying an after-dinner treat in the dayroom—a movie projected onto a large white sheet they've hung on the wall. Several benches have been arranged in rows for us. Georgie and I occupy the one in the back.

Lillian's hunkered down underneath us and being very quiet—her Soviets and their electro-mines must be close tonight.

There's tension on the bench. I finally told Georgie about my appointment with Sherman. About my new need to learn the addresses of the real Dorothy Frasier's hangouts before I can escape so I have a chance at tracking her and my purse down once I'm free. And I told her about refusing to play ball with the doctor by sharing my memory and his reneging on our deal.

So she's been ruminating. Definitely has some things she'd like to get off her chest if asked—which I make sure not to do.

The man we're watching on-screen is an actor I know I've seen before. He's got a kindly face that bears a striking resemblance to the sheriff's deputy, Officer Worthy. Right now he's gazing across a crowded dance floor at a woman he knows. When she spots him, her face lights up, and a series of emotions plays over it, like she's seeing their entire future together compressed into seconds—and it's exactly the life she wants. He's the one.

I wonder about the mystery man kissing me in my true north memory, those intense feelings in that moment with him. Was he the one? I replay the scene in my mind—the warm summer sun, the boy's laughter, the crescent-moon scar on the man's palm, the way his kisses on my shoulder sent a thrum through my body. Every known bit of the memory, hoping to draw more details out of my subconscious.

But my thoughts are interrupted by Georgie, who can hold in her lecture no longer. "All you had to do was give Sherman *something*, anything," she vents, the darks and lights of the movie playing over her face. The couple on-screen is dancing now, and as they do, the floor beneath them begins to hilariously split apart, revealing a swimming pool below. I pray Georgie will be done soon. "How hard is that?" she asks.

"Pipe down, Georgie," someone sitting ahead of us says. "We're trying to watch."

Georgie says, "No, I will not pipe—"

"You need to stop worrying," I tell her.

"And you need to *start* worrying, Bix," Georgie hisses back. "He's about to decide your ward placement—determining just how hard it'll be to escape from Hanover—and you can't cooperate just the slightest?"

A pitiful cry comes from Lillian below.

"Now you've upset the chronic," Georgie says.

"Lillian's a chronic?" I ask Georgie.

She nods. "Been here at least ten years. Relatives aren't exactly clamoring to take her," she whispers. "At this point Hanover's all she knows. The routines, the rules, what she has to do—who she has to please—to stay in A-Ward and keep her privileges."

"I didn't realize," I say. "Probably not what Lillian expected when she entered this place."

"No one *expects* it," Georgie says. "But a run-in with staff here, a bad diagnosis there, and you can find yourself down-alphabet, receiving 'state-of-the-art' treatments that leave you looking less and less like someone doctors would consider releasing. And it's not long till you agree with them. Before you know it, you're fully institutionalized, a permanent part of Hanover. Lillian's fortunate—she at least managed to luck into A-Ward."

"You're not being very subtle," I say.

"Not trying to be. You, with your need to fight authority, are exactly the kind of person who could run into deep trouble during a year at Hanover. You need to go—and soon."

"First you think I should stay, now you want me to go. Which is it, Georgie?" I say, laughing. But she just glares. "Relax, I'll have those addresses and be long gone before he assigns me to a ward."

Georgie levels her eyes at me. "You've already got a scheme in mind, don't you?"

On-screen, the couple falls into the pool, joined by the rest of the dancing crowd. Hysterical. Why can't she just let me watch?

"Spill it," says Georgie.

∗ ∗ ∗

Georgie was not a fan of the plan.

"Don't do it, Bix," she pleaded that night. "If you're caught, it's hello, D- or E- . . . maybe even F-Ward, locked down each night in a room full of Normas and Carols. I want no part of this foolishness."

When I pass her in the hallway, clutching the forged patient pass I managed to steal from the nurses' station a couple of days ago, Georgie looks the other way.

I arrive at the ward gate and find I'm in luck: the nurse on duty is preoccupied with taping up a poster that reads, "St. Aloysius Boys' Choir Christmas concert, Dec. 7 at 4:00 for patients from A to F Wards and guests. Women's main dining hall. Refreshments will be served." The nurse barely gives my pass a glance before buzzing me through.

The vicious *thwacks* of Miss Campbell's typewriter can be heard long before I reach Sherman's office. I pause short of the open door and make sure no one's watching before quietly depressing the door latch and securing it with some stolen tape. Then I duck around the corner and wait. It's not long before Miss Campbell emerges from the office for lunch. She shuts the door before heading down the hall to the staff dining room.

I slip into the office and ease the door closed behind me. It's quiet, just the clock on the wall behind the desk slowly ticking away as the second hand sweeps around. Next to it is the wall calendar with the boy in the big Pilgrim hat. Days one through eighteen are now checked off. November eighteenth—I've been in Hanover six days. Seems like more. The ringing in my ears I felt that first day is now nearly gone.

I fish the key to the enormous file cabinet from its hiding place in Miss Campbell's desk, unlock the E TO J drawer, then thumb through the F files till I find Dorothy Frasier's. I flip it open on top of the drawer.

Claim checks for my wool coat and the pennies taken from my shoes, are paper-clipped to the inside. The file's top sheet is pink and marked "Medical"—a copy of my infirmary visit write-up, beginning with the tetanus shot, followed by a cataloguing of my various scars, my barely uneven pupils, and ending with my punctured eardrums. After that, Dr. Sackler, the infirmary doctor, has jotted "Patient, a healthy 23 yr old female, is cleared for all treatments."

Below it are notes on my gynecological exam: "Cervical os presents as normal," blah, blah, blah . . .

I flip past it to the stack of yellow Dorothy Frasier's police reports. At the top of the pile are a bunch paper-clipped together, each with the heading "Culpeper County Sheriff Department Incident Report" and stamped with the word "Duplicate."

I scan the first: "Incident Report #93767 . . . Dorothy Frasier, female, Caucasian, 23 . . . Found trespassing and exhibiting loud and disturbing behavior on the grounds of a house of worship . . . Date and time of offense 4-19-54, 23:20 hours . . . After resisting officers, the individual was brought to Culpeper County Hospital for observation and evaluation. No charges of trespassing or disorderly conduct filed." At the bottom, I spot the word "Location" and an address: "St. Mark's Church, 169 West Eggers Avenue, Doyletown, VA."

The next few describe more trespassing incidents on the church grounds with no charges filed. But the last is different: "Received report of a break-in at the chapel. A broken door window was observed . . . Individual was found at the foot of the altar, bleeding heavily from a self-inflicted wound. She was transported to Culpeper County Hospital's emergency room and, after successful treatment, was moved to the psychiatric ward. Committed, per judge's bench order, to Hanover State Psychiatric Hospital for a minimum stay of twelve months. Criminal trespass and criminal damage to place of worship charges not filed."

The five reports all share the St. Mark's Church address—the first of Dorothy's haunts. I take a moment to commit it to memory.

I'm flipping to the next paper-clipped set of police reports, from the Metropolitan Police Department of Washington, D.C., for the address of Dorothy's other haunt, when some papers fall out of the file onto the floor. Two sheets paper-clipped together. I pick them up, about to shove them back in the file, when I notice the subject line on the top sheet: "Dorothy Frasier Directive."

It's a memorandum from Dr. Sackler to Sherman, dated November 15, 1954:

> Per your request, I have examined Dorothy Frasier thoroughly, and in light of both my clinical observations and her medical and psychological history, it is my opinion that the patient possesses a questionable capacity to responsibly govern her reproductive processes and sexuality. Therefore, should a decision be made to treat her with any procedure or regimen likely to further undermine that capacity, it is in the best interests of the patient that proper precautionary measures should be taken.
>
> Attached is the form signed by me so that you may obtain consent from the appropriate authority. But I caution against rushing into

initiating any treatment with such lasting consequences. Please keep me apprised of all developments.

I flip to the attached page. At the top are three words: "Directive for Sterilization."

What Dr. Sackler meant by "housekeeping."

I can't stop rereading these words that so clinically discuss the elimination of my ability to procreate. Till the *voice* intervenes —

Yes, that's bad, but get what you came for. The two addresses.

Right. The addresses. And I turn back to the file, about to flip to the Washington, D.C., police department reports — when I feel them return. The ghost bees. That buzzing I felt in the seclusion cell. It's quickly climbing its way up through me, and Miss Campbell's desk light is now crowned with a rainbow. The white roar is coming.

Shit, shit, shit!

Calm yourself. This is good.

No, this is bad. Very, very bad.

But it doesn't have to happen — because none of this is real. I just need to root myself in the here and now, let the painful vibration pass like a bad cramp while I hold fast to the details around me:

Dorothy Frasier's file.

The boy in the Pilgrim hat on the calendar.

The second hand of the clock just sweeping past the twelve.

But it doesn't matter what I do, what I cling to, the white roar comes to collect me anyway.

CHAPTER 12

WHEN THE WHITE roar withdraws, and I open my eyes, it's clear there is something not quite right with me. No concussion-fueled dream to blame this time, no excuse for what I see—

The lab. I'm back in that fucking lab.

With its looming shadows, those flickering blue lights, that snake-like web of cables crisscrossing the floor. And mere feet away, those figures: Kyung and Ethan.

Yet I'm wide-awake. This is not a dream.

It was never a dream. Or some doctor's test. This is real.

No. It's merely my brain telling me it's real.

So what *is* this exactly?

Both Ethan and Kyung look haggard. If figments of one's imagination can look haggard. And I guess they can. I suppose all of this—the lab, nerds, their glitchy machine—can look any old way my mind decides they should.

Ethan starts toward me, but I don't want *whatever* he is to come any closer. I start to back away, and he stops his advance.

But Kyung is undeterred. Takes out her little pack of gum–size device and aims it at my wrist till there's a *BEEP*. She peers down at the thing and smiles. "Looks like those latest adjustments Gideon made to the machine did the trick—Bix's fragging on this jump was minimal," she says to Ethan. "It's possible she could still help, go back—"

"No. Not up for discussion. We'll find another way to deal with the Guest," Ethan says.

The Guest. Those two words are again arousing such dread and curiosity in me. I need answers. Even if they're imaginary ones. "Who *is* the Guest?" I ask.

"The Guest isn't a who. It's a what," Ethan says. "A deadly virus here in 2035."

"2035?" I ask.

Ethan points to the stacks of black boxes with their glowing blue lights that surround us. "I know it doesn't look like it, but this is a time machine."

A time machine.

In the year 2035.

I can feel sweat beginning to prickle up under my plaid dress.

"We used it to send you back to 1954 Virginia," Kyung says. "So you could track down the doctor—a researcher there who we believe possessed a sample of an earlier strain of the Guest, when it was still just a benign rat virus. Before it mutated . . ."

I can see the brass pommel of her hunting knife peeking out from the sheath on her belt. Smell the odor of overheated electronics in the stale air. It all seems so goddamn real . . .

"If we had that rat virus, it's possible we could develop a cure for the Guest," Kyung says. "Your mission was to reach the doctor in time and get them to tell you where they hid the sample."

Sent from the future in a jerry-rigged time machine to get a doctor to part with their rat virus . . . It's breathtaking, all the bizarre details my mind has conjured up. "Outlandishly complex"—those were the words Sherman used to describe Lillian's visions.

Is this some kind of delusional episode? Fuck. "It's Hanover that's doing this to me," I say. "Being in this place is starting to mess with my head."

There is nothing wrong with you.

"No, no, there is *something* definitely very wrong with me!" I yell at the *voice*—

And realize the two figments are watching me argue with myself.

"Listen to her, Kyung," Ethan says, gesturing to me. "Is *that* also going to go away with time? You and that machine did this to her."

"But it's fixed now," Kyung says. "There's a chance if she went back to '54—"

"No. Bix has sacrificed enough for this mission. I'm ending this now," Ethan says, and turns to me. "We'll bring you somewhere safe, where you can get better."

A "safe" place where I can get better—sounds like my figment wants me in Hanover as well.

"You're letting your personal feelings cloud your decision, Ethan," Kyung says.

"Let's start with your link, Bix," Ethan says, ignoring her. "Why don't you hand it to me so we don't have to worry about it getting triggered again by accident."

"My *link*?" I ask.

"What you used to get back here to 2035," he explains. "It's a device keyed to your DNA's unique energy signature via your disc. Works on a delay: the jump happens fifteen seconds after it's triggered. But once you feel the vibrations, you're past the fail-safe and you're going to travel. With your tether cut, it's the only way you were able to return. The link was in your purse along with the solar recharger. Where is it now?"

I need to get out of here . . . or just get rid of *here*. End this.

But I have no idea how. Lillian said her visions would trap her inside them with no way to escape back to the real world.

A cage. And this time I'm the prisoner. Can feel my heart starting to race—

"Is the link in one of those, Bix?" Ethan asks, pointing to the large patch pockets on the front of my dress.

Would the figment like to frisk me? The absurdity of this thought, of this *everything*, finally just sends me, and all I can do is smile and shake my head. "Dorothy's the one in control now, I guess."

"Dorothy?" he asks.

"Ethan," Kyung calls to him. She's quietly gotten close, is eyeing my ID band. "Dorothy Frasier's the name on her patient identification." Kyung fixes her sharp brown eyes on mine, observing me like Sherman. "You know you're not her, right?"

"Why would Bix think she's some woman from 1954?" Ethan asks.

"If *you* woke there with this kind of neural damage, no memory of your life, where you came from, would *your* first assumption be that you were a time traveler from the future?" Kyung asks him.

But I don't hear his answer 'cause the buzzing's back. I squeeze my head as the painful vibration builds, shut my eyes, let it all wash over me.

Kyung shouting "Shit!" is the last thing I hear before the white roar drags me away—

✳ ✳ ✳

—back to the bundle of Dorothy Frasier's police reports in front of me.

To the boy in the Pilgrim hat on the calendar.

To the clock on the wall slowly ticking, its second hand still sweeping past the twelve.

No time has elapsed while I was "away." None. Like those moments in the far, fucked future never happened. And obviously they didn't. Obviously I'm . . . I'm what?

You're not a mental. Ethan and Kyung exist, and you heard them: Your mission is to find a certain doctor in 1954 before it's too late. Get the location of the virus sample!

You can't just ignore—

"Shut the hell up!" I hiss at her.

Then hear a noise behind me.

I turn to find Dr. Sherman in the doorway. Behind him are Miss Campbell and a guilty-looking Lillian. "I'm so sorry, Bix," she says. "I—"

"You can go back to the ward now, dear. You did the right thing," Sherman says, giving Lillian a smile-nod. She retreats just as an attendant appears, restraint in hand.

"Seclusion?" he asks Sherman.

I've at least got one of the addresses. And a hairpin in my dress hem. Seclusion, with its shitty locks, is exactly what I need. Whatever it is that's going on in my head will stop once I'm out of Hanover.

But Sherman says, "No, that won't be necessary," to the attendant, then whispers something to Miss Campbell.

∗   ∗   ∗

A couple hours later I'm summoned back to Sherman's office to "discuss" ward assignment. When I enter, the doctor is leaning against his desk, arms crossed, an expression of studied neutrality on his face. He's a regular Switzerland this afternoon.

I just want this day over with. Exhausted by that unsettling experience during the file break-in earlier. What the hell was that, anyway?

Focus on what you know: You saw the real Dorothy Frasier on that bus. That you're not the woman these people want to treat and sterilize.

Don't forget that part—the part where they clip your tubes.

Get the ward assignment. Get out. Plenty of time to debate what "really" happened earlier once you're out of Hanover's reach.

The *voice*—still mental enough to believe the future is real. But she's right about this: all that matters is getting free of this place. And once I learn what down-alphabet ward Sherman's banishing me to, I can adjust my escape plans.

Yes, adaptation. That's what'll keep you alive.

That Christmas Concert poster the nurse was hanging said it was for patients from A to F Wards. If you start a fight during it, as long as you're in one of those wards—

They'll bring me to A-Ward's seclusion and their crappy locks. Come sundown, I'd slip out of my restraint, use the stolen hairpin and my barrette to pick the locks, and run like hell.

But only if he assigns you to one of those wards. So keep it together, no matter what.

"Lillian's worried about you, dear," Sherman says to me. "It's why she told me about the plan she heard you discussing, to steal your file, somehow escape. Plans can often be good. They give us goals. Keep us busy. Productive. But you know the problem with plans?"

No doubt you're going to tell me.

"They can blind us to better plans. Better goals." Now he's looking at me expectantly. "What do you think about what I've just said, Dorothy?"

That fucking name. "I *think* you need to stop calling me Dorothy."

A hint of smug now creeps onto the doctor's face. "I'd hoped this meeting could wait, that given more time, you'd come to remember on your own, but your recent actions have convinced me it can no longer be put off." He presses the intercom button. "Send him in," he says into it, then turns to me. "You have a visitor who I believe will help clarify a great many things for you."

A visitor?

The door opens, and a man in a gray suit enters. He's good-looking, about my age, clean-cut, and lean. I can see a strong suggestion of deltoids under his suit jacket. He approaches with a tentative smile, an old shoe box tucked under his arm.

"Dorothy," he says softly, his hazel eyes locked on mine, like he's searching them for signs. Answers.

I turn to Sherman for an explanation, and he cheerfully provides, "This is Paul, dear. Your husband."

CHAPTER 13

T HE INSCRIPTION ON the wedding band this man, this *Paul*, has just put in my palm reads TO D, MY LOVE FOREVER, P.

"Here, Dee, let me help you with that," he says from the chair next to me, and reaches for the ring, but I close my hand tight around it. I'm considering using this ready fist I've formed to punch his lights out, but the *voice* counsels calm.

Keep your cool. See what this man is up to. What kind of enemy he is.

She's right. "Paul" holds all the sanity cards, and I hold none. I calmly place the ring on the desk, say to Sherman, now sitting behind it, "This man is not my husband."

"But—" the man starts.

"Mr. Frasier, remember what I said," Sherman warns.

So, they've chatted about me, my so-called doctor and my so-called husband.

"Right. Take it slow. Sorry, Doc." Paul turns to me. "I brought some things I thought might help jog your memory."

"About a husband who doesn't exist? Go ahead, give it your best shot."

Easy.

But then he pulls a square black-and-white photo from the shoe box—

And there we are, Paul and I, in swimsuits on the sand, hugging each other, big goddamn smiles on our faces. How is this possible?

"Virginia Beach, summer of '51," he says, then hands me another. In this one I'm dressed in a frilly apron, standing in an old-fashioned kitchen, proudly holding a platter on which sits a dome-shaped, gelatinous mound. And behind me, hands on my waist, is Paul. "That's your confetti lime Jell-O mold. Your nana's favorite. You used to make it every Christmas—"

"No way these are real," I say. "They've been faked using . . . the . . . the thing . . ." And I try to remember what snapshot-faking machine my faulty brain is so sure exists. But if it does exist, it's beyond the horizon of my recall. The men exchange woeful glances, fueling my rising anger. But the *voice* again urges caution.

Do nothing, say nothing that'll convince Sherman to assign you to a ward with high security.

So I wait silently for Paul to pluck the next rabbit from his hat.

"Did you know Dee's an ace bowler, Doc?" he asks.

"I do recall some mention of it in her file," Sherman says, and Paul pulls from the shoe box a bronze trophy of a woman in a skirt throwing a bowling ball. Holds it up for the doctor.

"First place in regionals," Sherman says, smiling. "It seems you have some real hidden gifts, Dorothy."

When Paul hands me the trophy, his eyes linger a moment on my wrist scar—and I feel something stirring inside me just beneath my skin, springing back to life.

Shame.

It's got deep roots, this shame, invasive and strong as kudzu. Nothing I want to unpack right now. I pull my sleeve down over the scar and examine the trophy. Inscribed on its plaque: "First Place, Mrs. Paul Frasier. Northern Virginia, Ladies Under 25's All-League, 1952."

"Someone's gone to a lot of trouble creating these artifacts," I say to Paul. "Why do it, why invent our life together?" I search his eyes for clues but find none. "What could you possibly be after?"

Careful. It's an act, but Sherman's buying it. Don't get drawn in.

"I just want you back, Dee," Paul says.

"Mr. Frasier, as you know, we've been assessing your wife's memory as well as her mental status the past few days. A bit of a challenge, given her limited compliance. But the results we were able to obtain through testing and conversation tell us a few things—and I believe it's important Dorothy also hear them."

Paul nods. "Whatever you think is best."

Now that he's gotten my fake husband's permission, Sherman continues. "Her procedural memory—how to perform a given task like darning a sock, chopping onions, driving a car—for the most part appears intact."

"That's good news, right?" Paul asks.

"Indeed. But her semantic memory—the recall of people, places, and things in our world—that's quite spotty. Some things she remembers, others . . ."

"I see."

Silently listening to the two men toting up my mental scorecard is—well, you can imagine.

"In spite of her coarse language," Sherman says, "it's clear Dorothy's highly intelligent. An IQ of at least a hundred and forty."

Paul smiles at me. "I always say she's the smart one."

"Do you, 'Paul'?"

Sherman ignores me. "Her vocabulary, both real and imagined, is quite extensive."

"Imagined?" I ask.

"Yes, what do you mean, Doctor?" Paul echoes.

"I'm referring to her neologisms," Dr. Sherman says, "words and phrases patients like Dorothy will make up or use in an odd new way—nonsensical to everyone else but all quite real to her. What makes your wife's case unique is the sheer number she's invented for things she believes exist. Such as 'quarter hour,' 'the guest,' 'grabble and snag,' to name just a few."

What is he talking about? Those are real phrases! I can feel my fury again starting to build, my need to defend myself to these men like an itch I can't scratch.

"Some of her terms are more worrisome," Sherman says. "'Leaning in' on someone, for instance, means a violent action specifically taken by a woman toward a man."

He and Paul exchange more looks of concern. More eyebrows pitched with worry.

"And still no personal memories?" Paul asks.

"There is one she's recalled," Sherman says.

"Oh? Can you tell me what it is, Dee?"

Let me get right on that.

"Unfortunately, she refuses to discuss it at present," Sherman says.

Paul's sad eyes roam over me. "I see."

"The good news is her medical exam confirmed there was no injury to the head. Just the perforated eardrums, which, as I've told you, were self-inflicted."

"That's a lie! That doctor never even ran tests—"

But Sherman cuts me off. "Dorothy, if you cannot remain calm, you'll need to return to the ward." No, no, no, that can't happen! I need to know where all of this is headed. So I redouble my efforts to stay seated and silent. Sherman turns back to Paul. "Because there's no physical injury, we believe her amnesia is dissociative in nature."

"Dis . . . ?" Paul asks.

"Dissociative. The result of her subconscious's efforts to block painful memories, deny truths some part of her doesn't want to face during treatment at Hanover. Which is perhaps why the amnesia emerged upon Dorothy's transfer here." What BS. "I know it's an upsetting development, but one I believe will ultimately resolve if we successfully treat the underlying condition. Her schizophrenia."

"The visions," Paul says.

Sherman nods, lights his pipe. "Yes. Can you tell me about them?"

Paul looks uncomfortable. It's got to feel awkward making up your pretend wife's delusions right in front of her. But he manages.

"Usually she believes she's someone named Bix on a mission."

He's definitely been clued in by Sherman.

"And how does this belief manifest?" Sherman asks.

"You mean what does she do?"

"Yes."

Paul swallows. "Well, there are times when Dee imagines she's arming herself against her enemies, gathering allies—I took to locking up the phone, things she could hurt herself with. Then there's often some sort of skirmish in her mind. Eventually she comes out of it. Sometimes near home . . . other times farther away."

"And does she remember her actions?"

"Not always," Paul says. "On those days she often accuses me of making it all up, that I'm somehow out to get her."

"Can't imagine where I'd get that idea," I say.

"That's the paranoia," Sherman says, "part of the disease. You shouldn't take it personally. Tell me, has she ever mentioned someone named Ethan?"

Ethan. Paul's eyes narrow just the slightest. He nods. "She started talking about an Ethan in her world soon after we hired a handyman by that name. Dee was . . . a bit sweet on the guy. Came to seek his attentions. She gets *attached* easily," he says, and the doctor gives him an understanding nod. "The man took advantage of her. After that I was careful about who was allowed near Dee."

Now I'm his slutty nutball wife. Every part of me longs to rise and do battle.

Don't worry, we'll make sure "Paul" gets exactly what's coming to him.

I ignore the *voice's* bloodthirsty promise. Bite my lip and stay in the chair.

"Actually," Sherman says, "it's quite common for patients to incorporate things, even people like this Ethan, from their real lives into their psychopathy." Doc is full of the ten-dollar words today. "Tell me, does she ever get violent during these episodes?"

Paul looks at me, hesitates.

"It's all right, Mr. Frasier," Sherman says. "You're not telling any tales out of school. I've personally witnessed her martial skills."

Paul nods. "Well, yes, sometimes she can get a little physical. When she believes Bix is a leader of some military group called the Kids'—wait, that's not it—the Child's Army, that's what she calls it. A soldier sent from the future back to 1954 in a time machine on a mission to help mankind . . ."

I never told Sherman about the Child's Army or the time travel! How the hell does this "Paul" know about them? I try to keep my face neutral, my jaw from dropping, struggling furiously not to get sucked into the vortex of mindfuck now swirling inside my head—

Till I remember just how out of it I was in seclusion, babbling to Sherman about my "dream" or whatever the hell it was. I must've mentioned time travel and the Child's Army.

"A time machine?" the doctor asks, jotting furiously.

"Yes, sometimes Dee will stand very still for a few moments," Paul continues. "Afterward, she believes she traveled to the future for minutes, sometimes even hours before coming back to 1954."

Minutes . . . like those minutes in the lab?

No. I shove the thought deep into a tansu drawer, pivot back to the men's conversation.

Sherman puts down his pen. "So, not just a foot soldier, Dorothy's in a position of command in this group. A leader, magically sent here to save the world," he says, tapping his pipe against the desk. "It's a fairly common delusional pattern for a man. A bit aberrant for a woman."

"It is?" Paul asks.

"Yes. Possibly speaks to a subconscious need Dorothy has to atone for something she's done—or left undone—that her mind is blocking the memories of. The proverbial ghost in the machine, influencing her actions and reactions. Dorothy feels tremendous guilt over something in her past, that much is clear. And there's a relief for her in not remembering it. Any idea what it could be, Mr. Frasier?"

Paul slowly shakes his head. Frankly, I'm surprised he didn't concoct some atonable deed I've done.

Sherman puts his pipe down, sits back in his chair. While he's gathering his quack thoughts, I contemplate the letter opener, partially hidden by papers on the desk.

But Sherman's big think is short. Soon he's sitting forward, elbows on desk, hands steepled. He wants to be frank.

"Mr. Frasier, can I be frank?"

"Please," Paul says.

"I believe your wife, as a result of her disease, is experiencing some powerful urges welling up from her subconscious. Violent, crude, sometimes sexual impulses fed by a disease that's left her profoundly disconnected from our real world and its norms and beliefs.

"And since these impulses cannot be acted upon in our civilized society," he continues, "what her mind has done is create a future, lawless and desperate, that allows her, as this Bix persona, to satisfy her need to lie, to fight, to lust—all in the pursuit of some fantastical mission to save the world. But as you can see, Dorothy," he says, gesturing out the window at the blue November sky, "the world is just fine. It doesn't need saving."

I wonder, if I acquired the letter opener and leaned in hard on Sherman, plunged it deep enough into his chest, would that satisfy my urges and prove his hypothesis?

Tempting. But stick to the plan.

"Dear," Sherman continues, "each time you pick up a weapon, real or imagined, each time you practice deception, or act on your baser carnal urges, you are, in essence, feeding your disease, pulling you even further away from the real world." He turns to Paul. "Have you given any more thought to what we discussed?"

"What you discussed?" I can feel rage creeping upward, about to boil over.

Don't do it—

"Who gave you two assholes the rum to decide anything at all about me!" I yell.

But Sherman just looks baffled, like I've spoken Swahili.

"'Rum' is one of her words," Paul tells him. "I believe it means 'power' or 'authority.'"

I turn to him. "Who the hell *are* you?"

"Capgras syndrome," Sherman says, jotting a note in Dorothy's file. "Where a patient believes that a loved one has been replaced by an imposter." Sherman reaches for the intercom. "I think it best if an attendant takes your wife back—"

"Please, Doc, let her stay," Paul says.

"Don't pretend you're on my side," I yell at him. "You are *not* on my side!"

"But I am, Dee," Paul says. "I love you. Please, try to remember—"

I lunge for Paul. He's surprisingly fast, out of his chair like a shot, but then he simply stands there as I pummel him, skillfully blocking blows but refusing to go on the offensive. His arms begin to encircle me, and as I feel the embrace tighten, a truly unnerving thought emerges—I am turned on by this struggle. When my forearms are pinned flat to his chest, Paul releases his grip, but we both stay there, eyeing each other.

He reaches for a loose hank of hair in my face, and I do nothing as he tucks it behind my ear. Then his hand drifts down to my earlobe and he tugs it gently.

It's a gesture that's alarmingly familiar.

Suddenly, my true north memory comes rushing back to me. Only this time it's fleshed out, like an artist has taken a brush and painted in the details of a sketch. Now I see:

> I'm standing near the edge of a quarry. It's warm. Summer. The sun's low, the shadows of nearby trees long and thready. Can hear a pair of mourning doves calling to each other through the sultry air.

And somewhere close by a boy is laughing.

My mystery man is behind me, his exquisite kisses advancing up my shoulder. I take his left hand, kiss the crescent-moon scar in the center of his palm.

And I am brimming with love.

When his lips reach the nape of my neck, a need, low in me, quickens. It feels tortuous, base, sweet, this desire, like the man is the key to one of my most twisted locks.

When he gently tugs my earlobe, I turn—and finally see his face. He's bearded, his hair longer, but there's no mistaking who it is.

Paul.

I blink away the memory. Pull away from him.

But the need to be sure forces me back and I grab his left hand, turn it over, hoping madly, stupidly, not to find what I do: that crescent-shaped scar.

A "no" comes out of me, but it's more exhale than rebuttal, because I know now with absolute certainty my mystery man is Paul. Was always Paul. I just couldn't—or wouldn't—see it. I've shared a life with this man. Loved him.

Which makes me Dorothy Frasier: housewife, bowler, schizophrenic, slut.

All that I was so sure about myself—that my visions were simply the temporary effects of concussions or of Hanover itself, that I couldn't possibly be an actual patient here. That I saw the "real" Dorothy Frasier escape on the transfer bus—none of it was true. My gut instinct has been worse than wrong; it's been lying to me this whole time.

And I come to one, inescapable conclusion: I cannot trust myself.

Bullshit! This is all a lie, even the memory's a lie. Has to be. Paul's the enemy—you're gonna need to kill him and soon . . .

As the *voice* issues her desperate denials and threats, I feel myself begin to come unstrung. Can almost hear each cord inside me as it snaps. Finally I say to Paul, "I don't care what the *voice* says, now I know it was you in my memory."

"'The voice'? Who's the voice?" he asks.

But Paul won't be getting an answer for a while. Ever, maybe. I just buried all my faith in myself. I need time to sit shiva, mourn my loss. When that's done, I'll decide when and with whom I talk about the *voice*. It's the one thing I can control now, and I won't give it up without a fight.

Tears are spilling over the banks of my lower lids, betraying me once again. Paul's watching them, spellbound and still, like he's come upon something incredibly rare and wondrous in the wild: a white tiger or a mother panda and her cub. When he reaches to wipe a tear from my cheek, I recoil, all twitchy and unbalanced by the adrenaline surging through me.

As I stand there shaking, Sherman approaches. Had forgotten he was even in the room. There's a glow about the doctor now—like he's picked up the scent of fresh breakthrough, gotten a whiff of all the shame and confession in the air.

"Do you know who you are now, dear?"

"I'm Dorothy Frasier. Now back the fuck off."

CHAPTER 14

THEY'VE BROUGHT ME a cup of tea and wrapped me in a blanket. My tears were legion, leaving whole swaths of darkness on the plaid of my dress.

Paul pulled Sherman away from me before things got ugly. Got him into the waiting room. They're out there now. The door's ajar and bits of their hushed conversation are finding their way through the crack. ". . . was sent here for a standard course of treatment . . ." I hear the doctor say.

He's right. I should be in treatment. Down-alphabet, maybe D- or E-Ward. I need to stop running away from myself, accept that I'm Dorothy and deal with my disease head-on. Adapt. That's what keeps you alive, right?

This isn't adaptation. It's capitulation.

You can't just pretend the future away by accepting Paul's lies.

The *voice* is going to be a problem. My fairy godmother's on the side of my disease. Of Bix. Hell, she *is* Bix, not a source of cold-blooded wisdom, merely a symptom. It's time to contain the schizophrenia, the paranoia. Make the *voice* and all the rest of it manageable—so I can leave Hanover, not end up a chronic like Lillian, doomed to a life inside these walls.

Make me manageable? Like Georgie and her fondness for women? Good luck with that.

Shut the hell up, I silently tell the *voice.* I take a sip of tea and try very hard to stuff her into my deepest, darkest tansu drawer.

That's just not going to happen, sweetheart. Ever. I won't be silenced like some errant thought because I am not one thought but all thoughts.

I am Bix and you are me, indivisible.

Her words, what they mean for me, my future—it's just too big to deal with right now, so I turn back to Sherman and Paul's conversation. "I can appreciate your concerns," Sherman says, "but in light of the recent escalation of her symptoms—the aggression, the paranoiac behavior, the delusional episodes—if we're to avoid serious measures down the road, something more global is called for."

Global?

I put the tea down and go to the door but run into Miss Campbell entering. She pulls it shut behind her. Waits till I sit back down before going to Sherman's desk to retrieve something. "More tea, Dorothy?" she asks.

"I need to talk to . . . to my husband." My husband. Jesus. It'll take time to get used to those words.

"Let's give the doctor and your handsome husband a chance to finish up their conversation," the secretary says as she searches through a drawer. "Then I'm sure you can speak with him."

That's not going to work for me. When Miss Campbell bends down to search the desk's bottom drawer, I quietly go to the door, ease it open, and slip down the short hallway.

Sherman and Paul are at the other end of the waiting room, by Miss Campbell's desk. Their backs are to me, Paul studying some sheet of paper.

"The elimination of outside distractions," Sherman says, lighting his pipe, "is absolutely critical to my protocol's success, to your wife's recovery."

Paul says, "I don't know about this—"

"The protocol was developed precisely for patients like Dorothy. It can address the structures of paranoid and disordered thought the disease has produced in your wife that have left her untethered to the real world. Enable me to reestablish normal, healthy behavior. Ultimately, your wife will return to you the easygoing, trusting, and happy woman she was meant to be. One who can live, even thrive outside of Hanover—"

"Dee's not going to want it," Paul says.

"Right now, she's in no position to judge what's best for her. But she'll come around in time, trust that we made the right decision for her—partly due to the effects of the protocol itself. You saw the remarkable and rapid changes it's capable of in those Unit patients you met."

The Unit?

"You want to put me in the Unit?" I ask, and the men turn around. Miss Campbell appears beside me, but Sherman nods for her to leave us and she exits.

"Dee," Paul starts, "let me explain—"

"I saw them in the dining hall, his Unit patients. Some could barely feed themselves."

"My protocol is just one of several treatment modalities being developed there," Sherman says, patting the air, trying to calm. "I'm sure the women you saw—"

"Don't you mean test subjects?" I say.

Sherman takes a long draw on his pipe. "I think we can agree, given these last few minutes, that you haven't been seeing things quite as they are for some time now—the future, with its time machines and missions, the 'real' Dorothy on the transport bus, even your husband, Paul. Your perception of those Unit patients is no different. It's likely been warped by your illness."

I hate that he has a point. How can I say the future was fiction but what I saw in that dining hall was fact? How can I know anything that feels real to me *is* real?

You know what you saw. Don't doubt it.

But I recently saw Kyung and Ethan—and they seemed as real as Lillian's electro-minefields, so I do doubt.

Paul leaves Sherman and comes over to me, still holding the sheet. I see the word "Commitment" on it. "Give me one good reason you'd sign that thing," I say.

"You getting out of here, Dee," he says. "Being home. Safe. I'm worried what a long stay in Hanover could do to you." Now the guy's sounding like Georgie. He points to a paragraph. "See this here? Dr. Sherman guarantees that after you're treated in the Unit with his protocol, he'll have your sentence commuted. Instead of a year or more locked up here, you'll be home in weeks."

"Weeks?" That is not nothing. Still . . .

"More importantly, the protocol might actually help you. Dr. Sherman allowed me to see some of his patients nearing the end of treatment with my own eyes. The women were completely lucid, happy—and going home. Whatever combination of therapies the doctor is using has worked for them. Maybe it could—"

"I don't want that asshole's protocol," I say.

Paul's head dips a moment, and when he looks up, his eyes have a tearful sheen to them. "Like you didn't want treatment last Christmas after you stole the Dells' hatchet?" he whispers. "Or in June after you broke into that butcher shop? Or . . . or . . . You never want treatment. And every time I say, 'Okay, Dee.' 'Cause I want to shield you, keep you safe at home. Everything I do, that I've ever done, has been to keep you safe."

Again the shame is stirring in me. For all the forgotten hell I've put this guy through—even if I can't remember the particulars.

Maybe I deserve the Unit.

There's not one goddamned thing wrong with you that needs fixing.

You can't believe a word he says. Paul's a liar—

Only now we know who the real liar is: the *voice*, who cares only that I complete the precious, fictional mission—and will tell me anything to keep me on task.

Sherman steps closer. "The protocol truly is the best thing for you, dear. The Unit provides a unique environment, away from the hubbub of a regular ward, where the right steps can be taken to begin silencing the voices, the delusions—"

"'Right steps.' What does that mean?" I ask.

"You're suffering from a serious illness, growing more intractable with each passing day," Sherman says, eyes leveled at mine. "We are long past the point where fresh air and warm baths will tame your symptoms, arrest the disease's development. So, there will be talk therapy in combination with adjuvant treatments I've found highly effective—"

"Can you give us a minute, Doctor?" Paul asks.

"Certainly, Mr. Frasier," and Sherman steps out into the hall.

Paul waits till Sherman's out of earshot to speak. "I can't begin to imagine how it feels to watch some stranger you've just been told is your husband decide your medical care along with that pompous windbag," he says, nodding toward Sherman.

Agreed. He can't.

"So, I'm not going to do it," he says.

"What do you mean?"

"I mean it's your choice," he says. "If you don't want to go to the Unit, say the word. I'll tell the doc no. You'll go to a regular ward, receive the standard therapies. And after a year, we'll see what Dr. Sherman says about the possibility of you coming home."

"You're really leaving it up to me?"

He looks into my eyes. "Yes, it's your life, your mind. You decide. But think for a minute." He holds up the paper. "Maybe his protocol in the Unit will work for you like it did for those women I saw. Help you get rid of this voice in your head that's making you see things that don't exist, like those people in the future and their time machine. I'm sure Dr. Sherman's protocol is no walk in the park, but it seems a small price to pay for wresting control back from the disease and being free of this place. Getting you home, back among your things—*that's* what's going to awaken your memories, reconnect you to your life. Our lives."

But before I can even respond, Lester approaches. Sherman must've sent for him. "Wait, we're not done here!" Paul shouts, but Lester doesn't slow.

And the *voice*? Her orders are simple:

He's a threat. Take him down.

Suddenly I'm roundhouse-kicking the shit out of the attendant. Lester recovers and counters with a backhand, hell-bent on repeating last week's Timex watch knockout. But this time I'm ready for it, feint to the left, dodging the blow.

And now I intend to pause, not let this start a chain reaction of strikes my body is lured into carrying out.

Only I cannot seem to stop myself.

I watch my elbow ram into Lester's face. See the blood, thick rivulets of it, in the spittle running down his chin. See him stumble.

I can hear the faraway sounds of Paul pleading with me. Of Sherman barking orders.

Still, I don't stop. Start to take Lester down at the knees —

Till I'm pulled off him by Gus and pinned to the ground.

As the attendants put me in the restraint, my mind keeps circling the same question:

Why couldn't I stop?

I replay the attack over and over, hoping each time to uncover some justification for my actions. But find none. Just the *voice*'s command and my violent response.

Was it the *voice* who drove me to slit my wrist in the first place — so I could be free of her? Was she urging me to do things I could no longer refuse? Things to Paul?

I'm sure they were necessary things.

There it is. Anything for the mission, right?

Yes.

When Lester and Gus have finished securing me, Sherman signals them to back off, give my husband and me some privacy.

Paul eyes Lester, who's blotting his split lip with a torn piece of tissue. "I'm not blind, Dee. I can see the guy's a bit too fond of his job. But you're not some hero trying to save the world, and he's not some minion bent on stopping you."

How do you know?

"You're a patient," Paul continues. "He's an attendant. What just happened, what you did to him—can you honestly say *you* were in control and not that voice in your head?"

I can't meet his gaze.

"I've always done what's necessary to keep you safe," he says. "But I can't protect you from yourself. And I'm scared, Dee, of where this disease is taking you. Where you're *letting* it take you." He pauses a moment, takes a breath. "I think you owe yourself the chance to see if the protocol can help. But the choice is still yours."

Could the protocol work?

Don't know.

What I do know is the *voice* will take over, take my identity and my sanity, if she's able. And doing nothing about her, about the violence, the visions, will mean a lifetime as a chronic under lock and key inside Hanover. The thought of that trapped half-life terrifies me.

The *voice* needs to die. I tell my husband to sign the paper.

CHAPTER 15

LOOK OVER MY shoulder at the figures of Paul and Dr. Sherman growing smaller as Gus and Lester escort me away.

You can still undo this. Tell them you've changed your mind, that you don't want the Unit. You're there for an important reason!

Yes, to erase all traces of *you*. Cheers.

Once in the basement, we pass through a locked door into the East-West corridor, the dim tunnel-like hall I saw the first day. Pipes running along its wall emit steam in periodic belches.

Eventually we come to an entry gate sheathed in steel mesh. The sign on it reads UNIT. NO UNAUTHORIZED ENTRY. Lester quietly shoves me up against the wall while Gus presses the nearby buzzer. Soon a door opens in the shadows behind the gate. "Here with Dorothy Frasier, ma'am," Gus says to someone on the other side. I peer through the metal webbing and see an approaching figure in white: Miss Wallace.

There's a calm, almost beatific smile on her face as she unlocks the gate. Like a drab Mona Lisa. She eyes Lester's bloody lip, then says simply, "Welcome to the Unit, Dorothy."

The attendants escort me into a vestibule whose far wall contains two doors: one marked W-UNIT, the other, M-UNIT.

"You can take off the restraint," Wallace says, then turns to me. "It won't be needed here."

Cocky. That could be good. Her overconfidence could present an opportunity if you can find a weapon . . .

I don't have the energy right now to fight the *voice*. I let her plot away. Maybe she'll tire herself out.

When they've removed the straitjacket, Wallace secures a new ID on my wrist: "Patient W8209, Dorothy Frasier. Schizophrenic. Suicide risk. Dr. Eustace Sherman. W-Unit." Then she unlocks the door marked w-unit. The lock's a brand-new Titan mortise—the Unit's security is on a whole other level than A-Ward's. We follow Wallace down the ward's main hall, which, like A-Ward's, is lined with benches.

But that's where the resemblance ends.

A-Ward was a constant buzz of women talking. To each other. To themselves. To their deities. It was a hive.

This is something different.

The hall is empty. No sharp-tongued ladies pacing around, getting in your face, telling you their nutter version of the way things are. And no one under the benches, hiding from the way things are. It's all deathly calm, the only noise the jangle of Wallace's keys and the clean squeak of her shoes.

"Where the hell are all the patients?" I ask, but Wallace doesn't answer. Soon we reach an open door marked DAYROOM. But it's more cave than dayroom. The windows running along the top of the far wall have been covered so that no daylight can enter.

Below them I finally spot patients, a half dozen of them with their backs to us, seated in a semicircle between two tall reading lamps that tower over them like streetlights. On the wall in front of them is a large, awful painting of a barn in a blizzard. White paint laid on thick in a desperate attempt to depict snow.

So you're just going to seek oblivion here instead of facing up to the mission? Don't do this. You're not like the others!

Not like the others—precisely the kind of thinking that's brought me to this moment.

We follow the nurse down the hall, passing an imposing, white-coated doctor. His coal-black eyes under a looming brow briefly scrutinize me before he opens a door marked WU-3. For just a moment, before the doctor shuts the door behind him, I can see the legs of a patient in there—male, I'd swear—squirming slowly on an exam table, trying to resist the ministrations of some unseen staff member.

Gus nudges me to follow Wallace and Lester into a room farther on marked WU-6.

Christ, it's even darker than the dayroom. While I wait for my eyes to adjust, I catch the faintest fuggy whiff of unwashed human, and squint for its source.

That's when I see them. The women.

A couple dozen lying in three rows of beds. And even though it's three in the afternoon, all are sound asleep.

Two nurses pull the covers of a nearby bed down, laying bare a patient with long, dark hair and a unibrow rivaling Frida Kahlo's. They take hold of the woman and expertly rotate her onto her stomach, smooth her arms along her sides, then re-cover her before moving to the next patient. Despite being flipped like a pancake, Frida never so much as stirs. Georgie was right about Sherman using the severely impaired as test subjects for some of his studies. Women too far gone to defend themselves.

Wallace walks down the aisle and I pursue. "What the hell is Sherman doing to these women?"

"*Doctor* Sherman, Dorothy," Wallace says, pausing at some shelves stacked with linens. "You are to call him Doctor Sherman. Addressing people by their proper titles, using 'please,' 'may I,' and 'yes, ma'am,' and above all not using profanity—these are the ways we show courtesy and appreciation for those taking care of us here in the Unit."

I've definitely entered Wallace's realm of respect now.

Nurse Gibbs appears with my meager belongings from A-Ward: my cardigan and books. Puts her hand on my shoulder and says, "Don't worry, honey, I'll make sure they're all safely stored away till the day you need them."

"Why wouldn't I need them now?" I ask.

"Let's get you more comfortable, Dorothy," Wallace says, and pulls something gray off the shelf. Lays it on an empty bed nearby. It's a nightgown, basic and faded with wear, like those worn by the zombies in the dining hall.

And each of these sleeping women.

I can't explain why it took me so long—Sherman would say I've once again been in denial. But the thought finally registers: Wallace intends for me to join these women in their collective coma. Now.

Run! Get the fuck out of here while you can!

Now the purpose of my double escort becomes clear. Before I can even turn, Lester and Gus have me by the arms. Objects like cotton balls and vials suddenly make their appearance and things start happening fast—Wallace lifts my sleeve and swabs my arm with rubbing alcohol while Gibbs fills a syringe with amber-colored liquid.

"I never agreed to sedation!"

"That decision was never yours, sweetheart," Wallace says. "You're here because it's what your husband and Dr. Sherman agreed is the best treatment for you. It won't be long before you'll begin to see that for yourself."

"No! Paul gave *me* the choice!"

She calmly exchanges the used cotton ball for the syringe. "I'm afraid I don't know anything about that."

"Ask him, he'll tell you," I yell, but she just flicks the syringe, squeezes a couple golden drops out of the tip of the needle, then sinks it into my arm.

The drug hits before she's even driven the plunger home. My legs turn to warm honey and give way, but Lester and Gus hold me up, swing me around, and deposit me on the bed. The room is beginning to spin, and I try like hell to raise my arms and stop its rotation but they're too heavy to lift.

"You boys can go," Wallace says. "We'll take it from here."

"You sure? She can be a handful," Lester says, looking down at my dress, hiked up to my hips in the process of getting me on the bed.

"I'm aware," Wallace says.

The men turn, and I watch their retreating figures fade to blurs.

Now it's just me and the sisterhood. There's a tugging on my feet—Wallace and Gibbs taking off my socks and shoes. They roll me on my side, and I feel the cold metal zipper on the back of my dress being pulled down. I try to speak—to protest the taking of my dress and free will—but my tongue feels leaden, and I lie mute while they raise my arms above my head and lift my torso.

The scratch of the dress fabric as it's pulled over my cheeks is the last thing I feel before I slip down into the black.

CHAPTER 16

Awake is so close. Just out of reach.

I fight hard to get to it, really I do. Can almost see the light, almost make out the words being spoken around me, but it all keeps slipping away . . .

At some point there's a loud rattling in my head like out-of-control castanets. When I bite the side of my cheek and taste blood, I realize it's my own teeth chattering, slamming into each other again and again with fever-filled abandon.

My whole body is quaking, shivering uncontrollably, and everything—my muscles, my skin, my head—feels raw.

Sometime later . . . or maybe no time later, I smell something sour. Feel a burning in my throat and nose. Vomit, I think. Then more voices. More hands undressing me, pulling off my soiled gray nightgown.

Someone is wiping me down with a scratchy washcloth, short, rough strokes that graze my goose bumps.

Cold air bleeds over my damp, fevered skin.

Someone cover me. Please.

*   *   *

My eyes refuse to speak to each other. Each has a mind of its own and I put all I've got into harnessing them together like a good pair of plow horses. The first thing that registers is Nurse Wallace's pasty face, inches from mine, looking into my wandering eyes, feeling my forehead. "She's coming around. You can get her up."

Nurses lift me out of the bed and float me past the rows of sleeping women to another room, where they lower me onto something cold. A toilet. Cajole me to do my business. "Come on, sweetie, we don't want to have to catheterize you . . ."

The next thing I know someone's saying, "Good girl," and the nurses are gathering me up off the porcelain, bringing me back to my bed in the slumber room and tucking me in.

Kyung said you have a purpose in 1954—locate the doctor!

You need to find a way out of the Unit!

But there is no Kyung, no purpose. Just the golden syringe, the prick of the needle, and the familiar black nothing. On and on it goes like that . . . rinse and repeat . . . time stretching like taffy between my moments of awake—

Till I feel them, the ghost bees buzzing in my feet.

∗   ∗   ∗

"What's wrong, why won't she wake up? Is she fragging again?"

"No. See these needle tracks on her arm. They're sedating her."

"Jesus."

"Probably better this way. We can pull the disc while she's out and harmless. Just let me get a quick scan first."

"Make it fast, Kyung. We don't know how much time we have."

"Never enough time," I say, lift my heavy lids—and see I'm in a forest. Not a real forest, must be one of my imaginary ones. The ground is damp. Can feel slippery leaves under my fingertips. Ethan and Kyung are kneeling, hunched over my right hand. Next to Ethan I see something that looks like a black lunch box.

Above us are a trillion stars. And the tops of fir trees, swaying slowly in the moonlight, murmuring like they do when the wind weaves through them just right. "I miss the outside," I say to my figments, before letting my eyelids slip back down where they should be—shutting out this delusion.

But then I smell rubbing alcohol and my eyes snap back open, searching for its source. A cotton ball. Ethan's wiping down my wrist while Kyung points her little wand at it.

"Hurry it up, Kyung, she's starting to wake up," Ethan says.

"Just a couple more seconds," Kyung says, then there's a *beep*. "Got it."

Ethan looks down at me, says, "You're going to need to hold very still, Bix."

"Not Bix . . . Keep telling you I'm . . . Never mind, the protocol will take care of all this," I say.

Then I spot the knife in Kyung's hand.

I try to get away from my armed figments, but my muscles are too full of Wallace's golden liquid to move, and Ethan pins my arms while Kyung brings the blade closer. "Sorry for the grabble 'n' snag, Bix," she says, "but there's no time for niceties. It needs to come out now."

"What?"

"Your disc. We need to cut it out," Ethan says, "sever the connection before whoever it is in '54 who's got your link triggers it again and you jump back there."

The woman on the bus . . . the real Dorothy . . . she's the one with my link . . . but she doesn't really exist. None of this exists . . .

Kyung puts the cold blade to my skin. "We don't want you stranded there if the Tabula Rasa—"

"Tabula Rasa?" I ask.

"It's a cult," Ethan says, "and they . . . well—"

"We'll explain everything once the disc is out, Bix," Kyung says, cutting him off as she presses her cold knife to my skin.

"It was never going to be easy for you to reach the doctor, get their help," Ethan says. "Now it's virtually impossible—"

"But the doctor *is* helping . . ." I say.

Kyung pulls back her knife. "Wait. You two have spoken?"

I nod. "Dr. Sherman's helping me get rid of you . . . this fake future . . . the *voice* in my head . . . All of it. That's why I agreed to come down here to his pit . . ."

"Dr. Sherman?" Kyung asks, and grabs my wrist, looks at my ID band. "Ethan, this says she's now a patient in the Unit! We can't pull her, not when she's so close — "

But the rest of her words are lost in the white roar as it hauls me away from my figments.

And drops me back in my bed. I look at the scar on my wrist, where Kyung almost cut me open in my fictional future forest.

It wasn't a delusion. They said the doctor with the viral sample is close. That means he's in the hospital. Maybe he's the one with the coal-dark eyes you saw in the Unit hallway. You need to find a way to get to him.

Don't you dare go to sleep!

But I ignore the *voice*, let the deep breaths of the sleeping women pull me back down with them.

✳   ✳   ✳

I rub my aching jaw with the palms of my hands, then lay them back down on my chair's big wooden armrests and return to gazing at the painting of the wintry barn in front of me . . . Snowflakes falling in thick white swirls—

I'm awake.

How long was I not awake?

How long have I been sitting here like this, watching the shitty swirls of snow? I try to remember how I came to be in this chair. The time before this moment.

But there's just a big, blank nothing before this moment.

The lamp above me flickers and there's a *buzzzz* coming from below. Something, maybe a mouse, has chewed a hole in the lamp's ancient cloth cord near my feet. Can see some of its silvery live wires peeking out like whiskers.

I'm not alone. There are three of us tucked under gray blankets, gathered around the bright and shitty snow painting, like moths by a porch light.

I remember the moth to my right—the woman with the pointy glasses I defended in the dining hall against Norma. Glasses looks up from her newspaper at me, eyes huge behind those lenses. She seems a helluva lot more with-it than she was in the dining hall that night I saved her from Norma.

Or was Glasses always with-it, but the *voice* warped my perception of her?

I wait for some menacing retort from the *voice*, but there is none, and in the blessed silence I turn to get a better look at the moth to the right of Glasses. She's asleep, head lolled to the side, face covered by a chunk of gray hair no one's bothered to tuck out of the way.

A couple nurses guide a dazed patient to a seat near me. It's Betsy, the squirrelly girl from the transport bus, the one so convinced her brother had inserted a transmitter into her head. I wouldn't want whatever treatment they're giving Betsy. Her hands are balled up in tight little fists that tremble in her lap like scared kittens.

And her speech—something's drained all the chirpiness out of it, left her syllables all stretched out and flattened, words all slurred. It's a horror show: "Whyyy wooon somonnne geddih transmehhhtterrr outtah my hehhhd?" she shouts at the nurses, who ignore her paranoid transmitter accusations.

After the nurses leave, Glasses nods to the now-sleeping Betsy. "Betsy's treatment doesn't seem to be agreeing with her." No shit. "It happens with some patients. Their emotions become too big to control."

Unlike Betsy, Glasses's speech is clear and calm, with just the slightest modulation to it. Like a metronome . . . the kind that sat on a piano so you could keep a steady beat . . . Whoa, my mind drifted off there for a moment. Might need a little more rest.

I'm about to close my eyes when I see my wedding ring. Someone's placed it on my finger.

I pull it off and toss it. Hear the satisfying *clink* followed by the sound of it rolling and settling somewhere in the shadows beyond our circle. "*I'll* decide when I'm ready to wear it, not them," I say to Glasses.

"I know, silly. You've told me. Three times."

"No. That's not possible."

"Don't worry. Lots of things get forgotten in the Unit," she says, holding out her hand. "Alice Wechsler, pleased to meet you. Again."

"Dorothy Frasier," I say, shaking her hand as I trot out my newly embraced name like I've known it forever. "How long have I been here?"

"Since the last meal."

"No, I mean how long have I been *here*, in the Unit? What's today's date?"

"Oh, I really shouldn't say." Then she leans over and whispers, "But I do happen to know. They're easing me back into things, now that I'm doing so well in my recovery. Like reading the paper." Alice holds the newspaper up, practically bursting with gratitude and pride. "Don't tell anyone I told you, but it's November twenty-ninth."

"Bullshit!"

"Language!" Alice shakes her head and tsks. "The doctor's certainly got his work cut out with you."

"They brought me down here the eighteenth. That can't have been more than a day ago, two tops."

"What's the last thing you remember?"

"Wallace giving me a shot."

"Oh, you've had scads of those. Look at your arms."

I pull up my gray sleeve and see an upper arm littered with bruises and needle marks. "Christ."

"Dr. Sherman explained the protocol to me during our talk sessions.

It calls for at least a week of continuous sedation and sensory depri-
vation in the narcosis room to disorient the patient. No daylight or
clocks, nothing to hold you to where—or when—you are. You're
woken just long enough to eat and use the bathroom."

Murky memories of vomit, sponge baths, and cold porcelain
briefly bubble to the surface. Narcotic-induced sleep in the dark—
that's Dr. Sherman's miracle treatment, what was going to vanquish
the *voice* and the visions?

There will be no cure.

The disappointment hits with almost physical force, and I'm
shocked by how much I'd allowed myself to believe the protocol
would work.

At least I'll still get my freedom. "Now that the protocol's done,
how soon can I leave—"

"No, silly." She laughs. Her chuckle is low and polished, like a
Bing Crosby version of a laugh. "You're not done. The sedation was
just phase one. You're well into phase two."

"Phase two?"

She nods. "Regression. They start it while you're still sedated so you
stay calm, don't fight the process. Once you're far enough along and
more *agreeable*, the doctor lifts the drugs. You've been awake for days."

"That's impossible."

"You're just forgetting 'cause you're already partially *there*."

"'There'?"

"Regressed, silly." Alice returns to her newspaper, and I try to wrap
my head around having been conscious for days. What the hell have
I been doing? Thinking?

I put my hand down on the newspaper, blocking her reading.
"Tell me about regression."

She sighs. "It's how Dr. Sherman addresses the diseased brain
pathways in a patient. Those causing all the paranoid thoughts, delusions, and what he calls 'antisocial tendencies' that limit our trust
and distance us from the real world."

"How?"

"With ECT. Electroshock—but not the old-fashioned kind of shock sessions, twice a week, one charge a session. Dr. Sherman's ECT is state-of-the-art: two treatment sessions a day, consisting of three shocks each. Except Sunday, of course."

Christ.

But Alice nods knowingly, like she's just shared the location of a prime hunting spot or stash of choice canned goods. "He starts you out low, then gradually raises the voltage and number of charges a session till you're at the very best dose for getting you where you need to be. 'Ramping up,' they call it."

"I don't remember any of that," I say.

"Memory loss, an unfortunate side effect of the shocks."

I remember Georgie saying how ECT would make agitated patients forget what they were even upset about. Like my memory's not broken enough already.

"It's unpredictable," Alice continues. "You never quite know which memories you'll lose and which you'll hold on to. Often whole chunks of time will disappear and suddenly it's hours—even days—later . . . Which is really for the best, though, makes the time go by faster."

Just about the shittiest pep talk ever.

I rub my throbbing temples. "This is all a lot to process . . ."

"Confusion, another side effect," she says. "Right after a treatment is when you'll feel the foggiest. But then things become clearer. Don't you feel better than when you first woke up?"

She's right. "Yes."

"See." She smiles. "Because the shocks affect the muscles and nerves a bit, meddle with one's coordination and such, I've found one will generally look worse off to others than one feels on the inside. Of course, when you're far enough along, heading toward full regression, you'll be foggy all the time, inside and out, mind hopscotching between awake and asleep. But that's good. It means you've reached the point where you're most open to change. Soon you'll start to feel yourself transforming, getting better."

Transforming? What the hell? As the panic starts to rise in me, I squeeze my Latin medal tight, like it's a totem that will somehow shield me from what I'm hearing. "Your memories, did they come back?" I ask her.

She nods. "Bits and pieces. Started returning once they stopped the shocks. Not all. But those that didn't, well, they couldn't have been very important, right?"

Pretty sure that's not right.

"I wouldn't worry, hun," Alice says dreamily. "It truly is for the best. By the time you're ready for phase three, you'll feel so much younger, unburdened. Honestly, it's been a godsend—"

"Phase three?"

"The repatterning. That's where the doctor can really make a difference—by reintroducing healthier, happier habits of thinking and acting in the patient," Alice says, sounding scarily like Sherman. "That's how he helps you become the best version of yourself. I'm almost done with my repatterning, just about fully recovered. So I'll be going home soon with Bill, that's my husband . . ."

The best fucking version of me?

I try to focus on the fact that Alice seems to have come through the protocol intact. But that fact fails to calm me, and I can no longer just sit here, mothlike. I pull my blanket off, stand up—and oh, the head rush. When the purple spots subside, I wander past Alice to get a better look at the sleeping woman with the hair in her face. Pull it away—and see she's Mary Droesch.

And she's not sleeping.

"Mary?" I say, but her sharp, vigilant eyes of three weeks ago now just stare vacantly into space. I snap my fingers by them. Not a flicker of response. "What happened to her?" I ask Alice.

"Not entirely sure. Medical progress is never a smooth road," she says. "The doctor's bound to run into a bump every now and then. It's all part of the process."

"What kind of bump hit Mary Droesch?"

"I heard she got a little too much treatment. Had a seizure. These things happen from time to time."

"Sure, if you continually electrocute a person, I imagine things *do* happen."

"But they're still hopeful she'll recover," Alice continues. "Sometimes they give her special treatments in room three to try and wake her."

Alice disappears behind her newspaper—and I spot a headline on its back page: "Ernest Hemingway Bags Leopard in Uganda." Underneath is a photo of the bearded author of few words crouching by the late, unlucky beast.

"I remember this," I say, grabbing the newspaper.

"Ernest Hemingway on safari? He's apparently quite the marksman. Bill told me he—"

"Uganda 1954. I think that's when he was in that plane crash . . . Then *another* plane crash the next day."

"What are you talking about, silly?"

"Sounds far-fetched but it's true. The guy was in two plane crashes in two days and survived both. Communication in the bush was spotty and everyone thought Hemingway had been killed in the first crash . . . Or was it the second? . . . Newspapers even published his obituary. But days later he miraculously showed up in Entebbe, alive and well and—"

It's happened again: me drifting away from serious worries about the doctor's brain-damaging protocol, only to end up chattering on, this time about Hemingway. Must be another side effect of the ECT.

"Dorothy." Wallace. She somehow snuck up on me. She takes the newspaper from me and gives it back to Alice. "Come, it's time for your next treatment."

"I'm not going anywhere till I talk to Sherman!" I shout, and my words wake the *voice*:

Sherman and his staff are the problem, not the solution.

And you know what to do with problems—

Find something sharp. Get creative.

Wallace interrupts the *voice*'s latest threats. "Then by all means, let's go see the doctor," she says, and nods to someone behind me.

I turn to find a ready and waiting Lester and Gus.

CHAPTER 17

G ET YOUR HANDS off me! You've got no rum!" I scream as the attendants hoist me onto the table, hold down my arms and legs.

The Unit's treatment room is identical to the infirmary's: green-tiled walls, cabinets, and an examination table at its center. But this one contains something more: a box of switches and knobs. Electroshock.

Wallace, now standing at my head, dips a tongue depressor into a jar of viscous gel that smells like iron filings and gasoline. She spreads the stuff on my temples as I squirm.

"Don't do this!" I say, looking up at her.

"Still fighting it," Lester says. "A week of shocks hasn't made a dent in her crazy. Doctor shoulda kept her knocked out longer—"

"Lester, that's enough," Wallace says.

Sherman enters the room. "And how are we feeling today, Dorothy—"

"You lied!" I shout, but the doctor says nothing, just takes my pulse and watches me, assessing. "You lied about the protocol! I demand to speak to Paul now!"

He squeezes my shoulder. "Now, you don't want to do that, dear. You'll interrupt all the progress you're making. I'm guessing you've already noticed a diminishment of your symptoms."

The *voice* has definitely been less present. And my last vision of the future seems a long time ago. But the risks—ending up like Mary Droesch? "I don't want this—"

"Not to worry. You're in good hands. It won't be long before you come to realize that." He pats my arm and walks over to the ECT control box.

"No! I need to talk to Paul! Once he knows what you're doing down here, he'll—"

Lester whispers, "Go ahead, darlin', tell us what he'll do again."

Again? So this scene has played out before? Jesus.

"Don't you want to get well enough to go home?" Dr. Sherman asks as he adjusts his dials.

"By inflicting brain damage to remake me?" I lift my head, the only part of me able to move, and level my eyes at him. "My memory's already in tatters and you're about to send an electric current through it. What kind of dumbass thinking is that—"

"Lester," Wallace instructs, and the attendant crams a rubber bit into my mouth, silencing me. Then the nurse fits something padded onto my greasy temples. "We're ready to proceed, Doctor," she says.

"Good. I'll be administering a hundred and fifty volts. Three charges of point six second duration. Note the change in Mrs. Frasier's chart."

"But those are full-dose levels," Wallace says, "and we haven't finished ramping her up—"

"She's obviously handling the dosage just fine."

"But—"

"I don't recall asking for a consultation, Miss Wallace," he says as he turns on the unit with a *THWICK* of a switch.

"Yes, Doctor."

There's a second *THWICK* from the machine.

Followed by a *CRACK* inside my skull, as a lightning bolt, violet blue and hot, whipsaws me around till my bones are shards and my brain, a fine puree.

* * *

I feel it all the time now, the protocol.

There's a heaviness in me, on me, like a lead apron, and I half expect at any moment to sink through my chair and the checkerboard floor, straight to the center of the earth. And my hand, the right one, it's begun to curl in on itself . . . But it's all part of the process, necessary, Dr. Sherman explained in one of our sessions, if we're going to truly extinguish the *voice*. And it's working, the shocks continuing to weaken her, as Dr. Sherman promised they would. There are whole slices of time now when the *voice* is silenced completely, giving me a break from her violent urgings.

So, I'm free to drift here in the Unit's kitchen, contemplate the meal in front of me. Breakfast . . . dinner? The bowl contains something beige and something brown, pureed then dumbwaitered down in covered pots from the main kitchen above. Definitely corn this time. And the brown? Beef stew? Hard to tell.

At the table with me are Alice and a couple of other silent ambulatories, along with Miss Gibbs, busy feeding Mary, while she stares unseeing through her thicket of overgrown bangs. The catatonic's a grim reminder of the risks involved in reclaiming my sanity. But Miss Gibbs hasn't given up on her. As she slots a spoonful of mush into Mary's half-open mouth, the nurse gently rubs her hand and speaks to her softly. Asks her how she's doing today and shares news about her sister like the gork is listening.

I push the brown slick into the lumpy corn sea with my spoon while I take in Miss Gibbs's details—her pale, porcelain skin . . . her delicate-looking hand with the grip of a longshoreman . . . the splashy drop of dried blood on her white shoe . . .

"Hun, you should eat something," Alice says to me. "You're getting awfully thin."

"I'm not very hungry right now." Whoa, my voice. It's hollowed out, measured, syllables all weighted and pitched the same. How long has it been that way?

They're taking you apart, piece by piece.

You can't let that happen.

The *voice* is awake, my break over.

"Sure am glad this is my last meal of mush," Alice says.

"Why is that?" I ask in my new monotone.

"Today's the big day. I'm going home. You know that, silly."

I do? Facts float in and out of my recall like the tide here in the Unit. I'll miss Alice. Even with her alarming explanations, she was someone to talk to. But her going home is a good thing. Sure, she's still a bit too composed and agreeable, still parroting Dr. Sherman, but she seems to be doing fine. Happy, even.

Is that what you want, happy?

Happy won't solve your problem. Angry and armed, now they might solve your problem—

Shouts and the sharp smell of mustard interrupt the *voice's* desperate suggestions. I look up and see Betsy standing a few feet away, swaying unsteadily, the shattered remains of a broken mustard jar at her feet.

But it's her face that's of most interest.

A red valley extends from her forehead to her cheek and blood trickles from the gap between the two flaps of skin in a steady drip onto the floor. One shaky hand's gripping a jagged piece of jar, while the other frantically probes the wound.

Gus enters the kitchen and Betsy shouts, "Teh . . . teh me wuhrr izzit? Dah teh . . . teh . . . transmeh . . . mehter?" But agitation has only worsened Betsy's verbal horror show and there's little chance the attendant understands her words—or cares about her missing transmitter. He's far more concerned about the bloody shard of glass she's brandishing in her hand. So Betsy shouts even louder, desperate to be understood. "Nee tah geddih outtah my heh . . . head—"

But Gus overpowers and disarms her.

As she's escorted out I can hear her begging to speak to Dr.

Sherman, to explain her actions, apologize, like a child seeking forgiveness from a father. Strange.

"What'll happen to her?" I ask Alice.

"Now that Betsy's used a weapon, shown she could be an immediate danger to others, I imagine the doctor will go a more traditional route." Betsy's going down-alphabet, and I remember what Georgie said that night at the movies: no one plans on becoming a chronic.

Now I see — how hard it could be to leave this place.

That Hanover might win.

A custodian enters, pushing his cart full of cleaners and buckets. It's Joe, the guy who lent me his handkerchief that first day to clean the blood off my ears, the latest to draw the short straw and have to come down here to clean up after us moths. "It's a shame the protocol didn't work for her," Alice says as we watch Joe begin to clean up Betsy's debris.

"Betsy's not protocol," I say.

"Yes she is, silly. You're forgetting again." Betsy's paranoid horror show is from Sherman's protocol? "Bill will be here any minute now, so give me a hug goodbye," she says.

"Buh . . . but what the protocol did to Betsy — what if — "

Alice takes my hands, her giant eyes behind the glasses fixed on mine. "Hun, when you get near the end, that last, most difficult part, when nothing makes sense anymore, just know you're getting better — even if it seems they've made you so much worse."

Worse? How much worse? Betsy worse? But before I can ask, Alice is out the door. Gone.

Joe picks up a piece of glass near my feet and tosses it into his wastebasket. Then he points to my Latin medal. "That's a handsome pendant you have there, miss. May I take a look?" I nod, and he examines it. "Georgetown Country Day Latin Award," he reads, then turns it over. "*Memento Audere Semper.*" He looks at me. "'Remember, always dare,' right?"

Must be some Catholic school in Joe's past. I nod.

"That's a fine accomplishment, miss," he says.

"Dorothy," Miss Wallace says from the doorway, "you shouldn't still be in here. Come, it's time for your treatment."

"Yes, ma'am," I answer, and go to her.

CHAPTER 18

D OROTHY, ARE YOU with me?"
Dr. Sherman's wondering where I've drifted off to. Drifting is easy in these sessions after the shocks. His office down here in the Unit is dull and dark, just a desk and chairs. No butterflies . . . busty clay figures . . . spiral shells . . .

See? Drifting is easy.

Especially now that the *voice* has gone quiet. I can still feel some of her in me, lying low, hoping to outlast Dr. Sherman's protocol. But it won't work. Each time the lightning strikes me, I can feel it scrubbing more of her out. Making room. Every bit of *Bix*, her trips to the future, her nerds with their links and lost tethers — most of all, her raging paranoia — will be scoured clean till nothing remains.

Then I'll be free. And I'll leave Hanover with all the marbles left to me.

So it's worth it, this feeling, like someone's reduced my voltage, cut power to all noncritical circuits. Only essential portions of my mind running while Dr Sherman rewires the system. The nurses promise my brownout will soon be over, most of its damage temporary. They say it's best not to fight it. Fight them. Just let go.

Surrender, Dorothy.

So I'm mostly calm. The drifting helps.

"Would you like me to repeat the question, dear?" the doctor asks. "I know the regression can make it difficult to remember things."

Regression. What's been trickling in, as Bix trickles out . . . urging me not to get so worked up, have faith in those trying to make me better. Its simple message of trust is making more and more sense.

"I'm talking about that day in my office," Dr. Sherman presses, "when you told Paul you didn't care what the voice in your head was saying, that you knew he was the man in your memory. Tell me about the voice."

"I don't want to talk about her," I say, worried he'll be mad.

But Dr. Sherman just smiles and writes his notes. "That's fine, Dorothy, plenty of time for that when you're further along in your recovery. I can see the protocol's getting you where you need to be. That's what matters most."

"What do you mean, 'getting me where I need to'—"

But Miss Wallace is at the door. "Now it's time for you to go with the nurse. All right?" he asks, and I nod back, feel the pleasant glow of contentment in the agreeing.

Miss Wallace takes my good hand and helps me out of the chair—my coordination's not great these days, muscles doing things I can't predict.

In the tunnel hall I start to turn back to the Unit, but the nurse stops me. "Not yet, sweetheart," she says, and guides me the other way. "We're going upstairs."

* * *

Upstairs.

Almost forgot about upstairs. I wonder what Georgie's been up to in A-Ward. If she's still making up things to confess to Dr. Sherman. Does she know I'm down in the Unit? How long have I been here, anyway? The questions are piling up, trying to break through my drift.

Halfway down the long hall, I see a man walking toward us: the doctor with eyes like bits of coal who I saw that first day in the Unit. The one the *voice* thought might be the doctor with the virus sample.

When we get close, I see the man's eyes sweeping over me like a searchlight and I start to slow down.

"Come, Dorothy, let's not tarry," Miss Wallace says, pulling me past him.

"Why upstairs?" I ask her.

"You have a visitor. Unit patients aren't normally allowed visitors, but an exception's being made for you today."

I'm hoping it's Paul.

I've been wanting to tell him about what they're really doing in the Unit. But maybe it's better he doesn't know. Don't want him stopping them from killing the *voice*.

It's hard keeping up with Miss Wallace. The walls are spinning, screwing with my balance, making me wobble. Finally, she unlocks a door with a big key, and we wait for an elevator.

That's when I see my reflection in some glass.

I'm a ghost.

Thin and pale, almost powdery, like someone's blown chalk dust over me. My face is gaunt, full of deep shadows that make my eyes look too big. Nocturnal.

And my head: it's tilted slightly to one side, mouth gaped open like a bass on a hook.

Is it always that way now? I shut the thing. Stand straight as I can. But I still scare me.

✳   ✳   ✳

When the elevator doors open, the light from the first-floor windows is blinding after so long underground. Feels like it could burn a hole right through me. Miss Wallace gives me a moment to adjust so I don't fall again before walking me out. I don't remember my tumble, but the nurses told me about it. Showed me the bruises down my leg.

The hallway's busy and loud, crowds of patients, staff, and too many strangers shouting "Happy Holidays" and "Merry Christmas."

I can just make out the gate to A-Ward in the distance. I hear Christmas music coming through the scratchy hallway loudspeakers:

Chestnuts roasting on an open fire
Jack Frost nipping at your nose
Yuletide carols being sung by a choir
And folks dressed up like Eskimos . . .

Suddenly a scene flashes into my head—

I'm standing in a living room, next to a Christmas tree, breathing in its pine smell. Wrapped presents lie on the floor by my feet.

In the background, Nat King Cole is singing, trying hard to make the season bright, but the Guest has arrived, and the world is turning . . .

And now my heart's pounding away. I try to calm it, tell myself the world didn't really turn, that a virus called "the Guest" isn't real, just another imaginary figment of my schizophrenia. Like this made-up memory.

"Let's go, sweetheart," Miss Wallace says, tugging on my arm to get me walking again.

Soon teenage boys in long, red robes are passing by us.

The St. Aloysius Boys' Choir. The concert. My escape plan.

I remember.

I know it's for the best I didn't break out of here. That I need to be at Hanover to recover. But knowing something and feeling it are such different things. My eyes begin to fill, and the crowd feels like it's closing in on me, cutting off my exits. But I set my sights on the visitors' room and put one foot in front of the other till we reach it.

"Stay right here, Dorothy," Miss Wallace says, seating me on a bench outside its door. "I need to check if your visitor's meeting you here or in the conference room."

"Okay," I say, and watch the choirboys go by, their eyes darting round the hall, looking at us patients—I think we're maybe their first lunatics. A couple boys whisper and point as they pass by.

"Would you like one, sweetie?"

An old lady in a reindeer apron is holding a basket out to me. It's filled with cookies in different shapes. Drums, Christmas trees, gingerbread men. She places a cookie in my good hand, a star topped with red sprinkles. It's beautiful.

How long has it been since I ate something not from a spoon?

A long time, I think.

I'm about to take a bite when I hear, "Well, look who's here— Wonder Woman." It's Norma, the woman I beat up in the dining hall to help Alice.

Norma seems bigger. Or maybe I'm just smaller.

"Just another Unit gork now, eh, pretty?" she says, laughing, then takes my cookie and walks away.

All of a sudden anger's cutting through the drift, making my thoughts so much sharper: Give it back, you bitch! But "Give it" is all I get out before the crowd swallows up Norma.

"Holy smokes!" I know that voice—Georgie. I turn around, and there she is.

"So good to see you, Georgie. I've been getting better in the Unit downstairs," I say.

But she just stares at me, mouth open wide in the shape of an O. I think my night creature looks have surprised her. "Bix?" she says, stepping closer.

I shake my head. "Not Bix. You were right, my name's Dorothy Frasier. My husband, Paul, he's visiting—"

"Georgie." It's Miss Wallace back from the visitors' room. "You know you aren't supposed to be near the Unit patients. Why don't you return to A-Ward and take your seat for the concert."

But Georgie doesn't move. "They've done something to her," she says to Miss Wallace. "What did they do to her?"

"I said you should return to A-Ward," the nurse tells Georgie. But

Georgie still won't go. Takes my hand instead. Her eyes are glassy with tears now. "Georgie," Miss Wallace says, the nurse's stern voice full of threat.

Georgie squeezes my hand, gives me a final look, then walks back down the hall.

"Come," Miss Wallace says, and guides me around the wet patch of floor Joe's mopping, into the visitors' room, where people are sitting at tables. I check all the faces, looking for Paul.

Then I see him.

Not Paul. The sheriff's deputy, Officer Worthy.

CHAPTER 19

T HE DEPUTY'S EYES go wide when he sees us, turning them extra blue. Suddenly the drift is gone, replaced by so many thoughts: I don't want to be seen like this, in my gray gown, all ghostlike. Wish I was somewhere else. Not seen.

But he is here, and I am here, so there is no choice.

All I can do is hope this is over soon.

I straighten up, try hard not to wobble when Miss Wallace walks me to his table. Sit down before she can try to help me. "I'll be right over there, Dorothy," she says, pointing to a spot near the entrance. I nod and she goes.

"You're letting them call you Dorothy now?" Officer Worthy asks as he sits. I nod. "So things are . . . better for you here? Clearer?" I nod again, but he looks puzzled. "After our last encounter, I was expecting at least a cutting remark, if not a swift jab from you," he says, and smiles. First time I've seen the deputy's smile. Crooked but kind. I'd smile back but I'm not sure those muscles are working right. "*Is* everything all right?" he asks. "And I'm afraid I'm going to need more than a headshake."

Time to speak, kill his concern so he'll go. I close my eyes, take my time to string together the right words. "Yes, I'm fine," I tell Officer Worthy on the other side of my eyelids. "It's tiring to talk, 'cause of the treatment. But Dr. Sherman's protocol is all to make me better."

That should satisfy him—only when I open my eyes, there's no satisfaction on his face. His brows are pinched together tight, his lips now an O like Georgie's.

But it's not till I hear "Christ" slip out under his breath that I realize what's happened—

The deputy's just witnessed *my* horror show.

Dr. Sherman, Miss Wallace, the rest of the staff, they've acted like I was speaking just fine, with their smile-nods. But all the time my words have been getting less and less fine, more and more slurred. Stunted. And I never noticed it changing—like the frog who doesn't know it's slowly boiling to death 'cause it's happening bit by bit. Realizing I'm the frog fills me with shame and rage—fear too—and I turn away to stuff it all back down.

When I turn back, pity's replaced alarm on Officer Worthy's face. And I don't want to settle for pity.

So, I try even harder to speak right. Show him I'm fine. "Dr. Sherman says I'll be recovered real soon and then I can go home!"

But it's like cut-open Betsy, blood running down her face, wanting so much to make Gus understand about her transmitter. The harder she tried, the worse her horror show got. Officer Worthy's leaning close now, trying hard to understand my words. I see his eyes go to my wedding ring.

"Your husband, he agreed to this treatment?" he asks.

Explaining Paul doesn't know what they're really doing downstairs—it's too many words. So I nod, and now the deputy's looking around the room like he's searching for someone to arrest.

"Why are you here, Officer Worthy?" I ask, slow and careful.

The deputy's fingers drum softly on the table.

"After the attendant took a crack at you that day on the driveway," he says, "I decided to check in on you, make sure you were getting on okay here. But you were not an easy person to see. When I contacted Dr. Sherman, he said it wasn't the right time yet for you to have visitors. So I waited. And waited. Weeks passed, but it never seemed to be the right time. So finally, I called Hanover's superintendent, explained that I'd witnessed possible excessive force being used on a patient by a member of his staff. And as an officer of the court, I needed to officially follow up with a welfare check on that patient to ascertain she was okay, that there had been no more incidents. Otherwise I'd need to turn my report over to my superiors."

"Lone Ranger rides again," I say, and we laugh at my words from that day on the driveway. Feels good to laugh, like none of what's happened has happened.

"So, you're sure about this protocol of Dr. Sherman's?" Officer Worthy asks.

"Used to think I was from the future," I say, and he nods. So he knows. Dr. Sherman must've told him. That doesn't seem right but maybe the doctor had his reasons. "I want to get better. Leave here."

"Good," he says, nodding. "That's what I needed to hear." He reaches into his pocket. "I have something for you," he says, and pulls out a wrinkled piece of yellow paper. "Found this on the driveway after that attendant took you away. Pretty sure it's yours." The balled-up yellow note from my coat pocket. I remember. He pushes it across the table to me.

I'm sure what's in this note is no good for my recovery. But the *voice* comes out of hiding to issue a last command before she flickers out of existence:

Look at it. Maybe it says who the doctor is!

And before I can smother the urge, smother *her*, I'm unfolding it. First word is three letters: *B* followed by *i-x*. Bix. Great, a note addressed to the *voice*.

But I wonder what I'd write her, so I move to the next word: *u-n-d-o-u-b-t-e-d-l-y*. So many letters. I sound each out, trying to form them all into a word, only it refuses to form, and now I'm jumping from word to word, looking for one I can crack—but find none.

Reading is mostly gone.

I feel my face growing hot, shame and anger rising again from this newest shrinking of me. Push the paper back across the table. "Can't."

On Officer Worthy's face, new pity. I need this to be over. Miss Wallace is just across the room. I could call to her—

"Would you like me to read it to you?" he asks.

No. He should definitely not do that.

Only "Yes, please" escapes me, and he starts.

Bix,

Undoubtedly, you don't want to hear any more from me about this mission to hunt down the doctor in '54—and all the reasons why you shouldn't be the one to go, so I'll desist.

You were right, I should've been more understanding of your desire to opt out, become Kyung's volunteer.

I'm still angry she went behind my back to enlist you. Still think her mission is premature. But it *is* your choice, your life, and I'm trying to make peace with it. Trying.

So now the housekeeping:

I reminded Kyung you've got over a year till your quarter hour, but our little control freak likes to be prepared, insists you carry a list of the addresses below. If things go south with the tether or the devil's kiss comes early, you'll have options for doing what's necessary. Horrible options, but options:

35 Braddock Road, Norfolk, Virginia

644 Tilbury Street, Manassas, Virginia

892 Twin Forks Road, Alexandria, Virginia

Just promise me when you make it to 1954 in that jerry-rigged machine, you'll be careful. As you know, 1954 has its own dangers.

—Ethan, your favorite twin ☺

I invented a twin brother. And the rest of this gibberish.

"I've been wondering about these terms," Officer Worthy says, "'devil's kiss,' 'tether,' 'your quarter hour.'"

"Your wife know what you do with your free time?" I ask.

He ignores my kidding. "Do you remember what they mean?"

Bix's words. Soon they'll be gone. "'Quarter hour' means twenty-fifth birthday," I tell him, "and tether's a . . . a connection between times . . . I think. Don't remember devil's kiss, or why those addresses."

Now his eyes look like they want to hide. "What?" I ask, but he doesn't answer. "Tell me."

"I drove out to them," he says finally. "The addresses."

"And you find?"

"Crematoriums. All three."

Like the yellow note said: my "horrible options." It's all so, so dark. Why couldn't I see how sick I was in A-Ward? Guess the frog was cooking too slow.

"I'm sorry," Officer Worthy says. "I didn't mean for you to learn—"

"How nuts I am? Already know. But you're still here, asking questions. Digging."

"I like a good puzzle."

"All just things my sick mind made up. Like time travel, the Guest . . . even people"—I hold up the yellow note from "Ethan." "I was starting to believe they were real." The deputy's eyes are hiding from me again. "What is it?" I ask.

He shakes his head. "It's . . . It's nothing."

It's definitely something. And I want to not care what that something is, drift past it like I have everything else on the way to killing the *voice*.

But I can't.

"Tell me," I say, and notice him looking over my shoulder at something behind me. Done it a couple times. I turn around and see Dr. Sherman and Nurse Wallace by the doorway, watching us.

What is the cop not telling you?

Maybe he's working with Sherman and Wallace. Trying to keep you from the mission! Stop you from finding the doctor!

I'm trying to stay calm, let the drift take me away, but the *voice* won't stop.

You're gonna need to force him to talk—

Shut up! I silently shout at *her*, then reach my hand across the table, toward the deputy. "Please. Tell."

The deputy's eyes come back to me and he nods. "To hell with them. You deserve to know," he says.

"Know what?"

"You've been lied to here," he says.

"No, no one here's lying to me . . ." I can feel my face growing hot, my thoughts prickly at his unwelcome news. My circuits are starting to overload. I don't want Dr. Sherman and Miss Wallace to see me all agitated like this, try hard to jam all that Officer Worthy's just said into a drawer.

But my drawers are too full. And now my head is filling with an awful high-pitched whine.

The deputy's still talking, I can see his lips moving—but all I can hear is *eeeeeee.*

CHAPTER 20

M Y HANDS.

Like nautilus shells, fists clenched in tight spirals that rest in my lap. Only the left will open. Use it to uncurl my right's frozen fingers, and now I see it—a bandage taped over my palm spotted with old brown blood. Did I fall again? Cut my hand?

"Heh . . . how did I get this? Was there a fight?" I ask the doctor. My words sound weak, raspy. Voice worn down to a whisper. Have I been screaming?

"Let's try not to get so worked up this time," he says.

And now my heart begins to race, fear rising like floodwater, threatening to engulf—

Something's happened. Something bad I can't remember.

I pull up the bandage and see letters cut into my skin. Wounds scabbed over. "Why're there letters—"

"Dorothy, please put the bandage back in place," the doctor says. But I need to look at the letters. Figure them out. Remember what's happened. "Dear, when I instruct you to do something, it's because that's what's best for your recovery. So you can go home with Paul. You want that, right?"

"Yes."

"Then you must cooperate every time, like we've talked about," he says. "Not just here with me now, but long after you've left this hospital, always doing what's asked of you by Paul and others in charge of your care. Trust that we know what's best for you and comply. Living outside of Hanover depends on it. Do you understand?"

I nod and feel the calm spreading through me like warm honey . . .

"Good," the doctor says. "Then say the words as best you can, dear. You remember the words?"

"Yes." I've repeated them for him many times. I close my eyes, say them slow to get it right. "Freedom depends on my cooperation."

"Very good. And again," he says.

"Freedom depends on my cooperation."

"One last time."

"Freedom depends on my cooperation."

"Excellent," he says, and picks up my file. It's thick now, my file. I must've been very sick . . . "The protocol's truly done a remarkable job breaking down those bad thought patterns in you these last few weeks." Breaking my thoughts? "Done it so well, in fact, that I've already been able to initiate your repatterning. Begun laying the foundation for healthier habits of thinking and behavior, along with instilling new interests in you that we'll strengthen and build on in phase three—"

"Interests?"

"Yes, a greater concern for things like hygiene, dress, and appearance, for cordial manners and the state of your household. A woman's enthusiasm for these things is a sign of her healthy engagement and connection with the real world."

My household? "I . . . I need Paul now. Please can I—"

"Soon, dear," he says, and squeezes my hand. "Once phase three is complete, Paul will take you home and help you with all those new ways of thinking and being, those new concerns of yours. Make them so strong in you they never go away. So you can be a new, sunnier, calmer Dorothy. Then you'll see just how much easier life can be."

"When I'm new? Th . . . that's not right—" I start to say, but the doctor's hand goes up, so I know to stop talking.

Miss Wallace is here. "Despite the recent upset, she's progressing well," he says to the nurse. "There's now a clear disruption of intellectual faculties—comprehension, learning, abstract reasoning. And a far greater level of compliance. It won't be long before she's at full regression and can begin stage three."

"The husband's still begging to visit," the nurse says as they look at me.

Paul is trying to see me.

"Nothing that man should witness," the doctor says. "I'll call later, reassure him."

The fear waters are rising up, about to choke me. "I want to go home now," I say. "Please, please let me go!"

"Dear, what do we do when we feel ourselves getting anxious?" the doctor asks.

"Focus on good?"

"Precisely, Dorothy! We don't linger on our bad feelings. Instead we focus on all the good in front of us, like seeing Paul soon and going home. Can you do that?" I nod and feel more calm filling me, forcing the fear down. "Good girl. Now let's continue. You were about to tell me about the voice in your head. About Bix . . ."

Thoughts that used to be just mine. Ones I sat shiva for. Never thought I'd give them up, but the *voice* is dead, and to become the best version of me, the one they'll set free, I need to share it all.

So I start.

* * *

"Come on, sweetie, open your mouth."

Nurse won't let me sleep. Wants to put more green soup in me. I'm her last patient to feed. The other moths are asleep, except Mary, staring blank across the circle.

The big lamp above me is sizzling again, flickering light bouncing off Nurse's big, shiny bowl. "Just a couple more spoonfuls of soup, then you can rest," Nurse says, "and I can go home, get ready for my date. Lord, let him be a decent kisser . . ."

She holds the spoon in front of my mouth. I shake my head, but she just waits till I remember about cooperation and freedom and open up.

"That's it, sweetie," she says, and slides the spoon up against my lip till soup dribbles warm and salty onto my tongue.

Feels like I'm almost there—that moment Alice said when you know you're changing . . .

"This time you need to swallow, like we talked about," Nurse says. "Can you do that?"

Swallow. Yes.

Now Nurse is smiling. "You did real good, sweetie. Just one more—"

But before there can be more, there's a CRASH somewhere. Nurse leaves her big bowl on the chair's fat arm and disappears.

Alone. I uncurl my fingers to look at the letters—but the bandage is gone. Letters too. Just a couple scabs left. I drop my useless hand— and it hits Nurse's bowl, flipping it into my lap. Now a pea soup river is flowing down my gray gown to my knees, spilling over the gap between them like a waterfall.

I feel the splashes hitting my ankles, see the green river running past my feet, heading for the lamp cord's sizzling silver wires like a Road Runner cartoon.

I know this cartoon is bad. Fatal even. But if I can just rest my eyes a little while, I know I'll come up with a plan to stop it—

But then something makes me forget the soup about to electrocute me like I'm Wile E. Coyote:

Mary Droesch, looking at me.

Really looking, face all alive—and angry.

Her eyes flick to the soup. To the buzzing cord. The sleeping moths. The door. Back to me.

"Goddammit," she says. No slur. No stutter. She pushes off her blanket and creeps over to me. Pulls out the towel Nurse has tucked in my collar and wipes the soup away from the sizzling wires.

Now her face isn't so angry. She wipes all the green off my chin, and I start to ask, "How'd you—"

But she pinches my arm hard. "Not a word, or you'll get us both killed." That's right, Mary's crazy like me. Put a man in the hospital, Betsy said.

Now there are voices in the hall. Getting louder.

Mary drops the towel by my feet. Gets under her blanket just before Nurse comes back.

"Dammit," Nurse says, and starts to clean.

I look over at Mary, full of things I want to know, but she's back to her stare.

CHAPTER 21

IN THE SLUMBER room tonight, the women breathing in and out don't pull me down to sleep.

I'm too excited about Mary and her secret in the next bed. When the night nurse sneaks off with her cigarettes, I whisper, "Mary. Mary." But Mary doesn't open her eyes. So I lean closer. "I know you're awake."

Mary's eyes flick open. "Shhhh!"

"Thanks for saving me."

She's frowning. "If I'd known you could still speak, I might not have . . . You need to keep your mouth shut. If they find out, it's dangerous for both of us."

"Why're you faking?" I ask.

"The less you know, the better. They're already suspicious. So stop talking. Go back to sleep."

"You're good at it. Faking," I say.

"You're still talking."

"Your stare. So real."

Mary leans close, looks at me. "Sherman's just about got you fully cooked, hasn't he? Just a few more days till you reach full regression, ready for reshaping. Do you even understand what I'm saying?"

She thinks *I'm* the gork. Pot, kettle, black. Can't let her think I'm the gork. "Yeah, and I'm getting better. Gonna see Paul soon—"

She laughs. "Not sure I'd put too much stock in Paul. Sure sounded like you had your doubts."

"Doubts?" I ask.

"Forget I mentioned it, which you will. All part of making you better, right? You'll forget all you've seen and heard come that first treatment Monday. Just need to keep quiet till then," she says, and closes her eyes.

"Tell me about Paul," I say, but she doesn't. "Tell!"

"Shhhh! If I do, you'll go back to sleep?" I nod. "The other day, for some reason they let you upstairs to see a visitor."

Now I remember. "Officer Worthy."

Mary nods. "Same sheriff's deputy who delivered me here. Local boy. Earnest, chock-full of integrity and principles." I shut my eyes tight, try to remember the officer's visit, but there's nothing. "When Wallace brought you back down here, you were yelling," Mary continues, "rattled about something the deputy told you about your husband. And, boy, were you desperate not to forget it."

"What?"

"That Paul lied to get you into the Unit."

"No. No, he wouldn't," I say.

Mary shrugs. "All I know is what I heard from my chair. You wouldn't say exactly what the lie was. When Gibbs heard the commotion and came into the dayroom, you begged her, of all people, to convince Sherman and Wallace to hold off on your next shock treatment till you could confront your husband, demand he get them to stop the protocol, transfer you out of here and into a regular ward. Of course that effort was doomed to fail."

"Stop the protocol? No, I need it."

"Not how you felt then. Or you'd never have written that painful little note to yourself," she says, and points to my hand.

I open it. Nothing there. "The letters?"

She nods. "Before they could take you for treatment, you got hold of a pen and started writing them on your palm: *P-L-I-E-B-A-B-T-W-M-A-N.* When the pen ran out halfway through, you were so desperate you carved the rest right into your hand."

Now I remember—the feeling of the pen cutting my skin. All the blood.

"What a mess you were," Mary continues. "As the nurses cleaned you up, they puzzled over what you'd written like it was the Sunday crossword. It took more than a few shocks before you forgot about the letters. Stopped pulling off the bandage, screaming till you were hoarse."

"Just gib . . . gib . . ."

"Gibberish?" she asks, and I nod. "Seems so—unless you wrote a 'b' when you meant a 'd.' Wouldn't be surprising, given the state you were already in. I think you intended to write P-L-I-E-D-A-B-T-W-M-A-N. Short for 'Paul lied about a woman.' Maybe a woman he had an affair with. It happens. My late husband lied about more than one. Maybe you found out, flipped your lid, and ended up here."

I shake my head. "No. Mind musta made it up."

"I'd think you'd place a little more faith in that sharper, smarter you of a week ago."

"Was sicker then." I tap my head. "A voice here made me think things. But she's dead now."

"Well, sometimes you need to trust that lunatic voice, 'cause she's the only one in your corner," Mary says. "No matter, after your first treatment Monday, a dimmer you won't even remember we had this conversation. But at least your faith in good ole Paul will be magically restored. As you happy protocolled ladies like to say, 'It's all for the best.'"

Witch. But right. Dimmer and dimmer I'll be. Did Officer Worthy really tell me Paul lied? Or did I imagine it? Like Betsy's transmitter in her head. Need them to stop shocking me till I remember. But they won't stop shocking till I'm cured—

And then I won't care what Officer Worthy said.

Mary's just a blur now behind my tears. "For Chrissakes, pull yourself together!" she hisses. "The nurse'll be back any minute."

Mary's too mean to be regressed. And smart. Must be a while since they stopped treating her. "How'd you make 'em stop shocking?" I ask.

"Nope." She shakes her head. "I've got my own problems. Can't be—"

"How?" I ask louder, and a couple moths start moving in their beds.

"Shhhh!" Mary says.

Hear the tunnel door opening—Nurse's coming back. "Now, or I tell Nurse."

Mary's eyes are angry slits. "You're too far gone to pull it off."

"Tell me. Please."

✳ ✳ ✳

"You sure you've got it down?" Mary asks. "You won't get a second chance tomorrow."

Two nights Mary's been teaching me during Nurse's smoke breaks. "Yes. Ready," I say.

Mary frowns. "If they find out you've been faking, you're right back here, only now you'll be under the care of a ticked-off Sherman, ready to shock even the slightest hint of doubt or rebellion right out of you. A reset. It's done all the time here. Alice was a reset."

"Alice?"

"Brought back by her husband when she 'relapsed,' which according to nurse gossip meant she caught him cheating again."

Poor Alice. Bill had them reshake her Etch A Sketch.

"You think the doctor or Paul will see my faking?"

"They won't have to—not if you tell them first."

"Me tell?"

She nods. "Through its brain-damaging regression and behavioral conditioning, Sherman's protocol etches into the minds of his subject new ways of thinking, of acting. And a temperament inclined to obey authority. That's the protocol's true purpose, to render difficult patients—defiant, mouthy women like Alice—more manageable, to the point they no longer question the rules or the rule *giver* of the institution—whether that institution is Hanover or their marriage. And with all that compliance comes a drive to confess all, then ask for forgiveness."

Like Betsy, wanting to apologize to Dr. Sherman for slicing up her face. "I won't."

"You sure? That programmed deference is hard to shake. Let's say you get your mind back and remember what was said during the deputy's visit. Do you think while still in that obedient state of mind you'll be able to summon the will to confront your husband about his lies?"

"*If* he lied. Yes."

She shakes her head. "Just promise me that if by some miracle you pull this off and they send you to the infirmary to recover, you won't rush into confronting Paul. Wait a few days, till you've recovered enough of your wits that you can handle yourself. Otherwise you'll just look paranoid, that voice in your head back running things. You need to tread lightly up there."

"I will."

"Let's hope so, for both our sakes," Mary says, lying back down in her bed.

"Mary, why fake? Why not take treatment. Get out?"

"Because I wasn't sent here for treatment," Mary says. "I was sent for interrogation. By the ones who *really* run this place. Government agents."

More Mary crazy. "You imagine," I say.

"Wish I did. Two spooks from some deep, dark pocket of the CIA are running the show using Sherman and his protocol to soften up their subjects. Most of their 'interviews' are conducted on 'patients'— more accurately, prisoners from the Men's Unit, but they made an exception in my case. They're pretty certain they've gotten all the information they can out of me—and it needs to stay that way," she says, looking all serious. "I've got to protect those caught up in this mess till my interrogators decide they're done with me."

"Who's caught up?" I ask.

"Never mind. I've already said too much. Those agents could easily have another go at you."

"Someone had a go?"

Mary nods. "They're convinced Soviet agents are trying to contact me here. So when you claimed hubby lied to get you into the Unit—that's when the agents shot you full of happy juice and dragged you off to room three for a little question-and-answer session. Your lying husband probably has no idea they even did it. That's how it works."

"No one shot me with juice," I say.

"Yes, they did. But apparently you told them you were sent from the future in a time machine on a mission so a doctor could help you get rid of someone called the Guest and save the world."

"Just my deh . . . deh . . ."

"Delusion?" she asks, and I nod. "The spooks agreed with you, decided pretty fast you weren't some trained Soviet operative subjecting yourself to brain damage in order to obtain government secrets from me. Just another protocol patient sure their doctor had all the answers."

More Mary crazy.

Just hope her plan works.

✳ ✳ ✳

Inside the green treatment room, there's a war going on in my mouth. Juice from the lemon Mary had me take off the nurse's teacup is mixing with the baking soda from the custodian's cart, and now the bubbles want out.

But I'm waiting for him. Dr. Sherman.

Finally, he comes in, and when he reaches for the switch, I start: grunt and gurgle, clench and twist, then roll my eyes back the way Mary coached.

"She's seizing. Keep her still," Dr. Sherman yells, but I'm off the table and onto the hard floor, thrashing and jerking round. When

Miss Wallace and Gus crouch down beside me, I make the choking noises, let the foam out the corners of my mouth and stiffen my arms and legs.

They turn me on my side and Wallace slips a blanket under my head. "I'll call the infirmary," Gus says. "Get Dr. Sackler."

"No need," Dr. Sherman says. "It'll be over soon."

The doctor kneels down next to me to take my pulse. Now comes the worst part: I push and push till I feel it—the warm wet flooding between my legs. Can smell the sour. Feels horrible. Mary's right, nothing a person would do on purpose.

"Dammit," Dr. Sherman says, so I know I soaked him. Good.

Now the clonic part. Begin to blink, shake. Tiring. Hope I keep it up long enough.

When the doctor opens my eyes, I keep them pointed down, away from his light. "Pupils are still equal, reactive."

Gus asks, "You sure we shouldn't call Doctor—"

"I said that's not necessary."

Miss Wallace puts her cold stethoscope on my jumpy chest, and I hardly breathe like Mary told me. "Breathing's shallow. Dorothy, wake up."

"Shouldn't be too much longer now," Dr. Sherman says. But I make sure it is much longer. Eventually I stop shaking, close my eyes and start the pretend-sleep part, hoping they'll think it's status epilepti-something and send me up to the infirmary. Mary said no opening eyes. No matter what.

Mary had lots of rules.

After a bit, Dr. Sherman pinches my arm hard but I don't move. "Dorothy, dear, I need you to—"

But before he can tell me what he needs, I start singing a song I must've learned a long time ago. Not out loud. Just in my head. Enough to block out his words. And it works. I don't hear what the doctor wants.

Soon lots of hands are picking me up, putting me back on the table.

"Twenty-three minutes of status epilepticus, Doctor," the nurse says, and I fight to keep my smile inside.

"I'm aware, Miss Wallace," says the doctor. "Get an IV drip of saline going and start her on thirty ccs Dilantin and sixty phenobarbital."

Someone wipes my arm. Then come the needle sticks and the drugs trying to flatten me, but I stay focused on the next part, what Mary called the waking but not really waking. I open my eyes but keep them blank on the ground.

Mary said staring at the floor wouldn't be so hard. She was right. Must be something I've been practicing a lot. Dr. Sherman takes my hand. His is cold and damp. "Dorothy, it's time for you to open your—"

But all I hear is my song:

> Wa saw the forty-second
> Wa saw, gone to war
> Wa saw the forty-second
> Marching through the brambles raw.
> Some the men got boots and stockings
> Some the men got none at all
> Some the men got boots and stockings
> Marching through the brambles raw.

The doctor drops my hand. "Get her to the infirmary and tell Dr. Sackler I said not to call the husband."

CHAPTER 22

DID IT.

Proved Mary wrong, fooled them all into bringing me up to the infirmary, pausing my treatment.

Has it been two days? Three? Not sure. My mind still feels cottony, not quite my own. But even with the antiseizure medication they're giving me through my IV, each hour I feel a little more awake. Sharper. I've already regained a memory from the Unit: being on the treatment table, Dr. Sherman and Nurse Wallace above me, discussing the beef stroganoff they just had for lunch as I'm prepped for ECT.

It won't be long before the memories of Officer Worthy's visit resurface. Then I'll learn the truth about Paul's lie — if there even was a lie. Could be I made up the deputy's words and Mary just overheard my babbling. I just need to keep fooling the doctors and nurses, lie very still behind these white curtains that separate us patients here, and wait. Don't hear much from the others. Most must be dying chronics nearing the end.

Mary warned this part's tricky, being more awake but still regressed. Said be careful. But so far I've kept my blank stare, eyes pointed down when Dr. Sackler and his kindly horse-faced nurse, Miss O'Brien, check on me. He's outside the curtain right now, dictating notes to her. ". . . Patient still minimally responsive after a prolonged grand mal seizure with status epilepticus. Extent of neurological damage yet to be determined."

Guess I'm still fooling them.

Dr. Sherman hasn't come by—and he hasn't let them call Paul. I'm relieved. Not yet up to deceiving my husband.

I can see the doctor's brown shoes under the curtains now. He's checking on my neighbor, the mouth breather in the next bed. "And how's she doing this evening?" he asks Miss O'Brien.

"She's stable."

"About the best we can hope for at this point. Another of Sherman's questionable outcomes. If he wasn't protected by his government work, I swear the man would've been shown the door by now. In a couple days she'll be ready for transfer."

"Yes, Doctor. I'll check with G- and H-Wards, see who can take her," she says as they leave.

Soon the night nurse comes on, turns down the lights, and goes back to her desk around the corner. Bedtime. But my woken-up mind's had enough of sleep and waiting.

It wants its body back.

I loosen my covers and start small, lifting my butt off the bed with my arms for a few seconds, then lowering it back down. Up, down, up, down, over and over, resting when I have to, then beginning again.

During one rest, I think I hear something. Listen for the night nurse, but there's nothing but the slow, thick breaths of my neighbor in the next bed.

And I get curious.

I swing my legs around, dangle them over the side of the bed. They're like sticks now, all shrunken. I carefully stand on them and catch my breath, let the sick feeling from my medicine sink back down. Listen again for the night nurse. Nothing. So, dragging my heavy IV pole behind me, I go to the curtain dividing us. Peer around it.

Even in the dim moonlight, I can see the twin shiners, both eyes swollen and bruised—it must've been some vicious fight my neighbor was caught up in. But then I notice her hair—uneven, chopped short with complete indifference. Like a sheared sheep.

Lobotomy.

I should turn away, leave the woman some privacy, but something draws me closer. Gets me to risk leaning over her, as far as my brown rubber IV tube will allow. Till I see it: the jagged line of stitches running down the far side of her face.

It's Betsy. Was Betsy.

So this is the more *traditional* route Alice said they'd take with her. The one to better address her *tendencies*.

There's a medicinal smell to Betsy now—like she's somehow been absorbed by Hanover, become part of it. But a part no longer useful, something vestigial, like an appendix or a tailbone. "Betsy," I say, squeezing her hand. But there's no response, only the steady in-out of her breath. How could Sherman do this to her? How could anyone think *this* was a solution?

My heart's pounding away, and the purple spots begin to float in front of me. I'm about to faint. Panicked, I clutch the IV pole for support. Not smart. It teeters above me, big glass bottle swinging back and forth like a lantern in a storm. But I somehow stop both of us from crashing to the ground. I freeze, letting the faint pass. Listening for sounds of the approaching night nurse as the bottle slows its careening.

I'm lucky. There are no sounds.

When I get back to my bed, I try to smooth out my breaths, my thoughts. But smooth doesn't come easy.

* * *

The voices wake me just past dawn. One is the night nurse, thanking the other for bringing her cigarettes. "No problem at all, Miss Jankowski. Had an extra pack and remembered you're a fellow Marlboro fan." I recognize the voice. Lester. "I've got a half hour till my shift, if you want to sneak away for a smoke. I'd be glad to watch the ward."

There is no work Lester is glad to do, so I wonder. The nurse must take him up on it. Her footsteps are getting fainter.

But Lester's are getting louder. Closer. Keep my eyes open? Closed? Open, I need to see, but pointed down.

He steps into my bay, draws the curtain closed behind him. The scent of his mouthwash and tobacco is overwhelming when he bends over me. "Hey, darlin', still trapped in never-never land, eh? That's okay. We'll make do."

He kisses me on the lips, then pulls the blanket down to my knees and slides in beside me.

Now I contemplate my choices.

If I fight him, I lose my gork status, sent back to the Unit before I can remember what Officer Worthy said that day. All of this for nothing. Worse, they figure out I'm a seizure faker and start to wonder about Mary.

And if I don't fight him?

Lester takes hold of my nightgown at the neck. Yanks it downward, and I feel the stitches popping at the shoulders, *thup, thup, thup*, as the seams give way. Next his other hand slides past his silver key ring to unzip his pants. His movements are smooth. Well practiced. Now the hand is drifting up my leg, drawing the gown with it—

But there's a noise.

A blessed noise—

The sound of a metal bucket crashing to the floor in the hallway, followed by the exasperated curses of Joe, the custodian.

"Son of a bitch," Lester mutters. He jumps up from the bed and yanks the covers back over me before slipping through the curtain and out into the hall. I can hear him berating Joe for his clumsiness as I lie very still in my bed and try to sweep these last minutes into one of my drawers.

But there's none big enough to hold what just happened, what almost happened. The tears just flow, and flow. Till I hear the footsteps of the night nurse back from her smoke—and realize I have a problem:

Gorks don't cry.

I've barely blotted my tears and shut my bloodshot eyes before she pokes her head in for a bed check. She must see something off, because she comes to my bedside and lifts the loose covers, revealing my torn-open nightgown.

There's a long pause before she gently straightens the gown, pulls up the covers, and tucks them back in extra tight.

CHAPTER 23

I STARE PLACIDLY AHEAD through the opening in my curtains while the kindly infirmary nurse, O'Brien, begins removing my IV. I'll be getting my antiseizure medication by injection from now on.

In the next bay, an attendant is helping Betsy up, escorting her to her new home in H-Ward. As the man walks her slowly past the curtain opening, I catch sight of the shiny metal key reel clipped to his belt loop—

And the image of Lester sliding a hand past his key reel to unzip his pants flashes through my mind.

I gasp and blink away the vision.

"Dorothy?" Miss O'Brien calls out to me—and before I can stop myself, I look up at her. The nurse smiles wide. "There she is. Sleeping Beauty's coming around!"

No! I can't be sent back to the Unit. Not yet.

But I've responded to her voice and there's no walking that back to full catatonic. All I can do is contain the damage from my slipup. Not let her think I'm fully recovered: I keep my gaze unfocused and say a slow and slurred, "Water. Please."

Staff spends the rest of the morning trying to rouse me more: slow walks around the ward, attempts to engage me in conversation. I give them just a few more words.

Sherman's still against informing Paul, but Dr. Sackler does it anyway, and my husband demands to see me immediately. A nurse's aide quickly readies me, brushing out my knotted hair and propping me up to sitting with pillows. Then she holds a mirror to my slack face. "See how pretty you look," she says.

A lie. But it sparks my first memory of that day the deputy visited: seeing my thin, powdery ghost reflection on the way upstairs with Miss Wallace. I'm getting closer; soon I'll remember what exactly Officer Worthy said—or didn't say.

I just need more time. And more wits—can feel the regression still permeating me, thickening my thoughts, weakening my will. I'm not ready to face Paul, but time's up: voices are approaching—Dr. Sherman's, Dr. Sackler's, and Paul's—and my heart starts to race.

"Dorothy, you have a visitor," Dr. Sackler says at the curtain as they enter my bay. I keep my eyes unfocused, a half-blank smile on my face. The doctors come alongside the bed, but Paul stays at the foot, watching me. What does he see? Can he tell I'm faking?

"Mr. Frasier, would you like some privacy?" Dr. Sackler asks.

Paul doesn't answer. Comes over and places a bouquet of flowers in the crook of my arm. I let my eyes float slowly down to them. Pink roses. Their beauty and scent are overwhelming after so much time underground. Feel a tear trying to escape.

"Your favorites," he says, and hugs me tight, but I stay still, like a sack of potatoes.

He sits down on the bed. "Dee?"

But I keep my eyes on the flowers.

"Understand, Mr. Frasier," Dr. Sherman says, "these transient symptoms from your wife's seizure are no reason to stop the protocol." No, no, no, no! "Admittedly, she appears a bit unexpressive right now, but it's been a tiring day for her. Earlier she was walking, speaking. There's been no indication she's sustained any permanent damage. Tests show normal reflex responses. Neurologically she appears to be fine."

"'Fine' might be overstating it," Dr. Sackler says.

But Dr. Sherman ignores him. "For the protocol to achieve its maximum effect, it's vital the patient be at full regression, absolutely pliant and receptive—"

"I think it wise not to talk about this here—" Dr. Sackler warns.

But Sherman keeps going. "Dorothy must depend solely on me to guide her through this process, like an impressionable child would a trusted authority figure," Dr. Sherman says to Paul. "She needs to be willing to do everything I ask of her."

Like a child? Jesus! I bite my cheek to keep myself still.

"Dr. Sherman," Sackler says, "we really should move this discussion . . ."

Paul ignores the fighting doctors, leans in close to me, and whispers, "I don't think I can do this without you, Dee. Please come back to me."

What could Officer Worthy have possibly said that would make me distrust this man, who speaks to his out-of-it wife like she's the most precious thing in the world?

Maybe he said nothing at all.

Maybe the *voice* made it up before the shocks got around to killing her.

"Dorothy," Dr. Sherman says, "tell us how you're doing today. Just a couple of words, dear. Go ahead."

But I fight the doctor's want, think only of my want: time. To clear my head. Remember the deputy's words.

And I'm fighting so hard I don't notice Paul's taken my hand—till he says in his husky voice, "I need you to do something for me, Dee, if you can. Just this one thing."

Then he gently uncurls my gnarled fingers, kisses them. Something's stirring inside me at his touch. Just not sure what that thing is. What am I feeling? "I need you to look up at me," Paul says. "Right now."

No! If I look at him, he'll see it in my eyes. But I can feel my husband's simple request, made out of both love and fear for me, beginning to tug at my frayed free will, attempting to unravel it, and I try to smother his want with my want like I did Dr. Sherman's.

Only this time Paul's desire trumps mine, quickly reaches the treated part of me—the part that knows what Paul's asking for is perfectly reasonable, that he deserves my acquiescence. My trust. After all, hasn't he suffered enough because of my disease?

This part of me is seriously considering Paul's request. No!

"Dee, do you hear me?" Paul asks.

I can do this. Keep my head down. Refuse to give in—

But it turns out the treated part of me has made a decision—and I begin lifting my chin one degree at a time.

Stop!

But I don't stop. Five degrees, ten, twenty, thirty, till there we are, face-to-face, and it takes all the focus I've got to keep my expression blank, eyes adrift. There's a moment where I wonder if he sees. Knows.

"Marvelous!" Dr. Sherman says. "That kind of compliance indicates she's quite close to full regression. At the point she's most open to change. All the more reason to get her back to the Unit."

No, that can't happen!

"There, away from the disruptive influence of other people, the repatterning of phase three can begin in earnest," Sherman says, "where, aided by medication and additional behavior modification techniques, I can deepen the new habits of thought, action, and belief I've already begun to establish in Dorothy. It's been days since her last ECT session. Any further delay in treatment would needlessly—"

Suddenly things get physical.

Paul jumps off the bed, comes after Dr. Sherman, roaring, "Are you out of your mind? After what your treatment's already done to her!"

Dr. Sackler steps between Paul and Dr. Sherman. "Gentlemen, outside!" he shouts, and ushers them away—

Leaving me alone to ponder my frightening discovery—that Mary was right. There's a part of me, the stronger part of me, that is utter clay, waiting to be molded by whoever's in charge.

Eager to be told the next thing to do. To be.

CHAPTER 24

'M GOING HOME.

I try to process the news as Miss O'Brien and the aide help me into my long-lost plaid dress and starched petticoat, along with my cardigan, socks, and loafers.

Paul raised holy hell with the doctors and Hanover's superintendent for irreparably harming his wife, threatened to go public with our story, and they agreed to get the forms signed by the court and release me to his custody as of this morning, December 21.

No more hiding behind the curtains in my infirmary bed, playing for time, hoping not to be sent back down to the Unit for more treatments. Paul's rescuing me from all that, from future Lester "visits," from Sherman's brutal protocol.

Free. So why aren't I happier? More relieved?

Because my rescuer is the person Officer Worthy might have said lied to me. But according to who? Mary? Some Unit paranoic who put a guy in the hospital?

And her source? Me, a maybe-recovering schizophrenic. Hardly a sure bet.

So I ignore my nerves as Gus walks me slowly down to the lobby, try to focus on the good right in front of me—I'm going home to familiar surroundings, where my memories will soon return like lost sheep, including the one I crave most: Officer Worthy's visit. Not a hint of it has returned yet.

Hanover's lobby is like nothing else in the hospital. Palatial. Filled with potted palms, velvet-covered chairs, and oriental carpets that feel soft under my feet. On the wall is a portrait of an old white man, probably the first of many to run this place.

"Morning, Dorothy," Miss Wallace says, walking up. She nods to Gus, and the attendant leaves.

"Good morning, ma'am," I say slowly, letting my flattened syllables slide into each other. Need my recovery from the seizure, not to mention my emergence from the protocol, slow enough to be believable. Protect Mary. Whatever her crazed reasons for faking her fugue state, they should be honored.

In the nurse's hands are my coat and a tiny manilla envelope with my name on it. "Aren't you lucky you get to go home in time for Christmas." She opens up the envelope. "The pennies from your loafers," she says. I remember a nurse confiscating them that first day in reception. "Put out your hand," she says, tilts the envelope, and the coins fall into my palm.

I slowly place them in my sweater pocket, then look up and swear I see Wallace eyeing me strangely, face even paler than usual. Does she know I'm faking my damage?

"Dee!" Paul shouts, coming through the big double doors, and as he runs toward me, grinning, I feel my stomach twist with nerves. He picks me up and swings me around, then gives me a kiss. Just on the cheek, but now I feel something thrumming through my body, overruling my anxiety.

Desire.

When he puts me back down, I say slowly, "Good morning, Paul."

"You *are* speaking!" he says, unbuttoning his gray wool coat. "That's . . . that's wonderful, Dee! They said you were . . . but I didn't believe—"

"As I tried to explain yesterday, Mr. Frasier," Dr. Sherman says, approaching the three of us, "protocol patients recover quite rapidly once the ECT is stopped." Paul glares at him and Sherman turns to me. "So nice to see you up and about, dear."

I keep my gaze hazy, sense the doctor's eyes still assessing me. "Thank you, Dr. Sherman."

He hands Paul some papers. I spot the words "Commutation of sentence" on the top one—and realize I can read again! My heart quietly soars as the doctor speaks to Paul: "Release forms for Dorothy signed by the court and myself. You'll need to present them at the gate."

Paul nods curtly and slips them into his coat pocket.

"And here are her prescriptions. To help keep things on an even keel," the doctor continues, handing him some small slips of paper. "May I have a word, Mr. Frasier?" he asks, then walks a dozen feet away and waits for Paul.

My husband frowns. "Be right back, Dee," he says, then joins the doctor.

I strain to hear snatches of the doctor's words to Paul as Wallace shakes out my coat. ". . . so for both your sakes, I urge you to continue the conditioning I've initiated with your wife . . . With the right reinforcement from you, those new beliefs and habits of thought in her, that new reluctance to act out or distrust, will strengthen and build till it becomes her new status quo . . . won't be long before Dorothy will cease to question her new inclinations, think about how she used to be . . . But without the right support from you, I fear she'll be back here within weeks—"

Paul mutters something I can't make out, and Sherman responds. ". . . and given you've cut her treatment short, it's unclear just where we stand in terms of her illness. Too much undue stress could precipitate a return of her symptoms." Is that true? Is my recovery that precarious? "So, you need to manage how much she's exposed to—"

"Dorothy, time to put your coat on," Wallace says, interrupting my eavesdropping. She holds it up and I spot a small rip at the elbow I'll need to sew. Must be from my tumble onto the pavement with Officer Worthy after he yanked me away from the speeding car. Almost six weeks since that day. The thought of all that time gone makes me almost queasy. But I push it down, slip my arms into the waiting coat, and watch as the nurse buttons it.

"Thank you, Miss Wallace," I say, and see that odd look in her eyes again. Maybe she *does* see through my act . . . Or maybe it's just paranoia still lingering in me that the protocol didn't have time to treat. But the nurse simply says, "Have a pleasant holiday, Dorothy," and walks away, off to impose her rule on other hapless patients.

I turn back to Sherman and Paul. ". . . so if something *serious* should come up, don't hesitate, call the sheriff's office. They're equipped to handle these situations—"

"She's clearly no threat to anyone, you've seen to that," Paul snaps at him, and walks back to me. Holds out his hand and smiles. "Ready to go, darling?"

I take his hand, and he walks me slowly away. At the door, I glance back at Dr. Sherman and his pursed lips. "Forget about him," my husband says, and holds the door open. Such a simple act, yet impossible without him.

I need to not forget that. Paul has forced them to release me into his custody, and as I walk out of here, I am in his hands. Loving hands, but all the same, his hands. He's my legal guardian, the one determining each day whether I belong outside of here. I need to be careful. Not give him any reason to doubt.

The snowfall last night has dusted the lawn in white, and the sunlight on it temporarily blinds me. I dip my eyes a moment, and when I look up, Paul's grinning. "If you'd like to stay . . ."

"No thanks." I smile, step outside into the bracing winter air, and am overcome with teary exhilaration and relief at my new-found freedom: I'm out of Hanover. And I'm never going back!

I slip my hand out of Paul's and head for the steps.

"Wait. Let me help you," he calls to me.

"No, I can do—"

"Dee, stop!" Paul shouts—

And I freeze without a second thought, or even a first. No thought, just the knee-jerk, obedient response etched into my mind by the doctor's shocks. Has the protocol merely substituted the *voice's* commands for Paul's?

I turn back to Paul, feeling a mix of shame, irritation, and unease at my latest act of compliance.

He walks up, holds out his hand, and I take it. "Look, adjusting to what's out there," he says, sweeping his arm across the horizon, "a world, a life that, for now, you largely don't remember, is going to be difficult—especially with you still recovering from the protocol. We need to be smart. You understand?"

No. But I don't want to argue. Just want to get as far from Hanover as I can. So, I say yes, and we walk slowly down the long steps.

Once we reach the car, Paul looks back at the hospital, then at me. "I didn't know, Dee . . . What was happening to you in Sherman's Unit. I thought I'd be allowed to see you. But Sherman refused. Said visits were 'detrimental to the protocol' and I'd be invalidating the terms of our agreement if I saw you before it was finished . . . I should never have trusted the guy."

"*We* should never," I say. "I trusted, too."

CHAPTER 25

Our Pontiac Chieftain glides like a gentle blue beast down Hanover's driveway—the same one the deputy tackled me on that icy day in November.

Officer Worthy. What did he tell me in the visitors' room about Paul? About our marriage. Maybe nothing. Maybe my disease invented his words. It could be he never even visited me at all. I just wanted him to.

I open up the little triangle window on the car door, let the fresh air wash over my face as we turn and head north. It's time to start getting answers.

"Tell me 'bout you. That," I say to Paul, pointing to the tattoo peeking out from the cuff of his jacket.

He pulls it up, revealing an anchor on his wrist. "This? From my stint in the navy. I'm from Michigan originally. Saginaw. After I left the service, I took a sales position with Apex Pens covering Maryland and northern Virginia. Not very glamorous, but with my salary and a small inheritance from my parents, we're quite comfortable."

"We met how?" I ask.

"On a train to Philly. Thought you were the most beautiful girl I'd ever seen," he says, and I see in his eyes that he's serious. "Wasn't long before I knew I wanted to spend the rest of my life with you."

I wonder if he still feels that way—this is probably not been quite the life he pictured spending with me. "My parents?" I ask.

"Sorry, hun, your mother died when you were a teenager. Cancer. And your father passed from a heart attack soon after we were married."

Dead parents. It feels sad but correct. "Brothers? Sisters?"

He shakes his head. No siblings. Feels like someone's robbed me. Paul's my only family. "Where do we live?"

"On the outskirts of Littleford, not too far from here. Moved there a few weeks before . . . before you went to Hanover."

I continue to question him in my slurry drawl as we head up Route 15. The scenery grows more and more rural, till we finally turn onto a narrow dirt road called Birchwood Lane.

"It's just the Clarks and us on this road," Paul says.

A half mile in, trees give way to hilly pastures. When we pass a driveway leading up to a house, a barn, and a green truck, Paul says, "That's the Clarks' place. I think they're in Florida right now."

Down the road a half click, we come to another driveway. "This is ours," he says, and turns into it.

Home. Will there be magic like Paul says, here among my treasured belongings? Enough to start that cascade of memories I've been waiting for? God, I hope so.

Through the trees, I spot a large log cabin–style house with a big front porch and two dormer windows above.

It's not the slightest bit familiar. A big fat zero of recognition. How can *nothing* about this house stir a memory? Paul sees my disappointment. "You were only here a short time. Maybe that's why it doesn't ring a bell. But your belongings inside—I'm sure they'll begin to spark something."

At the front door he asks, "Ready?"

"Yes," I say, and he opens it.

Inside is an entrance hall whose wood floor gleams. There's a staircase and rooms off to either side. I recognize none of it. Wander toward the half-open door to my right and see a telephone on a desk.

As I approach the door, a beautiful woman emerges from it.

She resembles the ham-lung woman on TV: flawless makeup, pert breasts, a tiny waist, and short, perfectly coiffed hair.

"Dee, this is Eloise. She's a trained nurse, not to mention an excellent cook and housekeeper. She'll be helping us out for a little while, staying in the study."

Eloise smiles. "It's lovely to meet you, Mrs. Frasier."

She's the first person outside Hanover who's spoken to me, and I'm feeling extra timid. Or is it frightened? The protocol seems to have rewired my comfort for conversations with strangers, made me self-conscious. I nod but say nothing, and it's up to Paul to break the awkward silence. "This way, darling," he says, and walks into the large living room to the left. Before following him, I glance back and see Eloise pulling a key from her pocket and locking the door to the study—with its telephone—up tight.

I can't be trusted near a phone—which I understand. I don't trust me either.

In the living room, a lovely sofa and chairs are arranged in front of a brick fireplace where a couple logs burn brightly. Above the mantel is a painting of a four-masted schooner caught in a storm. I walk slowly around the room, taking in details, scanning for the familiar but find none. I can sense Paul and Eloise behind me, my watchful pit crew, alert for any signs of trouble or upset.

I wander over to some bookshelves nearby, where I see a slew of cookbooks. I guess that gelatinous dessert in the photo Paul showed me at Hanover wasn't my only culinary endeavor. But nothing about Betty Crocker and Fanny Farmer is ringing a bell. The shelf below them contains novels. I pull a couple out: Hemingway's *For Whom the Bell Tolls* and *The Old Man and the Sea*. "Hemingway's your favorite, but Virginia Woolf runs a close second," Paul says, holding up *Orlando*. I know these books, but there's no personal memory anchoring me to that knowing.

On the top shelf are several trophies of women in skirts releasing bowling balls. I start to reach for one and Paul says, "Careful, Dee.

Here, let me get it," and he pulls it down for me. Its brass plaque reads: "1951 Northern Virginia League, Ladies Under 25, Second Place, Mrs. Dorothy Frasier."

"Only second place?" I ask with a grin, and Paul smiles.

I walk over to some framed photos nearby. Two are familiar. Paul showed them to me in Dr. Sherman's office. But two I haven't seen: a shot of a smiling older couple and another of the same couple younger, on their wedding day. "Your parents," Paul says, handing me the picture and looking at me expectantly. I feel no hint of recognition or love for these ghost parents of mine. They are strangers. But Paul's undaunted, points to the last photo, this one of a pudgy infant. "And this one is you," he says.

"Chubby baby."

"Evidently your mother liked you well-fed," he says, and we both laugh.

"More?" I ask, scanning the room for additional photos.

"How about first I show you the rest of the house?" he says, and we go up the stairs. At the top, I head toward a door on the right. "That's just a spare bedroom we use for storage. Our bedroom's this way," he says, and leads me down the hall. Strange to be guided through my own house like a tourist. But I'm grateful he's here, helping me with this transition from inhabitant of Sherman's Unit netherworld to normal person.

Paul stands just inside our bedroom. "I'll be sleeping down the hall, give you your space," he says, and I wonder if that's the state of us. We sleep apart, our marriage less about passion than obligation, Paul wanting to do the right thing. Maybe those sexual feelings we had for each other in my true north memory are long gone—at least on his part. Could Mary's guess have been right? That Paul had an affair and when I found out about it, I had a breakdown? Was that the lie that led to my time in the Unit?

I pivot away from my dark thoughts, stop borrowing trouble, and wander past one of the dormer windows to a chest of drawers, picking up various objects: a porcelain cat, a wooden box, an embroidered pillow, touching each like some Vegas psychic, hoping for a hit.

But nothing. No cascade of recall.

Maybe those memories of life before Hanover are gone, wiped out by disease or the protocol's electroshock. And maybe the same is true for the memories of Officer Worthy's visit. It could be I'll never remember what he said about Paul that day.

"Just give it some time, Dee. It's all gonna come back, now that you're home, you'll see," Paul says, putting his arm around my shoulders, and in his warm embrace I feel a certain sense of safety. But not fully, 'cause there's a shadow lurking at its fringes: that question about Paul's possible dishonesty—I'm going to need a plan B.

"How about you freshen up and then we'll make plans?" he says.

"Freshen up?"

"You know, shower. Clean clothes," Paul says, eyeing my plaid dress.

I peer down at it and see what I somehow hadn't before: the unsightly stains, the hem pulling out. The dress I wanted so badly to keep in the Unit, and only recently regained, is looking a little forlorn. And possibly smelling a bit ripe. It's embarrassing to think I've been in front of people looking so disheveled.

"Good idea?" Paul asks. It *is* a good idea that just didn't occur to me. I've a feeling a lot of things about living outside Hanover, things like freshening up, might not occur to me—and realize for the first time just how much I will need Paul to help me navigate my way back to this world. It's unsettling; that kind of dependence makes my stomach churn. But it's temporary, just till I get used to this life in the real world.

* * *

After the shower, I towel dry my hair and emerge in my bathrobe from the bathroom—and find my old clothes gone. On the bed are new ones: stockings, a skirt, and a white bra whose cups are so pointy they could take out an eye if someone's not careful. Next to it lies something resembling a jellyfish: a white crotchless panty-type item from which dangle ties that each end in a little metal jaw.

"Mrs. Frasier." I jump and turn to find Eloise holding a couple of powder-blue sweaters. "So sorry to scare you. Mr. Frasier thought you might want some assistance, so I took the liberty of laying out some clothes for you. Would you like some help?"

Dr. Sherman said that caring about my appearance was a sign of mental health, of a connection to the world. I want that. To feel connected. Normal. "Yes, please, Eloise."

"Let's start with the bra. The one you had on was doing nothing for you. Let's try this one." Not quite sure what exactly my bra has not "done" for me but trust that Eloise knows, so I stand still while she puts the new one on me, then bend to *pour* my breasts into the cups as instructed. "Next we'll do the garter belt," she says, picking up the jellyfish, and quickly wrangles me into the thing, using its metal jaws to secure the slippery stockings I've coaxed up my legs. Paired with the twin-peaked white bra, I'm now looking virginal but racy, just like the women in those magazine ads in A-Ward's dayroom.

Eloise helps me pull the sweater set and a narrow skirt over the undergarments, and now my pointy powder-blue breasts stand out like heralds, proudly proclaiming the arrival of the rest of my body. Next she helps me into a pair of shoes with heels and says, "Come," before starting for the bathroom. I attempt to follow, but the heels and narrow skirt are conspiring to hobble me. "You need to take small steps, Mrs. Frasier, and use your hips," she coaches, making an exaggerated wiggling motion to illustrate.

It takes a few tries but I finally get the hang of it and reach the bathroom, where the nurse applies my cosmetics: foundation, rouge, mascara, and eyeliner. It's a revelation, the makeup, like assuming a new identity.

Eloise hands me the lipstick, and I attempt it, but there's absolutely no muscle memory there. Have I gone lipstick-less my whole life? Sad. Eloise intercedes and expertly applies it, then takes on my hair, curling it with an iron, then whipping it up into a ponytail on the crown of my head that cascades down my back in shiny reddish-brown waves.

I look in the mirror at the polished woman standing before me — and feel a deep sense of satisfaction, possibly even pride, from having achieved this semblance of normal.

Then I remember another reflection — in the glass on the way to my visit with Officer Worthy weeks ago. The pale, slack-jawed ghost with the too-big eyes. And I wonder which one's the real me — the ghost or the polished woman.

Or if there is a real me left.

Tears are beginning to well up in my eyes but I manage to shut them down before Eloise sees. "Beautiful. Thank you, Eloise," I tell her, and we head for the stairs.

Paul gazes up at me as I carefully descend the steps. "Dee, you look . . . amazing," he says, and I feel that pride wafting up again inside me. "You must be getting hungry. I was thinking Eckert's soda fountain for lunch. How does that sound?"

"Fountain? Of soda?"

"You know, a place you go for hamburgers, fries."

Sounds fantastic. Every taste bud in my mouth is screaming with me, "Yes, please!"

"Great," he says, grabbing our coats.

But Eloise doesn't look happy. "Mr. Frasier, I'm worried it's going to be too much for her first day, that she's simply not ready for it. All the strangers and stimulation after . . . you know," the nurse says to him.

"Oh, it'll be fine, Eloise," he says, winking to me and opening the front door.

"But she hasn't had time to get her bearings, adjust to her life here."

He ignores her. "Shall we, Dee?" he asks, then takes my hand, and we slip out the front door, into the cold, bracing air, laughing like coconspirators making our second jailbreak of the day.

CHAPTER 26

T HE TOWN OF Littleford is a living snow globe. Giant snowflakes hug each lamppost, trailing tinselly arches that stretch between them. Bundled-up townsfolk walk its freshly shoveled sidewalks, balancing boxes and bags of holiday purchases, their excited, red-cheeked children in tow.

Unfortunately, none of this charming town is familiar to me.

Paul is careful to match my slow pace as we walk through the crowds, past shops all decorated in garlands and red bows, their front windows painted with wintry scenes of snowmen and holly. At the corner we pass a man in a Santa suit standing next to a red bucket, ringing a bell, then walk under two reindeer pulling the sleigh of another Santa high above us. "The town Kiwanis sure went all out with the decorations," he says. Whatever town Kiwanis are, they definitely have gone all out.

It's all so beautiful, this world. And I'm free to go where I want, when I want, in it. No waiting on doctors, nurses, attendants, or the *voice* to tell me what's permitted. All I've endured since waking on the bus has been to reach this moment of autonomy—

Yet I can't imagine ever feeling a part of it, in my past or my future.

I'd thought that if I could just be free of Hanover, reach the outside world, things wouldn't seem so *off* to me. That I'd feel more like I belong. But my sense of disconnect is only stronger here on the outside, the gulf between me and these rosy-cheeked, well-fed pedestrians far greater than any between me and my fellow unfortunates in the Unit.

Sherman told me that the feeling of not being in the right place was part of my disease, but unlike the *voice*, it was something the protocol couldn't get rid of. But it's time to shake off my dour thoughts, look only for the good in front of me till I forge a connection to this life in the real world.

Two boys in bushy-tailed fur hats tear past us, laughing. They're heading toward a giant Christmas tree in the town square. I stop a moment to appreciate the tree, the goofy boys, and my liberty. All the good. Only as I gaze at the tree, two words float to the surface of my mind: the Guest. And I see that make-believe memory, the one I conjured on my way to see Officer Worthy in the visitors' room that day—

> Standing in the living room, by a fragrant Christmas tree, unopened presents piled beneath it. Nat King Cole plays on the stereo.
>
> But in the background, there's a quavering voice. My mother's voice.
>
> I look across the front hall to her study. On her desk a laptop plays some choppy video footage in lurid colors. I can hear her talking on her cell phone. And crying. The great gasping sob sort of crying, where your breath shudders from you for hours afterward.
>
> Now there's a sound of sirens in the distance, growing louder, beginning to overtake Nat's beautiful singing and my mother's sobs. Something whizzes past our front window—

And like that, the vision is gone, leaving me with a residue of alarm, a racing heart, and a familiar nagging feeling in the pit of my stomach that there's something important I should be doing.

The Guest, laptop, cell phone—my made-up things. Nothing I can share with Paul. I squeeze my Latin medal tight, willing this moment of panic to pass.

"The tree's sure something, isn't it?" Paul asks.

I manage a smile and a slurred, "It's so beautiful," and we continue slowly down the sidewalk, passing a butcher's and a toy store before Paul pauses at the window of a cheese shop.

Up ahead is a storefront painted with words I can once again read: MAE'S LUNCHEONETTE in gold. A smartly dressed Black woman, loaded down with shopping bags, stands by its front door, keeping warm by deftly rocking back and forth in her pumps, heel to toe, toe to heel. I try the motion and nearly fall over. I'll need more practice to master advanced moves like that.

Two pale women exit the luncheonette and hug goodbye before splitting up. One passes us, accompanied by the Black woman toting the bags. As we pass the restaurant's window, I spot in smaller letters: WE CATER TO WHITE TRADE ONLY. I stop. Check it again to be sure.

Segregation, right there in fancy gold writing. Alive and well. Jesus.

Countless things feel not quite right about this world: its big, curvy cars, garter belts, giant typewriters. But those are just objects — neutral on the moral relativity scale. Segregation's a whole other thing, a giant festering sore of evil, knocking over the scale and turning my stomach.

But my disquiet doesn't just stem from its wrongness. There's a far more selfish reason running through my unease — my belief segregation doesn't fit in my world, this world, is yet another sign I remain disconnected from it. Untethered. Unwell.

I try to keep my face from revealing all the churn inside me, but Paul sees. Looks down at the writing. "It seems wrong to you because it *is* wrong," he says. "And you're not alone. I feel that way, lots of others do, too. The world just hasn't caught up. Feeling it shouldn't still exist doesn't make you crazy. Okay?"

Once again, Paul has read my mind, managed to say just the right thing at just the right moment, his words a balm for my raw emotions. His tender support feels good after so long alone in the dark.

So, naturally, the tears come. Fucking tears.

Paul puts his arm around my shoulders, enveloping me in the warmth of his long wool coat, and I want to relax, let in the feeling of security that's trying to embrace me as well. Only the doubt still lingering at its edges won't let me.

Paul hands me his handkerchief, and I dab my eyes to keep the mascara from running as he continues. "But, Dee, there's plenty about this world that isn't messed up, that is, in fact, incredible. Paris. Rome. The Greek isles. And we can travel there, discover it together, you and I."

Then he hugs me tight, and I feel so understood, so loved—

And so desperate to confess.

Tell him everything: how I suspected he was lying to me because of what the deputy might have said and how I faked my seizure with Mary's help so I'd recall what Officer Worthy told me about him.

Mary said I might tell on myself, divulge my misdeeds to Paul. I thought it was more Mary paranoia, but here I am, on the verge of spilling my guts and risking my freedom before I've even been home a day.

"Something you want to say, Dee?"

All I've done can't have been for nothing. So I stuff down my need to divulge and atone, shake my head, and we continue walking till we come to a thicket of Christmas trees, each mounted on a wood cross, lining the wide sidewalk in front of a hardware store and spilling out into the street. The smell of evergreen is everywhere, intoxicating, overwhelming.

And those two unsettling words again rise up from my unconscious: "the Guest."

A cocktail of dread, panic, and guilt again pours through me, knees going soft, stomach knitting itself into an afghan. I can't let Paul think I can be undone by a stand of Douglas firs, so I turn away from them, toward the hardware store.

Everything from hammers to saws to snow shovels hangs in its front window. I spot a couple rifles mounted on the pegboard wall and draw close for a better look. Both are Remington .22 caliber, single shot, bolt action. Next to them is a poster of a boy happily holding a similar rifle. Below the picture are the words: "Christmas lasts a lifetime when it's a Remington .22."

"Damn," says Paul, looking at his watch. "Forgot to pick up my navy suit from the cleaners, and Olson's closing early today. Taking his wife to Bermuda for the holidays. I was planning on wearing it to church on Christmas."

"Go. Get it. I'm fine," I say.

But he hesitates. "You sure?" he asks, his hazel eyes meeting mine. "You'll stay right here till I come back?" I nod. "It's important you not move from this spot. You understand?" He's looking at me like I might wander off with the first stranger with candy who comes along.

I roll my eyes. "Not a child. Go."

He nods. "Okay. I won't be more than five minutes." Then he jogs off through the Christmas trees and darts across the street. Those trees. Definitely a trigger I should avoid. Likely to bring on another made-up memory.

But if it's not real, why be afraid?

So instead of turning away, I step into the mini forest, breathing in the amazing pine air, till the vision returns—

I'm back in the living room, Nat King Cole singing of chestnuts roasting while my mother wails in the next room.

I see the blur whizz by outside and go to the window. It's a drone, circling back around as sirens get louder, and flashing lights appear up the street. The drone slows as it approaches the window, then hovers a few feet off the ground, bobbing up and down slightly like an overexcited puppy—

Then it's over, and I'm again left with the sickening sense I should be doing *something* that I am not.

And drones now. Awesome.

I turn back to the hardware store, trying to shake the feeling of imminent threat now roosting in my belly.

What I need is a distraction. Spot a flyer taped to a pane of glass on the store's front door and take a look: "Know you're safe with a Wooster Fallout Shelter." Below the words is a shot of a mother and her two children running for a large hatch in their yard, smiles on their faces, not much concerned nuclear winter's just around the corner.

As I ponder the oddness of this, a man exits the hardware store. He holds the door for me, but I stay where I am. "Come on now, honey, I won't bite," he says, winking. I don't feel like explaining to this stranger that I'm waiting dutifully for my husband, so I enter the store. The place smells of blood meal, oil paint, and kerosene. The man calls to me, "What? Not even a smile for my efforts, sweetheart?"

Smiles, the currency of assholes. I slip down an aisle to evade him, intending to turn back around once he's gone.

But I don't. Because something's caught my eye.

I head past shelves of garden tools and cans with labels like DDT and CREOSOTE till I reach the back of the store, where a sign hangs high above a long counter. It reads GUNS.

Below the sign, an old guy in rolled-up shirtsleeves, suspenders, and a tie is showing a customer an electric drill. Behind him, next to the fishing poles, is an impressive rack of rifles housed in a locked wire mesh display.

But by the time I reach the counter, something else has claimed my attention: a glass case containing pocketknives of various types — flip, hunting, switchblade. They're all closed, blades safely nestled in their hiding places. In the center of the display lies its star: a balisong knife.

The man in suspenders comes over. "Good afternoon, ma'am. See you've got your eye on the balisong. Very fine workmanship. Would you like to take a closer look?"

Another stranger and I'm again rendered speechless. I nod.

"Let me guess, Christmas gift for the husband?" He unlocks the display's glass door and pulls it out. "Also called a butterfly knife. Comes from the Philippines. This one's a real beaut," he says, and hands the folded knife to me.

"Arthur," the customer at the end of the counter calls to the salesman, "where's the hex key for this drill?"

"Be right there, Frank," the salesman says, and turns to me. "Now be careful, ma'am. It's very sharp. Takes a fair bit of training to handle one safely. Wouldn't want you to get hurt."

Then he walks back over to the other customer.

He's right, it's a nice one. The two brass-tipped wooden handles are inlaid with bone. I take it in my left hand, between my thumb and index finger, bite handle containing the latch end facing outward. Flick the latch off, uncurl my fingers, and let the handle drop.

The blade emerges cleanly. It's sharp, single-edged, decent stainless from the looks of it. I curl my fingers around the safe handle and flip the knife upward, swinging the bite handle around till the tang pin locks the blade in the open position. I wrap my thumb around it to feel its balance.

"Ma'am. Ma'am, you want to be careful . . ."

I'm vaguely aware of the man's warnings as I flip the thing around, handles and razor-sharp blade flying around my skillful fingers in a burst of shiny, autonomic action, my hands performing motions they must've repeated often enough in my forgotten past to achieve bloodless mastery. Was this a skill I picked up in my delusional wanderings?

When I pause I find the men staring, slack-jawed.

I flip the knife shut. I should head back outside. Paul will be back soon—

But the salesman approaches. "I didn't want you to get hurt, but it seems you have things well in hand," he says, and laughs. "So you've some experience with a balisong. Where did you ever learn to handle one? Bet that's a good story—"

"Dorothy, there you are!" It's Paul, breathless, eyeing the balisong in my hands. "I've been looking all over for you. You gave me such a scare."

I want to defend my actions, but I don't want to explain I ended up in this store, looking at knives, because I was trying to get away from a stand of Christmas trees.

Paul takes the knife from me and hands it to the salesman. "Hello, Arthur."

"So, this is your lovely wife, Mr. Frasier." The man turns to me. "Arthur Morris. So pleased to meet you, Dorothy." Arthur's smiling with that hint of pity and sweetness I've come to know well—Paul has told him about me and my *difficulties*. Have all the locals been apprised? Was there a town meeting around the cracker barrel?

"Dee, Arthur's the owner of this store," Paul says.

I so want to say to Arthur "Pleased to meet you," clearly and crisply, show him I'm fine, but that's not an option. So I say a slurry and flat, "Nice t'meet you, Arthur," and he smiles again.

"Darling, why don't we let Mr. Morris get back to his customer, and you and I go get that lunch I promised you," Paul says, then waves goodbye to Arthur and silently walks down the aisle with me.

"Your suit?" I ask.

"Closed already" is all he says.

Outside on the sidewalk, amid the holiday shoppers, I feel compelled to explain: "Just wanted to see the knife." I know saying I was only browsing the weapons sounds hinky, given my psychological history, but it's the truth . . . At least, I'm pretty sure it's the truth.

Paul looks at me long and hard. "This is my fault," he says. "I didn't think to make sure you understood the ground rules. Grasped the stakes." Ground rules? Stakes? What is he talking about? "I just assumed you'd stay where I left you . . . God, when I didn't see you . . ."

Part of me feels awful to have worried this man yet again. Made him wonder one more time when he would be getting that call from the local sheriff's department or mental ward. But another part of me is thinking, Get over it, Paul, roll with the punches.

That's the part that says to my husband, "Not a big deal."

Paul stops walking and turns to me, face suddenly grim. "Dee, you want to live your life outside, free, not in an institution like Hanover, right?"

"Of course, I just—"

"Then you need to take this more seriously, respect my concern. My experience with all of this. With you . . . The two of us have got to work together," Paul says, his voice ticking up a notch. "Do you understand why that's so important?" Pedestrians are glancing at us as they pass by—and I wonder how many painfully public discussions like this Paul has had to have with his wife in the past. I look at the man, guilt sluicing through me. "If we don't work together and agree to some basic ground rules like always making sure I know where you are—"

"Always? That's ridiculous."

"Without your cooperation," he says, his voice rising even further, "we could have problems I won't be able to solve. You could lose your freedom, end up back in the hospital."

For a moment I think about what that would be like, to be returned to Hanover, the slow-burn horror and humiliation of being stripped down, inspected, deloused, then locked away in some down-alphabet ward. And the phrase just spills out of me, unbidden: "Freedom depends on my cooperation."

There's something oddly familiar about my words.

But they're the right words, and just like that it's over. Paul smiles, and it feels like storm clouds lifting. "Yes, Dee, that's exactly what I mean," he says, and I feel this intense rush of relief at his appeasement. To be back in the fold, forgiven. God, it's almost joy rocketing through me, and I hate myself for it as we walk to Eckert's soda fountain.

CHAPTER 27

A LL THAT'S LEFT of my sundae at Eckert's is the bright red cherry. I pick it up, and Paul warns, "I wouldn't. They're nasty." I frown at him. "But I believe I've bossed you around enough today, so I'll be quiet."

"That's better," I say, and bite into the cherry. Immediately, I regret my decision. The thing has the consistency of a rotting, sticky eyeball, and I gag.

Paul bursts into laughter, and when I can't help joining him—right in that moment—I think I could make this work, this wonderful life right in front of me with Paul, our home. Maybe I could even get a job. Gradually those nagging feelings of doubt and disconnect would lessen, till finally they disappeared altogether.

But first, plan B.

I scan Eckert's and spot a sign over a doorway at the back of the store near a kid restocking napkins: RESTROOMS AND TELEPHONES.

"Bathroom," I tell Paul, gesturing to the sign, and start to stand. He rises, too, but I put my hand up. "No. Myself."

"Okay, honey," he says. I sense a little concern in his voice, but he sits back down, and I slowly make my way to the hallway. But once inside it, I bypass the ladies' room and head for the telephone booth at the end of the hall. "Booth" is the wrong word. It's a whole tiny room lined with dark wood paneling. Inside, a man is rising from its bench. He hangs up the phone and exits the booth, giving me a lingering once-over and a tip of the hat as he walks past—a credit to Eloise's makeover efforts and my tight sweater.

I slip into the booth and skip the phone, going straight to a brown book on its shelf: *Directory of Subscribers. Culpeper, Bixby, and Hanover, VA.* Mary said the sheriff's deputy was a local boy. I flip through whole chunks of pages as fast as my fingers will go, trampling through the alphabet till I get to the W's. There, at the bottom of a page, I find it, Officer Worthy's address and phone number: *Worthy, Thomas R., 14 Foxtail Ln. . . . Bixby 4–5733.*

But then I hear Paul talking to the kid restocking. He's seconds from the hallway. I rip out the bottom of the page, slam the book shut, and bolt. Barely manage to stuff the scrap in my bra and reach the ladies' room door before Paul appears.

"There you are." Paul's talking to me, but his eyes are taking in everything, including the phone directory, now on the floor. He holds his hand out, and I take it. "You all right?"

"Tired," I say. It's true. I'm exhausted.

"Don't you dare tell Eloise she was right, that I've run you ragged," he says, smiling. "Let's get you home."

* * *

Eloise has her arms crossed when we come through the front door. "Dorothy's going to take a little nap," Paul says to her, and the judgy look on her face ratchets up a notch.

In the bedroom, while Paul folds the covers back, I quietly stash the stolen scrap of phone book in the bottom of my lingerie drawer and kick off my shoes. I'm struggling with the fastener in the back of my skirt when he comes up behind me and unhooks it, giving the zipper a slight tug to start it for me.

His hands rise to my shoulders, and he speaks softly by my ear. "So good to have you home, Dee." The vibration of his words travels down the little hairs on my neck like they're telegraph wires. "I'll let you get some rest now," he says, and turns to walk away, but I grab his arm. He looks at me, head cocked in question, and I pull him closer, till our lips brush against each other, then kiss him.

And there in the kiss is all the recognizable and real that have eluded me today.

A thrill begins working its way through my body, down paths it's well-acquainted with.

I know sexual attraction shouldn't be the bedrock of a marriage, but what I feel when he touches me is certain, quantifiable. It promises nothing more than itself. And in a world where I'm surrounded by the unknown, its simple, strong, and familiar declaration is a welcome thing.

My lips travel up to the single freckle on Paul's left cheek.

I know this freckle well. More than I know this man.

So this freckle and the rest of my husband's body—that is where I will start my rediscovery of Paul. Grow back my knowledge of him. Of us. It's as good a place to start as any.

My lips begin to explore his face, his neck, seeking out other landmarks. His do the same. But when I start to unbuckle his belt, he stops me. Looks me soberly in the eye. "I'm not sure we should be doing this so soon—"

I kiss him to silence his sensible words while my hands work his buckle open, get his zipper down. He breaks off the kiss long enough to ask once more, "Are you sure?" before I push him onto the bed.

* * *

Eloise has been instructed to fatten me up and has cooked accordingly: roast beef covered in gravy, creamed spinach, and roasted potatoes. And for dessert, a slice of heavenly chocolate cake, which I cannot inhale fast enough.

But when Eloise takes our plates and disappears through the swinging door into the kitchen, I turn to Paul. "When can she go?"

"You can ask that after eating this cake? Have you ever tasted anything so delicious in your life?" he asks, grinning. I do not grin back. Just wait for his answer. "Soon, assuming things go smoothly, and we get you settled. Give it a few days."

"I'm fine. Don't need a nurse. You're treating me like a child," I say, getting up from the table.

Eloise comes in carrying a glass of water. In her hand are two capsules for me, one blue, one green. I look to Paul. "The green one's your antiseizure," he says.

"And the blue?" I ask.

"That's your sedative, Mrs. Frasier, to help you sleep," says Eloise. "Come, take them," and she holds the glass and pills out to me.

"No thank you. Don't need a sedative."

Eloise frowns. "Dear, the hospital advised—"

"See? Like a child," I say to Paul, whose face is inscrutable. He's quiet for a few moments, thinking. "Okay, we'll try no sedative tonight."

Eloise shakes her head, "I don't recommend it, going against the doctor's advice—"

"Duly noted, Eloise," Paul says, and she purses her lips in displeasure. Hands me just the green pill.

✳ ✳ ✳

It's chilly in the bedroom, but I've ample blankets, and Eloise has laid out a heavy flannel nightgown and thick wool socks on the bed for me. As I change into them, I think about my next move. Tomorrow, I might talk to Paul about my getting a job. Do it while he's still feeling guilty about losing it today, lecturing me on the sidewalk about ground rules and freedom depending on cooperation . . . which obviously is true, cooperation *is* the price of freedom . . .

Anyway, tomorrow I'll convince Paul I can handle a job. That I'm fine.

The only problem is the lie—putting it to bed.

Plan B. Find a way to call Officer Worthy. I pull out the torn phonebook page from its hiding place in the lingerie drawer and commit it to memory: *Worthy, Thomas R., 14 Foxtail Ln. . . . Bixby 4–5733.*

Is this crazy?

Yes. If Officer Worthy's words don't come back, maybe they weren't meant to. Maybe whatever Paul's lie was, if there even was a lie, it doesn't merit my dishonesty. My defiance. I need to stop dwelling on the deputy and what he said to me, on my doubts. Let go of plan B. Toss this shred of paper I've secreted away like a criminal and cooperate. Let Paul and I restart our lives on solid ground. I owe him that, don't I?

But that's the regression talking.

The truth. That's how Paul and I find solid ground.

And I need it soon. Now that I'm home, I can't live with this uncertainty hanging over me. If I don't remember what Officer Worthy said by the end of the week, I'll find a way to call him.

That's how I say yes to this life in front of me.

I slide the scrap back into its hiding place and climb under the covers.

CHAPTER 28

M RS. FRASIER? MRS. Frasier, wake up."
A man's voice calling me. Paul? Why would he call me Mrs.
Frasier? Is that one of our weird married couple kinks? He calls me
"Mrs. Frasier," and I call him "The Commodore" or something
equally pervy? Too early in the morning for roleplay.

And too cold. Some of the blankets must've slid off during the
night, but I'm too tired to retrieve them.

I ignore Paul, ignore the cold, and drift back down to sleep.

"Mrs. Frasier." Now he's jiggling my arm.

"What?" I open my eyes—

And see I'm not in my bedroom. Not at all.

I'm lying on a worn plywood floor smelling of wax and linseed oil.
Above me are shelves stacked with paint cans, brushes, and buckets that stretch all the way to the ceiling. Chains trailing from giant
spools above dangle around me like Spanish moss.

The hardware store.

How? Is this real? A reasonable question—I've been burned before.
I reach out to touch a chain and see the balisong knife gripped tight
in my left hand.

Blade out. Locked in position. Ready.

How is it that I am holding this thing, in this place?

What the hell is going on?

"Why don't I put that somewhere safe." The man's voice again, gentle and warm. I look up—and find the store's owner, Arthur Morris,

crouched by my shoulder. He reaches over, nice and slow. Takes the balisong from my hand and places it on the nearby counter.

"H-h-how did I get here?" No need to fake the stutter-slur. Panic, my recently fried brain, and the early hour have all taken care of that.

I sit up and see I'm still in my nightgown—but it's now a muddy mess, the bottom six inches solid wet brown like I've been out slopping hogs.

And there's blood on the right sleeve, near the wrist.

I yank the cuff up, scared of what I'll find—my artery reopened? Its contents rapidly departing me? But thankfully that's not the case. The scar's intact. The blood's coming from a small cut, higher on my forearm.

How did I get that? Is it a defensive wound? Did someone come after me, and I defended myself with the balisong? But how did I get the balisong? And how did I get here?

The last thing I remember was turning out my light. Then nothing till I woke miles away in a hardware store. Not much to go on.

Looking down, I see my socks are mud-soaked, burrs and twigs buried deep in the thick knit. Can feel something cold and clay-like squishing between my toes. I must've escaped my attacker by running through mud. A lot of mud. But what happened to that attacker? Are they still nearby? I look around the store, searching for signs of another. But there's only a single set of muddy footprints.

"Is someone else here?" I ask Arthur, more slowly and clearly this time.

"Who would that be, dear?"

Time to find out for myself. I hold on to a shelf, start to pull myself up. "Let me help you," Arthur says, and takes my arm. As I stand up I feel something heavy hanging from my shoulder, weighing me down—a long duffel bag I must've been lying against. Arthur lifts it off my shoulder, and we both spy the butt of a rifle peeking out from it.

He puts the bag on the counter, and I open it. Not one but two .22-caliber rifles and a machete inside, price tags still on them. In the bottom are several cartons of ammo.

Arthur quietly pushes the bag down the counter, out of reach, and two big shards of glass are revealed in its wake. Arthur carefully tosses them in the trash. Their source is the nearby pocketknife display case. The top's been shattered. Glass all over the floor and counter.

Then I see the nearby gun case's wire mesh door is ajar, a bent hairpin still jammed in its lock. Someone's picked it.

That someone was not—could not—have been me.

"I didn't do this!" I say.

"It's okay, Mrs. Frasier. Nothing at all to feel bad about. I've called your husband, and he should be here any minute."

Paul. So he knows I'm here. Like this.

Arthur pulls out two stools. "Let's you and I have a seat," he says, and I sit down. "We'll wait for him together, split this Hershey bar I've kept a secret from Mrs. Morris." He winks and smiles, produces a chocolate bar from a drawer.

It's a nice offer, but something's happened to me that chocolate won't fix. Someone did this and maybe they're still nearby. Maybe right outside. I look down the aisle to the front of the store. The sun's up. I'm guessing it's about 7:00 a.m. I need to get out there. Find whoever's responsible.

I start to stand—but Arthur lays his hand gently on my arm. "He wants you to wait here for him, dear."

Paul wants me to wait. Yes, that's a good idea. I'll need his help to figure this out, get my hands on whoever messed with me. So I sit back down, and the old man smiles, tears open the wrapper, and breaks me off a piece.

* * *

We're finishing up the last of the chocolate when the bell on the store's front door rings, and Paul comes running down the aisle toward us, breathless. "Thank God," he shouts as he wraps his arms around me and squeezes tight.

"Someone took me from the house and brought me here. I think we fought. We need to—"

"It'll be okay, Dee. Everything's gonna be just fine," he says quietly to me. "We'll talk about it in the car."

"But they could still be outside—"

"There's no one out there after you."

"But—"

"We'll discuss this later when we're both calmer. Okay?" he asks, nodding.

I nod back—and immediately feel more relaxed. More secure. Breath lengthening, nerves and muscles backing down on their terror alert levels, heart slowing, like I've taken a fat bong hit. I hadn't been aware of it before, this neural shortcut the protocol has forged in me: a connection between agreement and this buzzy feeling of ease.

Paul puts his wool jacket around my shoulders, and I let its musky warmth enfold me. He turns to the old man. "Thank you, Arthur. I've been out looking for hours. Ever since we realized she was gone."

"No trouble at all. Dorothy and I have been enjoying some early-morning chocolate."

Paul smiles, but it's a weak smile. He's seen the damage, spotted the gun bag and the balisong on the counter. "Can I speak with you a minute?" he asks the shopkeeper.

"Sure thing, Paul."

"Dorothy, stay right here, okay?" Paul says, nodding his head.

I echo the nod and my breath lengthens further, my fist begins to unclench.

Arthur follows Paul just out of earshot. They glance over at me occasionally as they talk. Then I see Paul pull some cash from his wallet. Jesus, he's trying to pay Arthur for the damage he thinks I caused—which I, for sure, did not.

But I also know that I should wait till we're alone in the car to convince him.

Arthur's patting Paul's shoulder as the two come back to me. "You sure I can't help you with the cleanup, Arthur?" Paul asks.

"Won't hear of it. You go take your pretty bride home," Arthur says, then turns to me, smiling. "Goodbye, Dorothy. It was a pleasure dining with you."

The man's gone out of his way to be kind to a woman he believes trashed his store—spelling out just how little personal responsibility he thinks I bear for what he's certain I've done.

Paul takes my hand, and as we walk down the aisle, the mud squishes from my socks, trailing more footprints.

When we get near the open front door, I notice the pane nearest the knob has been shattered, glass all over the floor. A small streak of blood runs down one jagged piece still attached to the doorframe.

I scope out the street for any sign of my attacker. "Dee, careful," Paul warns, and lifts me in the air, deposits me on the other side of the broken glass. As a couple of men pass by us on the sidewalk, their curious eyes drift down to my muddy nightgown and socks.

I feel on display. Misunderstood. In danger.

CHAPTER 29

O N THE DRIVE home, Paul's quiet, not upset like yesterday, when I didn't stay put. This time he simply looks sad, which feels worse.

"We need to find who did this to me," I say finally.

"Who did this to you?" Paul asks, turning to me. "Dee, *you* did this to you."

"No. Someone—"

His hand goes up so I stop. "I'm going to explain what I think happened," he says, "and I need you to stay calm, not get upset, not interrupt till I'm finished. Okay?"

Do I get so agitated that he needs to issue a warning preamble? I guess I do. Or did. I nod.

"I believe you snuck out, hitchhiked once you reached Route 15. Probably a trucker picked you up, dropped you in town. I didn't see any other store windows broken, so it looks like you had a plan. Usually do. You went straight for the hardware store and cut yourself breaking in. Must've gathered the weapons right before you blacked out."

"That's not right," I say. "I just can't remember . . ."

Paul shakes his head. Guess I can't blame him for being so sure I did it. He's been to that rodeo a few times.

But this is not that rodeo. "Someone took me—"

"You have no idea how lucky we are Arthur called me and not the sheriff. I trust him not to say anything. Promised we'd make certain it wouldn't happen again."

My husband is too concerned with sweeping my crazy under the rug to listen, and I'm too angry for a second attempt at making myself heard. So we drive the rest of the way in silence.

When we pull up to the house, Paul says, "You know, I offered Arthur money. For the repairs and his discretion. He wouldn't take it. Said I should donate it to the Kiwanis. I suppose so they can buy more flying reindeer." Paul looks at me and smiles. He's trying to leaven the moment after all the drama. Get us past this.

But I refuse to be leavened. "Maybe the sheriff's office *should* be called. Let them dust for prints, collect DNA."

"DNA? What the heck is DN— Never mind." He shakes his head. Shuts the car off. "You're imagining things."

And I remember Mary saying I was on the CIA's radar. What if she wasn't so crazy? "The people who took me, maybe they're with the government."

He slaps the steering wheel. "Do you hear yourself? This is how it escalates, Dee, with you inventing conspiracies to explain your actions."

He gets out of the car, slams the door.

I start to follow him but spot a big stretch of mud just to the side of the driveway. Walk over to it and see human footprints cutting across the deep brown slurry, disappearing into the woods.

Just the single set. My size.

I turn and see Paul there, eyeing them. The two of us walk silently back to the house.

* * *

Eloise took me upstairs and helped me get cleaned up. I'm grateful she hasn't said a word about their all-night search, or Arthur's call. She's just put a Band-Aid on me when Paul pops his head into the bathroom.

"Dee, would you come with me?"

I follow him down the hall, past the staircase, till we're in front of the storage room. He pulls out a key. "There's something I need to tell you. Was hoping I'd never have to, but I just can't see a way around it."

Is he going to confess his lie about the woman?

As he unlocks the door, Paul looks at me, serious as pox. "It's time you learned what we're up against."

What does the woman he lied about have to do with "what we're up against"? With what really happened to me last night?

Only one way to find out. I follow him inside.

The storage room's filled with random pieces of furniture and shelves stacked high with cartons and junk. I spot a bowling bag on a high shelf, in early retirement.

"Up till a couple years ago, things weren't that bad. You had your struggles, but the symptoms were mild. Then it changed. You became more excitable, restless. Something inside you began seeing threats, enemies it needed to guard against."

The *voice.* Urging me to resist, goading me to arm, consigning me to battle.

All for a mission she could never quite name.

"You started talking about the future," Paul says, "and something important you needed to accomplish. Your purpose."

"I've heard this, in Dr. Sherman's office—"

He puts his hand up. "I told myself I could handle it. And I did for a time," he says, "smoothing things over with neighbors, keeping the police from getting involved."

Paul the fixer. Evidently, he's had a lot of practice.

He digs through objects on a nearby shelf. "When you remembered what you'd done, you were mortified. But other times, like last night when you had no memory, you'd look for some enemy to blame."

"Last night was different," I say. "How can I make you see—"

"You started traveling, first to a church in town." I remember from the sheriff's department reports in my file: St. Mark's Church, Doyletown, Virginia. My memory of the address from Dr. Sherman's file managed to withstand the ECT. "But then you went farther, to Washington. And you began stealing. Things that voice in your head must've said you needed for your mission. Weapons."

He moves a wall clock that's been cleaved in half to an empty shelf. Pulls out the carton behind it. "It became clear you needed more supervision. So, I cut down my hours on the road, hired help, and for a while, we made things work. But you're *resourceful* . . ."

"What do you mean?"

He gives me a doleful look. "Come," he says, picking up the carton, and I follow him to a desk where he puts it down. "Yesterday you wanted to know why we didn't have more photographs. This is why," and he opens up the carton. "I kept a few things in case I needed them."

In the box is a collection of scorched objects. I pick up a large, blackened book. "A fire?" I ask, and he nods. "What happened?"

"Not entirely sure," he says. "Mrs. Engels, your caregiver at the time, was in the house with you."

My caregiver. Christ.

"Neighbors said the place went up like kindling. Mrs. Engels was trapped upstairs. Escaped by jumping from a window. She sustained some burns and a broken leg in the fall."

"Where was I?"

"Nowhere to be found."

"And you think I started it?"

"Not according to the official report. It states Mrs. Engels accidentally burned down the house by operating our kerosene space heater too close to the living room curtains. I quietly paid the woman three thousand dollars and all her medical bills so she'd agree to that story." He hands me a small stack of canceled checks made out to Helga Engels.

I sit down on the desk and try to wrap my head around the idea I might have tried to kill another human being. Not merely heard a voice in my head urging me to. Actually attempted it.

And I realize with a cold chill that it's not so outside my ken, not completely unbelievable. But still I fight it. "If I wasn't there, how do you know?" I ask.

"When I saw the ruins, heard you were missing, I knew where to look. Found you at the church. You reeked of kerosene but had no memory of what you'd done. Like this morning. You accused me of lying, said I was part of some vast conspiracy keeping you from fulfilling your mission. Eventually you realized the truth, and you were devastated."

My eyes are filling up. I don't fight it.

"Soon you started hurting yourself. Small ways at first. I tried to convince you to get treatment, but you wouldn't. And even with the help, it got more and more difficult to keep you at home, out of trouble. The police would bring you to the local hospital's mental ward, hold you a few days. It started to get commonplace. We needed a fresh start."

"So you moved us down here?" I ask.

He nods. "I thought new surroundings, far from your *places*, would help. And at first you *were* better. I was starting to have hope. But one night you found a way back to that church, and this time you broke in . . ." I see him eyeing the scar on my wrist. "Because you damaged church property, the courts got involved. The judge looked at your records and drew his own conclusions. Ordered a minimum twelve-month commitment to Hanover and had you transferred."

Paul sits on the desk beside me. "Then I get a call from Dr. Sherman saying you'd arrived at Hanover with no memory of who you were, of your life up to that point. So I decided not to tell you—or anyone—about the fire and Mrs. Engels. When Dr. Sherman asked if I knew what memory you might be blocking, I lied. Told him no. I didn't want you locked away in their violent ward with no hope of release."

I rub my eyes, let all this good news settle in.

Mrs. Engels was the mystery woman Paul lied about to get me into the Unit.

So my husband's big deception, the one I etched into my hand so I wouldn't forget, the one I faked a seizure in order to uncover—was all to protect me from learning the worst about myself: that I tried to kill an innocent person in order to accomplish my nutjob mission. *Her* mission.

That feels . . . exactly right, confirmation of a fact some part of me has known all along. My guilt-riddled heart makes sense now. I finally have my truth. About Paul, about us.

Yeah? Well, I call bullshit.

The *voice*. She's alive?

CHAPTER 30

Y OU, A PYROMANIAC *psycho-killer? Right. Tell me the Unit didn't soften your brain so much you believe that crap.*

The protocol didn't kill the *voice.*

If I hadn't faked the doctors into stopping it, would the treatment have had time to work? Would *she* be dead?

Would you?

Paul's lying, this is all a plot. He's trying to throw you off your purpose. Your mission.

Purpose. Mission. Here we go . . .

He's trying to make you think you're insane.

Funny, I was thinking that was the *voice's* job.

And now she's back to continue her work—which begs the question: How long, exactly, has the *voice* been back? Maybe she didn't just emerge. Maybe the *voice* resurfaced last night and decided I should take a little trip to town to arm myself.

No enemy dragging me out of this house.

No government conspiracy.

Just me. Just *her.*

And like when I torched my house and nanny, I was powerless to stop it. Turns out my sanity and freedom are on a lot shakier ground than I thought last night when I told Paul I was fine.

Fine is definitely off the table.

"Dee, are you listening?"

Paul. What did he just say? I look up. Eloise has joined us. Both are watching me closely. Maybe Paul knows the *voice* is back. But how could he possibly know? Don't get paranoid—

"You okay?" Paul asks. I should tell him she's back. I owe him that. Honesty for once. Full cooperation. Freedom depends on my cooperation.

What kind of BS has he been drilling into you?

Ethan and Kyung, the Guest—they exist. Or will.

Nope. I can't let Paul know about the *voice*. She's too big. It would be the end of any hope for Paul and me. For his trust in my mental state. And then where would I be? At Hanover, locked away in a chronic ward.

So I gather my wits and answer calmly, "Yes, I'm fine. What were you saying, Paul?"

"I said I know what I've told you, after the night you've just had, is a lot to take in."

"Being found like that in the hardware store, it's bound to be upsetting," Eloise adds. She knows the whole story. Great.

"But there's reason to be hopeful," he says. "You're so much better than you were. I think the protocol really did help . . . calm things. Most importantly, the voice in your head, Bix, she's gone now. That's going to make a big difference."

Did they see me flinch? Hope not.

"We can make this work, Dee," he says, "your life outside the institution, but we'll need to take greater precautions."

"Like what?"

Paul nods to Eloise, and she leaves the room. "I made a big mistake," he says to me. "I see that now. Rushed your exposure to the outside world with all its triggers. The strain was too much. I think that's what brought on last night. So what we're going to do is pull back a bit. Slow things down so you can adjust to your new life. Its requirements—"

"What requirements?" I ask.

"The first would be limiting interactions with outsiders, strangers who could witness your . . . lapses. People less understanding than Arthur Morris, who might tell the police."

Or might help you . . .

"What else?" I ask him.

"I need to know when you're feeling it," Paul says, "that dangerous belief you're a savior meant for greater things. So, no secrets. You need to be completely honest with me."

Really? Is that a mutual thing?

"Anything else?"

"Yes," he says, eyes leveled on me. "For the time being, I think it best if I make the decisions involving your welfare."

"What do you mean?"

"Your medical care. Eloise was right: It's time we listened to the doctors. Use the medicine they prescribed to make things easier."

Keep you under their heel.

Paul goes to the door and calls to Eloise. The nurse reenters the room, now holding a glass of water. She reaches into her pocket and pulls out two capsules, one green, one blue.

"Sedation. During the day? There's got to be another way. Couldn't we—"

Paul takes my hand. "Maybe last night's events were actually a blessing. Now that we've seen what could happen. How easily you could end up back in Hanover if the right choices aren't made about your care during these early days. So it comes down to trust. Do you trust me to make those choices now?"

Hell no! He's trying to keep you from the mission. Stop you. You're gonna need to kill him now. It can't wait any longer.

And there it is—no better illustration of the truth in Paul's words than this homicidal voice in my head trying to lure me over the edge in broad daylight. Coaxing me to kill my husband. There is no other way. I need to let Paul be in charge for now. Tie me to the friggin' mast. Dose me.

I take the pills from Eloise. Swallow each with the water.

"Let me see, Mrs. Frasier," Eloise says. Is she serious? Yes, she is. Waits till I open my mouth wide, then moves my chin around, checking every angle. "Now lift your tongue up." Christ. But I do it.

Back in our bedroom, Paul shuts the curtains, blocking out the daylight so I can get some rest after my long night.

A slumber room of one's own.

I get in bed, and he pulls the covers over me. "I'm hopeful we won't always have to be this strict, Dee."

"You are?"

He nods. "After some time has passed, and you're feeling more stable—no more 'episodes' like last night—we can look into lowering the dosage, even begin taking some trips together. It'll be a whole new beginning for us. We just need to be patient, not rush it. Allow things to stabilize, let the positive effects of the protocol have a chance to take hold," he says, then kisses me and walks out the door.

Maybe he's right. Things could get better. With time I might become less of a nutter, less in need of containment. There's a chance my wings won't always need to be clipped. That someday I could have a job, travel alone—but it's not happening anytime soon.

The notion that if I could just get out of the Unit, out of Hanover, I'd regain my self-rule—that was just another lie of the mind. I'll always be the lunatic wife the townsfolk have been warned about, kept safe up here. A protectorate of Paul and his good intentions.

That's where we differ—his intentions.

I don't think they're good.

* * *

The first days were bad, but it's getting better. I'm settling in, making peace with the new medicated normal. Paul's taken some time off from work so he can be close by during this period of adjustment to help reacquaint me with my life.

And Eloise has been keeping me occupied with little projects where I can be useful: baking, putting up holiday decorations around the house. She makes sure it's nothing too taxing. I know I wanted her gone when I first got home, but now I'm honestly so grateful she's here, keeping the house running smoothly. Not sure how we'd make this work without her.

Things are definitely more peaceful, my keel more even. One day, not sure which, I came down the stairs and found Paul wrestling a Christmas tree into its stand. I froze, bracing for the holiday scene to engulf me in panic. But only brief flashes came to me, all nebulous and vague. Nothing substantial enough to launch a panic attack. The pills are doing their job, coating my nerves, breaking down my big, fearful ideas into bland, bite-size thought kibble. Best of all, they muffle the *voice* enough to make things tolerable. She only emerges at the fringes of my pill schedule, when the meds are lapsing.

So I slid past Christmas and have been wending my way through these last days of December *mostly* fine—but there are still those times when I need extra help. Like a moment ago—

We were watching the news on TV. Some senator speaking to the cameras from the steps of the Capitol. And I noticed a man in the crowd behind him who looked so much like the doctor in the Unit, the one with the wary, bits-of-coal eyes. The man the *voice* thought might be the doctor with the key to saving the far, fucked future.

Now adrenaline is surging through my body. I can feel it slamming into the tips of my fingers as my nerves are hijacked by the fear I'm not doing what needs to be done—about a problem my mind has invented. Pure fiction.

But my nervous system doesn't care what's fiction. It's gone into angst overdrive, and the dread is overtaking me. Heart's racing, mouth's gone dry, and I'm struggling to get enough air. Paul takes my hands. "Let's you and I say the words, okay?"

Paul's mantras. He came up with them to help me when the drugs aren't enough. Been reciting them with me, helping me learn. They're a bit self-helpsy, hippie woo-woo, but they do seem to relax me. I nod, and he starts us off. "How do you find peace right now, in this moment, Dee?"

"By not craving a life I don't have," I answer, and immediately feel the call-and-response begin to work its magic, my nerves starting to back down.

"That's right," Paul says softly. "And what must there be instead?"

"Acceptance. I need to say yes to this life that's right in front of me."

He nods. "And what about the sadness and anger? What about the fear?"

"They're just emotions," I say. "Not real. So I let the feelings come and go, not resisting or opposing."

"Good. Now tell me how you will stay free, be able to live your life outside Hanover."

"By respecting you and others like Eloise caring for me, trusting you'll know what needs to be done."

"And how do you show that respect and trust?" he asks.

"By always cooperating. Freedom depends on my cooperation . . ."

We go through all the phrases, Paul's whole mindfulness catechism, and when we finish, there's such a lightness, such a sense of relief. The feelings of panic and desperation to do some mysterious *something* have all fallen away.

"Feeling better now, Dee?"

"Yes. Thank you."

CHAPTER 31

SEX. IT'S BECOME our late-afternoon activity, something Paul and I truly excel at, even in our present circumstances. I look forward to it because, for those few minutes, all else recedes and I can utterly lose myself in the act. That quest to learn the truth about Paul through our bodies—turns out it wasn't needed. I was the one with all the secrets.

So now I can just relax.

We hold off on my evening meds, letting the morning dose wane till there's a minimum of drugs circulating through me, blunting my sensations, my down under. He sets the two pills and the glass of water on the nightstand for after.

I unbutton my dress, my bra, my panties. Let it all fall to the floor, then join Paul on the bed.

* * *

When we've finished, Paul kisses the back of my shoulder, tracing the line of my scapula with his lips, then slides off me and grabs his shirt. I turn over and take his hand, tracing the blue anchor tattoo on his wrist with my finger before he stands up. He's feeling good, singing some song about blueberries on a hill.

I'm sitting on the edge of the bed, starting to put my clothes back on, when Paul throws open the curtains on the front windows. The brightness of the clear blue winter sky is a shock to my eyes, already reaccustomed to a life inside.

Suddenly images begin to surface from the murky depths of my brain, shaping themselves into bits and pieces of memories:

Wallace leading me out of the elevator into the bright sunlight of Hanover's first floor. As we walk slowly down the hallway jammed with holiday visitors, I can feel the sluggishness of regression already in me, weighing me down, dulling my senses, my awareness. The red-robed choirboys smirking and pointing at me as they pass by barely registers in my mind.

I remember a kindly old lady handing me a cookie shaped like a star—and Norma promptly stealing it out of my hand. Remember Georgie's shocked face looking at me, mouth shaped like an O, demanding Wallace tell her what they'd done to me down in the Unit, till the marly nurse scared her away.

Then finally it comes to me. The memory I've been waiting for: Officer Worthy in the visitors' room, rising from his seat as Wallace and I approach.

And now bits of memories from my meeting with the deputy start to come back:

Officer Worthy trying to understand my horror-show words.

Me calling him the Lone Ranger when he told me how he'd forced Hanover's superintendent to let him check up on me.

Him quizzing me about my yellow note, asking what all my odd phrases meant. And me teasing him about his curiosity, asking whether his wife knew how he spent his free time.

When he tells me the addresses I'd written in it were all for crematoriums, I confess all the other things my sick mind had made up, whole people it had convinced me were real—and he gets an odd look on his face. There's something he's not saying.

"Tell me," I plead, and notice his eyes glancing over my shoulder at something behind me. I turn around—and see Dr. Sherman, now standing with Nurse Wallace by the visitors' door, watching us.

The discovery brings the *voice* out of hiding. Close to death now from the protocol, she's desperately grasping for a new conspiracy theory: *Maybe the deputy is working with Sherman and the nurse, trying to get information out of me . . . All to keep me from my mission—finding the doctor . . .*

On and on she rants, so loudly I can barely think.

I stretch my hand out across the table, again beg Officer Worthy to tell me. His eyes flick one more time to the doctor and nurse. Then he says, "To hell with them. You deserve to know."

"Know what?"

He levels his blue eyes on mine. "You've been lied to here."

"No. No one here is lying to me . . ." I say to the deputy, who is trying to pull the rug of trust, so carefully woven for me by the protocol, right out from under my feet.

I'm trying to stay calm, not get agitated in front of Sherman and Wallace. But the pitched battle for composure going on inside me begins to produce a high-pitched whine inside my head, like a pipe bomb's just gone off.

I can see Officer Worthy's lips moving, no doubt saying more things I don't want to hear, but the whining sound is keeping me safe from those things.

The problem: I need to know those things.

So I close my eyes, press my hands to the table, and focus till I tamp down the squealing noise in my head. Then say to the deputy: "Tell me."

He takes a moment, gathering his thoughts, glances at Sherman and Wallace, then starts. "I do think they meant well when they made the decision."

What decision?

"There was real concern for you at the time—that you were in such a delicate state . . . Which I found so strange to hear because that day we met on the driveway you seemed anything but delicate. There was this strength about you. Even without your memory, you seemed to possess a certainty about yourself at your core. And about what you'd seen."

Seen what?

"But as I said, there was a genuine fear in those days that you might never come to embrace who you really are. But clearly that's no longer the case. You've now fully accepted that you're Dorothy Frasier. Even submitted to this . . . *extreme* treatment of Dr. Sherman's in the hopes of getting better." He puts his hands up. "So I can't in good conscience go along with the continued deception. The woman I met that day on the driveway deserves to know the truth."

"Truth about what?"

"The woman in braids on the transport bus with you," he says.

"The one I made up."

"That's just it—you didn't make her up. I saw her, too," he says. "She was crouched down, waving to us with your purse from the back of the bus as it was driving away."

I blink, pull myself away from the memory to fully absorb the deputy's long-forgotten news.

There *was* a woman in braids on the bus that day who took my bag. I didn't invent her. Neither did the *voice.*

You bet your ass we didn't invent her.

As I sit here on the bed, it feels like . . . like there's a rocket racing through me. Hands shaking, fingers fumbling wildly as I try to button my dress.

I glance over at Paul to see if he's noticed. He hasn't. Still singing about blueberries as he pulls on his pants.

I close my eyes again, hoping more flotsam from Officer Worthy's visit will come to the surface of my mind—

And it does:

"I called Hanover that day," Officer Worthy says. "It took a few tries, but when I finally got through to Dr. Sherman, I told him what I'd seen and asked if they'd double-checked your identification. He laughed at even the suggestion, reassured me you were indeed Dorothy Frasier. That he'd not only spoken at length to your husband, Paul, he'd even seen a photo of the two of you at the beach that Mr. Frasier keeps in his wallet."

"Then who *was* she? The braided woman?" I ask.

"The doctor thinks she was just a drunken vagrant who'd snuck onto the transport bus the night before to sleep one off, then woke the next morning to find herself taking a ride up to Hanover with you patients. And he's probably right. She stole your purse, then hid in the back of the bus till the driver parked it back at the lot and she could sneak away unseen."

"Dr. Sherman never told me I'd been right," I say.

He shakes his head. "I just assumed he would, once he knew the truth. Only learned he hadn't this morning when he called to warn me not to say anything about the woman during my visit, that it could confuse you unnecessarily."

"So Dr. Sherman was lying to Paul and me the whole time." Officer Worthy is quiet, his finger nervously playing with the corner of the yellow note. "What?"

It takes him a moment but he answers. "According to Sherman, he told your husband the woman on the bus really existed shortly after he heard it from me—but strongly advised Mr. Frasier not to risk a further worsening of your mental state by telling you. And your husband . . . well, he agreed."

"Paul knew? All this time? No!"

But Officer Worthy nods.

And now sadness, anger, and fear are tearing through me, unbounded, emotions no longer mine to control. Can feel myself coming undone—and the deputy sees.

That's when Worthy takes my hand.

His hand feels warm and safe, an island of calm in the middle of my raging sea of emotions. For a moment in my head nothing else exists but Worthy and me. And I want so much to stay there alone with him— but there isn't time. Sherman's talking to Lester and another attendant, and their eyes are all on me.

"Worthy," I say, "their shocks are gonna make me forget what you told me."

"Shocks? Is that what they're doing to you?" he asks.

"Part of it. I need to get Sherman to stop them till I can talk to Paul . . . Cuh . . . confront him." I grab hold of the table and get to my feet, try to steady myself as the room whirls around me like a top.

"Wait!" Worthy says, starting to rise. "Take a minute, think about—"

But he's interrupted by Lester and the other attendant, who each grab one of my arms. "Worthy!" I scream as I'm dragged away from him, past the other visitors watching the spectacle.

Worthy and Sherman yelling at each other is the last thing I see before the attendants pull me around the corner.

I open my eyes and take a deep breath. Try to stay calm, reason this out.

Paul knew all along the woman in braids was real. *She's* "the woman" he lied about.

The reason I carved those letters into my hand.

And if he lied about her, what else has he been lying about?

Nothing! You heard Worthy, Paul only lied to me on the advice of my asshole doctor. He was just trying to help me.

That's the regression. You need to fight it. Stop making excuses for Paul!

"Dee, you okay?" Paul asks.

"Y . . . yes. Okay," I say. I think I say that. Things are . . . This is a lot . . .

Stay with the conversation. Don't let him know you know.

"You sure?" Paul says, eyes leveled on me. "You look like you've seen a ghost."

"No, I'm fine," I say.

But he watches me a few moments more before checking his watch. "Damn, I need to go," he says, and heads for the door.

"Where?"

"I promised Eloise I'd make a trip to the liquor store over in Chatham before it closes. Get the bourbon she needs for her pecan pie," he says, kisses me, and leaves.

Soon there are voices out front. I go to the window, careful to stay hidden by the curtain. Paul and Eloise are talking by the car. He looks up toward my window once before getting into the car and driving away.

This is good. He's left you alone and undrugged—you've been handed a chance to find out the truth. Seize it.

The *voice* is the one seizing chances, taking advantage of my overexcited, undermedicated state to make the lie into something bigger. She's trying to lure me over the edge, off my even keel. The clock on the bedside table says four fifteen. Next to it are my pills. I walk over to them.

Don't do it. This thing is more than one lie. Maybe he's made it all up, your whole life!

Right. Like someone would go to all the trouble of faking *my* life—the hospital visits, the photos, the house, the bowling trophies. No one would do that.

Exactly. So, why did he? What's the story?

I hear Eloise walk back into the house, followed by the jingle of her keys and the *swick* of the front door's new keyed dead bolt locking smoothly into place. Moments later she's climbed the stairs and stands in the doorway. "You look a bit tired, Mrs. Frasier. Why don't you lie down and take a little nap till Mr. Frasier gets back from Chatham."

"With the cognac you need for the pie?" I ask, naming the wrong liquor in some lame attempt to test her.

But then she says, "Yes, an old family recipe. The cognac is part of the secret. Wouldn't be the same without it."

They really should get their booze stories straight.

"I'll be right downstairs starting dinner if you need anything. Okay?" She nods.

And I nod back. But the nod fails to relax me because I can't stop thinking this:

Fuck!

Fuck indeed. Lied right to your face.

I close the door and lean my forehead against it to think. Maybe it's just a mistake. Bourbon for cognac. Paul got it wrong, and now he's driving across the county for the wrong pie liquor.

You should be asking yourself what he's really doing.

The sun's just dipping below the tree line. The clock on the bedside table says four twenty-seven. Eloise has put a record on. I can hear Frank Sinatra rising up through the floorboards.

Twelve minutes gone. Get moving. The doors may be locked but you've got a perfectly good window.

No. There will be consequences. The new beginning Paul spoke of, his hope that someday soon we'd be able to loosen the precautions, lessen the medications—that promise of an almost-normal life will surely disappear if I escape out that window. Leaving is insane.

What's insane is ignoring your gut. Something's off and you feel it. Screw consequences. Go learn the truth.

The truth? The woman in braids was just a vagrant, and I am just Dorothy. That's the truth.

Then prove me wrong. Find someone, some stranger, who actually knew Dorothy and ask them a simple question: "Am I her?" If the answer's no, who does that make you?

I'll give you a hint. Starts with a B.

Here we go, Bix and her fictional future.

Then I remember Mary's words that night before I faked the seizure: "Sometimes you need to trust that lunatic voice, 'cause she's the only one in your corner."

She was right. Go while you're still capable of acting on your own. Not yet a complete pod person.

Screw you.

Ticktock.

Fuck.

CHAPTER 32

GO TO THE window overlooking our side yard and scope out the roof of the porch below and a nearby tree.

It's doable—if I've got enough strength. Big if.

I glance down at my dress. Not gonna cut it.

I run to my closet, search till I find a pair of wool pants.

As quickly as I can, I shed the petticoat and dress, then pull the pants on. Too big, but I grab a belt. Cinch it tight.

Shoes. The penny loafers are the only ones lacking a heel. I pull them on, then a turtleneck, knit hat, and gloves. My coat's downstairs, so I take a thick Irish knit sweater hanging in the closet.

Now for tools. The bathroom's medicine cabinet has been cleared of all useful items in advance of me and my suicide risk, but I do find a fingernail clipper in the deep recesses of a vanity drawer. Snag it.

I ease the window open. It's almost sundown. Just a little light hitting the bare trees surrounding the house. The cold air has that ice-rink smell it gets when snow is imminent.

Get on with it.

I ease myself out the window, onto the sloping roof. Sitting there, catching my breath, I'm both proud and horrified by my actions in a way I haven't been since the early days of Hanover.

I slowly crab crawl downward—till I hit a patch of ice and begin sliding toward the roof edge. I'm wildly grasping for anything to stop me when, as I fly off, my left hand finds the gutter.

I'm swinging back and forth, heaving great, giddy sighs of relief—

when I realize I'm dangling right in front of the living room window. Eloise is just fifteen feet away, her back to me. When she starts to turn, I drop quietly to the ground, out of sight, and a thrill cartwheels through me.

I don't look back. Sprint around the corner of the house and through the backyard, blood pumping through all my body's forgotten highways and byways, like I'm only just now fully waking from my Unit slumber.

But by the time I get to the split rail fence dividing our property from the Clarks', it's clear how out of shape I am—hard, cold air freezes my windpipe on the way to my starving lungs. I pause on the fence a moment, catching my breath.

That's enough. Get moving.

I push on through the Clarks' woods, parallel to the road, till I reach the rust-red barn. Creep around its corner, past the chicken coop, till I find what I'm looking for: the green truck.

I watch. Listen. The chickens know. They're making disturbed clucking noises from their pen. Fifty feet away there's a light on in the house. Someone's home.

It's a risk.

Then again, this whole thing's risky, misguided—

Enough. Plenty of time later to ponder how I've screwed myself. I need to keep going.

Eyes on the house, I inch up to the truck. Ease its door open. One tiny squeak. Not bad. The truck's parked on an incline, halfway up the hill. I release the parking brake, put it in neutral, and give it a hard push, then jump in as it rolls, easing it quietly down the hill before stopping it. In the rapidly ebbing light, I get to work:

Under the dash I find the three wires I know to look for—and I wonder if this knowledge was gained from repeated attempts to elude my caregivers or from another source.

I use the nail clippers to cut the two red wires, then nip their cloth casings a half inch from the end of each. After stripping them, I twist the bare ends together, then clip and strip the brown starter wire before climbing into the driver's seat.

Moment of truth. I touch the starter wire to the twisted reds and—magic—it starts right up with a low cough, and I haul ass down Birchwood Lane, praying not to run into Paul. I don't think I breathe till I've turned onto Route 15 and have put a quarter mile between me and our road.

Now to find a stranger who knows me.

My haunt. The address listed on the police reports in my file was 169 West Eggers Avenue, Doyletown, Virginia. But where is West Eggers Avenue? Or Doyletown, for that matter? There's only a few minutes of light left—and who knows how much time before the truck is reported missing.

I pull off on a side road, check the glove compartment, and find inside a clutch of maps.

Apparently, my map-reading skills are still intact, because thirty minutes later it's dark, and I'm pulling into Doyletown. The church is a Gothic structure of gray stone on a large, wooded lot. I drive past the flood-lit Christmas manger scene still up on its front lawn and into the parking lot.

It's just beginning to snow, the first big puffy flakes hitting the windshield as I sit here, not moving.

What am I doing? I don't have to get out of this truck. I could turn around, go back home, throw myself on Paul's mercy. Hope we can forget about this latest *episode*.

Nope.

I quickly exit the truck before I can talk myself out of it. Head for the floodlit manger scene, where an older man in a gray jumpsuit stands amid the life-size figures. He's straightening out a shepherd who someone has turned backward.

Talking to a stranger—not a real strength for me right now. And definitely not on Paul's list of approved activities. But I claw past my tetchy nerves, approach the man and blurt out, "Excuse me . . . sir . . . are you . . . are you the groundskeeper here?"

He's blinded by the floodlights in his eyes and the falling snow. Puts his hand up to block them, get a better look at me. "That's right. Name's Clarence Scrubb."

"And . . . and you've worked here awhile?"

"Over twenty years," Clarence says, now struggling to pull the robe off Joseph's face where the vandal has wrapped it. "Darn kids. If I don't do this before we get those sixteen inches of snow, poor Joesph'll be covered like this for days. What can I help you with, miss?"

"Do you remember a woman named Dorothy Frasier? She liked to come here."

He nods immediately. "Poor woman. Not quite right in the head. From time to time, I'd catch sight of her on the outskirts of the grounds, in disheveled clothes, hair all in knots, talking to herself . . ."

And I can't help remembering waking up, mud-caked in the hardware store . . .

"She always kept her distance, so I let her be unless she created too much of a disturbance," he continues as he readjusts Joseph's position. "But then one night, late October I think it was, she broke into the chapel and did some injury to herself. Neighbors heard the commotion and called the sheriff's department. Officers got her to the hospital. I heard she was sent to the lunatic asylum down in Hanover."

Ask him if you're her. This is your chance.

It is what I risked this idiotic breakout for. But I'm paralyzed. While I dither, Clarence steps out of the glare of the floodlights. Takes a good look at me. "Are you kin?"

"Why do you ask?"

"Your hair. It's the same auburn shade as hers."

He recognizes me. I may be proving the *voice* wrong very soon, heading back to Paul to figure out my penance.

Not so fast.

"Do you think . . . Am I her?" I ask him.

"Strange question. Shouldn't you know if you're her?"

Yes, I really, really should.

"I've been having some problems with my memory. I . . . I know it's an odd question, but it's important. Please."

Clarence studies the topography of my face carefully. I should pray—but for what? A yes gives me the certainty I need to finally, fully embrace my life as Dorothy Frasier. Be at peace with it. And no? What does no give me?

It gives you hope. Us hope.

"The problem is," Clarence says, "she always kept her distance from me, and she wasn't at her best, always a tangle of hair in her face. Yes, you could definitely be her, but I can't say for certain."

Not yes, not no. More of the same uncertainty.

You're relieved. Admit it.

"But, miss, if you *are* her, whatever treatments they gave you at that hospital must've done you a world of good. You're alert and taking good care of yourself from the looks of it, clean clothes, clean hair, no longer wandering around building your little altars. So if I were you, I'd stop worrying about—"

"What altars?"

* * *

Minutes later, Clarence is leading me down a path that's rapidly being covered in snow to the yard behind the chapel. The space is littered with various pieces of church refuse: rusted wrought iron candelabra, stubs of candles, a broken lectern. Atop the remains of an ancient furnace next to the back fence sits the stool-like bottom half of a wooden angel statue. I can see the carved sandaled feet peeking out from under its swirling robes and the bottoms of long-gone wings.

There's a rumbling sound quickly growing louder—a train approaching on the railroad tracks behind the fence. As it passes, I feel it sucking the frozen air through the fence slats. "The local to Washington," Clarence says, and we continue our trek through the sacred debris to a vine-covered alcove in the chapel's rear wall, sheltered from the falling snow. He points his flashlight down, revealing in the shadows a small shrine. "Here it is. Discovered this one about a month ago but never got around to clearing it out. Do you . . . remember it?"

A piece of lumber lies across two upturned milk crates, and on top of it are jars holding long-dead flowers, several candles, and some seashells, arranged in a line from largest to smallest. Next to them is a bowl whose bottom holds some rusty brown powder. Dried blood? None of it is familiar—though I'm keenly aware that means next to nothing at this point. I could easily have been here. Done this.

Or did the real Dorothy, fresh from switching places on that bus and sacrificing you to Hanover, come back here and arrange this little shrine?

Clarence starts to go, and as I turn to follow him I spot several train ticket stubs tacked to the wall with candle wax. Take a couple down. The dates have been washed away, but the destination can still be seen: Washington, D.C.

* * *

Five minutes later, the snow is picking up, and I'm back in the truck, just approaching the highway entrance, when I glance back at the set of headlights behind me. The car's remained exactly the same distance from me for a few blocks even as I've slowed.

Could this guy be following me? Is it Paul? If it's Paul, why hasn't he tried to catch up to me? Talk his wife out of the stolen truck? Probably just my paranoia, I think as I pull onto the highway.

Even so. Nothing wrong with being careful.

True.

A few seconds later, when the road curves, I gun the truck. Then, when I'm out of sight of any pursuers, I put on the brakes and pull a one-eighty. The car fishtails across the painted divider into the deserted opposing lanes, but I regain control and drive on. With the snow coming down, I'm not sure which of the headlights going the other direction are the ones that triggered my alarm. Out of caution, I take the nearest exit ramp and use side roads the rest of the way to my destination.

CHAPTER 33

Foxtail Lane, the street in Bixby listed for Thomas R. Worthy on the tattered scrap of phonebook I stole. I'm thinking, as I drive down it, that it's probably a mistake showing up at the house of a sheriff's deputy who thinks I'm mentally awry, who last saw me screaming his name hysterically as I was being dragged back to my ward after he told me about Paul's omission.

Paul. The repatterned part of me is aching to go home right now, beg Paul's forgiveness, and face the consequences. It's laid out a reasoned, compelling argument:

Yes, it'll take time to win back my husband's trust and its privileges. But that beats the repercussions that will surely come from this visit I'm about to make: a call from local law enforcement informing Paul that his wife drove a stolen truck to the home of a sheriff's deputy, where she proceeded to ramble on to the officer and his wife about truth and bourbon and all manner of utter fuckery before being subdued by said deputy.

Talk about burning bridges.

But does all this reason stop me? No.

I park the truck behind some bushes in a nearby patch of woods, just short of Worthy's house, and am tucking my hair into the knit hat when my mind finds its way back to that day in Hanover's visitors' room. Those fraught, chaotic minutes after he told me Paul knew all along about the woman in braids on the bus.

Then, just as my emotions were skyrocketing, him reaching out and holding my hand. How warm and safe his touch felt amid my frenzy. That was the moment I realized the nature of our relationship had fundamentally changed. I started calling him "Worthy." We were no longer arresting officer and perp; we'd become—what? Concerned acquaintances? Maybe even friends—

Pull your head out of your ass and get what you need from the guy. That address in Washington.

Fine. I cut silently across Worthy's front lawn, already dusted with snow, passing his patrol car parked off to the side of the driveway. Other than that, there are no signs of life.

Maybe they're out in the family station wagon—do he and Missus Deputy have kids?

I walk around to a side window, look inside, and see an empty living room lit only by the dim, flickering light of a TV—

"Freeze! Hands up high, where I can see them."

Worthy. He managed to sneak up behind me. Despite the ambush, an odd brew of adrenaline, relief, and glee is flowing through me at his proximity. I raise my hands.

"Turn around slowly," he says.

I obey and find a .45-caliber Smith & Wesson aimed squarely at my chest—which should bother me but does not. He's in street clothes, a plaid flannel shirt under a wool car coat. It's funny seeing him out of his sheriff's deputy uniform, naked of all the law and order. Except for the gun trained on me. There is that.

"Dorothy?" he says, shock on his face. And something else there, too. Relief? Joy? Something. He turns, eyes the street for clues about my transportation, but I've hidden the truck well.

Of course you have. One of your many skills.

"How? . . . How did you get here? . . . Get out?" he asks.

"Lower your gun first. Please," I say, and his face breaks out in that crooked grin. I'd forgotten about his grin.

"Your speech . . . It's . . . You're better. Recovered," he says, sliding his gun back in the holster.

I nod, shivering just the slightest bit. My sweater is no parka. "Come, get out of the cold," he says, and I follow him into the house.

The living room's been decorated in good taste by Mrs. Worthy: floral drapes with fancy tassels, a couch and chairs with velvet throw pillows, a coffee table, and a television in a carved wooden cabinet. But at some point she seems to have turned the space over to a fraternity. On the coffee table are stacks of unopened mail, a half dozen empty beer bottles, peanut shells, and the remains of a couple frozen dinners.

Worthy turns on a lamp and leads me through the living room, snapping off the TV as we pass by it.

"Your wife, is she here?" I'm thinking Mrs. Worthy has left her husband and tasteful living room for greener pastures.

"My wife died last year," he says, and keeps walking.

Mrs. Worthy is dead?

"I'm . . . so sorry," I say as I follow him, wishing my words weren't so anemic, that I hadn't kidded him about whether his wife knew what he did with his free time that day in the visitors' room. We walk past a dining room table. On top of it sits what must have been his late wife's sewing machine, surrounded by sewing boxes and piles of fabric, all shrouded in a sad, thin layer of dust.

The kitchen, on the other hand, is aggressively sunny. Everything's yellow: cabinets, floral curtains, refrigerator, stove, wall telephone. Even the table in the middle of it is yellow. Less cheerful is the ample collection of liquor bottles on the counter.

Worthy moves a tackle box off the table and pulls out a chair for me. "Tea?"

"Yes, please."

He turns on the burner under a kettle, and I gladly drop into the seat, exhausted from my adventure after weeks of vegetation. There's a small space heater under the table, glowing orangey-red and giving off that oddly comforting smell of roasting dust. The warmth feels good on my feet and I'm filled with a sense of safety

I don't think I've experienced since waking on that transport bus back in November.

I want to close my eyes for a moment and rest, but Worthy's impatient. "So, how *did* you get here? You didn't . . . You couldn't have—"

"One question at a time, Worthy."

He smiles. "Okay, should I be expecting the arrival of Dr. Sherman's men in white at my door, wanting to take you back?"

He's asking if I escaped the Unit. It's flattering. He clearly has no idea what the security is like in that place. "No. My husband made them release me when the protocol . . . didn't go as planned." I don't elaborate. Pretty sure that after seeing me dragged kicking and screaming away from the visitors' room, Worthy's got some idea what "didn't go as planned" means.

Worthy's expression now turns serious. "I need to apologize for what happened that day I visited. It was never my intention to make things worse for you there, set back your recovery in any way." He shakes his head. "Don't know what got into me, that bullheaded certainty that I needed to tell you about Dr. Sherman and your husband keeping the existence of that vagrant woman on the bus from you. I overstepped my bounds. So after that visit I resolved to keep my distance, not cause any more upset—"

"No, I'm grateful you told me. Trusted me."

"I'm just glad you're better. So, *did* the shocks make you forget my visit? What I told you?" he asks, and I nod. "Christ."

"But today, pieces of memories started coming back. About you seeing the woman on the bus, about Paul and Dr. Sherman not telling me."

"And you came here . . . How?" he asks.

"I borrowed a truck."

I can see Worthy's wondering at the meaning of "borrowed." "Does your husband know where you are?" I don't answer. "He's got to be worried. Probably already called the sheriff's office. We should let them know you're safe—"

"No . . . We can't. Not yet. I need your help first. There's an address in Washington, D.C., a place I would go to. I was picked up by the police there many times when I was sick. It must be listed in the Metro Police's reports."

"What is it about that address that's so important?" Worthy asks.

Can't tell him I need to find a stranger who can positively identify me as Dorothy because I don't trust my husband. No, that would be a bit of an overshare.

"It's . . . It's for closure," I say.

"What do you mean, 'closure'?"

Damn. "Closure" must be one of my made-up words. "What I mean is I want to see the place . . . now that I'm recovering . . . to better understand my illness. Can you call, ask someone there for the information?"

I think I was convincing. But pity's once again overrun Worthy's face like ants at a picnic.

"Honestly, I'm not a big fan of your husband and the choices he's made," Worthy says, "enrolling you in that 'protocol' of Dr. Sherman's, not telling you about the woman on the bus. But according to the law, he *is* your legal guardian—which means he gets to decide if you can see your records. I'm so sorry, Dorothy."

So, permission from my husband is required to pursue information that could tell me if I even need his permission?

That's some real patriarchy bullshit.

Worthy looks pained but resolute. The Lone Ranger's not budging. Mary was right about him: chock-full of integrity and principles.

And I'm pretty sure Paul's not going to be okay with granting permission to his runaway wife.

Which means I'm out of leads *and* time.

Worthy sits down across the table from me. "How about we have some tea and then we'll call Paul? Talk to him together about you seeing your records. Getting your 'closure.'"

It's becoming a familiar scenario, waiting with a well-meaning man for Paul to come collect me, convince me to stop my pursuit of some alluring conspiracy and accept the less sexy truth: that I have a protective husband who sometimes lies to me for my own good—because I am Dorothy Frasier, and I have issues.

In the words of Wallace that day on the transport bus, I've come to the end of my yellow brick road.

My eyes begin filling with their ridiculous tears.

Get a goddamn grip.

Worthy sees and takes my hand just like he did that day in the visitors' room. But I was halfway to regression then, already enveloped in its thick blanket that dulled my thoughts, dampened my emotions.

Now is a different story—I feel this charge at his touch. There's a tight, twitchy feeling sailing through me, and my heartbeat has kicked up a notch.

Not the time for this.

I'd wager it's never the time for *this* as far as she's concerned. But the *voice* needn't worry about any inconvenient feelings burbling up between the deputy and I. Worthy's eyes have already drifted down to my wrist—and the scar where doctors mended me.

I look closer at the thin, pink line and notice something I hadn't before, something that doesn't make sense:

The scar—it's blood vessel adjacent.

It runs not over the radial artery, where I should have cut, but on the other side of my palmaris longus tendon. Hmm, those are some pretty specific medical terms my mind's tossing around. I'm definitely someone with knowledge of the local anatomy.

Here's another definite about me—I'm a closer. Getting myself straitjacketed and locked in a padded cell in order to escape, breaking into Sherman's files, pissing myself to fake a seizure, my recent excursion out the window—I'll do what it takes to get the job done. If I was serious about killing myself that night in the church, I wouldn't have failed.

So, was I after something other than death in slitting my wrist? Maybe it was a cry for help, for needed attention, and I purposely cut in the wrong place.

But cries for attention? That doesn't sound like me, feel like me— at least the me I've experienced these past few weeks.

Maybe it wasn't about killing yourself or attention.

"So, tea first and then we call Mr. Frasier?" Worthy asks.

"Okay," I say, nodding. "Can I use your bathroom?"

"Sure." We walk into the dining room, and he points down a hallway. "First door on the right," he says, and leaves me to make my way.

It's funny, I think as I step into the bathroom. Worthy, my arresting officer, trusts me more than my own husband.

He shouldn't.

I lock the door, quietly ease the nearest medicine cabinet door open, and get to work.

CHAPTER 34

THE KETTLE'S WHISTLING when I return to the kitchen, forearms scrubbed to an angry shade of pink.

On the table are two empty mugs and spoons. Worthy takes the screaming kettle off the stove, pours the boiling water into each mug, and leaves a box of Earl Grey teabags on the table. "Help yourself."

But I'm not looking to make tea.

When he turns back to the stove, I peel the paper off the straight razor blade I took from the bathroom and drop it into the mug's roiling water, then pull a dish towel off a nearby hook and drape it on the tabletop.

"Going to heat up some leftover meatloaf," Worthy says, his back still to me, messing with the dial on his oven. "You look like you could use some food."

"Thanks," I say, silently snagging the gin off the counter. I regret deceiving this kind man. Not in an I-should-cooperate way. More in a what-a-shitty-person-I'm-being way. Though maybe the two aren't so different.

Deception's a necessity.

You can't trust the Lone Ranger not to do the "right" thing.

While he wrestles with a stuck rack, I quietly pour a liberal amount of gin over my hands and forearms, letting the excess fall silently onto the towel. Then I fish the double-edged blade out with my spoon and douse it with alcohol as well. The light bounces off its notched corners and teeth-like inner cuts as the liquor drains off it.

Sterilize twice, cut once.

Worthy gets a whiff of the gin. Turns and sees me holding the blade.

"Don't do it!" he yells, and starts for me, total focus in his eyes, his deputy mind silently, swiftly coming up with the sequence of steps required to disarm.

But before he can reach me, I draw the blade's corner to the distal end of the scar on my wrist. "Not one step closer!" I say, and he freezes.

We eye each other, caught in a draw.

"You don't want to do this," he says.

No. No, I do not. I am definitely entering new territory here, about to cross yet another line in the sanity sand. "What I'm doing, it's not what you think," I say.

But I'm aware there's a decent chance it's *exactly* what he thinks — that I am once again delusional, carrying out this quest in the diseased belief that what I'm doing—trying to learn the truth about myself—is warranted.

"I want to help you," Worthy says.

"Good. 'Cause you're going to be my witness."

"Witness to what, you killing yourself?"

"No. That's not what I'm trying to . . . I know this looks bad, but for a few minutes you need to trust me. Can you do that?"

"You holding a razor to your wrist is making that a little hard. If you give it to me, we can sit down and talk," he says, holding his hand out.

The repatterned part of me — she would very much like to do what Worthy suggests. Be reasonable. Drop the blade into his palm, let him stow it safely out of reach and call my husband. With their help, I could begin to back away from this ledge I'm on. Over a cup of strong Earl Grey, things could be sorted out, medications adjusted. Better precautions put in place for the future. Resolution in the kindest, gentlest way for the patient.

But that part of me needs to chill the fuck out.

I'm doing this.

Worthy's quietly taken another step toward me. I'd do the same, ease forward while the crazed woman is distracted by the factions in her head duking it out for cerebral domination.

But still, we can't have that. I push the blade's corner into the skin, and a thick red bead of blood blooms around it, spilling over and running down my hand. Worthy steps back, retracts his hand.

"Sit down. There," I say, indicating the chair near me.

Worthy sits. "Explain what it is you're doing. I'm listening."

How to do that without sounding insane? There are no magic words, just the truth.

"I can't go home without knowing for sure who I am—who I'm not," I say. "When I thought I was in the future, the people there, they would point devices at my wrist, there'd be beeping sounds . . ."

Could I sound more crazy?

But Worthy is quiet. Not spouting solutions to fix it, fix me. Just listening.

"I need to see there's nothing in my arm. Know for sure it couldn't possibly have been real. Then I can accept being Dorothy Frasier once and for all. Have my peace. But if I truly went to the future, didn't just imagine it, then there'll be something in here. Some sort of tech."

"Tech?" he asks.

Another one of my made-up words. "Technology, you know, like a device." There's a note of desperation now in my voice. I'm starting to lose it just a little, the revelations and exertions of the day beginning to take their toll around my frayed edges.

I look down at the bloody wrist, think about what I'm about to do—and remember Betsy, so damn sure about that transmitter and the need to flay her face open to prove it. Am I about to join her in the ranks of the truly committed crazy—those willing to cut themselves open in the fruitless pursuit of proof?

"A device. Like a gadget?" Worthy asks.

"Yes."

He nods. "Okay. I'll be your witness."

Holy shit. I'm blown away by this man's choice to stand down and trust me. It's been weeks since someone has.

I'm so grateful for even this temporary show of good faith and waste no time, begin right away to draw the blade toward me, cutting my skin along the healed incision, careful not to go too deep. As the blade slices, it's leaving a small trail of open flesh in its wake, and the blood's running down the side of my forearm and onto the towel in a steady drip.

"How are you doing that?" Worthy asks.

How *am* I doing this? I do feel the pain as I cut. It's definitely registering, but the level's not incapacitating. I'm sensing my pain threshold is scary high.

I glance at Worthy and shrug. He's looking a little peaked, his head beginning a slow swivel away from the surgical field.

"I need you to keep looking," I tell him.

He turns back to me. "And I need you to know my lunch is hanging on by a very thin thread."

"Sensitive, Officer?" I ask as I guide the blade. Feels good to give him grief. Keeps my mind off all the crazy I'm committing.

"I'm not good with blood . . . or vomit."

"And you're a sheriff's deputy?"

"Not a whole lot of shoot-'em-ups in Culpeper County. I've never actually discharged my weapon. The only time I see blood is car wrecks. And farm mishaps. Those aren't good."

I've now completely opened up the incision, the two sides of it a narrow fault line down my wrist. I pull my skin back with the corner of the blade to better see into the dark slit—and catch sight of a tiny shadow, like a bruise or a clot, among vessels, bone, and tendon. I gently prod the bloody thing with the razor, trying to tease it closer to the surface, to the light.

"Can you pour some gin in there," I ask Worthy, and he obliges.

The liquor makes my flesh scream, but it clears away the blood, revealing a thin black disc the size of my pinky nail. As I study it, a tiny monochrome video begins playing, all in grays and blacks like an LCD. It appears to be a woman walking down a sidewalk. But before I can take a closer look, the disc goes dark again.

Did that actually just happen?

I'm so fearful it did not that it takes all the guts I can summon to ask Worthy: "Did you see it?"

He looks at me, his face drained white. "The woman strolling down the street playing on the tiny TV in your arm? Yeah, I saw it. Christ almighty."

Proof.

Proof. I am not Dorothy Frasier, suicidal schizophrenic housewife from 1954. That I am, in fact, Bix Parrish, a soldier from the year 2035 sent back in time to 1954 to find one of the doctors at Hanover.

I'd like to take the facts I can remember from my previous jumps to the future and process what all of this means in pieces, grasp the implications one at a time, in some sort of logical order.

But that's not what's happening.

Every bit is hitting me at once, a fire hose of ramifications big and small, practically blasting me into the late Mrs. Worthy's lemon-yellow wall.

The *voice* was right: I *am* on a mission for mankind.

Which I suspect is not going well.

No shit.

So many important questions whose answers I should now be concerned with are skittering through my head—like who the hell is the woman on the video playing inside my wrist? And how is she related to what I'm supposed to do here? And how could some doctor on Hanover's staff possibly possess the key to defeating a virus eighty years in the future?

The list goes on. But those global worries are so monumental. Distant. Abstract. And my mind is seeking a more tangible bad.

So, it keeps returning to one question:

Who *is* Paul? The man I entrusted with my care. My sanity. My sexual satisfaction. The man I've had some sort of relationship with in the past . . . or more accurately, the future.

I take my wedding band off. Lay it on the table.

Does Paul also want the virus sample from the mysterious doctor here in '54? Is that why he did what he did to me? To stop me? Use me?

It definitely feels more personal than that.

"If you take that thing out, we can study it without all the blood." Worthy says, eyeing the disc that is again obscured by blood still oozing from the cut flesh.

"I would, but there's a chance doing it wrong might split me into a trillion pieces," I say.

"Then it stays. But I'm not sure how we keep the doctor in the emergency room from seeing it when he stitches you up. He's going to be curious—"

"We're not going to a hospital," I say.

"No, we have to. It's just . . . I don't think I can stitch that—"

"Relax. You won't have to. Is there fishing line in there?" I ask, pointing at the tackle box on the floor.

"You're going to do it yourself?" he asks. I nod and he shakes his head—but goes over to the metal box and retrieves a fresh package of nylon fishing line and scissors from it.

"Now I just need the right needle," I say, and we both look through the doorway at the dusty table in the dining room with its piles of sewing. He goes over and starts combing through one of the sewing boxes. I grab the dish towel and follow. I try to be gentle, disturb things as little as possible as I go through Missus Worthy's notions. "What was her name, your wife?" I ask.

"Ellie. Her name was Ellie," Worthy says, turning to a new box in his search.

"What happened?"

"Leukemia," he says. "There was nothing the doctors could do . . . It was . . . It all happened very fast. I felt so . . . "

"Powerless?"

"Yeah. I would have done anything to save her, switch places . . ."

"Whatever it took?"

Worthy nods. "Whatever it took. Protect the people you love. But there wasn't a damn thing I could do except watch it take her."

The two of us continue our search in silence till he pulls a small, curved needle from the box. "How about this?"

"Perfect."

Worthy grabs gauze and a roll of tape from his medicine cabinet, and in minutes, with his queasy assistance, I've stitched up the wound with the sterilized needle and fishing line and bandaged it. A definite skill I possess. Am I also a nurse in the far, fucked future?

"Amazing job," Worthy says, eyeing my wrist as he puts a plate of warmed-up meatloaf in front of me. He might just be more captivated by my fishing line MacGyvering than the idea I've time-traveled. But it could also be that it's all his mind is currently allowing itself to process.

I tear into the meatloaf. My hunger, held at bay by my adrenaline rush these last couple hours, has returned with a vengeance, and I am wolfing down the meal at a crazy rate.

"You should chew more," Worthy says.

I should. Pretty sure the Heimlich maneuver won't be invented for another twenty years. Worthy wouldn't be of much help should I choke, so I try to slow down.

Now that I've tended my wound and stuffed my gullet, it's time to ponder options. But I don't have options, just *an* option—finding the link, my only connection to the future. And answers. "I need to find Dorothy Frasier. Now."

* * *

Fifteen minutes later, Worthy joins me by one of the curtain-covered windows in his darkened living room. "Got it, the location in Washington, D.C., Dorothy Frasier was partial to. My friend on the Metro force looked it up in their files. Union Station." He joins me in peering through the break in the curtains at the deserted street. "You think Paul could have followed you here?" Worthy asks.

I feel no prickling sensation running down my spine. See nothing amiss out there in the snowy suburban darkness. But all the same—

"We should go," I say, and we head for the door.

CHAPTER 35

WORTHY AND I split up, and I take the pickup into downtown Bixby. No need for the deputy to be caught driving a stolen truck. Every few seconds, my eyes flick to the rearview mirror, checking the other cars on the road through the falling snow for any signs of Paul, but I see none. If he's out there, he's keeping well hidden.

I ditch the pickup behind a liquor store near the train depot, then slip between buildings and descend to the railroad tracks. Run down them till I come to a crossing a quarter mile away.

Worthy's waiting there in his Chevy Bel Air. Elvis Presley's singing on the radio as I approach. The deputy moves some folded shirts from the dry cleaners to the back seat to make room for me. I get in the car and wait for him to drive. But he doesn't.

"Worthy, we really need to go," I say, then look at him. See his expression's gone dark.

"I need to say something first. How truly, truly sorry I am for not letting you go that day in Hanover's driveway, for not trusting the feeling I had that there was more to you than Dorothy Frasier. And that day in the visitors' room," he says, hands gripping the steering wheel tightly, "when you walked in on the arm of that nurse. It was obvious the damage they were inflicting on you. I should've fought harder with Dr. Sherman and the hospital superintendent—"

"Stop. There was absolutely nothing you could have done, except what you did—which was respect me enough to tell me the truth," I say, hoping to end this revisit of victim me.

But as we head down the road, he says, "Tell me."

"Tell you what?"

"All you've got the stomach to share."

I start my rehash as an effort to give the minimum of details necessary to satisfy Worthy's curiosity—a sort of *Reader's Digest* version of my tortures and humiliations that I can shed quickly.

But once I get going, I can't stop the unspooling. There's this comfort with Worthy that fuels my letdown. He doesn't interrupt my torrent of words with questions, just lets me talk. I tell him everything I've learned about 2035 and time travel. Tethers. Links. Nerds. My mystery mission to speak to some shrink at Hanover, convince them to give up the location of a virus sample that could hold the key to stopping the Guest. That time is running out. Maybe it already has . . .

And I tell the increasingly horrified Worthy what I remember of those last days in the Unit.

Of my battle to hold on to what he had told me in the visitors' room. Of Mary saving me from electrocution, then helping me fake the seizure to avoid complete regression. Of my time recovering—and dodging Lester—in the infirmary.

But when I get to Paul bringing me "home," my throat starts to tighten, and the *voice* tries to end my words.

Stop. Baring your soul to this guy accomplishes nothing.

The voice is a remnant of the old me. The Bix before time travel, the one who is fine with beating up nurses, hitting deputies with rocks, stabbing doctors, eliminating suspicious spouses—but can't handle sharing her feelings. Old Bix.

I'm no longer that person.

So I don't stop. I tell Worthy about Paul and Eloise gaslighting me, and by the time I reach the point where I distrusted myself enough to turn my care and upkeep over to Paul, the words are coming out half-strangled, each one draining a little more energy from me.

How could I have let Paul's bullshit happen? How could I give myself away like that?

Even with the damage from the machine and the protocol, how did I not see it? Sense it?

Route 29 is a four-lane highway lit only by the Chevy's headlights and those of the cars sharing the road with us. On either side are deep gray woods, freshly dusted in snow.

I close my eyes and try to forget my tale and self-blame, think only of the cool, gray woods.

* * *

It's the sound of my own voice that wakes me. A keening moan, ragged and feral, pouring out of me that I can't seem to control. So I let it have its way with me, rock back and forth, watching the butterfly-shaped stain on the wall slowly spin around.

No, that's not right—I'm the one that's spinning, writhing, twitching in perpetual motion on the padded beige floor.

I try to stop myself but can't find the off button.

The lock on the padded door CLICKS, and before it can swing open I scramble back to my corner, where no one can sneak up on me from behind. Two nurses are watching me from the doorway. One's Wallace; the other I don't recognize. She's new, maybe sent here by the people who really run this place . . . the ones who steal things from your mind and don't let you see any sky even though they could . . .

"What's her story?" the new one asks. Like she doesn't know . . . like she didn't write the whole book . . .

"Hasn't been lucid for months," Wallace says. "Somehow got hold of a sharp piece of metal and slashed both wrists. They found her sitting in a pool of her own blood, muttering something about 'proof.'"

"Seems docile. Why is she in J-Ward?"

"Docile?" Wallace smiles. "Just don't turn your back on her," she says, and the two begin to cackle like witches. So I speak my words of protection, unbroken syllables to keep *them* away, the ones who are after me . . . the ones who really run this place . . .

"Time to go, Dorothy," Wallace says, hands reaching for me—and I claw at her—

"You're safe. It's okay!" a voice says.

"Don't come any closer!" I scream.

"Bix! It's me, Worthy!" And I feel his hand on my shoulder.

I open my eyes, see Worthy's eyes shifting their worried gaze back and forth between me and the road ahead. He's got a fresh scratch on his cheek. I must've done that. "That was some dream you were having. You all right?" he asks.

Just a dream. I take a few deep breaths, let it fade away.

"So, how does it feel. To know you're her, Bix?"

"Good. The certainty's good," I say. I don't tell him it also feels like a yoke's been lowered onto my shoulders, but how much water I will be hauling in its buckets has not yet been revealed. What exactly *is* my mission here in '54? And what does that woman walking down the street on my disc have to do with it? "Did you recognize the woman in my wrist?" I ask.

"No, too small and too fast for me." He glances over. "So how long has it been since you last time-traveled?"

"Weeks at least. Maybe a month."

Worthy's quiet, probably thinking the same thing I am—that it's been a while. What if we don't find the real Dorothy Frasier and get back the link Ethan spoke about—so there *are* no more trips to the future? And I'm left wondering what all of this was for.

What I was for.

I turn up the radio, eager for a break from all the dread and speculation tumbling through my head. The announcer's talking about Hemingway and his ill-fated safari in Africa. Next he moves on to Khrushchev, Matchbox cars, and the Chevy Corvette. All appear to be taking America by storm.

We drive through the seedy Rosslyn section of Arlington, past its pawnshops, pool halls, and brothels, rounding a large curve in the road whose sign reads WELCOME TO WASHINGTON D.C.

We ascend a straightaway onto a beautiful moonlit bridge lit by old-fashioned pale green streetlamps spilling ghostly circles of light onto the snowy roadway—

And my heart just about leaps from my chest.

I know this bridge—unlike anyplace I've seen since waking on the bus. Its name floats to the surface of my memory with the certainty of cherry Life Savers: "Key Bridge."

"Yes, the Francis Scott Key Bridge. You remember it?" he asks, and I nod.

To our right, the lights of Washington twinkle with a warm incandescent glow.

To our left is a cluster of buildings clinging like barnacles to a steep slope. Georgetown University. Two church-like spires rise above the rest. I am certain I know these towers. Intimately. Like you would the playground of your elementary school. They are part of Healy Hall, a towering academic castle of granite at the heart of Georgetown's campus.

My home. The one I've searched for everywhere in Dorothy's life. I feel elation, vindication, a whole raft of ebullient thoughts—

But twisted up in them is dread, because I am absolutely certain some very bad things have happened there at Georgetown—or *will* happen.

Worthy sees me staring off toward the school. "That's Georgetown University. Do you think you know it?" Worthy asks as we turn toward Washington and the towers recede.

I do not wish to share my dread—which is an option, now that I'm out of Hanover. "That's where I grew up."

We head down M Street, a road in Georgetown lined with upscale stores with colorful awnings spanning their fronts. Like Key Bridge, the street looks very familiar—but different at the same time. Cleaner.

Soon we're veering down Pennsylvania Avenue, and the White House is coming up on the left. Eisenhower's behind those walls. It's not in any way barricaded, and I'm amazed how close we are to it as we drive by, like I could reach out and touch the portico. On our right is the enormous White House Christmas tree—which still prompts thoughts of drones and the Guest. But now those thoughts are more like questions, less like threats, and they do not derail me.

CHAPTER 36

U NION STATION IS a majestic confection of white marble arches
and columns, sitting in a field blanketed with snow like a vast
neo-Roman igloo. We park on First Street, a dark road running
alongside the high stone wall supporting the station's tracks above.

Walking through its long, arched portico, my eyes scan the station's
gray shadows for signs of Paul but see nothing.

Worthy opens a heavy bronze door, and we enter the station's
incredible waiting room. High above us, its barrel-shaped ceiling
stretches a block in either direction, lined with countless gold-
painted octagonal recesses. A thousand golden eyes shimmering in
the lamplight.

There's a hum to the space from all the holiday travelers trying to
get to their destinations, like putting a conch shell to your ear and
hearing a human ocean. A nearby clock reads ten after ten.

Above us, a string of marble Roman soldiers runs along a ledge
spanning the station. Each is dressed only on top and holds a shield
in front of their naked nether regions for chastity's sake. I remember
these skirtless Romans—I've been in this room before.

"The police report was sparse on details. Not exactly sure where
they found Dorothy," Worthy says.

So, we're methodical, check every room in the place for signs of
her, starting on the second floor and working our way down.

We also ask porters, ticket sellers, and other workers if any has
seen a woman with my hair color acting strange around the station

or railyard. I let Worthy do most of the talking. We finish with the platforms, quizzing conductors, porters, and maintenance men.

But no Dorothy. Several do remember her, but none has seen the woman in at least a couple of months.

Worthy and I are walking back up a platform, nursing our disappointment, when we pass an older man and a teenage boy wheeling their tobacco and candy cart down the platform. "Ex . . . excuse me, have either of you seen a woman hanging around the trains? Hair color similar to mine. Dorothy is her name."

The old guy says, "Oh yeah. A woman—unusual for an FRN."

Worthy and I look at him blankly, and the teen intervenes: "FRN, it's short for, pardon me, miss, 'effing rail nut.' Those people with a thing for trains."

"She was crazier than most," the old guy adds. "Liked to slip off the platforms and wander the yard. Every so often the police would have to come drag her out kicking and screaming."

"Have you seen her recently?" Worthy asks.

Both shake their heads, and I fall into a funk. My last chance at tracking down the woman with my link and getting back to the far, fucked future blown. Learning who's got the rat virus that could help save so many people is looking pretty damn unlikely.

✳   ✳   ✳

"It was always a long shot, finding her here," Worthy says as we walk back to the Chevy. The wind is starting to pick up, blowing snowflakes into our eyes. "If I'm Dorothy Frasier and I've been lucky enough to send some poor time traveler to Hanover in my place, I wouldn't come back here, where porters and candy sellers, not to mention police, could identify me. She'd get as far away from here as possible."

"If she could. But she can't," I say.

"She can't?"

"She needs to be near the tracks. The candy sellers said Dorothy was a rail nut and they're right," I say. "On the bus, when she was stealing my link, she said she had to be near the trains to watch over them, signal God. And today, near the altar she built by a railroad track, I saw what I think was a viewing platform she made by stacking the base of a wooden statue on top of an old furnace. It was just high enough to watch trains from. Trains are Dorothy's crazy-maker."

"Her what?"

"Crazy-maker. My friend Georgie's term. It means the thing a patient is so obsessed by that they're willing to risk everything for it. I think Dorothy's still nearby."

"Okay . . . But where?"

"Somewhere close to the tracks, where she can see the trains, but she can't *be* seen."

"She's thinking that strategically?"

"She may be mentally unbalanced, but she's not dumb."

"So, a duck blind for trains?" Worthy asks, grinning.

"Exactly."

And we both look up through the falling snow at the soot-covered stone wall supporting the west side of the station's railyard above. It must be thirty feet high—dwarfs the rowhouses across First Street from it. "But even from the roof of those rowhouses, there's no sight line to the railyard," Worthy says.

"What about the other side?" I ask.

* * *

We drive over to Second Street on the eastern side of Union Station's tracks. It's a dim road lined with aging brick buildings facing the railyard's other foundation wall. But on this side of the tracks, that wall's only fifteen feet high. The upper floor of these buildings could give Dorothy the right perch.

A truck hauling snow-covered firewood disappears into the dark of Second Street. "Turn down there."

Worthy's dubious. "It's eleven o'clock. You've been going for hours. After weeks of sedation . . . and worse. We should check you into a hotel so you can sleep. Regroup in the morning."

It does feel like days since I snuck out the window. I'm beyond exhausted.

But kinda done with people telling me to rest. We need to find Dorothy now.

"I'm fine," I say, and he reluctantly turns down Second. As we creep along past rowhouses and shops, I scan the windows for any sign of Dorothy Frasier but come up empty.

"There is another possibility," Worthy says. "She's dead."

"Paul?" I ask.

"Do you think he's capable of it?"

My *husband's* gone to great lengths to fake my life. Our lives. Subjected me to mental and physical torture. But murder? "Don't know."

And we lapse into silence for a few blocks. But as we cross L Street, a train passes us on the tracks above, slowly heading out of the station—and I hear the sound of a fifteen-pound ball of plastic crashing into ten pins.

"Listen," I say.

Worthy's quiet a moment. "Bowling?"

"Dorothy's got a thing for it. And she's good. Got a few trophies."

There's a neon sign that reads BOWLING AND BILLIARDS on the second floor of a nearby building, above a bar. I scan the frosted-over windows facing the tracks, see nothing remarkable.

But just around the corner is a church. Trains. Bowling. Church— the Dorothy trifecta. "Pull over."

$$* \quad * \quad *$$

I follow Worthy into the smoky bar, filled with a couple dozen revelers, and we approach a Black bartender drying a highball glass. He eyes Worthy with suspicion, his cop radar pinging away.

"Excuse me, I'm wondering if you could help us out," Worthy says to him. "We're looking for a woman."

"Good bowler," I say. "But a bit strange, with hair my color, maybe in braids."

There's an almost imperceptible rise in the bartender's eyebrows. "No, sorry. Haven't seen anyone matching that description," he says, and turns away from us.

"Really?" Worthy says. "You sure about—?"

"Thank you for your time," I say to the bartender, and strong-arm a confused Worthy through the crowd toward the rear of the bar.

"Why'd you pull me away?" he grouses. "That guy knows something."

"I know," I say, and point to the staircase near the bar's back door.

"Oh," he says, and follows me up the stairs.

On the second floor, sounds of crashing balls and pins bounce off the walls. Beyond the counter are four bowling alleys. A barrier wall extending down from the ceiling to a couple feet above the lanes hides the equipment that resets the pins.

I scan the bowlers but see no sign of Dorothy. Walk beyond the farthest lane to the windows we saw from the street. They indeed have a commanding view of the snowy railyard. Then I notice on one of the window sashes a line of seashells arranged from largest to smallest—like the altar behind the church—and the hairs on the back of my neck stand up.

I start back to Worthy, who's speaking to an old guy manning the counter, but then I spot someone's pant legs under the barrier. On their feet: saddle shoes.

Like Dorothy's.

"What'll it be folks, one game or two?" the guy asks us.

"Do you have a person resetting the pins?" I nod to the area beyond the barrier wall.

"Yup, we do it the old-fashioned way, with pin boys."

"In saddle shoes?"

He smiles. "Not all our pin boys are boys. She bowls herself. Knows what's what. You won't have a problem—"

"What's her name?" Worthy asks him.

"You here to bowl or ask questions?"

Worthy and I take off across the lanes and the guy yells, "Get off of there!"

Immediately, a head peers from beneath the barrier, hair in braids—

Dorothy Frasier! She disappears, and we chase her, slipping and sliding on the oiled wood amid more shouts from the guy.

As I jump over a bowling ball hurtling down lane two, a door slams somewhere behind the barrier.

"Fire escape," Worthy shouts as he avoids crashing pins on lane three and ducks under the barrier. I follow, entering a shadowy, dust bunny–ridden space of steel contraptions holding sets of pins.

I duck under one and through an open door into a tiny back room with a window now open to a fire escape. Random snowflakes blow in through the window, landing on a nearby cot—where lies my missing red purse. Inside it I find a small solar battery and some change. But no link, no object that looks like it could magically transport me to another time.

I grab the bag and head out the window. See through the falling snow Worthy now chasing Dorothy down the alley below.

The fire escape's metal rungs have iced over, forcing me to slow down to keep from sliding off. By the time I jump the final few feet to the slushy alley, Worthy's rounding its far corner onto Third Street.

I reach Third just as Worthy's tackling Dorothy to the pavement. By the time I catch up to them, he's got her upright, holding tight to the screaming woman's scrawny arm. Worthy looks at me. "This her?"

"My angel!" Dorothy says, staring at me with that venerating look she had on the bus. "Back from the devil's house to help me again. Another of God's miracles. Praise the—"

"Where is it?" I roar, and she flinches. Good. I drop the purse, shove my hands into Dorothy's pants pockets—

And pull out a dark, shiny object the size of a cell phone.

The link.

Fuck yeah!

"No! It's mine now. I need it to signal the Lord!" Dorothy screams as I take the link over to a nearby streetlamp for a better look.

The thing is sticky and smudged. Is that chocolate on the screen? I flip open the cover on it and see a keypad and a round button. I press it but nothing happens, and just when I'm thinking the thing is dead, a dim green spiral appears on the glassy screen, rotating on some invisible axis.

The image dims for a few seconds, then leaps to full strength, and immediately I feel it—the familiar buzz in my toes, rising up through my body—

And I can hear the first rumblings of the white roar, like the leading edge of a summer storm rolling in fast. I look up, see snowflakes falling in the rainbow ring of light cast by the streetlamp.

"Bix?" Worthy's staring at me.

"It's coming," I say, securing the link deep in the pocket of my pants. The vibration in my head is threatening to upend me, so I brace myself against the lamppost.

"What's coming?"

I don't answer—can't answer—as the white roar overtakes me.

CHAPTER 37

"GRAB HER! TRY to hold her down," someone whispers. A hand clamps over my mouth and suddenly I'm on the ground. More hands and body parts quickly lock me down, like at Hanover—only now it's Kyung doing the gagging. And astride me, like a cowboy on a roped calf, is Ethan, his Arctic Monkeys hoodie close enough that I can make out the tiny cracks in its fading decal.

I see trees high above Kyung and Ethan—we're in the woods again, in the middle of a thicket of overgrown bushes and trees. But this time there is daylight.

Nearby I spot a familiar beech tree charred and split by lightning, and I know exactly which woods these are: Glover Park, a narrow ribbon of woods, miles long but barely a thousand feet wide, that runs alongside Georgetown University all the way down to the Potomac.

Both nerds keep checking the trees. Something's got them spooked. Kyung brings a finger to her lips.

I nod, and the two release me. As Ethan helps me up, he says softly, "You need to know you're not Dorothy Frasier. Your real name is—"

"Bix, short for Beatrix, Parrish. I know now," I whisper back, and pull up my sleeve, show them my freshly restitched wrist.

Grins appear on their faces, and without warning Ethan's ambushing me with a hug. "Thank God!" he says, pouring all his words and raw emotions into my shoulder. "Jeez, you're so thin!" he says, and the intensity of this stranger's concern—it's all too much. I push him away, and now he and Kyung are eyeing me with fresh concern.

"Are you . . . all right?" Ethan asks softly. "We know about Sherman's research in the Unit. What you've been going through there." The guy knows jack shit. "It's okay. You can trust me, Bix."

Can I? Trust a twin brother I remember less than Paul?

And look how that turned out.

I've currently had my fill of loved ones foisted on me, demanding my affection. My faith.

"Here," Ethan says, offering me a protein bar. "A time jump does a number on the metabolism. Quickens the appetite." He does not lie. I barely get the wrapper off before I'm shoving the thing in my mouth. It's a little chewy but edible.

While I'm wolfing it down, I notice Kyung watching me. Observing. Like Sherman, she's on the lookout for any chinks in my mental armor. Can't really blame her. She's seen me at my worst in those quick trips I made here weeks ago. Probably thinking I might not be all there. She's in need of reassurance. I pull the link from my pocket to show I got it back, made the trip here of my own volition, and now relief floods even Kyung's face.

"Your battery symbol's flashing. Almost at zero," Ethan says. "You're lucky you made it back here, didn't end up lost somewhere in between."

That's a possibility? To be lost *in between*?

"Now that you've got the link back," Kyung says, "and we know you're not suddenly going to wink out of here, we've got time. We'll recharge it as soon as we reach safety." She starts to shove the black lunch box–looking object I saw on my last jump here into her backpack.

"What is that?" I ask Ethan.

"We call it the football," Ethan answers. "It's a remote beacon that lets us recapture you or some other traveler outside the lab."

"Why would you need to do that?" I ask Ethan.

Kyung answers instead. "It's just good to have the flexibility."

"Speaking of other travelers. There's something important I need to tell you as well, about what's happened in '54—" I start to say.

"You can tell us all about it later. When we get to a safe—"

A twig snaps somewhere in the woods nearby, and the nerds' eyes flick nervously to the trees again. "What's out there?" I whisper, but before either can answer, a guy in a hoodie emerges silently from the thick undergrowth. He's Black, no more than twenty, lean but built. Slung over his shoulder is a backpack—

And a semiautomatic rifle.

I grab the hunting knife from Kyung's belt and push her and Ethan back, brandishing the blade at the armed man-boy in a woefully outgunned attempt at defense.

"Fuhhhhck," he whispers, lowering his gun and watching me. "Nerds weren't kidding, you really are wiped. Bix, it's me. Kofi."

"It's okay, Bix," Kyung says, nervously eyeing her knife in my hands. "Kofi's one of your men."

"*My* men? Why do I have men?" I ask, handing Kyung back her knife.

"From what's left of the Child's Army," Kofi says, his eyes continuously sweeping the area as he speaks.

What's left of it? Is the Child's Army some kind of failed weekend warrior group? An unpopular militia? Maybe I was just some crazed doomsday prepper whose boasts about drinking her own urine and refusal to share her Bisquick drove all the others away. Would explain some of my skills.

"Those Reckoners'll be doubling back soon, so we need to get moving," Kofi says. "We'll use the woods then skirt along the border of campus to avoid them. Once we've gotten past campus, we can cut over to the safe house."

"What are 'Reckoners'?" I ask.

Kofi opens his mouth to answer, but Kyung beats him to it. "Shouldn't we be going, Kofi?" He nods but he's clearly pissed at

Kyung. Interesting. "When we get to the safe house, we'll explain things, Bix. And you can tell us your news."

She's right. I've got the link now. I'm not going anywhere. Neither are they. My news about Paul, a fake husband I somehow knew here in 2035, is big, full of implications and unanswered questions—like how the hell was Paul able to send himself back to '54 in the nerds' machine right under their noses? And why?

It's way too much to unpack while being chased through the woods by an unknown enemy. My news will need some quiet and calm to digest.

"Can you run?" Kofi asks me, and I nod. "Then let's go," he says, and the four of us take off through the woods.

It must be April or May. The leaves on the trees still have that bright yellow-green of new growth, and the place is teeming with wildlife. A wild turkey mother and her chicks scurry right across our path, fearless.

Glover Park is shaped like a cattle chute—and we're the cattle. As we head south down it, I steal an occasional glance behind me for any signs of the mysterious Reckoners but see nothing.

Soon we're coming up on Reservoir Road, an east-west connector on the northern end of Georgetown University's medical complex that bisects the park. It could use some repaving; I can see weeds sprouting through cracks in its asphalt here and there. We pause a moment behind the cover of bushes just short of the road while Kofi scopes out the trail on the far side of it that winds through a field of shoulder-high grass.

Reservoir Road is oddly devoid of cars—but not people. In the distance to our left, a steady trickle of them is crossing the road like army ants on the march.

"Who are they?" I ask, and swear I see odd looks passing between Ethan, Kyung, and Kofi. Or maybe I'm just imagining it, my mind still in paranoia overdrive after those last tense hours in 1954.

"They're members of the Tabula Rasa," Ethan finally replies.

Tabula Rasa. I remember the name from earlier trips here. "The religious cult?" I ask, and feel Kyung's eyes on me, once again observing.

Ethan nods. "They're cutting through the med complex to get to campus for a gathering on Healy Lawn. They call it a Reclamation."

"The Reckoners chasing us are the Tabula Rasa's security guys," Kofi says, "there to 'protect' the Tabula Rasa flock from its enemies."

"Us?"

He nods. "They almost caught these two earlier," Kofi says, pointing at Kyung and Ethan. "But I got them away, and now the goons are combing the area."

Suddenly there's a whoosh in the air: a dozen birds taking flight from somewhere deep in the woods we've just come from. Something's disturbed them.

Kofi and I look at each other. "Time to go," I say.

"This way," he says, and the four of us streak across the dusty road and lose ourselves in the tall grass.

✳   ✳   ✳

Minutes later, we've climbed a wooded embankment out of Glover Park, up to a narrow drive that skirts the backside of the Georgetown Medical Center—

Or what remains of it. The buildings near us have been torched recently, their brick outer structures still standing but their insides all blackened and hollow. None of the charred ruins have been fenced off yet.

As we jog south down the drive, I spot an old face mask on the ground. Then another one, and another, more and more till we're walking over dozens littering the drive. And not just masks. All around us lie the faded pastel remains of discarded PPE and surgical gloves. Whole piles of them have been blown by the wind up against a giant white medical tent we're approaching. The tent looks like it's been set up for patient overflow but the thing is empty except for a few stripped-down cots, some abandoned equipment, and more discarded PPE.

I see a squirrel jump onto the branch of a tree that is literally growing up through the *inside* of one of the charred buildings. That tree is at least five years old. These aren't freshly gutted buildings awaiting safety fencing and demolition. They've simply been abandoned.

"What the fuck has happened here? Where are they, all the doctors, nurses, patients?" I ask, and everyone halts. "And the police—why aren't they out arresting those Tabula Rasa thugs? I'm sure the cops have their hands full dealing with all the issues caused by the Guest, but they should at least be—"

"You haven't told her?" Kofi asks Ethan and Kyung.

"We thought she knew," Ethan says, and Kyung nods.

"Know what?" I ask, and feel a sickening dread spreading through me at just how grim the answer will be. Could Sherman have been right? That my subconscious has played a role in my memory block, protecting me from bad news with its shoddy recall.

"There are no cops, Bix," Kofi says. "Not anymore."

"Why? What happened?" I ask.

"The Guest happened," Kyung says.

"Come, we'll show you. Up ahead," Ethan says, and the four of us jog down the drive, picking our way through heaving chunks of pavement overrun with trees and shoulder-high grass growing right through them. A wall we pass is covered with graffiti, phrases like: "the Chosen shall inherit," "#TabulaRasa4life," "New Covenant= Salvation," "#Timeoftesting," "Areyouworthy?" And a final one someone's tried to get rid of: "the TR should STFU."

Soon we reach the end of the driveway near the observatory and I get my first look at Georgetown's campus. It's in worse shape than the medical center. Ivy, sprouting up through cracks in the pavement, has overtaken it. Most buildings, even the burned-out ruins, are covered in the vegetation. They look like enormous chia pets, and I can't take my eyes off the sight till Ethan calls to me.

He and the others are gathered around a woman seated on the bench. As I approach them, a foul stench hits me.

"This is the Guest," Kofi says, and steps aside, allowing me to see the woman. She's dead. And it wasn't a good death: pale skin covered in pocks, eyes open wide, bright red with blown capillaries. The blood around her mouth hints at last moments spent in a battle for oxygen. A fly lands near a pink mark on her neck that resembles a hickey, crawls over it, then up her jaw and into her mouth.

Without warning, the remains of Worthy's meatloaf and Ethan's protein bar come hurtling upward.

I finish puking and straighten up to find the others eyeing me with an odd mix of shock and dismay. Ethan hands me a water bottle, and as I rinse out my mouth I'm mulling which of the fifty or so questions piled up in my brain to ask first—but then I hear the sound of an engine. It's coming from the thick, overgrown hedges encircling nearby Cooper Field.

The smell of more death is overwhelming by the time I reach a break in the hedge. The artificial turf of Georgetown's football field has been rolled back like a sardine can lid, revealing the bare ground beneath it, now studded with dozens of fifteen-by-thirty-foot mounds and one open pit. A dump truck backs up to the pit, and a boy holding a pole waits as it tilts and releases its load.

At first I don't realize what it is I'm seeing fall from the truck. Or I don't want to realize.

Bodies. At least a couple dozen drop into the pit. They don't lie neatly. Don't behave. Rigored arms and legs stick out, akimbo, in whatever position they landed. The boy's been tasked with smoothing out the pile and prods a body poking up too high with his pole till it slides to the bottom.

There must be thousands buried here.

Crows fly out a broken window of Kennedy Hall at the far end of the gridiron graveyard. One bird peels away from the group, swoops down, and lands on the pile. Begins to walk over the bodies till the boy shoos him away with his pole.

It's a Hieronymus Bosch painting come to life.

"Newcastle Virus was the Guest's official name," says Ethan, now at my elbow. "Named for the Seattle suburb where it first appeared in early December of 2025."

Kyung joins us at the hedge break. "Nobody knew where it came from. It was like no virus scientists had ever seen."

"All over the world, they scrambled to understand it enough to develop a vaccine or treatment," Ethan says. "But the Guest was too fast. Within weeks it was everywhere. It spread through the air, so it was off-the-charts contagious."

"Airborne?" My body instinctively backs away from the field. "We were inches from that woman. Unmasked! We've all been exposed—"

"You don't need to worry about catching it," Kyung says.

"I don't? Why?" I ask her.

"You're already infected."

CHAPTER 38

The boy's now spreading lime over the bodies.

"I'm sick with that?" I do a quick check-in with my body but feel no signs of nightmare pandemic brewing in me.

"We all are," Ethan says.

"Not just sick, Bix," Kyung says. "Dying. The Guest is one hundred percent fatal . . ."

One hundred percent.

She said that, right?

For a few seconds that high-pitched whine invades my head like it did that day with Worthy in the visitors' room. But I beat it back. I need answers: "Why would you send me to '54? Risk me spreading—"

"You're not contagious. At least not right now," Ethan says. "It's . . . sleeping."

"Sleeping? What are you talking about?"

"The Guest has three stages," Kyung says. "Those twenty-five and older go right to stage three, get very sick and die in days. But those younger only get stage one: no symptoms in most—just extremely contagious the first week."

"And stage two?"

"Where we're at. The latency period between one and three," Kyung says, "where the virus goes dormant like chicken pox, beds down in your brain for a long stay." Whatever is left of Worthy's meatloaf is threatening to come up.

"That's why you call it the Guest?"

She nods. "And it sleeps till—"

"My quarter hour," I say.

"Yes," Ethan says, "roughly twenty-five years of age. It's thought that the timing has something to do with the maturation of the pre-frontal cortex—"

"How old are we?" I ask Ethan.

"Twenty-three years, nine months," Ethan says.

Life so precious it's measured by the month.

"Stage three starts with a warning," Kyung says, "a sentinel rash—that hickey-like mark you saw on the woman's neck. It's called 'the devil's kiss' around here. Once it appears, you've got only about twenty-four hours till you're contagious."

"That would explain the list of crematoriums in your note," I say to Ethan.

He nods. "If the devil's kiss appeared on your neck in 1954, and you couldn't get back here, you'd need to make *arrangements* quickly, before you became contagious."

Jesus.

Insane 1954 housewife is looking pretty fucking good right now.

"When you told me weeks ago the Guest was a 'deadly virus,'" I say, "I thought you meant COVID-deadly—a deadly that could be managed. But this"—we watch the boy climb out of the pit—"you meant civilization-ending deadly."

"We thought you realized," Ethan says.

"Why would I? In my trips here none of you appeared to be taking precautions. No masks. Distancing. So later, after I knew this was real, I figured you'd had the Guest but recovered. That it was largely survivable. Not to mention you had a goddamn time machine at your disposal! I just assumed—"

"That we weren't in the middle of a viral apocalypse?" Kyung asks. "Would've been nice. But unfortunately the Guest is an amazingly efficient killer. What usually limits a deadly disease's vector, its ability to spread, is its own lethality. Take Ebola. It sickens and kills its host before they can spread it far, containing an outbreak. But the Guest's initial stage let its young, asymptomatic hosts move freely, spreading the virus far and wide."

"Once they figured it out," Ethan says, "lots of grown-ups tried to wall themselves off from the children. Lockdowns. Martial law. Riots. It got ugly."

"And useless," Kyung says. "Within six weeks, everyone on the planet over twenty-five was dead. Doctors, scientists, police officers, power plant workers, grave diggers—all gone."

A world with no one over twenty-five. I think back to that first day at Hanover, when the sight of Wallace's and Sherman's wrinkles seemed so shocking, so impossible. This is why. I hadn't seen a "grown-up" in ten years.

"When the Guest struck," Ethan continues, "about sixty-five percent of the U.S. population was over twenty-five. But that was just the beginning. Lack of clean drinking water, lack of working sewers, lack of parents . . ."

"Turns out global chaos isn't good for the young," Kyung says. "We think at least ninety percent of the U.S. population is gone. At least two hundred and eighty million dead."

I need time to absorb all the nightmare facts and figures of the last few minutes but there is none—

"Shit, Reckoners," Kofi says, using his scope to peer through the overgrowth at the distant end of the gridiron cemetery. He hands me the scope and I finally get a look at them, a half dozen solidly built guys in leather jackets stationed between us and our escape route. Fuck.

"What now?" Ethan asks him.

"We should double back, take our chances on Reservoir Road," Kyung says.

"No. They'll be there. They're tightening the noose," I say with a certainty of their tactics I can't begin to know how I possess. But I can see in his eyes that Kofi agrees. We're fucked.

I turn back to the steady stream of Tabula Rasa believers pouring in for whatever a Reclamation is. The *voice* has been pretty quiet since I climbed out that window and launched myself into this. Guess she finally got what she wanted: me in action. But she pipes up now:

The only way out is through the fucker.

"The only way out is through," I say, removing the expletive. Can't believe I'm repeating *her* words, the chilling voice in my head I spent weeks trying to silence. "We need to join them, the crowds heading for the Reclamation ceremony . . . use their numbers to hide us while we climb the steps and cut through campus . . ."

". . . till we reach Copley Lawn," Ethan says.

"No, no, no. You both know she shouldn't be anywhere near those people, let alone a Reclamation," Kyung says to Ethan and Kofi, and I catch more weird looks being exchanged. What are they hiding from me about the Tabula Rasa?

"Unfortunately, Bix is right. It's the best choice, only choice we've got," Kofi says. "Once we reach Copley we'll slip out through the farmers market."

"Fuck," Kyung mutters.

Kofi turns and whispers to me, "You're not so damaged after all. Kyung made it seem like you'd gone completely mental, Humpty-Dumpty fell off the wall cracked." He smiles. "Nope. Still the old Bix."

Not sure what I think of that.

Kofi turns back to Kyung. "You two need to get your things on."

"*Our things?*" I ask Kyung.

"We'll need to blend in, look the part if this crazy plan is going to work. Put this on," she says, handing me a skirt from her backpack, before stepping into one herself. I pull the skirt over my pants. It goes clear to the ground. Next she hands me a dull brown scarf. "For your head. Cover everything."

"Seriously?" I ask. She nods and starts wrapping her own, so I start looping mine around my head. My muscle memory appears to be quite practiced in headscarf draping, and I quickly cover my hair and shoulders in the scarf's modest folds.

But Kyung frowns. "Nope. All of it," and she draws the tail end of her own scarf across her face and secures it. Now all that's visible are her eyes, watching me, waiting.

"Full fundamentalist?" I ask. She doesn't explain. Just waits. I unfasten the end of my scarf and rewrap it to cover my face, leaving only the narrowest of openings for my eyes. When I finish, I see Ethan and Kofi have pulled their hoods over their heads, throwing their faces into shadow. Hoodie up—that's the extent of the Tabula Rasa's demands on its men.

Kofi walks over to me as he unzips his pack. "You're in luck. Got your favorite with me," he says, and pulls something bundled in a teddy bear baby blanket from his bag. He unfolds it, revealing a SIG Sauer semiautomatic pistol.

I have a favorite gun.

Take it.

"Tuck it in your waistband, under your sweater, in case of trouble," Kofi says, and holds it out to me. The gun oil scent is reassuringly familiar but I hesitate. "Just like riding a bike, Bix. Trust me, it'll all come back to you."

That's what worries me. Sherman said each choice of violence would nudge me closer to my dark side. It was a warning meant for schizophrenic Dorothy, but it's feeling applicable. Old Bix was the one with the favorite gun and questionable moral compass. I wouldn't want to meet her in a dark alley. And I certainly don't want to *become* her all over again.

Whatever I was before, I am no longer a gun person.

We'll see, snowflake.

"No thank you," I say to Kofi. The polite demurral slips out, a relic of the protocol. One of the ruts dug into my mind during my time in the Unit. Wallace would approve of my repatterned manners. Kofi, Kyung, and Ethan are less taken. Surprise and concern show on the guys' faces and what little I can see of Kyung's.

Kyung says, "You really should take the gun—"

"Kyung, it's okay," Kofi says to her, reswaddling the thing, about to put it back in his bag when a pissed-off Kyung grabs it and stuffs it in her own backpack.

Kofi eyes the Tabula Rasa coming down the drive in the distance. "Crowds are big enough now to hide in. Time to go," he says, and the four of us start toward the throngs of true believers climbing the steps that lead to Healy Lawn. I catch up to Kofi ahead of me—out of earshot of Kyung and Ethan.

"Tell me about the Tabula Rasa," I say. Kofi glances back at Kyung and hesitates. "We're about to enter an ocean of them, Kofi, don't you think I deserve to know—"

"Okay, okay. They're a bunch of virulent antitech wafer-huggers led by a talented grifter-showman named Kameron Rook."

"Why all the followers? What is this guy promising them?"

"A long life," says Kofi. "He claims God cured him of the Guest and promises any followers devoted and worthy enough will be cured, too. It's all in his 'New Covenant,' a set of commandments Rook says he received from God in the woods." He rolls his eyes. "All who wish to be saved must live by them during these years he calls the 'Time of Testing.'"

"What kinds of commandments?" I ask.

"The rite of Reclamation, along with rules for dress, behavior, division of labor, food and technology, tithing, engaging in science—"

"Engaging in science?" I ask them.

"Rook says science and tech gone wrong gave us the Guest, climate change, nuclear weapons, so all of it must be closely overseen by Tabula Rasa leaders. Only 'sanctioned science' is permitted. Reckoners hunt down and arrest anyone practicing unsanctioned science. Confiscate or destroy any equipment they find."

"What a load of horseshit," I say.

"Horseshit that's selling," Kofi says. "'Cause Rook realized just how desperate people are to believe in something, to have *someone* in charge. And Stokes knew just how to weaponize that need—through guilt and rules. The stricter the better."

"Stokes?" I ask him.

"One of Kameron Rook's top lieutenants. In charge of psy-ops—indoctrination and general mind-fuckery to keep their flock of followers in line. Had a real gift for it."

"And people really believe this Rook guy's been cured?" I ask.

Kofi nods. "More and more each day. His birth certificate says he's now almost twenty-six, way beyond his quarter hour. But any day now the devil's kiss is gonna appear on his neck—and the Tabula Rasa's sadistic circus goes away."

We pass a guy and girl groping each other against the side of a building. Nearby, two girls are making out on an old couch sitting on the grass. And beyond them a group event on a mattress. Can't help wondering what Wallace would say if she could see it. Or Worthy. What would the deputy make of this feral world?

The first girl sees me watching. "What you looking at, Bible girl?" she snarls.

"Now, that's not very nice," the guy says to her, then calls to me, "You're welcome to join us—but first you're gonna need to lower that veil, lemme see your smile."

And there it is. Always some asshole demanding his smile.

I turn to Kofi. "So, a world of children with no future. Wouldn't people just—"

"Go crazy?" he asks, taking a last look at the sexual festivities.

"Yeah, each in their own way. Especially a person's yoloyear. No two of those alike."

"Yoloyear?"

"A person's last twelve months," he says. "Lots of people try to live out their fantasies. Like a bucket list on steroids. Going for that last thrill, some final bit of happiness . . . no matter how twisted."

CHAPTER 39

W HEN WE GET close to the Tabula Rasa walking down Tondorf Road, I finally get a good look at them. The men have beards, longish hair, hoods or hats on most. Baseball, porkpie, all kinds. Many carry guns.

The Tabula Rasa women and girls are all in long dresses and skirts. Every woman's head is covered, and many have also cloaked their faces.

"Women in headscarves, is that in Rook's New Covenant?" I ask Kyung, and I can see, even with the scarf, a definite tension around her eyes at the question.

She nods. "It started with headscarves. Recently, covering the face has begun to be strongly encouraged." Jesus. She shakes her head like she's trying to shake off the budding horror of the situation. "But it does make for a good disguise."

True. Anonymity's definitely an advantage of this most restrictive of fashion statements.

Ironically, freedom's another—I can react however I choose to people and events without being witnessed. After weeks spent under observation by nurses, doctors, Paul and Eloise, even Ethan, Kyung, and Kofi, all watching for any sign of mental meltdown in me, being unseen feels like a guilty pleasure.

Ahead of us is a large group of young children, most of whom's caregivers are pregnant adolescents.

"Procreation, is that also in the New Covenant?"

I mean it as a joke but Kyung nods. "Risking your life to bring a baby into this world—for the Tabula Rasa it's the ultimate show of faith that God, not science, is going to remedy this. And soon."

Heads bowed, we enter the stream of Tabula Rasa, and none of them gives us even a passing glance. Kofi and Ethan are in front as the four of us begin to climb the first flight of stairs leading up from the field.

"So, you sent me back in time to rewrite the past. Fix all this?" I whisper to Kyung.

"You're not there to rewrite anything!" she whispers back excitedly. "The inventor of the time machine, the late Dr. Cyrus Corbett, believed a traveler's smallest action in the past could cause changes that could ripple out, altering the timeline—and our present."

Ethan turns back to me. "That's why Corbett's number one rule for time travelers was interfere as little as possible with the lives of those around you."

I hadn't realized there was a rulebook. "So when the 'late Dr. Corbett' was killed by the Guest, you inherited his machine?" I ask Kyung.

"Actually no," she says. "According to data from the machine, he wasn't killed by the Guest. Died during a time jump."

Killed by his own machine in the *in between.*

"So, let me see if I have this right," I say as we start across the large patio leading to the next set of stairs. "You sent a woman with a dormant killer germ back in time to 1954 in your murderous machine on the off chance she could get information on a viral sample from a doctor there—while still managing not to alter the timeline and destroy your present? Seems like a solid plan."

"We had to take the chance, Bix," Kyung says. "We've still got the facilities and people to do something with the sample we get from 1954. Study it, hopefully develop a cure. But once we're gone, there'll be no one educated, or trained, enough for that. We're it."

"But if you didn't want me screwing with the timeline, why send me back to gather ingredients for a cure? Preventing the pandemic in 2025 will, for sure, change the timeline."

"The treatment wasn't to *prevent* the pandemic that happened in 2025," Ethan says. "That would create a paradox, and Dr. Corbett's rule number two for time travelers was no paradoxes."

The late Dr. Corbett is starting to get on my nerves. "Pretty sure I'll regret asking this," I say, "but how does preventing the pandemic in 2025 create a paradox?"

"By removing the reason we sent you back from 2035 in the first place," Kyung says. "So then we *wouldn't* send you back . . . so then you wouldn't prevent the pandemic . . . so then we *would* send you back . . . so then you . . . and so on."

Just shoot me now.

"If you mention the multiverse, I'm going to scream," I warn her, and hear Kofi snort ahead of us.

"Anyway," Ethan says, stepping between us, "in answer to your question, prevention in the past is not a possibility. But the present here in 2035 hasn't been written. We *can* bring the sample of rat virus back from 1954 to 2035 and produce a treatment from it. Save us and millions yet to be born."

"How do you even know this rat virus exists in 1954?" I ask.

"In 2025, scientists and governments around the world were desperate for a way to fight the virus," he says. "Many believed if they could find a weaker relative of the Guest virus lurking in animals or humans, they could come up with a cure."

"So they began the largest round of crowd computing in history," Kyung adds as we cross the terrace to the next flight of stairs. "People all over the world took part: the CDC, Russian spooks, librarians, Silicon Valley tycoons, Chinese intelligence, gamers in their parents' basements, all using pattern recognition software. They scoured decades of written material—from newspapers to agricultural reports to top secret NSA files—searching for any mention of a disease that shared the Guest's unique attributes, especially its three-stage pro-gression: juvenile, latency, then the sentinel rash signaling adult onset."

"And they found something in 1954?" I ask.

She nods. "The only lead that checked all the Guest's weird boxes: a July 1954 newspaper article. In it, a biologist from the Fort Detrick biocontainment lab accused the government of a cover-up. They claimed to have worked on something called Project Gambit. It was tasked with studying a virus, NQ-30, discovered when an Arctic ice core dug up by the Army Corps of Engineers melted during a power outage and wiped out the local vermin population—yet it produced only the barest of symptoms in humans."

"But while in the Fort Detrick lab, the rat virus mutated," Ethan says, "morphing into a deadly human virus they called NQ-31."

"You're saying some mutated virus from an army biocontainment lab in 1954 produced symptoms similar to a mysterious virus that wiped out all older adults beginning in 2025?" I ask.

"Not similar. Identical," Ethan says.

My brain somersaults with the implications of that news and I pause a sec to process, but Kyung puts her hand on my arm. "Keep moving," she says softly, and pulls me along. "The scientist in '54 warned the higher-ups that the mutated strain, NQ-31, could cause a global pan-demic far deadlier than the Spanish flu, that it had to be destroyed. And they assured the scientist the virus would be eliminated—"

"Only someone secretly kept it," I say, "'cause they thought they could study and tame it, use it as a weapon against our enemies."

Kyung looks at me, eyes all aglow. "Do you recall us telling you that?"

"No, I recall it's in every movie about space monsters I can remem-ber," I say, and now she glares.

Ethan slides between us as we mount the next set of steps. "After learning the higher-ups had lied, the scientist risked arrest and went to the press, even claimed there was proof—a sample of the original rat virus they'd snuck out of Detrick. But the crazy-sounding story of a killer Arctic rat virus and a secret government cabal was a tough sell."

"In the 1950s, people still trusted their government not to kill them," Kyung adds from behind us.

"And just to make certain no one would take the story seriously," Ethan says, "the military quietly reached out to the heads of the major news organizations, denied the existence of both NQ-30 and the devastating NQ-31. Said it was all the invention of an unstable Fort Detrick employee never even close to the biocontainment lab. After that, no print or television outlet would touch it."

"Except one," Kyung says, "the *Weekly World Post*."

I barely avoid tripping on the next step, turn back to her. "The *Weekly World Post*—the tabloid? That's your 'news source'?"

"Yes."

"So my brain-scrambling mission through time and space is because of a seventy-year-old tabloid story sandwiched somewhere between alien sightings and Twinkie diets?" I ask—

But that's when I see them, just entering the patio below us: a half dozen Reckoners, clearly in pursuit of someone, pushing their way through the crowds of Tabula Rasa faithful, heading for the steps.

CHAPTER 40

T HIS WAY. Now," Kofi says, and the three of us follow him up the last couple steps, then off the path to an alcove hidden behind overgrown bushes under the staircase of a nearby building.

The ground inside the alcove is strewn with random items left behind by previous tenants: a couple cans of peaches, a dirty blanket, a stuffed bear.

I peer through the bushes and thirty seconds later see the Reckoners reach the top of the steps. There are four of them, all armed and wearing leather jackets, each with a different image painted on the back: a dove, a hammer, a flame, a tree.

They look rattled. Scraps of conversation come over one of their walkies: "Negative. Not in the woods . . ." One of the Reckoners gestures for the others to follow, and they move on.

"What now?" Ethan whispers to Kofi.

"I'll go find out what the security situation is up ahead. Stay here," Kofi says.

Once Kofi leaves, I turn to Ethan and Kyung, whisper, "You were at the part where you sent me to 1954 because of an item in a tabloid. Keep going."

"Actually, the NSA in 2025 took the *Weekly World Post* piece quite seriously," Kyung says. "Searched the government's deepest vaults for anything connected to the rat virus or Project Gambit."

"What did they find?" I ask.

"A brief mention of the project in a redacted report and a requisition sheet for it with the whistleblower's signature—proof Project Gambit existed, and the whistleblower was a part of it."

"And the samples?" I ask.

"None—of the rat virus or its killer spawn," Ethan says.

"But, you see," Kyung says, "in 1954, those samples still existed, along with the whistleblower who knew of their location. So we used the time machine to send you to just outside of Hanover in '54, but the glitch screwed up the landing coordinates."

"And I ended up on a patient bus."

She nods. "Pretty much killed the plan for you to secure a job as a nurse at Hanover, then find a way to contact Dr. Pell in the Unit."

"Pell, that's the name of the doctor?" I ask.

"Yes," Kyung says.

Could Pell have been that coal-eyed doctor I saw in the Unit? I can't remember ever hearing his name. Once I get back to '54 I'll find where he lives, go to his house, and convince the shrink to reveal the location of the sample. "How did a Hanover psychiatrist end up with the whistleblower's virus sample, anyway?" I ask.

They're both staring at me, incredulous.

"Dr. Pell wasn't a psychiatrist at Hanover," Ethan says. "She was a patient there. She *was* the whistleblower."

The doctor was a patient? And a she?

I'm floored by the lazy-ass, sexist assumptions my 1950s-addled mind has been making.

"Here's a picture of her," Kyung says, and hands me a black-and-white photo. A still of the same woman walking down the street in the video clip that played on the tiny LCD inside my wrist. And for the first time, I can clearly see her face.

It's Mary.

All that time, and the motherfucking mission was right in the next bed. "Dr. Pell is Mary Droesch?"

"Droesch, yes," Kyung says. "For a time she was married to a man named Stanley Droesch." The philandering ex-husband Mary talked about. Figures Hanover would admit her under his name.

"Shortly after the article came out," Ethan says, "Mary Pell was arrested—"

"—on a trumped-up charge of assaulting a coworker she'd supposedly become obsessed with," I say, finishing his sentence. "She was soon declared insane and committed to the Unit at Hanover. Mary told me."

The nerds break into hopeful grins. "You two have spoken!" Ethan whispers excitedly.

I think about Mary saving me from electrocution by soup, about those evenings she coached me during the night nurse's smoke breaks, somehow managing to teach me in those slivers of time how to fake a seizure to get myself out of the Unit. Who knows where I'd be now if Mary hadn't intervened. Dead? Overtreated? Still being repatterned to Sherman and Paul's liking? *Have spoken* doesn't quite cover it.

"We know Dr. Sherman's research was covertly funded by the CIA," Kyung says, "part of their MKUltra project to identify procedures and drugs that could be used during interrogations to weaken people, force their confessions through brainwashing and psychological torture."

Ethan examines a can of tomato sauce he's pulled from a pile in the corner. "So Dr. Pell presumably underwent enhanced interrogation."

By the people Mary said *really* ran the place . . . That panic I felt seeing a man on TV who looked like the coal-eyed doctor from the Unit—I thought it was my illness causing it, making me worry over not completing my "fictional" mission. But maybe there was a different reason for it: maybe the coal-eyed doctor was a CIA agent. One of my interrogators. Mary's as well.

All Mary's talk about the mysterious "them" framing her to get her sent off to Hanover, her pretend catatonia to avoid any more of "their" questions—I dismissed it as just the crazed behavior of a paranoiac, when all along she was the sanest among us. What a little shit I was. "Mary was definitely interrogated," I say. "By the CIA, I think. She told me 'agents,' so at least two. I think one was posing as a doctor."

"Okay, so definitely steer clear of them when you return to '54," Kyung says. Sure, no problem, Kyung. "But you've got to get Mary Pell to give you the name of the person she entrusted with the viral sample before the night of December twenty-ninth."

"But that's tomorrow!"

"It's all the time you have left," Kyung says.

"But we're rolling in time—we've got a time machine! Give me a do-over. Have the machine send me back a few days earlier—"

"Can't," she says. "Password-protected code Dr. Corbett installed in the machine prevents anyone from traveling back any earlier than November twelfth, 1954. It also won't send a person back further than the most recent moment in the past they occupied. No do-overs."

Dr. Corbett, what an asshole. "Why the deadline of the twenty-ninth?"

"Dr. Pell dies that night," Kyung says.

"Mary dies? . . . How?"

"According to her death certificate, she slipped and fell in the shower the evening of December twenty-ninth. Died of a cerebral contusion."

"No. There's got to be a way to stop that from happening," I say. "I could warn her. Better yet, I could find a way to get her out of Hanover. She could help from outside—"

"You *cannot* save Pell!" Kyung whisper-shouts. "It could have a profound effect on the fabric of our timeline—"

But Ethan shushes us—there are footsteps. Close. The three of us flatten against the wall. I grab a can of peaches from the pile. Hold it overhead, waiting. Someone steps through the entrance and I start to bring the can down.

Kofi stops it inches from his skull. "We've got a problem."

CHAPTER 41

"THEY'VE BLOCKED OFF the Copley Lawn exit by the market," Kofi says.

"What do we do now?" Ethan asks.

"We'll have to cut through the Reclamation crowd," Kofi answers, "get to the exit at the far end of Healy Lawn." Kyung looks extra dubious. "It can be done if we keep to the middle of the crowd, far enough from the stage, but not too close to the Reckoners on the perimeter."

Not ideal but you are shit out of options.

"Let's go," I say, and the four of us wade back into the stream of Tabula Rasa.

Ethan sidles up next to me as we walk and pulls some photos from his backpack—like Paul's photographs only in color. Holds one out to me.

It's weathered, corners bent. A picture of two people, with a campfire and tent in the background. "Mom and Dad," he says. "Professors here at Georgetown. She was theology. He was applied mathematics."

Theology—that could explain my knowledge of the Bible. Maybe she taught me. I can't help myself; I grab the photograph. The couple is smiling, ruddy faced. Happy. The man looks like he's in his late fifties, tall, balding, with horn-rimmed glasses. The woman is younger, in her forties. She looks a lot like me, but I've no more recollection of these parents than the fake ones Paul offered up.

I hand the photo back, but Ethan persists. Holds out another

baited emotional hook. This one's of a boy and girl about ten building a sandcastle. I recognize Ethan, smiling, skinny, his too-big
SpongeBob trunks already halfway down his butt. He grins at the
girl, who's pointing a shovel at him and laughing.

My eyes roam over this long-lost version of me. Her buoyant smile,
jaunty polka-dot bikini, the cheeky angle of her sand shovel. I want
to protect her. Freeze her in amber.

"Nice half-moon," I say, passing the photo back to him.

"Mom had a real gift for capturing her children's most embarrassing moments on camera," he says, and I find myself wondering
about her. Mom. What we liked to do, just the two of us girls. Bake?
Tour museums? Spelunk? When he holds up a third shot, I pluck
it from his hand—no attempt at indifference now. It's of six people
standing on a lawn: my parents, then in descending height, two pale
boys in their mid-teens, Ethan, about ten here, and me on the end in
a yellow dress, that smile again blazing.

Ethan says, "Next to me, that's Daniel, and on the other side of
him is Luke. He was the oldest . . ." I look closer at the boy/almost-
man—and spot something wrapped around his wrist. A string of
wooden beads—like the ones flanking my Latin medal from Georgetown Country Day. Luke's beads.

My Christmas drone memory returns.

> I'm in the living room. Nat King Cole's still singing, but no one's listen-
> ing. The front door is open and loud voices out front are arguing.
>
> I walk past it to my mother's study, open the door, and approach
> the couch, where something is covered by a blanket. I pull it down and
> gaze at my father. Glasses are gone now. Body's still warm, the mark on
> his neck still pink.
>
> I put my head down on his still chest and sob, burying my face in his
> flannel shirt. I'm at least thirteen but in this moment I feel five.
>
> My mother calls to me from the door: "Beatrix, you need to come
> now. I've arranged it." She's so, so pale. There's a rouge-colored smudge

on her neck, a couple pocks blooming nearby. She walks over, gently coaxes me away from the body and replaces the blanket.

"I'm not going. I'm staying here with you."

"No, baby. You and the boys need to go with these men." Two marines have appeared in the doorway. "They'll keep you safe."

"No!" I shout, backing away.

Luke slips by the soldiers. Enters the room, trailing Daniel and Ethan. Luke's eyes are bloodshot but dry—he's recently wiped his tears, having been hurriedly initiated into adulthood.

He's still getting his parental sea legs. Tentatively puts his arm with the mala beads around my shoulder, his maiden attempt at being fatherly. "Hey, I'll give you my *Watchman* deluxe edition and two Crunch bars . . ."

I shake my head, refusing his pathetic bribe, run and hug my mother, certain in this moment I will never hold anyone so tightly again.

But the marines' patience has been exhausted, and now one is calling me "miss" and beginning to extricate me from her, limb by limb—

I stand very still amid the tide of Tabula Rasa filing past us, trying to assimilate this scene that has finally played out in full, all the blocks my mind had set up to protect me from its agonizing content cleared away. The wave of remembered heartache nearly flattens me.

"Bix?" Ethan asks, gently nudging me back into motion.

I describe the memory to him.

"That was the day Dad died," he says, "and the soldiers came for us—marines the NSA sent to retrieve the kids."

"What kids?"

"The ones from Georgetown's early-college program. They were doing this all over the country with kids enrolled in similar platforms. Kyung, Gideon, and others in our group, they were in it with us."

"You, me, Daniel, and Luke were all in this program?"

"Three of us were . . ." And I realize he politely means not me. "Not that you aren't smart, just different smart . . . You're an amazing writer—"

I wave off his verbal smile-nod. "But the marines took all of us?"

He nods. My mother, sending her children off with soldiers so they'd be as safe as she could make them in an impossible situation. Then dying alone. Like Worthy said: "You do whatever it takes to protect the people you love."

"Mom played hardball, said she wouldn't let them have the three of us if they didn't take you, too. They could have insisted. There was a lot of that happening, people with guns, insisting . . . But the marine in charge agreed to Mom's demands. Dad had just died; she was in bad shape. Maybe he took pity on her."

Now I know why that memory stuck with me through time machine glitches and the protocol's punishing voltage—hard to top being ripped by soldiers from my dying mother's arms.

So what about that memory of Paul and me and that laughing boy at the quarry?

What emotional land mine has it been trying to show me for weeks? What I've recalled can't compete with my nightmare Christmas memory.

What am I still not seeing?

CHAPTER 42

"HEY TOOK US to a secret facility near Quantico," Ethan says as we continue amid the Tabula Rasa heading up the dusty path. "Pinned their hopes for mankind's future on a bunch of pubescent college students. They assembled as many experts as they could by video to brief us, teach us, tell us their secrets."

"While you nerds were being given the keys to the kingdom, what was I doing?"

"Getting in trouble, mostly. We were all forced to grow up fast. But at least Luke, Daniel, and I had work to distract us."

"And I did not."

"No. You were smart, idle, and basically in emotional free fall. Books weren't quite cutting it anymore. You needed to be *doing*. In motion. Out there," he says, gesturing around us. "You started with arson and petty theft, moved on to burglary and black market trafficking."

That explains some of my more unique skills.

"But even those activities couldn't hold your interest. You took to dogging the marines. Begged and cajoled them to teach you, train you, put up with you. Eventually they relented, and you went with them." Ethan looks like he's swallowed something bitter.

"And you just let me go?"

"We tried to stop you . . . We should've tried harder . . ." His expression darkens. "After the grown-ups were dead, the remaining soldiers found themselves spread thin, trying to keep us safe while preserving as much of civilization as they could. So you began bringing them promising orphans to train."

"The Child's Army?" I ask in an even lower whisper, aware of all the ears around us.

He nods. "The marines' nickname, and it stuck. They taught you all tactics and weapons along with how to keep some semblance of society going—everything from hunting to farming to shutting down nuclear reactors. You started spending more time with them, less with us . . . And you grew from Beatrix Parrish into . . . Bix. Skillful, relentless, fearless . . ."

"Ruthless?"

He pauses a moment, choosing his words carefully. "You became our well-armed catcher in the rye, protecting us nerds squirreled away in the labs, trying to hold on to the science, the possibility of a future. And to do that, I think you felt you needed to be more soldier than sister or friend. To close off that part of your life."

Grim.

Well, you asked.

"We saw you less and less," he says. "After Luke died, you threw yourself into procuring supplies and building up the Child's Army. It was sometimes weeks before we'd see you. Eventually, you'd appear, always with some haul for us but no explanations. Then Daniel died . . . and you really went lone wolf. Not even letting your people in on what you were doing half the time."

Tears are about to roll. For these two forgotten brothers? For myself? I close my eyes, try to push them back down, not lose it here among the enemy. But when I feel my twin brother's arm around my shoulders, I let it stay, let the drops flow from my eyes, where they're quickly absorbed by the brown scarf.

Now we're almost at the entrance to the Copley Lawn market—and beyond it, the Reclamation. Ethan looks around at the crowd, then whispers softly, "Last March you visited me. Said you were going up to Baltimore. That you'd be gone awhile—"

"Ethan," Kyung whispers sternly from behind us.

But he doesn't stop. "You told me about a cult there called the Tabula Rasa—"

Now Kyung quietly pulls us out of the procession. Kofi sees and joins us. "You said they seemed awfully well stocked for a bunch of religious nutbags," Ethan says. "You told me you'd be going under a different name, so they wouldn't know you were *that* Bix, of the Child's Army. That you'd poke around till you got some answers."

"*I* have a history with the Tabula Rasa?" I ask, and Ethan nods.

"This really isn't the time—" Kyung says, glaring at Ethan.

"So, what did I learn about them in Baltimore, Ethan?"

He shakes his head. "When you got back, you wouldn't talk about any of it," Ethan says.

"What? Why?"

"Look," Kyung says, "what you've done these last few years, whatever you did in Baltimore, it was always to provide for us, protect us and what we're trying to do. What you do safeguards hope."

"Sounds lofty," I say. "And what's the going rate for saving hope? What have I been willing to do for the cause?" More furtive looks between them. "Never mind, I don't need to know. 'Cause that's not who I am anymore."

"It's not?" Kofi asks.

"No. For all the machine has cost me, it's also given me something: a do-over, wiped away the old Bix and her violent *proclivities*. It changed me, and new Bix won't go back to being her for any cause. And I don't need to; goals can be accomplished without bloodshed."

Kyung takes a deep breath, and I can see her scarf puff outward as she exhales. Then she speaks: "Do you know why we sent *you* to 1954, Bix? Because you were someone who would do whatever it took to get the job done."

Whatever it took. The *voice's* strong suit.

"I don't know if you'll ever remember *that* Bix. All I do know is, right now, *this* Bix," Kyung says, pointing at me, "with all her shiny new emotions, and gun phobias and 'no thank you's,' she's all we've got. So don't let this idea of some untainted 'New Bix' get in the way of what you were sent back to '54 to do. We can't afford that. You're *there* to save millions *here*. And if that means bashing some heads, so be it."

Brava!

Easy for her to say. "Are you finished?" I ask.

Ethan gets between us. "Let's all cool—"

"No, actually I'm not finished," Kyung hisses. "Two identical viruses seventy years apart *and* someone cleaning up their connection—that's no accident. That's a big-ass conspiracy with dangerous rogue military *and* CIA players at its core—part of it operating within Hanover. And you think New Bix is going to jump back there like some quantum Gandhi, waving incense at them when they come for you? No. When you jump back, you're taking a weapon."

Agreed.

"No," I say. "I get the information without violence, or I don't get it at all."

∗   ∗   ∗

On first glance, the market at Healy Circle looks like your average farmers market: tents, lots of people with handmade tote bags slung over their shoulders perusing the kale.

But then you see the postapocalyptic touches. People are hawking anything and everything: liquor, pot, sex, generators, canned goods, solar batteries, tattoos, gauze, books, gasoline, horses . . .

The crowd here isn't just Tabula Rasa. There's a whole spectrum of end-of-days tribes represented: folks who look like they've been hiking the Appalachian Trail too long—straggly hair, threadbare clothes. Skinheads in all black with elaborate geometric scalp tattoos. A group of women in what look like the faded remains of surgical scrubs, armed with bows and arrows.

Near the tents are a few battered flatbed trucks alongside the horses and wagons.

Off to the left I see what Kofi was talking about: fencing's been thrown up, guarded by Kameron Rook's Reckoners, that blocks off access to Copley Lawn—and any escape in that direction. More leather-jacketed goons are stationed on foot and on horseback along Thirty-Seventh Street's fencing.

We make our way past tables of goods: books, magazines, VHS tapes, and DVDs for sale.

Inside a locked cage in the center of a display are DVDs of the complete third season of *Friends*, *Liar Liar*, and *Uncle Buck*. "Comedies are by far the most sought after," Ethan says.

"*Old* comedies," I say.

He nods. "Technically, 2025 was the last year of global media—last movies made, songs recorded, TikTok videos posted. But most of that was in the cloud, lost when everything collapsed. The older stuff's on DVDs, VHS, still accessible if you can get hold of a machine—"

"What's my favorite movie?" I ask him. "I mean, if you know—"

"*Amélie*, hands down. You watched that movie over and over. I've got a copy somewhere . . . Hey, when all of this is over, and you're back for good from 1954, we can watch it together . . . if you want to, that is."

"Yes," I say, "I'd like that."

"I've missed this, missed you, the last few years," he says.

Near us in the crowd, a bearded redheaded man in an overcoat is conducting business with a pale-faced man. There's a devil's kiss rash on the customer's neck. "You've squeezed all you could out of your final year, reached your quarter hour," the ginger says. "Now it's time to opt out, let Blue Heaven take it from here. You have payment?"

The doomed man hands him three potatoes and a DVD whose case shows a man covered in yellow Post-it notes. Above him the title reads: *Office Space*.

The ginger nods appreciatively as he inspects the goods. "Very nice," he says, then whips open his coat, and I hear the sound of hundreds of pills rattling in bottles. He drops the potatoes in one of the many pockets sewn into the coat's lining, the DVD in another, then pulls a bottle of pills from a third. "You're making the smart choice," the red giant says as he taps three blue pills into the doomed man's waiting bandanna. "Quick. Clean. With Blue Heaven, there's no waiting around for the Guest to do the dirty work."

Beyond the merchant of death are several tents manned by Tabula Rasa. Their vegetables, canned goods, and definitely their pot look superior to the competitors'. But it's their electronics, under lock and key inside the fenced-in back of a flatbed truck, that impress me most: parts for solar arrays, generators, even a couple large-capacity storage batteries.

"Nice equipment," I say to Kofi. "Where's it coming from?"

"You asked that same question last year," he says, "just before heading off to Baltimore."

And whatever I did there . . .

I hear music—notes of Creed's "With Arms Wide Open" being sung in multipart harmony by a choir. The Creed cover makes it official—mankind is circling the drain.

"What kind of religious ceremony is a Reclamation?" I ask Ethan as we head toward the entrance.

"The kind you don't want to be part of, " Kyung says. "Stay covered up." She gestures to my scarf, which is starting to come loose. I redrape it across my face and tuck the slippery fabric in tight.

Kofi pauses near the entrance. "Remember, keep to the middle, don't stray too close to the Reckoners on the perimeter or the stage. Kyung, you go first, then Ethan, Bix. I'll go last. Keep some space between us and remember, walk slowly—like you're mingling, not like you're escaping. If one of us gets stopped, don't stick around. Get out of here. Meet up at Rock Creek Pumping Station as soon as it's safe." Kofi pulls me aside. "No matter what you see or hear onstage, keep moving." Jesus. I nod. "Let's go."

* * *

The enormous Healy Lawn is packed. Even the branches of its trees hold people. The crowds are so thick I can't even see the exit on the far side of the field. Here and there tents have been pitched and the smell of makeshift barbecues wafts through the air. From their clothing, I sense the crowd's a mix—everyone from fully indoctrinated Tabula Rasa to the merely curious. As I walk through it, "mingling," I keep the others in sight.

In the near distance a stage juts into the audience, constructed around Healy Hall's central entrance, below one of its towers. Its double doors are flanked by large white banners painted with the red letters *TR* inside a circle.

Extending from a balcony above the doorway is a giant wood beam rigged with an arrangement of ropes and pulleys. Around the stage are floodlights connected to large nearby solar generators. Amps and speakers are wired in as well.

Impressive setup for the end times. We slowly begin to weave our way through the crowd, ten to fifteen feet apart from each other, balancing our distance from the stage with our need to avoid the Reckoners on the perimeter. As the choir exits the stage, rhythmic clapping begins to break out in the crowd, growing rapidly till the whole audience is pounding their hands together in unison and a voice comes over the speakers: "And here he is, Brother Kameron!"

Two men open Healy Hall's doors—and a high-pitched scream now pours from this audience of children raised by each other, and I'm careful not to bump into any of the screaming feral fans.

Kameron Rook emerges—and he does not disappoint. East Asian, long and lean, he is dressed in a faded, snug-in-all-the-right-places T-shirt, black jeans, and boots. He descends the handful of steps and struts onto the stage, a glorious end-of-days amalgamation of rock star and preacher. Even before he's said a word, his charisma is palpable.

But I have zero memory of this man.

Much as I try to recall any past dealings with him, I'm drawing a complete blank. Suppose that shouldn't be a surprise to me anymore.

After the announcer hands Rook the mic, the preacher pauses, allowing the collective energy of the audience to build, and I find myself slowing to watch, getting just a little bit closer for a better look.

The clapping and cheering are now deafening. Finally, he walks to the front of the stage, maybe a dozen yards from me. "Brothers and sisters, God has made a promise to us during these years we are being tested." He pauses again before continuing. "Only the chosen will be saved. And . . ."

Now he holds the mic out to the crowd, and it shouts back in thundering unison, "Only the worthy will be chosen!" The expressions of hungry devotion on the faces of those replying take my breath away.

Kameron Rook pulls back the mic and nods. "Exactly so . . . It's a simple truth, one any child can see—which is a good thing, given this crowd."

The audience erupts in laughter and applause, and he waits till it's crested before continuing. "Believe me, God *wants* all of his children to be saved," he says, and begins a slow walk across the small stage, steering the crowd's mood back into more thoughtful territory.

"But there are some poor, misguided souls among us who've strayed from the path of salvation," he says, "because they haven't yet found their faith in God. Many kinds of sins among these folks. Some are practitioners of thievery, others of deception, still others are pursuing unsanctioned science, the kind that helped decimate our world."

Shouts of "Uh-huh," "That's right," and "Yes they are" erupt from the audience as Ethan nods to me to keep moving.

Rook stops and the last of his swagger falls away, leaving just a solemn man onstage. There's something so deeply compelling about this and I can't help myself, I draw a little closer. "And then there are those practitioners of treachery. In Baltimore last summer, we learned firsthand just how much pain and destruction can be caused by such a person, a *creature* pretending to be our trusted counsel, friend, lover, only to betray us."

At those words, Ethan, fifteen feet away, glances nervously over at me—and I realize in that moment that Kameron Rook is talking about *me*.

I'm the "creature" who wreaked destruction. Betrayed the Tabula Rasa.

Maybe so but ignore it. Keep moving.

I manage to resume walking but can't completely tear my eyes away from Rook, who is calling to his henchmen at the foot of the stage. "Bring up the *volunteer*."

Two Reckoners drag a figure, hands bound, head hooded by a burlap sack, up the steps. Once onstage, they lift the prisoner's tied hands onto a large meat hook on the end of a rope hanging from the beam above.

Fuck. This isn't a ceremony, it's an inquisition.

"Like last summer's betrayer, this one here has committed sins against the Tabula Rasa. But you and I are not judge and jury," Rook says to the audience. "We are simply witnesses to this *volunteer's* decision. They can reclaim their soul, willingly join us on the path of salvation, by choosing to purge their sins, reveal their coconspirators, and accept their penance in the camps . . . Or not." The Tabula Rasa have camps? That's not good. Rook now paces to the edge of the stage. "The decision is entirely theirs."

A Reckoner signals someone above to crank the pulley, and the hook rises, hoisting the poor "volunteer" onto their toes.

The second Reckoner produces a whip and a couple of bladed implements as Rook continues, voice smooth as glass. I look around to see how the crowd is reacting to this prelude to torture and notice, ahead of me, Kyung and Ethan both slowing, eyes on the stage.

"As Proverbs, chapter twenty, verse thirty, says, 'Lashes and wounds cleanseth away evil . . .'" The rest of the words come floating back to me before he says them: "'. . . beatings purge the inmost being.'" Maybe it wasn't my mother, the religion professor, who taught me scripture. Maybe it was the Tabula Rasa. Rook turns back to the crowd. "Thus, together, you and I must proceed."

Now the Reckoner reaches up, about to take the hood off the figure—and I see Ethan's now joined Kyung. Both are at a dead stop— and mere feet from me. They don't seem to have noticed, their attention completely focused on the "volunteer" about to be unmasked onstage. I glance behind me and see Kofi ten yards back, definitely not happy with our spacing.

"Do you think it could be him?" I hear Kyung whisper to Ethan, slipping her hand in his and squeezing it tight.

"Not sure. Gideon *does* have sneakers like those," he answers.

They think the prisoner "volunteering" could be Gideon? So the Tabula Rasa arrested him?

Onstage, the hood is pulled off, revealing a gagged man who is not Gideon—and I see Ethan's and Kyung's shoulders drop just a little in relief that this poor unfortunate is not *their* poor unfortunate. I pull up next to them and whisper: "How long has Gideon been their prisoner?"

Guilt washes over their faces at their lie of omission. Kyung shakes her head slightly at Ethan, but he shrugs off her warning, says, "Enough, Kyung. She deserves to know." He turns to me. "A few weeks ago Reckoners raided the lab. Kyung and I were in the back when it happened, near the tunnel entrance. We barely made it out with the football as the Reckoners were coming in the front. They locked down the building and took Gideon and a half dozen others prisoners. We don't know what's happened to any of them since."

The cult has been in control of the machine—and the people who know how to operate it—for weeks. And at some point Kameron Rook and his goons forced them to send my fake husband to November of '54.

Paul is Tabula Rasa.

But my spiraling thoughts on this new revelation are cut short by the stifled, animallike cries of the gagged volunteer onstage. His eyes are bugged wide with fear and when Kameron Rook unmuzzles him, he begins to plead, "Please, you don't have to do this!"

"Let's go. He won't last long," Kyung says to me. Then she and Ethan split up and head for the exit.

She's right. Go now. Before you're next.

But before I turn and follow my deceitful compatriots, I turn back for one last look at Kameron Rook. He's running his fingers through his hair. It's such a small, nothing gesture—

Yet it's managing to provoke feelings in me—shame, panic, guilt—stronger than any I've experienced since waking on the bus. I can feel my knees going weak, about to buckle.

I need to get the hell out of here.

So I bolt—no looking, no thought, just pure adrenaline and fight-or-flight instinct propelling me—and immediately crash into two bearded and hoodied Tabula Rasa men.

CHAPTER 43

WATCH WHERE YOU'RE goin', yah feggin' bitch!" one of the men yells. And now he's looking at me, head cocked like he's trying to place my face, which is weird, cause it's covered—

But no, it is not covered. The flap covering it has come loose in the collision, and now I'm standing exposed—and putting these pertinent facts together far too slowly.

"Wait a minute," the second guy says, and I can see it in his eyes— he's recognized me. He takes a step toward me. "You're—"

But he doesn't finish, 'cause I knee him in the nuts. As he sinks to the ground, the first guy grabs my wrist and tries yanking me toward him, but I resist and soon can feel my hand slipping out of his grip.

This is when I notice the quiet. The sounds coming from the stage—Kameron Rook's torture patter and the volunteer's begging— have stopped. I glance up and see Kameron peering into the audience near me. See his eyes flare wide a split second in recognition. "Beatrix, don't you take one fucking step!" he shouts, his smooth voice now one of pure rage.

Get the hell out of there!

But the part of me etched by Sherman's shocks doesn't comply. All thoughts—of escape, of defending myself—have been shunted aside, leaving just one resounding thought: Kameron has ordered me not to move.

My protocol-induced paralysis lasts just a moment. But it's enough. The guy holding my wrist is able to spin me around, wrenching my arm behind me and forcing me into a half bow. I hear Kameron summoning Reckoners from somewhere in the crowd.

But then I hear a muffled *crunnnk*. And my wrist comes free. I turn around and see the guy unconscious on the ground near the first one—and Kofi standing over him with a rock.

"Run!" he whispers to me, and the two of us take off in opposite directions. Amid Kameron's calls for Reckoners and all the whistles and shouts, I duck down and burrow my way through cultists, slipping behind a nearby tent to re-cover my face with the scarf, then weaving my way through the Tabula Rasa at a quick walk, slowing only when I get near the edge of the crowd. I spot Kyung and Ethan up ahead trying to appear casually not terrified as they pass by Reckoners manning the exit at the far end of Healy Lawn. They're headed for a large stone staircase a few yards away that drops down to the street below.

I follow, forcing myself to walk slowly past the leather-jacketed goons and down the stone staircase, even though I can now hear shouts and the squawks of walkie-talkies beginning to erupt nearby. Just before I've descended out of sight, I chance a look back at the crowd and see a Reckoner in a green baseball hat muscling his way through it. I sprint the rest of the way down the steps, joining up with Ethan and Kyung waiting on Thirty-Seventh Street North.

"This way," Kyung says, and the three of us run through a series of warren-like walkways and drives that thread between row houses.

When we turn onto Prospect Avenue, despite the immediate danger—or possibly because of it—I feel that charge again, no doubt helped by the double shot of adrenaline now rocketing through me.

But we make it less than a block down Prospect before I spot, over my shoulder, Green Hat and a second Reckoner running toward us.

So we zig down Thirty-Third. When we reach M Street, I get this gut feeling, before the *voice* can even chime in, that we should cut left onto it.

Now you're coming around.

"This way," I say to Ethan and Kyung, and lead them onto M Street with its ruins of upscale shops and ample abandoned cars to use as cover. We sprint at full speed down the raggedy road till shots ring out and glass shatters uncomfortably close to us. We duck behind a FedEx truck just as a bullet pings off its bumper.

"Come out, drop your weapons," Green Hat shouts at us.

Another bullet hits close and Ethan flinches. "Maybe we should surrender—"

"No!" I say. Captive of the Tabula Rasa doesn't sound terribly survivable.

"Well, we can't stay here," Kyung says. "I say we head—"

"Both of you do exactly as I tell you," I bark, no preamble, no pleases. "Kyung, hand me the SIG Sauer." She looks beyond relieved as she slips it to me. I examine the pistol, taking the moment to reweigh the costs and benefits of pointing this weapon at people with the intent to kill. Am I willing to do that? Sacrifice the time machine's do-over, the fresh start it's given me?

No, I am not.

"Just cover fire. I'm not shooting anyone," I tell them. And myself.

Time to see just what kind of muscle memory for gunplay I possess. Will it be just like riding a bike? First I check the pistol. Bank the SIG Sauer on its side, then quickly and smoothly rack the slide and check that the chamber is empty before closing it. Then I press the release and drop the magazine to check it. Full. Fifteen rounds. Good. Drop it back in. Done. It's unnerving to see what nimble, well-trained little fuckers my fingers are as they carry out these actions.

"Follow me, on three," I tell Kyung and Ethan. They nod and I aim the gun at the ground in front of the Reckoner. "One, two," I say, squeezing off a couple shots. "Three!" I say, and lead them in a mad scramble past the ruins of Pizza Paradiso and Dean & Deluca. We're just a hundred yards short of Wisconsin, about to pass J.Crew, when more bullets ping close by.

Green Hat is an excellent shot.

We duck behind a burned-out Range Rover some asshole double-parked a decade and a world ago, and I'm catching my breath when I hear the squawk of walkie-talkies coming from the other direction on M Street. I peer around the Range Rover and see two more men approaching.

We're about to be fish in a barrel. Crap.

There's an alley to our right, the entrance almost completely blocked with piles of junk. And thirty feet in lies an enormous red dumpster, further obstructing the view. There might be no door into the building behind it, no exit. But something about this garbage-strewn possible dead end just feels right.

Yes, it is. Do it.

Do I trust the *voice* and her maybe-knowledge?

Do you have a better option?

I do not. "The alley. Follow me," I say to Ethan and Kyung.

"Are you sure, Bix?" Kyung asks.

"Let's go," I say, and the three of us hurtle ourselves down the debris-choked alley, just barely reaching safety behind the dump-ster before bullets start pinging off it. But there, mere feet away, is a door. A door with a giant happy face painted on it. I know this smiling door; I'm sure of it.

But when I give the knob a try, it doesn't move. And the lock's a mortise. Can't pick it. Definitely can't shoot it.

Fuck. My mind races, scrounging around my dusty brain for any idea of how to make a locked door unlocked, hoping some thought will come to me.

And something does come. Not a thought, an action: my hand reaches up high, to the trim over the door, and it feels around till my fingers make contact.

A key.

I take it, shove it in the keyhole, say a quick prayer to the lock-smith gods, then try to turn it.

And it works! It fucking works!

"Bix!"

Ethan. In my excitement over the door, I'd forgotten about him and Kyung. I turn and see, clear over on the other side of the alley, a petrified Ethan and Kyung crouched behind some abandoned debris. There's a good twenty feet of open space, a virtual shooting arcade, between us. Shit.

How to retrieve Kyung and Ethan? I get down on the ground by the dumpster. Scan the shadowy mountains of refuse piled next to the building on the right. Pretty sure the Reckoners are near the shiny hubcap someone's mounted on the pile.

It's Green Hat I'm most concerned about. He's the one with the skills.

My eyes roam over the semistructure, searching. At first I find nothing. But then there's movement. A tiny flash of green. The sharpshooter's hat reflected in the neighboring building's transom window tilted open above him.

I grab hold of the bar on the dumpster's massive door to pull myself up—and get an idea. Take a closer look at its lever. It could work if the thing's not rusted shut. I reach down and pull hard on the lever, but nothing moves.

The second try's also a failure. I close my eyes and will my long-past bone-weary body to yank a third time with all it's got—and, lo, the lever flies upward, freeing the heavy door.

I swing it outward 180 degrees, bullets soon pinging off the steel. Opening it has bought us another eight feet of cover. And it's given me something else—a one-and-a-half-inch gap at the hinge to use as a gun emplacement. I point the SIG Sauer through it.

I hold my finger up in a wait-for-my-signal gesture, motioning for Kyung and Ethan to be ready. Hopefully my intentions are clear, but who knows.

I aim for the hubcap, hoping to force our pursuers to duck. Squeeze off two shots: one hits the top of the hubcap; another blows it off the pile.

"Now!" I whisper-shout to Kyung and Ethan.

Kyung charges across the gap, clearing it before the bullets come.

But Ethan's still on the other side. Shit. His face is brimming with apology and fear. I wave it off, put up my finger again, and he nods.

I check the sniper's reflection in the transom window. He's got his .22 rifle trained on the gap. Ready. I'm about to fire another shot to force his head down when he bats away some insect in his face—and his head pops right into my crosshairs.

Take the shot!

But I don't. I won't. Instead I squeeze off another warning shot, blasting the debris pile inches from his ear. Splinters of wood explode around him, his head goes down, and I whisper-shout to Ethan, "Run!"

Only, Ethan hesitates. Just for a split second, but it's enough. I'm about to shout for him to stop, but I'm too late. He's already launched himself across the gap—

The next seconds unspool in brutal slow motion. I watch as Ethan's body is rocked sideways by the force of a bullet entering his right back, exiting his right chest.

A bullet I could've prevented if I'd taken the shot.

Ethan's eyes go wide in surprise but his forward momentum propels him past the gap, and his body collapses onto me like a wave crashing on shore.

I hold him tight, and he whispers weakly in my ear, "Sorry, Bix. We should've told you . . . all of it . . . trusted you could deal . . ."

I'm aware of the sounds around me, Ethan's cryptic apology, the Tabula Rasa's bullets still pinging off the dumpster, Kyung's cries, but they're all muted, background noise to what I'm focused on: Ethan's quick, labored breaths and what they mean—that the bullet must've passed through his right lung. Blood is flowing from the exit wound on his chest. I can feel its sticky warmth spreading between us.

I stand there frozen, arms unwilling to relinquish their embrace till Kyung intervenes, takes one of Ethan's arms and slings it over her shoulders. I tuck the pistol in the waist of my pants, take his other arm.

"You with us?" I ask him.

He smiles weakly. "Yup, right here," he says, and we carry him into the building, shutting the door behind us. It's almost pitch-black inside, but I seem to know the building's layout, and soon we're weaving through the ruins of the J.Crew. Naked, ghostly mannequins hold court over the store's dusty remains, barely lit by the dirty skylights above. The place has been stripped bare. The only item of clothing still remaining is a lone pair of green pants, resort wear so luridly preppy they practically glow in the semidarkness.

I pop my head out the back door to check for Reckoners but see none, and we exit.

Outside it's dusk, a sliver of moon rising. We're on a brick patio overlooking the C&O Canal that is flowing somewhere below, under the thick tree cover.

As we haul Ethan toward a footbridge spanning the canal at the patio's far end, I listen for sounds of pursuit, but so far no one's figured out we're not still pinned down in the alley.

That won't last. We need to get to a hiding place soon.

When we reach the footbridge, Kyung doesn't have us cross it. Instead, she leads us down its attached stairs, to an overgrown footpath running alongside the canal. As we scramble through the tangled brush of the path with Ethan, my head's on a swivel, scanning every shadow for Reckoners—or witnesses—but I don't see a soul.

After a half click, Kyung leads us up a ramp to a dark, narrow street, then another till we reach a Federal-style house. While Kyung is unlocking the door, I gaze upward and see millions of stars in a sky undiluted by the lights and pollution of man. It's stunning.

"One perk of this world," Ethan says, watching my awe, and I smile.

My eyes sweep the street one last time before we carry Ethan into the dark house.

Once inside, door double bolted, Kyung flicks a switch on a beefy wall-mounted solar battery and light fills the space. And it's a familiar space.

This is my house. I'm finally home.

We're standing in its large kitchen, with its probably dead Sub-Zero fridge and other top-of-the-line appliances, with a long, marble-covered island that probably graced many an Insta feed in its day. But now it's stained and half covered with large plastic boxes containing what appear to be medical supplies.

Beyond the kitchen is a living room with a well-used stone fireplace that's surrounded by a patchwork of animal pelts, random chairs, and a massive pile of firewood. Bunches of strong-smelling botanicals are drying on racks nearby, next to stacks of more boxes.

Ethan looks around the room, smiles, and cracks, "What a disaster. When's the last time you cleaned this place, Bix?"

"Good one. Keep it up, nerd," I say.

Kyung leaves Ethan with me and goes to the island. "We can lay him here," she says, and pushes the boxes out of the way, spreads out a plastic sheet. The two of us heave Ethan up onto the marble as gently as we can and Kyung pulls out an array of medical equipment from a nearby box. Clips a pulse oximeter onto Ethan's finger and then starts to take his blood pressure.

My twin's breaths are rapid and shallow. Now in the quiet stillness of the house, Kyung and I can hear the telltale gurgle of a sucking chest wound: with each breath Ethan takes, air is being pulled in and out of his chest cavity through the exit wound. A stroke of luck in its way: at least the bullet went straight through. If the bullet had knocked around inside him or been a larger caliber, there would be no chance.

"Blood pressure's ninety over sixty," Kyung says, then checks the pulse oximeter. "Heart rate ninety-five."

Decent vitals, considering. I grab a stethoscope from the pile of supplies and take a listen. "He's stable," I say. "Let's monitor him for now." Then I turn to my twin. "Anything in your medical history I should know? Previous surgeries? Allergies?"

"No," he says weakly. "Fortunately, I'm not like you with penicillin."

"What do you mean?"

"You're allergic," Kyung says, "like full-on anaphylactic-death-show allergic."

"Good to know. I'll try to avoid the stuff." Ethan's looking pretty pale, eyes drifting closed. I pull Kyung away. "He could have a tension pneumothorax," I say softly. "You should be prepared to do a chest tube."

"Not me. You," Kyung says, grabbing some surgical instruments and plastic tubing from a plastic box.

"No," I say, shaking my head.

"*You're* the one with medical training, Bix. I'm a decent nurse at best."

Me put a chest tube in Ethan? "I . . . I can't—"

"You know how to do it. I've seen you," Kyung says, holding out a box of surgical gloves.

Shit.

Kyung grabs a nearby pair of scissors while part of her brain returns to job one: "Once Ethan's out of the woods, we need to come up with a plan for sending you back with proof you're from the future. So Dr. Pell will believe you and—"

My brain, which has been keeping all thoughts of the mission and what Kyung has been keeping from me for the sake of the mission in a sturdy drawer for the last ten minutes, suddenly pulls them back out.

"Kameron Rook," I say, cutting her off. "When he spotted me in the crowd, the look in his eyes . . . it was beyond angry. It was murderous . . . What the hell did I do to that guy in Baltimore, Kyung?" But she doesn't answer. "How did I become *the beast*?" Still no response. "I wanted the Tabula Rasa's secrets—so what did I do to get them?"

Finally, she says, "You got involved with one of his men last spring.

Someone high up. Cocky asshole, but apparently he fell hard for you. Pulled you right into the Tabula Rasa's inner circle, where you quickly managed to gain people's trust. And you must've learned something. We heard that one day last July you broke into a warehouse of theirs you'd tracked down, that they had you trapped but you shot your way out, somehow escaped."

"Who was the guy? Who was Rook's man?" I demand.

"Stokes," Kyung says.

"The psy-ops guy?" I ask, and she nods. Of course Paul is Stokes, the Tabula Rasa's master of mind games, gaslighter supreme. Makes all the sense in the world. But I need to be certain. "Are there any photos of him? Do I have any—"

Kyung goes over to the fridge and searches the various photos and miscellaneous objects taped to it. Finds a photo partially hidden under a pair of dangling baby booties. Pulls it off the fridge and hands it to me. On it are Paul and I, his arms around me. Behind us is the quarry. It's from that day, my true north memory day. "That's Stokes," she says. I can't stop staring at it, that fleeting memory of mine locked on paper.

"So, you're starting to remember things . . . from before your jump to '54?"

She doesn't look entirely pleased with that possibility.

"No, not exactly," I say. My tale of nearly being housebroken by Paul . . . Stokes—still not something I want to share, especially with Kyung, who I suspect is still keeping all manner of shit from me.

But it's long past time she knew.

CHAPTER 44

I TRY TO BE succinct.

Tell Kyung about my loving husband, Paul, appearing one day at Hanover.

It's fair to say her mind is blown.

The shocked and, for once, silent Kyung listens as I unspool the details: the slow spiral down into the depths of regression and muffled despair in Sherman's Unit as the doctor tried to remold me. Then I tell her about Paul bringing me "home" and all that followed, ending with this: "My 'husband,' Paul, in '54 — it's Stokes."

Kyung's gone almost as pale as Ethan, her eyes now making twitchy little movements back and forth as she takes it all in. "Jesus," she says, and puts her arms around me. Her movements are tentative, a little clumsy. Comforting each other is clearly not a thing we do — which makes her awkward gesture all the more powerful.

So, of course, the tears start.

I wipe them away with the sleeve of my sweater, while Kyung begins parsing out all the implications of my news. That the Tabula Rasa didn't just confiscate the machine as forbidden tech, that they've been using it with the forced labor of Gideon and the other prisoners. "So, shortly after they invaded and took over the lab, Kameron Rook and Stokes learned about the mission — and your memory loss — in '54, and forced Gideon and the others to send Stokes back in the machine, posing as your husband," she says as she starts to cut away

Ethan's shirt with the scissors. She looks up at me. "So, Kameron Rook wants Mary Pell's viral sample."

The two of us say nothing, dumbstruck by all the implications and our own conjecture.

But our shell shock is soon interrupted by Ethan. "No! Don't, Kyung!" my brother cries weakly. He's only semilucid, batting away Kyung's scissors while pleading with her. "Don't ask her to do it . . . Bix can't be your guinea pig . . ." he says before slipping deeper into unconsciousness. I take his blood pressure. It's just slightly lower. Still stable.

"Why *did* I volunteer to be your guinea pig in that iffy machine?" I ask Kyung. She doesn't answer. "Kyung, cut the crap," I say, and at last she relents.

"When you returned to Georgetown, you were dead set on opting out."

Opting out—what that ginger selling his death pills called suicide. So I did intend to kill myself. Before my quarter hour. Before time travel. It's why suicide felt so believable in Sherman's office that first day.

"Why did I want to die when I got back here from Baltimore last July?" I ask.

"Not July. You didn't return till this March."

"I was gone a year? Where the hell was I?"

She shakes her head. "Don't know. All you told me when you got back was that you intended to surrender to the Tabula Rasa. Which would've been pointless. They'd have killed you—very painfully— and it wouldn't have changed a thing. But once you heard about the mission, you decided that risking a long-shot trip in the machine—"

"Was a far more meaningful way to end things," I say, and she shrugs. I chose death by time machine. "You still haven't told me why I wanted to die. Pretty sure conning a couple of grifters in Baltimore wasn't keeping me up at night," I say, then catch her eyes flicking back to the dead Sub-Zero and its photos.

When I start to walk over to it, Kyung tries to stop me. "You need to get your gloves on, Bix . . ."

But I ignore her, eyes busy scanning the haphazard keepsakes and photos of my forgotten past for whatever Kyung was looking at.

Then I spot it, a printout of a selfie. In it are four people: Me, Stokes, Kameron Rook, and a boy on the brink of his teens. Shit-eating grins on all our faces, beers in our hands. Not the kid. The kid's drinking a Coke. Behind us are the familiar trees and far wall of the quarry.

This was taken that same day at the quarry.

And my true north memory floods back into my mind:

> My feet feel wonderfully warm. The late afternoon sun has baked the rock we're standing on. Below us is the quarry, filled with deep emerald-green water.
>
> Stokes, behind me, is kissing my shoulder. I pull his hand to my lips and kiss the crescent-moon scar on his palm.
>
> "Ew, gross!" I hear the boy exclaim, before breaking into those familiar peals of laughter.
>
> Stokes tugs on my earlobe, and I turn to face him. "Next time we go naked, in front of both of them," he says, winking at someone, then tilts my chin up, and we kiss.
>
> "No!!!" the boy shouts at this newest PDA assault on his senses, then giggles again. I turn to the boy, sitting on a nearby log, sipping his Coke. The kid grins at me, his toothy smile beaming from a sun-kissed face unspoiled as yet by adolescent hormones—and I'm awash with the same feeling of boundless love I've experienced with this memory these last few weeks.
>
> It was for this kid—the love I thought all this time was for Stokes. My time travel–damaged brain conflating and confusing the two.
>
> How colossally messed up is that?
>
> Arms wrap around both Stokes and my shoulders. They belong to Kameron Rook, now standing in between us. "Yes. Must we watch

while you two make a lunch of yourselves? At least spare the boy!" Rook says, running his fingers through his hair as he winks at me. He opens three bottles of deliciously cold beer and hands one to each of us. We clink them together and are taking our first pulls when a Reckoner approaches on the path.

It's Green Hat, the one who shot Ethan. "Brother Kameron, Brother Stokes," he calls to them, and the men leave to speak with him.

I sit down on the log next to the boy, keeping one eye on the men.

"Tomorrow, can you teach me how to shoot?" the boy asks me.

I muss his curly golden-brown hair. I can feel a certain desperation in my gesture, like I'm trying to ward off his looming adulthood. "Not yet," I say. "You're too young to be pulling a trigger."

"You said that last month."

"Because it was also true last month," I say, smiling, then steal another glance at the three men talking. Green Hat is handing Rook some papers. He glances briefly at them before slipping them in his back pocket—

I bring the photo over to Kyung, now swabbing Ethan's chest with Betadine. She's not happy to see that picture. "Tell me about this photo. Who's the kid?"

"This is not the time to get into this—"

"Stop fucking with me, Kyung. Just tell me who the kid is!"

She frowns. "Kameron Rook's little brother, Theo." Theo.

The name makes the hair on my arms stand up. "We were going to tell you everything, once your mission in '54 was over. Given the state you were in, all that you've been through, we just didn't know if you could handle it and still carry out the mission, get the information from Mary Pell in time—"

"What exactly is the *it* that you don't think I can handle, Kyung?"

Kyung can't meet my gaze, eyes going anywhere to avoid me. And when they finally alight on my brother lying in front of us, she gasps. "Shit. Bix!" she says, scrambling to pump up the blood pressure cuff.

I look down and see what she's talking about. The veins on my brother's neck are now distended, his ghostly white forehead clammy, his lips bluish. It's a tension pneumothorax: air is escaping from the hole in his lung into the chest cavity, crowding his heart and damaged lung.

"His BP's down to sixty-eight over forty!" she says. "Heart rate's one thirty."

Fuck.

"Bix, do something!"

I grab a pair of surgical gloves, snap them on, and pray that forcing a chest tube into your brother without puncturing anything vital is also just like riding a bike.

I breathe deep and let my hands take the lead, counting Ethan's ribs as I feel my way down his side. I stop at his fifth, take the scalpel Kyung is holding out to me, and make a small cut through the layers of skin, muscle, and sinew above the rib. Then I swap the scalpel for a pair of surgical scissors Kyung is offering, slide them into the incision.

Don't know how I know to do it. Like hot-wiring a car, handling a balisong, or shooting a pistol, I just do.

When I open up the scissors in the incision to widen it, the sound of air escaping the cavity accompanies the sight of blood gushing out onto the counter, my sweater, and then down onto the floor. It looks bad, but there's also an audible change in Ethan's breathing. Longer, deeper breaths. So, I *think* that's good. I hope that's good. I gingerly probe the hole I've made in Ethan with my finger till I reach his pleural cavity. He'll need the tube, or the pressure will build back up.

Maybe I can actually do this. Save Ethan . . . from an injury he wouldn't have if I'd just taken the damn shot.

Just don't make the same mistake again.

I grab a clamp and tubing, about to feed it into the incision, when I feel it. The slightest hint of buzz in my toes.

That can't be right.

I'm so tired, it's got to be my imagination.

But when I glance at the chandelier above, each of its lights has a rainbow halo. No, no, no!

"Kyung, it's happening!"

She looks up from the bloody battleground of Ethan's chest. Immediately sees it in my eyes. "Shhit!" Her hands dive into my pockets, frantically searching.

"But I've got the link," I say. "This shouldn't be—"

Kyung's hand emerges with the link, now glowing blue. "Someone set it to auto return after one hour," she says. "Which is—"

"Now." Dorothy and her sticky fingers must've reprogrammed the thing. "How can we stop it?"

But Kyung's expression as she shoves the link back in my pocket says it all: nothing can be done.

Because I've felt the vibrations. I'm past the fail-safe. Going to travel—and with a battery at close to zero. Will I make it to 1954, or be lost somewhere *in between*?

And what about Ethan?

"Kyung, douse your hands!"

She immediately understands. Pours some moonshine over them. "Tell me what to do."

The roar is building fast now.

There's no more time. I grab her gloved finger and push it into the incision. "Feel it? The pleural cavity?"

She nods, and I place the clamped tube in her other hand. "Don't screw it up," I say, and kiss my brother's forehead as the roar rips me away.

CHAPTER 45

OPEN MY EYES and see snowflakes, lit by the streetlight, falling around my feet; see my long skirt.

I've made it back to 1954.

Ethan!

Maybe there's another trip left in the link. I jam my bloody gloved hand in my pocket, pull the link out, and press the button over and over—but nothing happens. The battery's completely dead. Even if, come sunrise, I hook it up to the solar recharger in the purse, I'll still be hours from returning to 2035.

Meanwhile, the minutes just keep marching ahead in our two linked times.

I can't save Ethan.

Was Kyung able to, eighty-one years in the future? Could she get the chest tube in? Was that enough? Did the bleeding stop? . . . The questions cycle through my mind, faster and faster, till they merge into one giant ball of dread.

"Bix?"

I look up, see Worthy and Dorothy right where I left them when I jumped. The two are staring at me—or rather, at my suddenly blood-soaked sweater and surgical gloves.

Dorothy, ever adaptable, takes the strange sight in stride and is already creeping toward my purse on the ground nearby. "Get away!" I roar as I snatch up the bag, and the frightened woman takes off down the street.

Worthy's oblivious to his suspect getting away, eyes only on me as he runs up. "We need to get you to a hospital. Now—"

"The blood's not mine," I say, pulling off the gloves.

"It's not? Oh thank God," he says, and hugs me tight. "Wh . . . what happened there?"

So, so much. "I need to go back," I say.

"To 2035?" he asks.

"No. To Hanover."

*   *   *

As we drove, I told Worthy everything I learned in the future. Of the Tabula Rasa and what I could uncover about my checkered history with it. Of Stokes being Paul. Of the Guest and its origins. Of Ethan and his unknown status. Finally I told Worthy what he most wanted to know—why the fuck I would ever reenter Hanover.

Mary and the location of her virus sample that could save millions from death.

And now we're both silent, lost in our own thoughts as we head back over the frozen Key Bridge.

We stop just on the other side of it, in Rosslyn, where he gets us a room at the Rosslyn Motor Inn, a dive motel just down the street from a billiard hall and brothel. Worthy puts enough money down for a week of no questions asked.

While he makes calls from the pay phone up the street, I strip off my bloody clothes and step into the steamy shower.

*   *   *

I emerge from the bathroom in a big shirt borrowed from Worthy's dry cleaning, just as he walks in with two brown paper bags.

He looks at me and smiles. "You definitely look better in that than I do."

"Thanks. How did it go with your lineman friend?"

"It's done," he says, putting the bags down on the table. "Pete'll make sure telephone service to Birchwood Lane is down as of seven a.m. tomorrow. With the full force of the storm hitting later tomorrow, there's no possible way it gets restored till the next day. Paul, I mean Stokes, won't be getting any calls from Hanover."

"Impressive."

"Well, he owed me one," Worthy says.

"You're far better at extortion than I would have predicted."

"You and me both," Worthy says, producing a couple of cold beers from one of the bags. He opens them with the bottle opener on his key chain, passes me one, and we both take a long pull. I try to focus on how amazing the cold beer tastes and not on what it reminds me of: that day at the quarry with Stokes, Kameron, and Theo. And all my still-unanswered questions. "Hungry?" Worthy asks, pulling a sand-wich wrapped in wax paper from the other brown bag.

"Starving," I say, and take it over to the bed.

"From the house of ill repute up the street," Worthy says, sitting down with his own sandwich next to me. "Their pastrami on rye is apparently top-notch."

Between the time travel and losing both Worthy's dinner and Kyung's protein bar in 2035, my need to nosh is off the charts. I utter a quick thank-you before diving into my bordello sandwich.

"Oh, almost forgot, I bought these off the ladies for you." Worthy pulls a worn navy coat from the second bag, followed by a green dress. The dress is exactly what you'd expect of one scored from 1950s hookers—in a word, it's *suggestive*. "They called it a sweater dress," he says. "Not sure if it's the right size."

Not a problem. This dress was built to be flexible, designed to accentuate any and all curves. But it's got long sleeves that'll cover my stitched-up wrist and no bloodstains, so it'll do.

"Thank you," I say.

"Maybe we're rushing this. Maybe we should wait—"

"There's no time," I say. "According to her death certificate, Mary Pell slips in the shower and dies tomorrow night. So, when Hanover's reception desk opens at seven a.m., I need to be there—as Dorothy Frasier."

"And what if you're not fully past the regression? The repatterning?" he asks. "What if once you're back in there, the doctors and staff are able to control you, convince you—"

"I'm over it completely. Spell broken. Go ahead, ask me to fetch your slippers. I'll refuse," I say, shoving the recent memory of freezing at Kameron's command back into the tansu drawer it's trying to escape from.

"I'm serious, Bix. Those ECT shocks wiped my entire visit from your memory. And it didn't come back for a very long time. What if Dr. Sherman insists on restarting the protocol? One treatment and everything you know about the future, Dr. Pell, her viral sample—everything you know about *us*—could be erased."

"Sherman won't treat me without speaking to my husband first, and that's not going to happen tomorrow, thanks to your phone company friend."

There's a good chance I'm right about that.

Only we're talking about Stokes here, so there's at least a decent chance I'm wrong. If that prick's figured out I know I'm Bix . . . But no point in concerning Worthy with worst-case scenarios.

I know—pretty hypocritical in light of my recent demands for total honesty from loved ones.

You're doing what needs to be done. Stop apologizing.

"I could go there myself," Worthy starts, "convince the superintendent to—"

"No! You can't just roll in guns blazing. The only way I get anywhere near Mary Pell in time is as Dorothy Frasier. They can't know I'm not her till after I've gotten Mary to tell me who she's stashed that sample of rat virus with."

"Let's just say you do that, reach Dr. Pell in the Unit, somehow convince her you're from 2035, then get her to give you the information those scientists in the future are after. You'll still be alone in Hanover, under lock and key and overseen by people who think you're insane—some of whom are dangerous. You'll have no rights. No gadgets in your pocket to magically transport you to some other time. No weapon to defend yourself."

He forgot no future tech with me to convince Mary Pell I'm not some doomsday-spouting nutcase. Not great.

I can do nothing about my proof.

But I can do something about the weapon. I pick up Worthy's key chain lying on the table. On it, next to the bottle opener, is a tiny yellow pocketknife. Inscribed on it are the words: STONE CONTAINER CORP. CORRUGATED SETTING DISPLAYS. It's a box cutter, no more than two inches long and an eighth of an inch thick. But sharp. It'll do.

Do what?

Don't want to think about that right now.

"This could work," I say.

Worthy's dubious. "You think you'll be able to get people to do what you say by threatening one of them with a box cutter?" he asks.

"Unfortunately I do," I say as I wrestle the thing off his key chain. "In September 2001, men hijacked airplanes—"

"Airplanes, plural?" he asks.

I nod. "Four of them, using box cutters. Managed to fly three of them into buildings. Very big buildings, full of people. Thousands died."

Worthy stares at me in disbelief.

I carefully lift the pink inner sole of one of my loafers, slip the pocketknife in, and re-cover it. But the thing won't lay back down flat. "Crap."

"Give it here," Worthy says as he pops a couple sticks of bubble gum into his mouth. After chewing them, he carefully places the sticky wad under the inner sole and smooths it back down. Now it doesn't move.

I put the shoe on and try it out. "Wouldn't want to run a marathon in it, but it'll work."

"I still don't like this plan," Worthy says, "leaving you to fend for yourself in there."

I sit back down next to him. "Worthy, I need that time alone in Hanover, to get what I came for. No notifying authorities. No cavalry."

"You've got twenty-four hours, then I'm riding in like the Lone Ranger and getting you out."

"Deal," I say.

It'll all be over, one way or another, by then.

Worthy's leg is touching mine, and he's looking at me with those blue eyes . . . And even though I know, *I know*, this is precisely not the time for this, I am having some feelings. Large and unruly ones, like a wild animal has somehow gotten inside me and is knocking around, dislodging things near my heart . . . which is beating so, so fast now—

Go ahead. It'll help get rid of the jitters.

So you're ready for tomorrow.

The *voice* is all in favor of me bedding Worthy. A little missionary for the mission.

He's right there, inches away. I could so easily lean over and plant my lips on him. In seconds, between kisses, he and I could be fumbling with buttons, zippers, and belts, sweeping cheap motel bedspreads to the floor, taking in the glorious sight of each other naked—

But there's a problem.

With Paul—and Stokes, and others before him, I'm guessing— jumping into bed was easy. We were using each other to blow off steam, have a little fun.

Forget one of you was a virtual prisoner of her house . . .

True. But even given the truly sick situation at its heart, sex with Paul felt comfortably *transactional*. There was a quid pro quo tidiness to it.

This is different. This is messy.

Already it feels like gossamer threads are weaving through me, ligatures beginning to bind me to something I can't even fully see. So many reasons not to sleep with Worthy. I do not need another man in my life who could possibly screw up this mission. Blind me. Weaken me.

But the biggest reason is this: I never again want to feel what I felt that day the marines came and ripped me from my mother. Or hours ago, when I held my maybe-dying brother in my arms. I never want anyone to matter so much to me that I could suffer that kind of devastation again.

No. This can't happen.

So I get up, go and sit at the table with my beer.

CHAPTER 46

I T'S STILL DARK out, snow now starting to come down heavy, as we prepare to leave the motel room. I'm in the green sweater dress, gift of the working girls down the road. It's hugging me tight, conspiring with the bullet bra to raise my curves to Barbie levels. I throw the wool coat over it and walk out the door.

We stop briefly at Worthy's house, and while he changes into his sheriff's deputy uniform, I pull the solar recharger from my purse, plug the link into it, then set them on the windowsill in the kitchen. Before we leave, I phone "my" house and get that odd, continuous tone that lets me know Worthy's friend has delivered: the line is down.

Just before dawn, we head out in the patrol car and soon come to a familiar stretch of wrought iron fence.

"You sure about this?" Worthy asks me one last time.

I nod and we turn onto the road.

* * *

But when Worthy and I pull up to Hanover's gate and I look up at the bronze plaque reading HANOVER STATE PSYCHIATRIC HOSPITAL, I feel like the girl in a teen horror movie poised at the front door of the possessed house while the audience screams, "Don't do it!"

The guard approaches Worthy's window. "Morning, Officer. Can I help you?"

"I have a readmit. Dorothy Frasier. Patient of Dr. Sherman," Worthy says, indicating me in the seat next to him.

The guard eyes me before noting the name on his clipboard. "You can go ahead and take her up to reception. Speak with them," he says, then opens the gate.

As we round the final curve of the hill and the Gothic turrets and peaked roofs of the enormous hospital come into view through the falling snow, I take a deep breath and tell my thumping heart to stand. The fuck. Down.

Worthy pulls the car past the grand main entrance and its looming clock tower, to a spot in the nearly empty parking lot a short distance from reception. Turns off the engine. It's a couple minutes before seven.

I reach for Worthy's hand, and we sit in silence a few moments before he says, "After this is all over, and you've gotten those in 2035 what they need and they develop a cure, maybe you could return here to 1954. I know a guy who could get you papers, a new name. We could . . . At least give it a thought."

And now my mind is giving it all my thoughts.

Even though what has to be accomplished before I could return is huge, any thoughts to life beyond it more a wish than a plan, I can't help wondering what it would be like, an afterlife here in 1954 with Worthy. No one chasing me, no mission on my shoulders. We could take trains, ships, and airplanes. Travel everywhere. See the sights of this still-civilized world.

Or I could do nothing in particular with the deputy, just let each day unfold like the gift it would be . . .

I let my mind contemplate sharing the blissfully mundane with Worthy. New Bix and the deputy doing some deeply normal activity together, like going to the movies or yardwork. Maybe cooking . . . the two of us in his cozy yellow kitchen, sipping lemonade while we shuck corn to go with the hamburgers Worthy's going to cook out back. I even get him one of those aprons that says KING OF THE GRILL—

Ridiculous. For Chrissakes, the guy would be over a hundred years old in 2035!

True. It's strange to think about.

Another thing to think about—losing him and being devastated. Devastation's not good for survival.

But maybe Worthy's worth the risk. Deep down, it feels like that.

Enough with the feelings, snowflake.

Old Bix, the *voice*, they can't take any more loss. Not New Bix.

He's another man who'll blind you. Leave you weak. Look what happened with Paul.

That wasn't love. Enough of the self-talk—what I want has never been more clear to me. I look around the parking lot to see if we're alone. We are. "Worthy?"

"Yeah?" he says, looking at me. And I lean close and kiss him on the lips. It's an amazing kiss. When we pull apart, we're both grinning like idiots, and we stay like that for a long, wonderful moment.

Enough. It's time.

She's right. Worthy's watch says seven o'clock.

"Ready?" he asks. I nod.

Worthy exits the car, and I take those few moments before he reaches my door to prepare.

Time to redon the mask.

Slow myself down. Flatten my cadence. Dull my countenance. Back to the damaged Dorothy who left here with Paul. Then it was a variation on my actual state. I was still getting over the punishing effects of the protocol. Now it'll be a complete performance from the moment I step out of the patrol car.

Can I pull it off?

Worthy opens the door and holds out his hand. Before I take it, I say, "You need to be able to deny knowledge of what I'm about to do. So as soon as you turn me over to them, you leave. Okay?"

"Yes, Mrs. Frasier," he says, and "helps" me up, then holds my upper arm, all formal and cop-like, as he walks me slowly down the long path to reception. The wind's beginning to pick up, the last of fall's leaves blowing with the new snow across the path in front of us.

The guard at the gate must've called ahead because the door at reception opens before we even reach it and there's Wallace in the doorway, smiling stiffly.

I don't say a word. Keep my gaze unfocused, my affect flat. Let Worthy do his law enforcement thing. "Good morning, Miss Wallace," he says.

"Deputy Worthy," she answers with a frosty voice, and I remember she was there in the visitors' room when Worthy went against the doctor's wishes and spilled the beans about his and Paul's lie, sending me into hysterics.

"Mrs. Frasier's husband has been in an accident requiring surgery, and since we were somewhat acquainted, he left a message for me at the station, requesting I bring Dorothy here and secure appropriate accommodations for her, till he's well enough to contact the doctor himself."

"Morning, Dorothy," the marly nurse says, eyes narrow and peering into mine, like she's trying to divine something.

Is Wallace CIA? Dr. Coal-Eyes's partner in interrogation? And if she is, am I still on her radar?

If I wasn't, I am now.

"Good morning, ma'am." I think I slur it convincingly, but I could swear the maybe-spy is eyeing me funny, like the day I left Hanover. Does she see through my slows? Suspect the ruse Worthy and I have cooked up?

Stop. More likely, she's simply being her usual stone-cold imperious self, and I'm being paranoid. Whether you're sick or well, this place is a petri dish for paranoia.

Worthy hands Wallace an envelope. "This letter I was given from Mr. Frasier explains everything."

The deputy and I cooked up the note last night. It states Paul would like his wife readmitted to the familiar surroundings of the Unit since she's still in a fragile state, and he'll call as soon as he's able to discuss "possible resumption of the protocol."

Worthy fought that last part, worried Sherman would overstep the instructions and start treating me before hearing from Paul. But in the end I convinced him that to make sure they admitted me to the Unit, we needed to throw some chum in the water for Sherman. Entice him with the possibility he'd get to finish what he started with me. One last chance to be *instrumental*.

As the nurse reads over the letter, Worthy looks at me, uneasy. He's not comfortable with all the subterfuge. I, on the other hand, seem to be quite at home with it. Just hope Hanover will admit me on the basis of a handwritten note.

Wallace looks up from the letter. "I see. Very considerate of you, bringing her here, Deputy. Come in out of the snow while I write up the intake form. I'll just need a signature from you and then you can be on your way."

It worked! She's admitting me! I manage to contain my elation, catch Worthy's eye before we enter but see no hint of joy. Just worry.

Hanover's familiar medicinal stank greets me when we enter reception. I remember being frisked here my first day. Several lights, suspended from the ceiling, cast ghostly circular patterns on the gray-and-white checkerboard floor. As we follow Wallace over to reception's large desk, Lester enters the room. A slight smile briefly appears on his face when he sees me.

"Lester, would you help with Dorothy," the nurse says as she fills out the form.

Worthy glares at the attendant as he approaches, and for a moment I'm scared he'll lose it and go after him. But he manages to resist the urge, lets Lester take me over to a spot under one of the big lights.

I keep my eyes pointed down.

"All right, Missus Frasier," Lester says with exaggerated clarity, "open your mouth real wide for me and keep it open." I comply, but he still grips my cheeks and forces my jaws farther apart, orders me to lift my tongue, then shines a flashlight in my mouth.

When he's satisfied, he says, "Now give me your coat and hat, dear." I very slowly take them off. And as I hand them over to Lester, now getting an eyeful of my snug green dress, I notice Worthy watching and cringe.

I wouldn't have thought I'd feel embarrassed to have him witness this pocketing of my free will. After all, I'm just playing a role, right?

Only there's a part of me that feels it's not a role.

I've been that patient, struggling to make sense of the confusing world around her—which makes all of Lester's slow and sweet talk in front of Worthy excruciating.

The deputy signs the intake form and Wallace hands him a pink receipt for me, like I'm a load of bricks, then escorts him to the exit. At the door, Worthy gives me a last worried look before Wallace shuts the door behind him.

I'm alone. But I'm in.

The nurse goes back to her desk and picks up the phone. "Dr. Sherman's exchange, please," she says to the hospital operator.

"Take 'em off," Lester says, pointing to my weaponized loafers, and I slip the shoes off carefully, praying the Bazooka Joe'd inner sole on the right stays in place over the box cutter. True to form, Lester gives the left just a cursory glance before dropping it back on the linoleum.

But for some reason, he's more thorough with the right, peering at its inner sole a long tick. Now his hand starts to reach inside it.

I'm moments from being caught before I've even begun.

But then Wallace calls out, "That's fine, Lester. You can go ahead and take her."

Lester stops his search. Drops the shoe on the ground.

I step back in it and start breathing again.

But then Wallace adds, "She's been at home, so no need for delousing. You can bring her straight to A-Ward."

A-Ward? That's not at all how I need this to go.

"The Unit?" I ask her, trying not to betray the alarm beneath my slow, slurry words.

"The doctor would need your husband's signature on a special paper for that, sweetheart. But you'll be just fine in A-Ward for now."

CHAPTER 47

As Lester leads me past the door to the east-west corridor, I catch a glimpse through its window of the dim main tunnel. Somewhere in its distant shadows is the Unit. How the hell am I ever going to reach Mary in time if I can't get in there?

"Dorothy." I look up. Miss Gibbs is walking toward us, smiling. "I guess you missed us too much to stay away."

"Good to see you, Miss Gibbs," I slur to Doe-Eyes.

She squeezes my hand gently, and a memory surges forward:

> I'm strapped to the examination table. Coal-Eyes is about to inject me, when a woman's voice, warm and soothing, says, "If you tell me the truth, I'll get him to stop, honey."
>
> Then a delicate-looking hand squeezes mine tight.
>
> I look up and see Miss Gibbs. She leans in close, till she's inches from me. "Just whisper it in my ear . . ."

Gibbs?

Gibbs is CIA! She's the one in charge of extracting information from Mary.

Don't you dare react.

I will my face to stay flat and still, not show any emotional response to this revelation, while my insides roil. I give Gibbs a dull half smile and let Lester pull me down the hall.

* * *

I keep my eyes pointed groundward as we exit the elevator onto the first floor's main corridor. Just beyond the ward gate, I smell Sherman's cologne.

"Dorothy."

I turn to him slowly. The doctor's looking me up and down, assessing. "Doctor Sherman . . . it's nice to see you," I say slowly, trying to exude an air of benign compliance I don't at all feel. Now that I've regained my faculties and can fully appreciate the depths this man brought me to, I just want to grab him by the throat and lean in hard.

"I'm so sorry about your husband's mishap, Dorothy, but we'll be sure to take good care of you here." Then he walks on.

Lester deposits me in the dayroom, which looks unchanged. A few new faces but the same vibe of questionable incarceration mixed with mild madness. Germanic Nurse is watching my arrival from the nurses' station.

"Holy Toledo!" Suddenly Georgie's got me in a bear hug. Her fluffy pink sweater tickles my nose. Aware I'm being observed, I try to temper my reaction to this reunion. But damn, it's good to see her. My inclination to cry, though less than it was in November, is still present, and my eyes start to fill.

There's a distinct chance I'm becoming a bit of a gal pal.

Jesus.

Georgie puts her arm around my shoulders and steers me away from the nurses' station. I keep my eyes on the floor as I let her slowly walk me to an empty table at the far end of the room and help me into a seat. As she stops to push a hank of my hair that's slipped in front of my face out of the way, she says to herself, "What in heaven did they do to you?"

I smile up at her, eyes now sharp and focused, and whisper, "I'm fine, Georgie. Don't scream—"

She just about jumps out of her skin—but manages to do it

silently, not drawing Germanic Nurse's attention. She drops into her seat, dramatically clutches her hand to her chest and hisses, "You scared the living daylights out of me! Faker."

"Sorry, I had to."

"But that day of the Christmas concert, when you were so—"

"That was real. The Unit."

She shakes her head, trying to banish all the awful, then pivots to my clothes for some relief. "That's some getup you got there," she says, eyeing the dress and pointy bra. "You certainly know how to make an entrance."

"I try."

"So, if you're not really ill, or overtreated, then why on earth did you let your husband bring you back here?"

"He doesn't know I'm here," I say.

"You brought *yourself* back to Hanover?"

* * *

I relay the discoveries of my long, strange trip—from Hanover to my "home" with Paul, to the blighted future and back to 1954, on a mission to get information from a Unit patient before it's too late.

All the crazy weirdness. But none of the particulars. No mention of Mary's name, the virus sample I'm after, or the whistleblowing against the government that led to Mary's incarceration at Hanover. Certainly no mention of her interrogation by Gibbs and the mystery beady-eyed CIA man in the Unit.

I need to protect Georgie. Don't want to fill her with knowledge that would be of interest to whatever secret pocket of the CIA Gibbs and Dr. Coal-Eyes are part of.

When I've finished my story, Georgie sits silent.

"I know, it's a lot to swallow," I say. "I don't expect you to—"

"How can I help?" she says.

"You believe me?"

"Sorry, no," Georgie says bluntly, "but you are my friend who's come back here at great personal risk to accomplish something *you* believe in, and I will support that endeavor . . . As long as it won't land me in any hot water . . ."

Same old Georgie. Going along to get along.

* * *

We spend the next few hours spitballing ideas on how to reach Mary. The idea of pulling the fire alarm seemed promising before Georgie informed me they're locked. Stealing a staff member's keys also had its moment, but having seen one of those shiny key reels up close that night in the infirmary with Lester, I can attest to their strength. No one's slipping one of those off a belt without detection.

And so the day goes, me racking my brain, coming up with awful ideas, Georgie her own equally bad ones. At one point I spy Lillian looking at us from across the room. Wave for her to come over but she shakes her head.

"What's with her?"

"She's kept her distance ever since you were sent to the Unit," Georgie says.

I walk over and take a seat next to Lillian. She's not happy, seems extra nervous at my presence. I open my mouth, about to ask what gives, but she puts her hand up. "Don't say a word." I start to protest, but she again stops me. "Please. I mean it, Dorothy. After I told Dr. Sherman about your plan, I felt so awful. And, well, I've been trying to be better."

"By not talking to me?"

"By not telling Dr. Sherman things about people he might want to know . . . I'm getting better at it. Just this week, I didn't tell him Maren stole a dinner roll from Esther and hid it in her sweater sleeve," she says, and smiles.

"That's good," I say.

"But I'm still not great at it." Her hands are twisting her skirt like she's wringing it dry. "That's why I need to keep away from you. So I'm not tempted . . . to learn things . . . You should go now."

Lillian's trying with all her might to control what she can in her world. Not for me to screw with that. I get up and walk away.

* * *

Five o'clock rolls around without a decent plan, and my angst building, when Germanic Nurse's voice booms from the loudspeaker: "Ladies, tonight is Hanover's New Year's banquet. Those who'd like the chance to decorate a party hat beforehand should make their way to the dining hall."

"New Year's. I completely forgot!" Georgie says breathlessly as patients begin heading for the door.

"Probably because it's not really New Year's," I say.

"But don't you see?" she says. "There are sure to be Unit patients brought up for the meal. Maybe the woman you need to speak to will be—"

"She won't," I say. "She's not a patient they ever allow upstairs."

Georgie's looking at me, and I can see the little gears turning in her head. "Ever? Why would she never be al—?"

"Drop it, Georgie."

* * *

Different holiday, different pictures taped to the walls of the dining room's serving area. Now, instead of turkeys and Pilgrims, there are pictures of clocks, Father Time, and Baby New Year.

I follow behind Georgie in line. As the woman in the hairnet loads my tray with a fake New Year's feast of ham, peas, rice pilaf, and a dessert of apple crumble, I watch a kitchen worker opening the nearby dumbwaiter and placing two familiar covered pots inside. Pureed dinner for the Unit, though the women there won't know it's dinner. No such specifics of time allowed in that netherworld.

"Move along," the hairnet woman orders, and Georgie pulls me away, out into the deafening dining hall packed to the gills with patients—many of whom are not truly ill. Just inconvenient. Mouthy, embarrassing, unconventional women, swept up and deposited in Hanover so the normies won't have to deal with them.

Someone on the hospital staff has taken Fake New Year's Eve quite seriously. Tables are full-on festooned with confetti, streamers, noisemakers, and party hats, some of which industrious patients have decorated and now wear. Crayons, colored paper, and pens from the craft session still lie scattered about.

Lillian averts her eyes as I pass her table.

Limited to my slow Dorothy gate, I quickly fall behind Georgie in our trek down the center aisle. So I'm alone when I start to pass Norma and Carol's table. "Look who's back. Wonder Gork," Norma says to me, and Carol howls at her brilliant wordplay.

I'm so tempted to react. Funnel all my disappointment and rage at failing to reach Mary into pummeling the she-bully. But I manage to keep my dull half smile firmly in place—

Till she trips me.

My tray and I go airborne, and it's looking like an ass-over-teakettle situation is unfolding as I sail over the checkerboard floor. But then my body, like a cat, wrests back control midair—and I land on my feet, tray still in hand, not a pea out of place.

Reflexes are definitely back.

You know what's also back? Knee-jerk rage.

I turn toward Norma, about to go postal—when a hand gently alights on my arm. It belongs to Joe, the custodian. "You all right, miss?" he asks, and his concern manages to interrupt my chain reaction of anger and frustration.

"Yes," I say, and walk away.

When I reach Georgie's table, I take a seat on the bench, spy the big clock on the wall—and sink into a funk.

Five thirty. Time's just about up.

If Kyung's right, Mary dies in the next few hours. And I have over-come time machine brain damage, ECT brain damage, and gaslight-ing by a fake husband, not to mention marauding young religious thugs in the future, only to sit here, uselessly chowing down on pressed ham.

My eyes drop from the taunting clock to the table below it, full of Unit patients. The kitchen staff's decorated it like the others: hats, crayons, confetti, and streamers—but the gray moths seated there are oblivious to the festivity. They only have eyes for the slop in front of them, completely wrapped up in the attempt to feed themselves.

I recognize one of them from my time in the Unit: Frida, the woman with the unibrow.

As I watch Frida try to scrape up a spoonful of pureed ham, a brief flash of having done the same comes to me, and I remember how it felt to have one's whole world reduced to a spoon and bowl full of mush. To put all you had into a good swallow. So you could keep going.

Tears are rising and it's a battle to stuff them down, so it takes me a moment to realize who's sitting next to Frida—

Dr. Mary Pell.

CHAPTER 48

"S HE'S HERE," I say.

"Who?" Georgie asks.

"The woman I need to speak to." Georgie looks over at the Unit table. "To the left of the one with the eyebrows," I say, and she takes in Mary, staring blankly ahead, hair trailing over her face like a veil.

"Not a fan of the hairbrush, is she?" Georgie says. "Why do you suppose they let her up here?"

Exactly. How is Mary, prisoner of some rogue group within the CIA, sitting there unguarded? Has to be a trap. Maybe Gibbs wasn't so convinced I was just a crazy housewife, and when she learned I'd returned to Hanover, she placed Mary at that table to lure me over so she could pounce.

So, where is Gibbs?

I search the dining hall, from the observation window and entrance near us, all the way to the other end of the enormous room, where the kitchen and other entrance lie.

But Doe-Eyes is nowhere to be seen. Neither is Wallace—which also strikes me as strange and vaguely trap-y. But these concerns are irrelevant because I have no choice.

Trap or no trap, I need to speak to Mary.

The only staff in the vicinity, besides Joe doing rice pilaf mop-up, are Germanic Nurse and Gus. I watch the two patrolling the aisles, ever so slowly moving away from our end of the room, and my mind wills them to move faster.

Georgie nudges me. She's holding up a shapeless gray cardigan with pockets. "Put this on. The gray will help you stand out less over there," she says, nodding at the Unit table full of gray moths.

"Where'd you get this?" I ask, and she nods toward Maren, the blond Norwegian alcoholic and dinner roll thief, now proudly wearing Georgie's beloved fluffy pink sweater. "Oh, Georgie. No."

She shrugs. "What's a little angora for the cause. What else can I do?"

"Nothing else," I say, slipping my hand into a sweater sleeve. There's a couple of crumbs inside, no doubt from Maren's last pilfered biscuit. "Gibbs can't see you helping me."

"Gibbs?" Georgie asks. "What's she got to do with—?"

"Do *not* get involved. Understand?" I say with rather too much intensity, and she solemnly nods.

When Gus and Germanic Nurse are far enough away, I slip off the bench onto the floor, then scramble across the aisle and past the next two empty tables to the Unit's beyond.

I check behind me for indications I've been spotted, signs of Gibbs or Wallace, but seeing none, I slide into a space on the bench between two Unit patients.

And am now face-to-face with Mary Pell.

She stares dully into the distance behind me through her stringy hair, hand gripping a spoonful of pureed peas. Frida and the equally out-of-it woman on Mary's other side have her boxed in tight, and I imagine that beneath the vague gaze, Mary's going crazy over her neighbors' boundary issues.

"Mary, I need to talk to you," I say. "Before Gibbs shows up."

Mary's eyes still hold their thousand-yard stare, but she says softly, "So you figured it out, that our meek little kitten's actually CIA, there to hold our hand and coax our secrets out—she and her beady-eyed partner in the doctor coat."

I nod, glancing behind me again for any signs of trouble. Gus and Germanic are still at the far end of the room. Joe, now sweeping pilaf into his dustbin, is the only staff on this side. "Why would those agents let you up here?"

"I suspect *they* didn't. Someone else has had a hand in setting up this meeting. Making sure we're left alone," she says cryptically.

"Someone else?" I ask.

But she doesn't elaborate. "I'm guessing your visit home proved educational," she says, eyes now laser sharp.

"It did. I—"

"Finally started listening to that lunatic voice in your head . . . and discovered you're more than Dorothy Frasier," she says, again all prophetic and inscrutable, like some goddamn Delphic oracle.

"Yes," I say. Now the hard part: the convincing without proof. Despite the fact that we're surrounded by barely there Unit patients, I lower my voice. "Okay . . . this is going to sound really insane, but I *am* a time traveler from the future."

No reaction from Mary. Probably decided it's best to retreat into catatonia till the crazy lady's forced by staff to return to her table. Shouldn't be long now.

That's when a last-ditch, desperate idea comes to me: what worked before could work again. I quietly take the box cutter out of my shoe and extend the blade. "I'll prove it," I say, and pull up my sleeve, revealing my new fishing line sutures—the ones I'm about to cut off.

But Mary leans forward, puts her hand on mine.

"Put it away. I know."

I freeze. "That I'm a time traveler?" She nods imperceptibly. *What?* "How—?"

Her eyes sweep the room. "I suspect we don't have time for 'how,'" she says. "Best we get right to it. So, tell me, H. G. Wells, what are you risking life and limb to speak to me about tonight?"

As quickly as I can, I tell her about the Guest virus, how it had appeared out of nowhere and decimated humanity in 2025. Mary's face behind those greasy bangs looks quietly devastated. I tell her about how the NSA uncovered Mary's interview in the *Weekly World*

Post, where she warned about the government hiding a virus virtually identical to the Guest. And I tell her I was sent to 1954 Hanover to speak with her.

"I'm guessing those searching in 2025 found all the records from Project Gambit missing, along with the samples?" she asks.

I nod. "Someone cleaned house," I say.

Suddenly there are shouts erupting from the other end of the room. I twist around and see the figures of Norma and Carol fighting in the distance, and Gibbs caught in the middle.

Gibbs. Shit.

Curious patients are beginning to gather, blocking my view of them—and also Gibbs's view of Mary and me. For now.

"We need the name and location of whoever has the sample of rat virus you mentioned in the tabloid story," I say. "Will you help us?"

Mary doesn't hesitate to reveal the name she's suffered torture and faked catatonia to keep from her interrogators these last few weeks. Leans toward me, about to speak—

When she stops, eyeing Frida next to her. Or rather Frida's hand, which is paused in the middle of bringing a spoonful of pureed pilaf to her mouth. Mary's wondering if Frida's listening.

Given how far into the protocol Frida is, it's far more likely she's simply forgotten about the spoonful of food in her hand. But Mary's taking no chances; she plucks up a nearby coil of pink New Year's Eve streamer. Rips off a small piece.

"Get me that pen," she says, nodding to a red felt one in a basket of arts and craft supplies down the table. "Hurry."

I reach across a couple patients, nab the pen, then hand it to Mary, who hunches over the scrap of paper, shielding it from prying eyes.

As she writes, I look behind me but can't see through the knot of patients now gathered around the fight at the far side of the room.

Mary finishes quickly, turns the piece of pink streamer over and looks at me, deadly serious. "Read, then swallow it."

Sounds very *Spy vs. Spy*, but under the circumstances, it's just common sense. "I will," I say, and she pushes the snippet across the table to me.

"Thank you," I tell her, picking it up.

Holding the flimsy scrap to my chest, I peek at it cautiously, like a poker player eyeing her hand. Everything that's happened since waking on that bus has led to this moment, and I half expect to hear Beethoven's Ninth as I look at the neatly written name of the loyal friend Mary entrusted with the rat virus. Who she was talking about when she said she had to "protect those I can for as long as possible." I don't recognize the name. What I do recognize are the two words after the name: "Fort Detrick." Ground zero for this whole shitshow.

I close my eyes and take a quick mental picture of the words on the slip. Commit them to memory. When I look up, Mary warns, "Be very certain you're not followed when you make contact. No one's to be trusted."

Including me. This woman will be dead by midnight and I'm not going to warn her. Just letting her die . . .

Don't start.

For the mission.

Remember what you're here to do—save millions.

And if that means watching Mary Pell die—

Shut up.

You've got the name, now go! Don't mess with the timeline.

But at this point hasn't the timeline already been pretty damn messed with? By me. By Stokes. No telling how many people's lives here in 1954 we've impacted. And we're all still here. The universe hasn't imploded. Mary saved my life, my mind. It's time to return the favor.

I put my hand on Mary's. "I need to tell you—"

But something behind me has stolen Mary's attention. "Get back to your table. Now!" she whispers.

"But—"

"Go!" she growls, then returns to her blank stare.

I shove the pink scrap into my sweater pocket, slip off the bench, and scramble across the floor to the first empty table with its meager cover. Peering up the aisle, I see Norma and Carol still lunging at each other as they're dragged away by attendants.

And I spot Gibbs's white cap in the crowd.

She's trying to get through the knot of onlookers, yelling in a decidedly un-Gibbs voice for them to return to their seats.

Georgie's watching me crouched behind the table. She looks nervously back at Gibbs, who's about to break free of the clot of patients.

Then she does a truly unexpected thing: jumps up from the table, pulling Maren along with her. Drags the confused woman by her fluffy pink sweater over to where Gibbs is just emerging from the crowd and begins shouting to the nurse, I'm guessing about how Maren stole her sweater.

Then an even more bizarre thing occurs. Go-along-to-get-along Georgie puts her hand on Gibbs and shoves her.

Yeah. Holy shit.

Gibbs's response is swift and rough. Before Georgie even knows what's happened, she's received two quick blows and is on the ground locked in a choke hold. Moments later two attendants arrive with a restraint and Gibbs orders Georgie be put in it.

I don't waste this sacrifice Georgie has made. The privileges that will be taken from her. The extra days and state-of-the-art treatments that could be added to her stay here because of this brave act. I make damn sure I'm back in my seat, chewing placidly on my ham, by the time the pissed-off Gibbs marches up the aisle toward the Unit table. She appears unaware of Mary and my meeting, not even a glance my way as she passes by.

I sneak a look back at Georgie, now in the straitjacket. The punch-drunk debutante grins at me just the slightest as she's led out of the room.

Time to eat Mary's words. I reach into the pocket of the gray cardigan for the scrap of pink streamer.

But there's nothing.

I check the other. Empty as well. I look around my feet, under the table, then farther afield—

Till I spot it lying in the middle of the main aisle. Face up.

I can see the red writing from here. Gibbs is getting ready to march Mary and the rest of the Unit patients right past it. If the CIA agent happens to glance down as she walks by, that "Fort Detrick" will certainly catch her eye. A scrap of paper with the name of the army's primary bioweapons lab written on it is not your typical patient doodle.

I need to reach it before Gibbs does.

I snatch a party hat from the table and quietly toss it into the aisle close to the streamer.

Then in my best Dorothy, I rise from my seat and walk slowly into the aisle. I don't look at Gibbs now coming down it with the Unit patients, focus only on the hat, reaching for it with both hands, like it's a prized possession—while, at the same time, making sure to land my loafer on top of that piece of pink streamer.

With great and deliberate care, I place the party hat on my head, securing it with the elastic band under my chin, while Gibbs leads her charges past me. I don't look at Mary passing by, bury the urge to run after her shouting warnings about her impending death.

When Gibbs is far enough away, I chance a look. She's at the far entrance, exchanging what look like heated words with Wallace.

I casually bend down and cup the pink snippet of streamer, stuff it back in my sweater pocket, out of sight. When I straighten up, Gibbs is exiting the far door with the Unit patients.

I exhale a sigh of relief, marveling at having obtained this prize right under Gibbs's nose.

Time to contemplate next steps. Maybe I complain of stomach pains so they bring me to the infirmary tonight—where I find some object to serve as a lockpick then escape out a cooperative exit door while the night nurse snoozes at her desk. Or I could simply wait for Worthy to arrive, all Deputy Badass with the cavalry, and he and New Bix ride off together into the sunset. But first I need to eat Mary's words.

Only as I reach into my pocket, I see Lester, heading straight for me down the center aisle.

Something's wrong.

Gibbs left, oblivious to my actions. So what's going on? I quickly scan the room, trying to piece it together—

And see Stokes, standing at the observation window with Sherman.

Watching me.

How did he know I was here? The phone line's down, so the hospital couldn't have reached him at the house . . . Has Stokes been following me since I climbed out the window? Does he know about Worthy? Does he know—

No doubt he knows many things. But what's pertinent right here, right now?

Think.

He knows if I've risked coming back here, then Mary must not be a gork. That she's awake and has the information he—and Kameron Rook—want.

When Stokes turns to speak to Sherman I get a glimpse of his plan: the bandage on his cheek, the bright red bloodstain on his collar— and the fuck-ton of concern on the men's faces as they watch.

Just how long has Stokes been there?

Long enough to see me talking to Mary? Retrieving the streamer?

I've got to get rid of it. Chew it, swallow it. So there's nothing he can get hold of.

Ten seconds alone is all I need.

So I sprint for the far end of the dining room near the kitchen. If I can get past Lester and out of Stokes's sight line, I can swallow the scrap without him seeing. Then wait for Worthy to ride up on his white steed.

Lester lunges for me, and I dodge him like I did Gus that day I escaped the bus. Like Gus, his momentum carries him to the floor.

Only once there, Lester manages to grab my ankle as I'm running by.

There's a *CRACKKK* as my head hits the ground and things get fuzzy . . . Sherman and Stokes by my side . . . Stokes leaning over me, calling me Dee—while I feel his hands quietly sliding into the pockets of the gray sweater . . . Then Lester and Gus scooping me up and bearing me away . . . Squares of checkerboard floor sliding beneath me till it all fades to black.

CHAPTER 49

T HE CLOUD OF mint green around me gradually comes into focus and I see the familiar tiled walls of the Unit treatment room. Its big, bright light blares down on me from above, amplifying the painful throbbing now going on in my head, and I try to rub my temples for relief.

But find I can't.

My arms and legs have been strapped to the examination table. The right sleeve of my dress has been pulled up—someone's discovered my new fishing line sutures.

And my feet are bare—they've removed my weaponized loafers and set them in the corner. Shit.

Yet I'm still in the green dress. No one's taken the time to put me in a Unit gown yet—Sherman in too big a rush to restart my treatments, plug me back into the Tennessee Valley Authority's electrical grid.

Pretty certain the doctor's not taken kindly to being duped. No doubt it's a heart-wrenching tale Stokes has told him about his wife's relapse and deceit, filled with details both false and true. And now the doctor's more than ready to shake my Etch A Sketch, wipe away my latest delusions with a triple shot of 150 volts.

But Stokes would first want whatever information I've gotten from Mary.

The scrap of pink streamer.

I madly crane my head around, trying to peer into the pocket of the gray cardigan. Twist and contort myself till I see what I feared—both pockets empty.

He's got the name. I need to get out of here. And I scan the room for ideas.

That's when I see the Dalmatian in a fireman's hat picture on the wall.

I'm not in the green treatment room of the Unit. I'm in its twin: the infirmary's procedure room.

The door swings open, and Nurse Wallace enters. "Miss Wallace," I say, free of slur. No point in pretense now. "I've got to talk to the doctor. Please!"

She approaches me, about to respond, when Sherman enters. "Dorothy, I think it's time you and I had a frank discussion," he says, and Wallace withdraws to the storage cabinets on the far side of me, busies herself pulling various items from them.

Convince him without giving the whole truth.

"Doctor, I need you to listen, really listen, to me. I'm not Dorothy Frasier, and that man who calls himself Paul, he's not Paul Frasier. He's probably killed the real Paul Frasier."

That's a bit too much truth.

Sherman looks at Wallace. "Return of her Capgras syndrome," he says soberly. She nods, and he jots a note in my nearby chart.

"I know, I must sound deranged," I say, "but someone with proof of this will be here tomorrow—"

"Is that so?" he asks, a trace of facetiousness in his doctor voice. Prick.

"You don't understand. There's something extremely important I've got to do, information I need to get to certain people before it's too late, and that man posing as my husband, he's trying to stop me . . .'Cause he wants it for himself—"

"I can only imagine how upsetting it must be to think that's what's happening here," Sherman says. "But I assure you, dear, everything's going to be just fine . . ."

Just fine. Yeah. Got it.

"You see, Dorothy, we're blessed to live in a time of tremendous advances in the treatment of mental illness. Which means we now have choices in how best to help a patient. There's no one right approach for everyone . . ."

"Doctor—" I start, but he puts his hand up and I knee-jerk stop talking, my brain still a tangled mess of lost connections and new reflexes Sherman has wired into me.

While I'm temporarily struck dumb, Sherman continues. "And after learning the truth from Paul today, about his injuries, about the struggles you're clearly still having with your illness, then observing you firsthand . . . Well, it's clear a new approach is needed."

"You're giving up on the protocol?" I ask.

"Yes." He turns to the nurse. "You can go now, Miss Wallace," he says, and the nurse sets a cloth-covered tray down on the table beside me, then leaves the room.

On the tray are an array of items: squares of cotton gauze, rubbing alcohol, a scalpel, a hammer—and two long, ice pick–shaped tools with heads shaped like mushrooms.

Lobotomy. Fuck.

Stokes has set me up. Told Sherman I attacked him with a knife. Even slashed himself to back up the story. And now that the doctor thinks I used a weapon, he believes I pose an immediate danger to others.

So he's going the "traditional" route with me.

Like Betsy.

"No. No, no. You can't do this!" I plead with Sherman as I strain against the leather restraints binding me.

Sherman's unperturbed by my response. "In a short while, with these specialized instruments called leucotomes, I'll be performing a minor but, I believe, life-changing procedure on you. It's called a transorbital lobotomy—"

"You have no fucking right!" I scream.

He pats my squirming shoulder. "It's time to put an end to this struggle, dear. Let you get on with your life—a life lived with far less conflict. The lobotomy might not be able to free you of your delusions," Sherman says, "but it'll dampen your emotions, weaken the urges associated with them. Give you and your husband the peace I know you're both looking for—"

"I told you, he's not Paul Frasier. He's taken his place! You're making a huge mistake!"

"A brief shock to sedate you and then the procedure. The whole thing will take less than ten minutes. And after you've recovered, you'll get to go home, do all those things you love again. Bowling, cooking—"

"Like Betsy?" I ask. "Is she home doing all the things she loves?"

"Not the outcome we'd hoped for with Miss Apel. It happens from time to time. But that's nothing you should worry about," he says, and turns to jot another note in my file. "I know it seems scary, Dorothy, but trust that we're making the right decision for your needs."

"My needs? This is about *my* needs?"

"Try to relax, dear, you're in good hands," he says, flipping my file closed and heading for the door. "When you wake tomorrow, you're going to feel completely different about this."

"No shit! I'm also going to be drooling and pissing myself, you quack! What kind of dumbass fuckery is this?" I yell as he steps out into the hallway.

You need a better exit strategy.

The scalpel on the tray.

The one lying next to the long, pointy thing Sherman's going to shove through my eye socket, into my brain . . .

Focus.

The scalpel.

I pull hard against the restraint strap on my left wrist, fingers stretching, trying to reach the corner of the cloth covering the tray Wallace has left so tantalizingly close.

But I fail. It's just out of reach.

So try again.

I give it a second go, manage to touch the cloth with the tip of my finger. But I just can't grasp it.

Again.

This time I strain against the thick leather like some rabid dog on a leash, the strap cutting painfully into my arm. Don't care. It can have my arm if I can keep my mind.

And I succeed! Manage to pinch the corner of fabric between my fingertips!

I ever so gently draw the cloth toward me till the tip of the scalpel is hanging as far off the tray as I dare bring it. Then I reach up, grasp the blade's cold metal between my sweaty fingertips.

Carefully, I lower the instrument, bring it down to my side.

Seconds later, I've manipulated the scalpel into the backward angle required to bring its blade against the leather strap and begin to saw away at it as quickly as I can.

Out in the hall, Sherman's speaking. "She's a little hysterical. There's always some amount of upset before the procedure. Perfectly normal, Mr. Frasier."

Stokes. He decided to stick around. Make sure the procedure is carried out. His wife's struggle ended. I can hear him laying his earnest-husband act on thick: "I just regret not listening to you earlier, Doctor. Things might have been so different."

"I suppose we'll never know if it would've made a difference," Sherman says. "Or if her illness was simply too advanced, the delusions and violent urges too entrenched for the protocol to work. But you're making the right decision now, Mr. Frasier."

"If it's okay, I'd like to wait here . . . till it's done."

"I understand. I'll come down, let you know when it's over. There *is* one more thing we need to discuss. The directive."

"For Dorothy's sterilization?"

"I know you were against it when she was entering the Unit, and I understand the reluctance to commit to something so permanent at the time. But now that she'll be undergoing lobotomy, I urge you to reconsider. There's a certain lack of 'pushback' in patients after the procedure—"

"'Lack of pushback'? What do you mean?" Stokes asks.

"More often than not, they simply aren't capable of governing their own bodies, of saying no. And given your wife's tendencies, her history . . . Well, undesired pregnancies can and do result. Reproduction needs to be prevented in women such as your wife, with mental disabilities."

Jesus Christ.

"I suppose you're right, Doctor," Stokes says.

"Glad we could come to an understanding, Mr. Frasier. Here are the consent forms for both the lobotomy and the sterilization via tubal ligature. I'll just need your signature—"

"First I want to see her."

"Oh . . . Yes, certainly."

I cease my sawing, quickly slide the scalpel under my hand and out of sight before the two enter. In Sherman's hands is the paperwork required to end my critical thinking and reproductive abilities. The doctor sits down at a nearby desk and busies himself with my file while Stokes puts his hat on the counter and comes over to me.

"Hello, darling," he says, the portrait of a loving husband.

I want to kill him.

"I know how hard this is," he says, gently taking my captive right hand in his. I force his hand around for a closer look at his wrist. And now I see it: hidden beneath the anchor's indigo lines, a two-inch-long scar like mine. Blood vessel adjacent.

Stokes smiles and twists my hand violently back around. Kisses it. "This will all be over soon, Dee."

"You can't let them do this, Stokes!" I plead, and he and Sherman exchange looks.

"Don't worry, darling. Dr. Sherman's a real expert at this surgery.

Takes no time at all when he does it. And afterward, none of today's *unpleasantness* will matter."

"Motherfucker."

Another look passes between them. Stokes waits for the doctor to return to his reading, then quietly reaches over and picks up the ice pick–like leucotome. Examines it briefly, then smiles at me and returns it to the tray.

Nausea begins to build in me as the enormity of what's about to happen hits home. What my life will be like after Sherman performs the lobotomy. Badly. Each day unfolding like the last, as I recover from my "procedures," dully waiting in some chronic ward for the day my fake husband comes to bring me "home."

And kill me.

There's a knock at the door, and when Dr. Sherman exits to speak with whoever's there, I say to Stokes, "If I used you, our relationship, to obtain information last summer, I'm sorry. But there's too much at stake here in 1954 to—"

"Ah, your mission. Saving mankind. That valuable scrap of paper you obtained for me. Can't believe you actually got Dr. Pell to give up the name. Kudos for squeezing it out of that poor, doomed woman."

I did that, didn't I? Squeezed Mary for information, then discarded her like a tissue.

"Well, no sense in dragging this out, Beatrix," Stokes says, and walks over to the forms. As he begins to sign, my fingers quietly feel out how far I've cut the leather strap. So close.

Dr. Sherman reenters and sees "Paul" has signed the papers. "Ah, good timing. The attendant is here to prep Dorothy, cut her hair," he says. "We find it best to keep hygiene postsurgery as simple as possible for the patient. Makes for an easier transition."

Fuck.

Sherman gathers the signed consent forms and exits just as Lester enters carrying heavy-duty electric hair clippers and a cloth to catch my hair as it falls. He gives me a smile.

"Ah, here he is, Dee," Stokes says, "the nice man who'll be giving you a brand-new hairdo." He leans over me. "Good night, darling. I'll be bringing you back home very soon." Then he kisses me on the lips as Lester looks on.

"She's all yours," Stokes says to Lester, then picks up his hat and walks out the door, whistling "Blueberry Hill."

CHAPTER 50

L ESTER CLOSES THE door. Drapes the cloth around my neck, tucking it behind my head, then leans in close. "Doctor's finally going to make things right up there," he says, tapping my forehead. "Then you and I can get better acquainted, baby doll."

Time's up. It's now or never. I begin yanking on the partially cut restraint, pulling with all that's in me.

"Tug all you want on those straps, darlin'. Won't do you no good. They's tough."

He flicks on the metal clippers, and with a loud *thwock*, the thing hums to life.

As Lester grabs a section of hair in his hand, some rabid force takes over me, and one last time I try with all my might to wrench free of the table's grip—

And I finally feel the slightest give in the remaining leather. I pull again and again and again, till the thing *rrrrrips* open, and my hand flies free, knocking the clippers out of Lester's. The thing lands on my stomach, where it rumbles and vibrates.

While Lester's caught off guard a moment by the failure of the tough strap, I madly fiddle with the buckle on the cuff holding my right hand, fingers desperately trying to undo the thing.

But Lester rebounds. Grabs my free hand and slams it and me back down on the table. "You bitch!" he yells, and I see in his eyes something primitive stirring. His other hand goes for my throat and begins to strangle me with raw ferocity.

As he squeezes the life out of me, I try to scream, but there's no air to produce one, and a panic over my situation begins to set in —

When I remember the scalpel.

I know it's somewhere near where he's pinned my wrist.

My fingers paw desperately about for it, feeling around within their limited reach —

Till they touch metal.

I grab hold, point it up toward Lester's forearm, and jab.

He yanks his hand back. "What the hell!" he screams, aggrieved, like I've broken the rules of our match. He drops my wrist but tightens his grip on my throat. Everything quickly starts going fuzzy.

So I bring the scalpel up to his neck, to where the carotid is closest to the surface. But it has no effect on Lester.

Go deeper.

To the river of red surging below the skin? No. I don't want to kill him. That's not something Bix with her new code does.

And yet, you're choking to death.

True. Blackness is closing in. Mere seconds of consciousness left to make a choice.

Plan A: kill. Plan B: die.

And I choose . . . I choose . . .

Plan C. I drop the scalpel and grab the vibrating clippers off my stomach and slam the heavy appliance into the side of his head. *Cruncck.*

Lester's eyes roll up, and he slides to the floor in a heap.

Get his keys.

I quickly undo the straps restraining the rest of my limbs, then, bending down, use the scalpel to saw away at the thin metal cord connecting the key ring to Lester's reel. It comes free surprisingly easily and I pocket the keys in my sweater before yanking the plug of the clippers from its socket. Grabbing hold of Lester's white pants, I heave the loathsome prick onto his stomach, bind his wrists behind him with the cord, then lash them tight to his ankles.

A quick rifle through nearby drawers produces a roll of gauze and spool of first aid tape that I use to gag him. Then I put my loafers on, and I'm heading for the door when it opens—

And there stands Joe, the custodian.

I should blow past him. Get out of here. He is, after all, a member of the hospital staff. Probably disapproves of my hog-tying Lester.

But something about the smooth way he enters and locks the door makes me pause. Joe rubs his chin, taking in the unconscious, trussed-up Lester on the floor behind me a moment. "Right. Well, I suppose it couldn't be helped."

Those words coming from this man, in this moment, are strange enough. But even stranger is the way he's said them. Gone is the deferential southern drawl, replaced by a clipped British accent stuffed with professorial pomposity, and my brain's on overdrive trying to come up with a reason for this one-eighty in demeanor.

Joe's kneeling by Lester, taking his pulse, checking his eyes, clocking the cut-off wire on the attendant's key reel. "He'll be fine," he says, casually pulling a syringe from his pocket and injecting the attendant. "Some insurance he'll be out long enough for our purposes."

Next, the custodian steps over Lester and goes to the counter, grabs my medical file and stuffs it under his shirt.

What the hell is he doing?

"W . . . why are you taking my file?" I splutter as he tucks his shirt back in. "And why are you helping me?"

"Unfortunately, there's no time to explain. We have maybe fifteen minutes at most till Dr. Sherman and Miss Wallace return to perform the lobotomy. And there's much to do."

We have? "Who *are* you?" I ask him.

"When you're safely out of here, I'll answer all your questions," he says, before opening the door a crack to check the hallway.

I don't move.

"You can trust me," he says. But still, I don't budge. He crosses his arms, his eyes leveled at me. "Have you a better option, some caped superhero about to arrive and sweep you away?"

Fine. I follow him into the hall, where I see the back of the night nurse down at its other end, just entering the infirmary ward.

"Come," Joe whispers, and I follow him in the opposite direction, to a door marked CUSTODIAL. Joe unlocks it, and we slip inside.

The small room is filled with floor buffers and various other pieces of equipment. Rows of shelves are stocked with cleaning supplies.

"Lester's keys," Joe says, holding his hand out, and I reluctantly place the key ring in it. The custodian flips rapidly through them till he gets to the one he's after, the one that says EAST ST. Holds it up to me. "This is the key to the east stairwell down the hall. Take it to the first floor, then use this key"—singling out a second, beefier one— "to exit the fire door near the entrance to the dining hall. When you get outside, cut down the hill and head toward the wooded area to the east. Once you've scaled the perimeter fence there, wait in the bushes by the road till I come for you."

He hands me back the keys, then grabs a large brown paper–wrapped bundle from a high shelf. Rips it open. Inside is a nurse's uniform he's stolen, complete with starched cap.

This guy's been planning.

"Put this on," he says, and hands me the pile and a flashlight.

"Someone will definitely recognize me in this," I say.

"Let me worry about that. Give me three minutes."

CHAPTER 51

I T'S BEEN MORE than three minutes.

Maybe the custodian is just another mind game Stokes is playing on me, a final screw-you—letting me think I have an ally with an escape plan. Then when I'm all in and chock-full of hope, he rips it away. Hands me back to Sherman and Wallace and their ice picks.

I extract the box cutter from my shoe just in case. Pull it open and drop it into the uniform's front pocket along with the keys, scalpel, and flashlight. But I don't move.

My heart's thudding away, beating the drums for action.

Keep your shit together.

I dip my lids, clutch my Latin medal tight, and draw a couple of deep breaths. When I open my eyes again, it's happened, what the custodian promised—

A blackout.

I ease the door of the custodial closet open and find the hallway lit by a single anemic red exit light, like some lesser corridor of hell. The faint chatter of the infirmary nurse calling the switchboard for information comes from down the hall.

Time to go.

I grip the key ring by the two keys Joe showed me and slip into the hallway, heading toward the east elevator.

But as I pass an opening marked INFIRMARY KITCHEN, I spy, inside the room, a small metal door with a little round window in its center.

The dumbwaiter.

I remember when I was a patient in the infirmary ward hearing Nurse O'Brien talk about checking the infirmary kitchen to see what food the cooks downstairs in the main kitchen had dumbwaitered up that morning. This tiny elevator connects the main kitchen to its satellites in the infirmary above and the Unit below.

Where Mary is.

The Unit could be just a few yanks on a pulley rope away.

Hmm. Bad idea?

Yes, a very bad idea.

If you go now, you get out clean. No more skirmishes. No more run-ins with staff. A decent chance of escaping here with the name Mary gave you.

Remember the name?

The whole goddamn reason you're there?

I leave now and the nerds get the intel they need. Without me having to resort to violence. Without sullying New Bix. Worthy and I might still have a chance at a life . . . if the person on that scrap of streamer has the sample, if I can reach her before Stokes . . . if Kyung and the others can develop the cure . . . if I can get back here. So many ifs. But there's a chance.

Down in the Unit, on the other hand, nurse's whites or not, blackout or not, the staff will know who's supposed to be there. I'll be recognized, forced to fight them.

But also down in the Unit, Mary—still alive.

I could get her out. At least I could try. Wouldn't New Bix try?

And before the *voice* can rebut, I'm opening the door of the dumbwaiter. It'll be a tight squeeze. On one side of the car is the rope controlling it, leading to a pulley wheel somewhere in the shaft above.

I manage to fold myself into the cube, then shut the door, making sure none of my parts or clothing are sticking out, before pulling on the rope. The carriage drops slowly downward through the ink-black chute.

When the dumbwaiter passes the main kitchen, I see, through its porthole, two cooks having a blackout smoke, the embers of their cigarettes glowing in the dark.

Another dozen feet down, I reach the basement level.

I look through the window at the darkened Unit's kitchen, searching for staff, but it's empty, so I ease the door open, quietly step out, then creep to the door. Turn the lock and open it a crack. Like the infirmary's hall, the Unit's is bathed in the dim scarlet of its exit lights.

I say a silent thanks to Joe, whoever he is.

The Unit is its usual mausoleum quiet. Little difference for its patients between a blackout and their normal endless night. As I creep past the closed door of the slumber room, I hear two nurses conversing behind it, a few feet away.

Batshit madness, what I'm doing here.

I pass the empty dayroom, turn onto the Unit's main hallway— and lay eyes on a cluster of naked patients standing around. There's not a nurse in sight.

The women are soaking wet, drops of water sliding down the bony ripples of their rib cages. Damp towels lie at their feet, dropped and forgotten. Frida's among them, agitated, pounding her wet head with her fist and making a low moaning sound. These were the Unit patients in the dining hall earlier.

But Mary Pell is not among them.

Under the sound of Frida's moan lies something else—the hiss of showers going full blast. It's coming from the closed door of the nearby lavatory.

I try the door and find it unlocked. Inside, steam from the showers and the dim red exit light have produced a crimson-tinged cloud my eyes can't penetrate.

As I creep past the doorless toilet stalls, sinks, and benches, the sound of the showers grows louder. I pull out Joe's flashlight and point it ahead, but its beam merely spotlights the vapor, turning it even more opaque—like high beams on a foggy night.

At the entrance to the showers, I hear a splash and a muffled cry. Then a hard *thunnnck*.

"Mary?" I call.

Another splash.

I crouch down, aiming the beam below the red cloud at the less dense air near the floor—and spy a naked figure lying on the tile whose legs are still being hit with the shower's spray.

I run over, kneel down, and turn the figure's head toward me.

Mary. Staring at me with lifeless eyes. I'm too late. A quickly expanding halo of blood is coming from a wound in the back of her head. I put the flashlight down on the wet tile, and its beam throws Mary's face into grotesque high relief. I gently coax her lids closed.

I could have prevented her fall if only I'd warned her. Or gotten here sooner . . . Gotten her out of this place . . . So many ways I have failed her. "Mary, I'm so sorry . . ."

Tears begin flooding my eyes for this prickly woman who saved my life. Maybe, hopefully, many lives—

Only if you get out of there alive with that name.

Someone needs to beat Stokes to her.

Otherwise it's meaningless. All of it. I kiss Mary's forehead, grab the flashlight, and am rising from the floor when I hear the squeak of rubber soles. A shadowy figure wielding a massive wrench emerges from the steam cloud.

Gibbs. The spatter of blood on her uniform appears black in the ruby darkness. Mary's blood. The death certificate was wrong: Mary didn't slip. She was killed by Gibbs.

She continues toward me. "What are you doing here?" she demands.

I don't answer. Instead I slide my hand into the pocket of the nurse's uniform. Grasp hold of the scalpel.

Feet away from me, Gibbs begins swinging the enormous wrench in an upward stroke toward my jaw like some unhinged golfer.

I dodge the tool at the last second then grab a hunk of the surprised woman's hair. Yank her head back while my other hand brings the scalpel upward.

It would be so easy. One quick slash and I could avenge Mary. Start to make amends.

Don't do it for Mary.

Or your guilt-fueled vengeance.

Do it 'cause Gibbs will kill you if you don't kill her first—and the clue will die with you.

Do it!

But the *voice* isn't in charge. New Bix is.

And she's getting herself and Mary's clue the fuck out of Hanover without more bloodshed.

As I shove the nurse down, her quick, grasping hands knock the scalpel from mine. I leave it. Race for the lavatory door.

"Come back here!" Gibbs roars from behind me, already in pursuit as I streak through the lavatory to the entrance. She's no more than ten feet behind me when I leap through the open doorway, and I brace for the impact of her wrench—

But then the door miraculously slams shut behind me. A split second later, Gibbs and her wrench crash into it.

I turn to see which naked Unit patient has been able to pull this off.

But it's not a patient.

It's Nurse Wallace, already dead bolt–ing the door with her key.

CHAPTER 52

Y ou?"

It's all I get out before Gibbs starts pounding and screaming, "Open this door!"

As Wallace pulls me away from it, I tell her, "She killed Mary Pell."

She nods. "You need to go. Now," she says, hustling me through the naked Unit patients and down the dark hall till we reach the door to the Unit's vestibule. Wallace starts to unlock it.

"Why are you helping me," I ask, "against her, risking—"

"No other course of action to take . . . now that I know what you are."

"What's that?"

"A time traveler," she says, opening the door and walking toward the Unit's entry gate.

"How . . . how long?"

"Have I known? Not long. At Hanover, more than a few patients think they've been sent here from the future. Or the past," she says, unlocking the gate, then pulling me down the dark east-west corridor toward the main building. "You didn't strike me as any different. The things you'd mumble about while groggy—being someone named Bix Parrish, sent from the future in a time machine to get a doctor's help fighting some illness you called the Guest. It all sounded like the usual patient babble. Even that day I gave you back your pennies in the lobby. I thought for a second I saw the date 2021 on one of them, but I dismissed it."

"So what changed your mind?" I ask.

"Ernest Hemingway," she says.

"Huh?"

"Weeks ago, I overheard you telling Alice and the other Unit patients seated around you some wild tale about the author surviving two plane crashes in Uganda in a day, turning up alive even as obituaries were being written about him. You remember?" the nurse asks.

"Yes."

"I thought it was just another delusion. Till a couple days ago when the news exploded with headlines about Hemingway showing up alive in Entebbe after miraculously surviving two plane crashes. The exact same story you told Alice." Wallace glances behind us to make sure no one's coming. "But time travel, it's a lot to wrap one's head around. I was still trying to accept it when you showed up this morning with that deputy. No husband, just a note from him asking us to readmit you to the Unit. I knew that moment it was all true—and that you'd come back to speak to Mary Droesch. Dr. Pell."

"So you knew who Mary was?" I ask.

"I'd heard the gossip: lady biologist from Fort Detrick who'd suffered a psychotic break, accusing the army of some germ warfare cover-up, then attacking her boss in a delusional fit of rage."

"Did you have any idea Mary was faking being a catatonic?" I ask.

"None," she says. "But I figured if you were risking reentering the Unit, you might know something I didn't. And need assistance."

Assistance. Wallace was the unseen hand in all of this. "So you were the one who helped keep Gibbs and her partner away so Mary and I could speak?" I ask.

She nods. "As a veteran, I find Miss Gibbs's brand of patriotism hard to stomach."

"Were you the one who convinced Mary I was from the future?"

Wallace grins—which is jarring, the sight of a smile on that dour face. "I made sure a newspaper with the headline about Hemingway was 'left' on the chair next to her this morning."

Then it occurs to me: "That tray of surgical instruments you put on the table in the treatment room—"

"Did I place it close enough for you to reach the scalpel? What do you think?"

When we reach the door to reception, the nurse turns to me. "Were you able to get the information you needed from Mary in the dining hall . . . before Gibbs—"

"Yes," I say, trying to ward off the tears.

"Good." She opens the door. We're halfway to the exit when we hear voices—

And retreat back into the tunnel. Wallace gestures for me to follow her down a side hallway to a door she unlocks marked TOWER STAIRWELL.

The staircase must have really been something once. A grand carved wood affair gracefully ascending to the upper floors. But at some point, the people in charge of this place sacrificed beauty for safety and fenced in its center. Now it's a bleak tunnel, curving upward, all steel mesh and dimmed hopes.

"These stairs service the main hall—lobby, doctors' offices, and the tower. It's deserted at night. You should be okay," Wallace says, flipping through Lester's keys. She doesn't ask me how I got them. Quickly picks out one with a *T* on it, unlocks the stairs' entry gate, and hands the keys back to me. "That key with an *L* on it unlocks the lobby door."

"Thank you," I say.

She nods stiffly. "Good luck."

I nod, then sprint up to the next floor. Unlock the staircase's gate and door and enter the lobby. Wallace was right: the place is empty. To my left are the main entrance doors. The same ones I strode through a week ago on the arm of my fake husband. I run for the doors and unlock them, about to disappear into the snowy night.

But then I hear the double click of a revolver's hammer being cocked. And Stokes's voice instructing: "Turn around."

I do as he says. Find him pointing a .38 at me. "Was waiting here for Sherman to come tell me he'd finished dumbing you down when the lights went out. Knew right away it was you. Your persistence has really gotten tedious, Beatrix. It wasn't long before I heard voices in the stairwell." The lights come back on, Joe's blackout over. Stokes clocks the bloodstain on my borrowed nurse's uniform, then points his gun toward the tower stairwell. "Let's go."

We begin climbing the steps, Stokes's gun at my back. "What are we doing?" I ask.

"That blood on your nice new uniform, whose is it, the friendly attendant with the shears?" I don't answer. "No . . . You went back for Pell—but got there too late to save her from Miss Gibbs and her fellow spook. Am I close?"

"Fuck off." Seeing Stokes's cocky assholeness unfiltered and free makes it clear just how gifted an actor he is to have pulled off the role of gentle and caring Paul Frasier in 1954.

He chuckles behind me. "Amazing the lengths you'll go to convince yourself you can be *that* person."

"What person?" I ask.

"Someone good," he says. "Really can't blame you. I thought the same—that you could be *domesticated*. But you couldn't change, even with half the voltage in the state sent through you. It's your nature. And you can't fight nature, it'll surface eventually—like yours is beginning to, Beatrix."

Ignore his mind-game bullshit.

Keep him talking. And look for an opportunity.

"As long as we're asking questions," I say, "why are you here?"

"Same reason as you. Getting the location of that rat virus sample from the esteemed Dr. Pell."

"What use does a cult that believes its members will be saved by God have for Mary Pell's sample?" I ask, glancing back at him.

He smiles. "I managed to snag a look at Dr. Pell back in November, on that tour of the Unit I convinced Sherman to give me before I saw you in his office. There she was, drooling in her soup. Looked like a complete vegetable. I was sure she wouldn't be telling *anyone* where her viral sample was before she died. The last hope for a cure, gone. A low point. That left just one job for me in 1954. Tie up loose ends."

"Kill me."

He nods. "Kameron had wanted a violent, painful, public end for you in 2035. But he's practical, all about the big picture. Said keep your death here small and forgettable. No flags raised. No timelines fucked with. So I came to that office armed with—"

"Those doctored photos of us," I say, "to convince me you were my loving husband."

He laughs. "Convince you, my crazy wife no one's gonna listen to? No. I just needed to convince Sherman. So he'd give me a few minutes alone with you to use the *other* item I came with: a syringe of penicillin."

CHAPTER 53

M Y ALLERGY."

He nods. "You once told me you nearly died when you were younger. Airways closed right up. Only a swiftly administered EpiPen saved you. And with the medical care in this place, well, you wouldn't be so lucky this time," he says, smiling. "All I needed that day was a moment alone with my Dee . . . And when it was over, I'd 'find' a few peanuts in your pocket and accuse the hospital of gross negligence for letting you anywhere near them with your rare peanut allergy . . ."

"Then quietly clear out of 1954."

"A simple plan," he says as we pass a door marked SECOND FLOOR. "And satisfying, getting to watch you in Sherman's office, no memory, trapped like a caged animal. Denying you were my mental wife, while trying like hell to figure out what was *really* going on . . . But then came that moment when you realized I was the man in your one memory. That you had to be Dorothy. Seeing you, of all people, break down in tears like that . . . So frightened. Vulnerable . . ."

"At your mercy," I say. "Must've been quite the turn-on."

"For sure," he says, "but it was so much more. I could suddenly see the possibilities of this *unique situation*. The opportunity to obtain a more tender, agreeable, and trustworthy version of you, one not driven by your merciless save-the-world agenda. A you I could enjoy this not-yet-fucked world of 1954 with . . . at least for a little while."

Stokes's yoloyear fantasy: living out his last months here with an "improved" version of me. He must've gone AWOL from Kameron Rook and the Tabula Rasa to pursue it.

"Mr. and Mrs. Paul Frasier," I say. "You just needed Sherman to damage me enough to accept it."

"Exactly," he says. "I already had a couple factors in my favor—your brain damage from the botched time travel. And all that free-floating guilt and fear swirling around your subconscious."

"The perfect candidate for your fucked-up mind control experiment."

"A brainwashing challenge worthy of my talents and expertise. So when Dr. Sherman begged me to let him treat you in the Unit, I gave my consent."

"All the while letting me think it was *my* choice."

"Absolutely. The most crucial factor in a successful reeducation is that the subject believes they're making their *own* decisions, even when they're not. That illusion of free will—that's what gets them to double down on choices you've *already* gotten them to make. To really *own* them. So the subject won't question a situation, a belief, an authority figure. Because they think *they chose* that situation, that belief, that person exerting control over them. And therefore, to question it would be irrational."

I remember the repatterned part of me urging me to be sensible, presenting all those solid, grounded reasons I should comply. Christ.

"I knew if I raised the right fears, dangled the right rewards, I could get you to choose the Unit," he says. Cocky motherfucker. "Just needed something you were so desperate for, you'd do anything to get—and keep it."

My crazy-maker. "Freedom," I say.

Stokes is hardly able to contain himself. "It was perfect. You wanted out of Hanover so damn much, I knew you'd cooperate."

"Freedom depends on my cooperation," I say, repeating the line that's inhabited me, like a tapeworm, these last weeks.

Stokes chuckles. "That governing phrase Sherman embedded in you. Still firmly in place, I see."

"You knew everything he was doing to me in the Unit?"

"Of course. Sherman got off on all my adulation and interest in his work. Kept me well-informed on his progress with you," he says, as we pass a door marked THIRD FLOOR. "The doctor has a workman-like grasp of mind control. Nothing spectacular, but between his protocol and your existing issues, it was definitely working, you were accepting the changes being wrought on you, becoming habituated to your new role. Your new you."

"Till I faked the seizure." I wonder if I suddenly turned around, could I get that gun out of his hands before he pulled the trigger? From what I've seen of his reflexes, I'm guessing no.

"Bold move," he says, "and convincingly done. Still don't know how you pulled it off. Fooled Sherman. Even I was sure they'd over-treated you—and gotten you close to full regression. It made taking you out of Hanover too tempting to pass up. To be in total control of your reprograming, not have Sherman muddying the waters . . ." We reach the fourth-floor landing, come to a door marked TOWER ACCESS. "Open it," he says.

"So you forced them to release me," I say, unlocking the door.

"Yeah," he says, prodding me down a hallway. "But once you were home, it quickly became clear a part of you was fighting the process, insisting on your independence. Still wanting to accomplish its 'mission'—even if it hadn't a fucking clue what that was. I needed to make you more afraid of yourself, of what your disease could make you do. So you'd let the mission—and your independence—go."

"The hardware store."

"A healthy dose of sedative added to your antiseizure capsule that night. Then an additional injection between your toes later so you wouldn't wake till Arthur Morris found you in his store the next morning."

That's some grade A gaslighting.

The hallway opens up on a set of narrow steps that hugs the four brick walls of Hanover's clock tower, as it rises upward like some M. C. Escher staircase. I could try to—

Not the ideal place for a fight. Wait for a better opportunity.

Stokes shoves the barrel in my back to get me moving up them. "I had Eloise slog through that mud outside the house in an identical nightgown and socks, then change you into them."

"Who *is* Eloise?"

"Out-of-work actress heavily in debt to a loan shark. You find the right, desperate people, they'll do anything. And I gotta say, she played the role of disapproving nurse quite well," he says. "But even though I'd scared you enough to agree to the medication, the limitations, you still had questions. I had to know where they were coming from. What you were keeping from me."

"So you left me alone, undrugged, yesterday. A test."

"Which you failed. 'Magically' healed enough to climb out a window, steal a truck. Now I knew you'd been lying. But I was curious. Wanted to see how close you'd gotten to the truth."

"So you did follow me."

"At a discreet distance. Too discreet—you managed to lose me after the church."

I knew I sensed the asshole. Thank God he didn't follow me to Worthy's house. At least so far I've kept him from knowing about the deputy and me.

Let's not congratulate ourselves yet. He's still about to kill you. Us.

"When you didn't return with your tail between your legs," Stokes says, "I spent the night wondering just where the hell you'd gone, my 'wife' with no friends outside a mental ward and fuck-all faith in herself. You'd either gotten your memory back or jumped—which would lead you where? Hanover? But Mary Pell's a vegetable . . . or is she?"

"So today you called Sherman."

"You *are* the smart one, Dee." Fucker. "When he told me you'd been readmitted, I realized Mary Pell must've been faking a little damage of her own. Could still share the location of her viral sample. What I didn't count on was how easy you'd make it, Beatrix. No need for me to torture it out of you back home on Birch Lane." He shows me the scrap of pink streamer. "You gave it up so willingly."

"Fucker."

"So now it's time to end my failed experiment."

I turn around to face him, stall him. For what I don't know. Worthy's cavalry is hours away. "You don't have to do this."

He smiles. "Isn't death what you wanted from the time machine? So you'd be free of all the guilt for your dark deeds?"

"Dark deeds? Conning you and Kameron hardly seems worth killing myself over."

A look of genuine surprise appears on Stokes's face. "The nerds didn't tell you. Didn't want their best soldier distracted from her job. That's cold."

"What are you talking about?" I ask.

"Haven't you asked yourself why some part of you is so damn driven to save us all? Accomplish its mission? What awful thing it's trying to make amends for? Eventually you'd figure it out. Enough memories would return—and then you'd know who you *really* are. What you did to Theo."

The boy in the selfie. Kameron's brother. What *did* I do to him? I can feel my knees going wobbly and grab the railing to steady myself. "The boy at the quarry that day."

"Darling, you've remembered something!" Stokes says in his Paul voice. "Yes. Kameron's little brother. God, that kid loved you. Followed you around like an overgrown puppy. And I think you actually cared about him. Not the BS you pretended with me. Real affection—which meant he was doomed."

"What happened?" I ask.

He gestures with the gun. Waits for me to resume the ascent before responding. "That night in June, after the day at the quarry, you managed to get hold of papers Kameron was carrying with the location of our nearby drop site. Theo must've seen you sneak away and followed you. I imagine when he caught you breaking into the place, he realized you weren't all you appeared to be. So you killed him to keep him quiet."

"No. That can't be—"

"But it can, Beatrix. It's what happens—people who care about you die. In the end, they're the ones who pay the price for all your hero-ing. Your missions."

Suddenly the creaky stairs, the tower's brick walls, and Stokes are gone. All I can see is darkness punctuated by the staccato of bullets pinging off metal nearby. The smell of gunpowder hanging in the humid night air surrounds me.

Then the bullets die down and I see the boy, Theo, crouched behind a large crate. "Beatrix, I'm here," he says, and starts to stand just as the sound of a single shot resounds through the air. Theo looks at me in surprise as he crumples to the ground.

Theo . . . That's why Kameron was so intense on that stage. Why he so badly wants me dead. I killed his brother.

I keep climbing steps, feet still going through the motions, but I'm not entirely in my body. My mind's floating somewhere in the stairwell.

Do I really need to remind you Stokes is a psychopath and not to believe a word he says?

But I saw Theo go down. I know that happened.

"Theo was just another expendable loved one to you," Stokes says. "But not to Kameron. He took off into the woods like John the fucking Baptist. Gone for weeks. That's when he came up with his New Covenant. Started believing his own bullshit. You were the inspiration for it all, Beatrix. The Reclamations, the camps, the misogynistic rules and restrictions."

"Christ."

CHAPTER 54

A HEAD OF ME, the final flight of steps ends at an opening in the ceiling from which pours a din of mechanical noise. Next to it is a sign that says CLOCKWORKS.

I grab hold of my Latin medal, squeeze it tight.

Stokes pulls up next to me. "That medal—it's how I tracked you back to Georgetown. Discovered who you really were: notorious Bix of the Child's Army. And when Kameron returned from his powwow in the woods and heard my news, he decided it was God's will the Tabula Rasa relocate to Georgetown. Begin the work of Reclamation *there*—starting with anyone connected to Beatrix Parrish."

Including the Child's Army. How many friends did I expose to Kameron's vengeance? How many were hunted down, sent to his camps, or killed for my little trip to Baltimore?

This is why the memory of that day at the quarry and Theo's laughter wouldn't let go, why it clung to me like a burr till I remembered all of it.

It's why I volunteered for the nerds' deadly machine.

Because that day—and its bloody aftermath—broke me.

You don't know what really happened—

I know this is what Kyung and the others were desperate to keep hidden from me. So I wouldn't go off the rails before completing the mission. I know it's what I've kept locked away in my tansu drawers, what I've used death and the Unit to escape from.

What I've been blindly trying to atone for, feeling around in the dark of my soul for a clue to it.

"Don't let it go to your head, Beatrix," Stokes says. "It's not *all* because of you. Kameron needed a way to eliminate potential rivals—to consolidate power, acquire those assets—and minds—of use to us. Most of all, to energize the flock and recruit new members with a convenient new enemy they could band against—science. The New Covenant has proved more than handy for all of that."

Stokes waves the gun at the stairs. "Let's go."

I climb through the opening into a square room. Each wall contains an enormous clockface connected by a shaft to a large, motorized clockworks clattering away in the noisy center of the room. With every advance of its huge gears, a sharp *tick* punctuates the din. Stokes gestures to a ladder near the clockworks that leads to a small wooden hatch in the ceiling. "There."

"Can we just take a minute to talk about—"

Stokes rams the gun barrel hard into my back, till I duck under one of the metal shafts and start up the ladder.

At the top, I open the hatch and climb up into the tower's attic.

On each of its walls is a single tall casement window starting a foot off the floor. They rattle against their steel frames, buffeted by the December wind forcing its way inside. Can feel the ribbons of cold air whipping around me.

Now we've come to the point of this climb. How Stokes ties up his last loose end. Shooting me would be too messy, flags would be raised. Timelines affected.

Stokes pushes me toward the nearest window. Pulls up its metal latch, shoves it open, and steps back. The wind and snow rush in, howling around me, plastering the nurse's uniform against my legs. "They'll never question it. Even Gibbs."

He's right. Desperate, suicidal patient gets loose and jumps to her death. No one at Hanover except Wallace and Joe will even bat an eye.

But first he needs me out the window.

The snowy ground far below is barely visible through the thick, swirling flakes.

"Don't do this," I say.

"Don't worry; it'll be quick."

True. Just one step into the winter air, and it's over. But then this asshole wins.

More important, everyone else loses.

Stokes will terrorize—or trick—Mary's brave friend into giving up the virus sample. Then Kameron Rook will force Kyung and the rest to develop the cure for him at gunpoint.

"Let's go," Stokes says, but I don't move. He's not pleased. "If you insist on making some pointless stand here, after you're dead, once we've squeezed a cure for the Guest out of your scientist friends, I'll have my men take your brother and anyone else you care about still left in 2035, and slowly—very slowly—gut them like fishes. But if you simply accept the reality of your situation and jump, I'll let them live. Think of it as one last opportunity to save lives."

I look out the window at the yawning snow-laced blackness. "Say yes to this death right in front of me."

Stokes smiles. "I knew those mantras weren't in vain. As the Buddha once said, 'Serenity comes when you trade expectations for acceptance.' Chop, chop, Beatrix. I've got work to do. The cure awaits." He waves the gun. "Time's up. Let's go."

Time *is* up, motherfucker.

I pretend to take a moment to weigh my decision, then mold my face into an expression of hopeless resignation, my body into the slump of surrender. I did a lot of that in the Unit. I know the move well. "Okay. I . . . I'll do it," I say solemnly, and step forward, lifting one foot onto the deep windowsill. Flakes of snow roil around me.

Stokes steps closer. Now that he's got me in position, the cocksure bastard intends to hurry this along, not wait for me to jump. But the gun leaves him with just one arm for shoving.

I bow my head, take a deep breath as if I'm psyching myself up, and wait for him to make the move.

It's not a long wait.

When I see his knee bend, about to spring, I duck and pivot away from the window, slipping under his arm that's already reaching out to shove me. Then I knock the revolver from his other hand. It slides across the floor.

Stokes sees me eyeing it. Pulls a switchblade from his jacket pocket, flicks it open, and steps closer.

All I've got is the tiny box cutter in my pocket.

But it's a box cutter he doesn't know about.

He takes another step as the knife begins an arcing slash toward me. But my hand thrusts the tiny box cutter blade into the oncoming path of the knife, slashing open the muscle at the base of Stokes's thumb. The switchblade falls to the ground.

Before he can recover, I've snatched his knife, regained control over how this ends.

You can't let him live.

I ignore the *voice*. New Bix gets to decide this. "Come," I say to Stokes, and gesture toward the stairs as my mind feverishly works on scenarios for how I'm going to keep him immobilized till I get him back to 2035.

But Stokes is having none of it. Backs away toward the window as he pulls something from his pocket. His link. He presses the button. Then presses it again. And again. But nothing happens. There's shock on Stokes's face—he doesn't know about the fifteen-second delay.

CHAPTER 55

A ND NOW I have a new choice.

New Bix lets this guy go. Keeps her clean slate, her second chance. Her potential for a life with Worthy.

But what about the person whose name is on the scrap of streamer? Stokes will come back to 1954, torture the rat virus sample out of them, then return to 2035 triumphant. And if we're lucky, very, very lucky, and the nerds can somehow manage to construct a cure, Kameron will decide who lives and who dies. Absolute power.

Then Stokes will move on to hunting down my remaining loved ones. I believe him on this point.

I don't realize I've made the decision till I'm already charging at him. I thrust the switchblade into his side, as deep as it'll go. A wound to the gut is surely fatal in 2035.

Stokes's eyes flare wide for a moment with pain. Shock.

But then he smiles. "There she is. There's the Beatrix I know. Welcome back, darling."

I hold tight to the knife and shove Stokes out the window.

His eyes stay on me as he plunges to the frozen ground—

But right before impact, he blinks out of sight, disappears from 1954. Poof. Gone.

The only proof he was ever here—that I killed him—is the dripping knife in my hand.

I shove it in my pocket. Wipe my shaking hands on the uniform.

I'm aware of distant footsteps getting closer, but it's like it's happening in some other reality. Not this one where I just killed a guy.

New Bix just killed a guy.

You killed him for a reason. Don't make it for nothing. Go. Get out of there with what you came for—

The name.

I grab the gun off the floor, add it to the growing arsenal in the front pocket of my nurse's uniform, then clamber down the metal ladder and out of the noisy clockworks room.

I fly down the narrow tower stairs, taking them three at a time, then sprint down the hallway, through the door, and have just started down the grand, caged stairs—

When I hear someone charging up the steps from two floors below me. I edge to the banister fencing and peer down. See through the mesh an arm in a white doctor's coat, using the railing to propel himself powerfully upward.

Not a doctor. This can only be one person: Coal-Eyes. About to intercept me. Shit.

In the dwindling seconds before he clears the third floor, I look madly around for somewhere to hide. But there is nothing.

Fuck.

I duck back through the fourth-floor hallway door. Flatten myself into the corner behind it moments before it slams open and Coal-Eyes charges down the hall. Once he disappears into the tower, I slip back out and bound, as quietly as I can, down the steps, not stopping till I reach the bottom.

When I ease open the stairwell door, I'm half expecting Hanover's entire staff to be waiting in the lobby for me.

But it's still empty—though shouts echoing through nearby halls are growing louder. I'm heading for the front door when I spy a familiar gray flannel overcoat hanging on a nearby coatrack. Stokes's coat. Sherman must've met him here in the lobby when he arrived earlier, bloodied and full of his woeful tale of a broken wife. I can see a spot of blood on the collar.

I grab the coat, then throw open the still-unlocked main entrance doors and sprint down the big steps out onto the snowy grounds.

It isn't till I've rounded the men's wing and am almost to the fence that I see the flashlights, hear the distant voices of staff beginning to fan out over the frozen expanse.

Keep going. Get to the fence.

It's just like I remember it from November: chain-link, about ten feet high, topped with coiled barbed wire. I throw Stokes's coat around my neck, then take a running jump at it. My pointy loafers help, their narrow toes fitting deep enough in the diamonds of fence wire to get a foothold. Momentum and some serious scrambling get me inches from the top—where I spread the coat over the barbed wire and drag myself over to the other side, then yank the coat free and jump to the snowy ground. I take a last look back through the fence at Hanover as I put Stokes's coat on. More flashlights now. One surely belongs to Coal Eyes. And another to Gibbs. She's probably already perfected her story of the crazed ex-Unit patient attacking Mary Droesch in the showers.

I scramble down the hill to the road below. It's deserted, just woods on the other side. I hide myself in a clump of bushes, shiver, wait—and hope that Joe, whoever he is, will be here soon. Before the search parties. The police.

Worthy.

I know he'll have been monitoring the police radio for any signs of trouble at Hanover. That was part of the plan. Has he heard? Have they even notified the sheriff's department?

We had an arrangement: if I escaped, I'd find a way back to the Rosslyn Motor Inn and he'd meet me there with my link.

A pair of headlights soon appears, belonging to an ancient truck coming slowly down the road. As it approaches, I recognize Joe in the driver's seat.

I run out of the bushes into the icy road, waving my hands, and he comes to a stop. When I open the passenger door, a rattled-looking Joe takes my medical file, lying open on the passenger seat, and closes it. I can see his hands shaking as he slides it onto the floor. The last half hour has taken its toll on the custodian. I don't think the guy's cut out for this kind of activity.

"Thank God! Do you know how many times I've circled this stretch of road? Where on Earth have you been? Get in," he says. I take a seat, and the custodian tears out of there—as much as an ancient truck can tear. He looks over at me. "So, were you able to get it from her, in the dining room? I couldn't tell."

"Get what?" I ask.

"What we've both been pursuing. The name of Mary Pell's contact."

Like a shot, the bloody knife is out of my pocket and up against his neck. The truck veers wildly back and forth before Joe manages to put on the brakes.

"Who *are* you? Tell me now!" I yell.

Joe eyes me nervously as he slowly unbuttons his cuff and rolls up his shirtsleeve. Then he turns his hand over, revealing a scar like mine on his wrist. I lower the knife.

"You came here in the time machine, too?"

"I invented the thing," he says, and holds out his hand. "Dr. Cyrus Corbett. Pleasure."

The asshole inventor with all the rules and the password-protected code? That tracks. I shake his hand. "Bix Parrish."

"I know," he says, and looks at me like he's seeing me for the first time. I guess that makes two of us.

"I did get the name from Mary," I say, then gesture to the road, "so, we should probably . . ."

"Right you are," he says, and we continue down the road.

I clock Cyrus's gray hairs, his wrinkles. "You're at least forty. You'd be dead in the future. How could you have come from there?"

"I'm from the future. Just not 2035. I'm from the year 2025," he says, then his eyes spot the brand-new stains on my nurse's uniform under the coat. "Is . . . is that blood?" he asks, and I nod. "Whose?"

"Mary Pell's. I tried to save her, but everything seemed to work against me. Maybe she was always going to die, no matter what I did. Maybe the universe is always going to self-correct and we can't change anything that's going to happen. To Mary. To those women still trapped in Sherman's Unit. To the human race . . ."

Cyrus stops at the intersection we've reached. "Not so. The man pretending to be your husband, he's changed plenty. Just ask the actual Paul Frasier." So Stokes did kill the real Paul Frasier. "It seems we *can* affect things. At least some things . . . Alter someone's fate. I already have," he says, looking at me, serious as pox.

I'm about to ask what he means when we hear a siren growing louder. Behind us the road is empty and dark. But red lights are emerging from the thick veil of snow to our right: a patrol car speeding toward us. Its left blinker is on and as it slows down to make the turn onto our road, I see Worthy at the wheel, his eyes laser-focused ahead. My heart starts beating like a drum at the sight of him.

I remember sitting in the car with him this morning, which feels like years ago, just before I reentered Hanover, kissing him, imagining our possible life together after all of *this* was done. Barbecuing hamburgers, him in the obnoxious apron, me with the tall glasses of lemonade.

But now I have thoughts . . . hopes . . . fears for another future:

This one with Ethan alive—saved by Kyung that day in my house.

And my twin is old, his face blessed with wrinkles that crinkle in the corners of his eyes when he smiles. Some bits of gray have begun to appear in his hair and there's just the barest beginnings of a middle-aged paunch to his belly. The two of us are sitting on a couch, surrounded by friends and family. And laughter. Even Gideon, now portly and bald, is laughing.

A little boy with Ethan's floppy hair runs up and jumps into my brother's lap as everyone begins singing "Happy Birthday to You." Kyung, long silver hair woven into a single braid, wedding ring on her finger, approaches us carrying a cake with two lit candles. She places it on the table in front of us. Large, sloppy letters of icing spell out *Happy Fortieth.*

A future where life contains more than mere survival.

I remember waking that November day on the patient bus, looking out the window at that fence of spears passing by, not a clue who I was, why I was there. My purpose.

I'm still not sure who exactly I am. Where Old Bix and the *voice* leave off and I begin. Or end.

But I do know my purpose: get hold of Mary's sample and the promise it holds of a long, full life for *all* of us. Give mankind back the gift of time, paunches, and wrinkles. Of children and the promise of rekindling civilization from its still-glowing embers.

Will I be able to pull it off? Find Mary's friend before Stokes's replacement can? Get the sample to the future and find a way to deal with Kameron Rook? Don't know. But I am sure of one thing now: Kyung was right. It's going to require my old skills, my old proclivities.

By the time it's all over, will I be back where I started? Reversion to the mean . . . to Old Bix?

Worthy turns onto our road and Cyrus gets a look at him. "Hey, that's your deputy friend. He dropped you off at Hanover—so he was in on your scheme?"

I nod.

"Then shouldn't I flag him down?"

It would be so easy. Lean on Cyrus's horn, get Worthy's attention. The three of us could get out of here, start making plans for how to approach Mary's friend, how to steer clear of Gibbs and Coal-Eyes.

Then I look down at the bloody front of my nurse's whites. The knife still gripped in my hand. Worthy deserves more than Old Bix.

Deserves more than joining the list of my loved ones on the Tabula Rasa's radar. I need to do what you do for the people you love . . . or could have loved: protect them. Protect Worthy.

And not just from Stokes and the Tabula Rasa.

From me.

"No," I say. "Go right."

∗　∗　∗

Cyrus stays in the car while I quickly slip around to the back of the house and lift up the pot near the door where Worthy showed me the spare key. I make my way through the laundry room to the kitchen—this place where I imagined my afterlife with Worthy.

I grab the link off the windowsill, then pull the folded note addressed to Worthy I wrote from my pocket. Put it on the yellow table, then head out the door.

I think Worthy will understand the choice I've made to keep him safe. He won't like it, but he'll understand it.

At least I hope so.

ACKNOWLEDGMENTS

Such a village it took to write this book:

Thank you to my amazing agent, Elisabeth Weed, whose enthusiasm, editorial eye, and unflagging confidence in this book—and in me—have changed my life. And to the rest of the Book Group team for all your efforts.

And to my editor, Micaela Carr, who, despite everything thrown at her, including my book, never lost her calm or her insight. And to all the Holt team, whose efforts are still underway as I write this: Allegra Green and Laura Flavin in marketing, Clarissa Long in publicity, as well as production editor Morgan Mitchell. To Emily Mahar for her incredible cover design. And finally, huge thanks to editorial director Emily Griffin and production designer Chris Sergio, whose tireless work and collegial spirit over those Zoom calls resulted in such a stunning book.

Thank you to Laurie Grotstein, my friend since Holmby Park and my latter-day career buddy, who first said, "This is a book, now go write it." May we both panel widely and well.

To Susannah Grant, who one day in the Loire Valley listened to my words and said, "You know, you are a writer." This is all your fault, Sue.

To Matt Ember, my TV pilot–writing mentor, there at the beginning of Bix, whose advice, "Don't listen to those idiots," has been my guiding light ever since.

To all my friends and family who became/were conscripted into being early readers and brutally honest cheerleaders for this book, especially: Mary Beth DeLucia, Corynne Corbett, Maren Stenseth, Stephanie Stanley, Cathleen Young, Vicky Van Zandt, and Kathryn Davis.

And to the 2024 debuts Slack and the 2025 debuts Discord communities, whose virtual support, stories (oh, the stories . . .), humor, and wisdom made this last year so much more sane. And fun.

To my soccer ladies: Twenty-four years of pure pleasure (and maybe a few bruises) on the pitch with you all. Thank you for letting me shout story ideas and various other non sequiturs at you while we played.

To my twelfth-grade English teacher at Westlake School for Girls, the immortal Joannie Parker, who first cracked open the door for me and so many others to a world of smart women and their words, asking questions, demanding answers, and encouraging us to tell our stories.

Thank you to Dr. Giuliana Repetti for growing up, going to college and med school, and becoming a doctor while I wrote this book so you could be my ace medical consultant.

Thank you to my in-laws, Jacqueline and Ray, for all the love, support, and good cooking those years on Thomasina Lane.

To my parents, who I know are watching and smiling. And to Frasier and Dewey, my pup muses who are also watching and smiling . . . and no doubt drooling from on high.

And to my sibs, Nancy Duggan Benson and Richard Duggan, for being my loving and ever-humorous compatriates in the clueless adult orphan club and my early, tireless readers.

To Lizzy, Maggie, and Andrew, my funny, wise, and wondrous kids, thank you for being my unflagging supporters lo these many years. And thank you for putting up with my endless rants about effing time travel.

And finally, to my husband, Chris: love of my life, partner in crime and not quitting, dairyman supreme, master of the core, and my rock. So glad I met you in Sci-Li that night, dressed in my green (it was really blue) jacket. Love you all around the fifty states and forever, BB.

ABOUT THE AUTHOR

Melissa Pace, a Wesleyan University graduate, is a former editor and writer for *Elle* and a past finalist in the Humanitas New Voices Fellowship for emerging television and screenwriters. She is a middling soccer player, an erstwhile oil painter, and a mother to three incredible grown children. Pace lives in Los Angeles with her husband. *The Once and Future Me* is her first novel.